LAST MAN ALIVE AND NOW HE IS LEGEND

Two Full Length Western Novels

GORDON D. SHIRREFFS

WOLFPACK
PUBLISHING
— EST 2013 —

Last Man Alive and Now He Is Legend
Paperback Edition
Copyright © 2022 (As Revised) Gordon D. Shirreffs

Wolfpack Publishing
9850 S. Maryland Parkway, Suite A-5 #323
Las Vegas, Nevada 89183

wolfpackpublishing.com

Paperback ISBN 978-1-63977-106-6
eBook ISBN 978-1-63977-601-6

LAST MAN ALIVE AND NOW HE IS LEGEND

LAST MAN ALIVE

had been smashed and driven back by the Oglala. During the war years it had reverted to the Sioux and their allies, and it had been that way for the ten years following the war.

There was another way, always used by the military when traveling west, to reach Fort Edgerton by passing well to the south of the hills that showed dimly to the west. There had been a little trouble with the hostiles, but hardly enough for a column such as Montfort's to worry about, *if he* had taken the prescribed route to the south.

Dallas slanted his faded campaign hat lower over his eyes and felt for a cigar. His throat was dust raw, and the taste was brassy, while the dust gritted between his teeth.

He lighted up and eyed Montfort as the tall officer spurred his gray away from the head of the column, urging on the three greyhounds he always had with him, as a big antelope jackrabbit broke cover and sped off. Montfort's view-halloo carried back along the column, above the jingling of trace chains, the thudding of hoofs, and the creaking of running gear. In an instant two other officers and a young women emerged from the column and raced after the commanding officer, the two younger officers slapping the dusty rumps of their horses with their wide-brimmed campaign hats.

The column kept on, led by dour Captain Jack Dutton, whose lined and bitter face glanced briefly after the hunters, then ahead to the trail that led true as a straightedge toward the dim hills. Dutton's disapproval seemed to emanate from his ramrod back and the set of his square shoulders. He spoke out of the side of his mouth to Trumpeter-Corporal O'Hara, and the wind-jammer kneed his gray away from the officer and rode the length of the column to the windward side where Dallas Lorimer rode just ahead of his Arikara scouts.

O'Hara saluted. "Sorr, Captain Dutton requests yere presence at the head av the column."

Dallas returned the salute, threw away his cigar, then touched his rawboned claybank with his heels. He rode past the supply and forage wagons, noting the second of the two ambulances that rolled with the column. Paymaster Jordan Nares dozed in the back of the vehicle beside his two locked money chests. Over fifty thousand dollars was said to be in those dusty boxes, back pay and expenses for the garrison of lonely Fort Edgerton and other sunbitten posts to the west. The column was escorting Nares, his money chests, and his blond niece Jean Ross.

Montfort and his coterie were almost out of sight now while the frightened jack raced on for his miserable life. It might have been different, Dallas thought, if meat was needed for the pot. Dallas was a hunter himself and he had dropped two antelopes just the previous day for the officers' mess. There was an ugly tale told about Montfort that had soured many a hard fighting man of the Army of the Tennessee of how in Georgia Montfort's clanking and powerful brigade had run into a pitiful ambush of Georgia militia composed of graybeards and boys. The ambush had been smashed, but a minie ball had killed one of Montfort's pet greyhounds, and the boy who had fired the shot had run for his life down the sunlit, dusty road with Montfort coursing after him, heavy Prussian saber outthrust, skewering the boy between the shoulder blades, and lifting him off his bare, callused feet to be flung lifeless from the road.

It was said that it had taken two of Montfort's officers to stop him from hacking the pitiful lifeless body to pieces. Montfort the Murderer, it had been whispered about the fire lit messes of his tough cavalry brigade that night. But Montfort led them well and disciplined them with a rod of iron, and they hated him even before he had killed that boy.

Dutton carelessly returned Dallas' salute. The dust had floured his mahogany-hued face and powdered his bushy gray beard, but nothing could dull the pewter sheen of his hard gray eyes. "How many Rees do you have out, Lorimer?" he asked.

"Five, sir. They left before dawn. Corporal Herr and a squad are riding point, and there are three flankers on each side of the column."

Dutton grunted. "Where is Leathers?"

Dallas almost shrugged. "I was told by the general not to bother Leathers with orders, that he was to take his orders directly from the general, sir."

Dutton nodded, then spat thickly to one side. "I've been suspicious of that windy old bastard ever since we came into this country, Lorimer."

Dallas nodded. Mordecai Leathers was the greatest scout in the West, next to Jim Bridger, and even Bridger had admitted a number of times that Leathers was his superior in some aspects of their intricate craft. Mordecai Leathers was an uncanny shot; he knew the Plains Indians like the palms of his hands; he could outrun, outfight, and out-Indian any hostile west of the Mississippi. If you didn't believe it, all you had to do was to ask him, then fill your pipe and settle back for at least an hour of bombast and blow. Trouble was, many a man believed Leathers, including General Arliss Montfort.

Dutton spat again. "All I know about Leathers is that he talks too gawd-damned much, he stinks, he drinks too much, and he's got the clap."

Dallas couldn't help but grin. Dutton had neatly packaged Mordecai Leathers in Dutton's own bitter way.

Dutton glanced toward the thin scarf of dust that had marked the passing of Montfort and his companions over a low, hardly discernible ridge. "Our esteemed commanding officer didn't think much of that arrow placed in our way, Lorimer. What do you think?"

"I would have turned south, sir."

Dutton nodded. He stood up in his stirrups and eased his crotch. "Seems to me that General Montfort is looking for trouble. You think the Sioux meant that thing back there at the Little Sunflower?"

"They weren't bluffing, sir."

"I agree." Dutton looked to the west. "We have enough men to hold them off out here. They won't charge infantry. They have a helluva respect for Long Tom .45/70's fired in volleys by well-trained beetle crushers. I wish I could say they had the same respect for our mounted troops. If we go into those hills trailing a streamer of dust behind us, making all this noise, the odds are that we'll never get out of there alive."

The statement struck Dallas Lorimer like the butt blow of a rifle, although the same thought had occurred to him again and again since dawn of that day, sparked by a slender shaft of wood, fletched and painted red, thrust into the way of the column.

Dallas looked back along the column at the dusty faces of the troops, at their half closed eyes peering over the yellow scarves they had tied about their mouths and noses. They looked taut and trim, but the fact was that almost two thirds of them were new to the Plains. Some had fought in the war, but most of them were little more than Johnny Raws from Jefferson Barracks. The infantry had a thicker leavening of veterans, but they'd be no match for the enemy in those confining hills. Infantry fights where it stands; as long as the ammunition and the water hold out. They can't outleg hard riding warriors like the Sioux, the Cheyenne, and the Arapaho.

"But our *political* General likes his coursing, his gay evenings beside the bivouac fires with his hardy troops, the feel of the wind on his handsome face, and saddle leather between his muscular cavalryman's thighs." Dutton spat once more.

Dallas glanced quickly at the bitter officer. He had known for some time back at Fort Locke that Dutton had little use for Montfort, but now the timbre of his voice held a strong tinge of venom in it, akin to utter hatred of the commanding officer. Back at Locke they had a saying that you were either a Montfort man or nothing, if you served under him. If you *were* a Montfort man, everything was just fine, but if you weren't...

Dutton shifted in his saddle. "I'd like to wring Leather's skinny neck if I didn't have to disinfect my hands after the act," he said sourly.

Dallas took out a cigar, then hastily returned it to the case.

"Go ahead," said Dutton. "I'll just have one, too. Anything to get the taste of this dust and Arliss Montfort out of my mouth."

They lighted up, and Dallas glanced back along the column, then to the left flank. Mordecai Leathers had been assigned to the column as chief civilian scout along with Seb Wallace, but Seb had taken sick the third day out and had returned to Fort Locke. According to practice, the scouting officer should have made some use out of Leathers, but Montfort had taken over control of Leathers, if there was such a thing, leaving Dallas in charge of the Ree scouts. None of the Rees had spoken much since they had left the Little Sunflower, but their dark liquid eyes had spoken volumes. They wanted no part of the Sioux if they could avoid it. Leathers had left the column shortly after the troops had pulled out of the bivouac, ostensibly to scout ahead.

"I'll bet Leathers is comfortably asleep in some coulee, waiting his chance to slip back with a voluminous report on his scouting activities," said Dutton.

It was almost as though the hard-bitten officer had voiced Dallas' own thoughts.

Dutton sucked in the strong tobacco smoke and then blew it out. "I'm going to lean heavily on you, Lorimer, if anything comes to pass."

"Yes, sir."

There had been an odd inflection in Dutton's tone. There was a grim story about Jack Dutton that had been rife for some time before the column had left Fort Locke; it had been told by a drunken sutler in the officers' club that was situated in the rear room of the sutlery. The sutler had known Dutton shortly after the war when Dutton, reduced in rank from the colonelcy he had held in the Department of the Trans-Mississippi, had been second in command of a column sent out to punish some raiding Kiowas. The commanding officer had panicked when the Kiowas had jumped them one dawn and had shouted out a gibberish of orders that would have swept his fighting command to bloody death. Suddenly, in the middle of the fight, the commanding officer had gone down as though pole-axed, shot through the back of the head; Dutton had taken over, whipped the frightened troops into order, and had driven back the hostiles with severe losses. It had been thought by many that Dutton had killed his commanding officer from behind to get him out of the way. But it was true that if Dutton had *not* taken over command, the column would have been wiped out.

Dutton's agate eyes swung to study Dallas. "You're a good officer, Lorimer," he said suddenly, "even if Montfort has little use for you."

There was a flush beneath the tan on Dallas' face. It was certain that *he* wasn't a Montfort man. For one thing he had not served against the Confederates in the Civil War but rather on the western borders, fighting Indians, serving as escort, garrisoning obscure outposts, chasing will-o'-the-wisp guerillas. He may not have fought against Johnny Reb, but he had come up the hard way from the rear rank of a volunteer company of Kansas cavalry to the rank of second lieutenant by '65 and had been promoted to the first lieutenant when he had elected to stay in the army after the war. Now, with ten years of hard service on the borders as a first lieutenant behind him, there was little chance of ever getting another silver bar as long as Arliss Montfort commanded the battalion.

"Still, Montfort has use for us, Lorimer," said Dutton thoughtfully. "There isn't another officer in this department with your knowledge of this country and the friendly inhabitants thereof, to wit, the Sioux, Cheyenne, and Arapaho." He grinned wryly. "Arliss Montfort will use a man to further his own ends, whether he likes him or not."

Dallas could not resist a comment. "Like the captain himself," he said dryly.

Dutton relighted his cigar and blew out an angry puff of smoke. "Aye, damn him! He has no use for me as a man, but as a Regular soldier and second-in-command, he has a great need for Jack Dutton!"

There was bitter truth in the officer's words. It was another fact of the Montfort Way. Arliss Montfort took along his hounds for sport and pleasure on the march, and he took along his little coterie of favored officers as well for companionship and as drinking and gambling companions, but he had long ago recognized the fact that the best sporting, drinking, and gambling officers, despite their pleasant company, did not always make the best field officers. He had need of men like Jack Dutton to regulate the march, pick out the night's bivouac area, secure the camp, and fight like a Spartan beside his commanding officer if the need arose. He also needed men like Dallas Lorimer to handle the mercurial Indian scouts, to pick the best routes, and to make sure the column was never surprised by the hostiles.

Dutton glanced up at the almost invisible trace of dust left by Montfort and his group. The man's thoughts were almost indelibly stamped on his hard face. Maybe, by a sheer stroke of luck, Arliss Montfort might *not* come back. But Montfort was known throughout the army for his luck; he had used it to save his hash, reputation, and service record many a time instead of his professional skill, upon which other and far better officers depended.

The 'fortunes of war' were no joke to Arliss Montfort; he lived by them.

Dallas rode back along the column when he was dismissed by Dutton. He sent out two more of his Rees in the general direction in which Montfort had vanished to keep an eye out for hostiles that might surprise the officer.

The sun was almost behind the western hills when the men of the column saw the Rees who had left before dawn. They were hunkered down beside the dim trace of the trail, stolidly eyeing the approaching troops. Dallas rode ahead of the column to talk with them; but there was no need for them to talk, for Dallas saw something in the center of the trail fifty yards to the west of the Rees.

The column ground to a dusty, brake-shrieking halt, and Jack Dutton rode up beside Dallas. "What is it, Lorimer?" he asked testily.

Dallas pointed to the objects in the trail. A pile of stones had been centered in the dust of the trail, and on one side of it was the skull of a buffalo bull while on the opposite side was that of a buffalo cow. A slender pole had been set into the ground, slanting toward the cow skull.

"So?" demanded Dutton.

Dallas shoved back his hat and wiped the collected sweat from his forehead. "It's the second warning, sir," he said quietly. "It means when we met the Sioux and their allies, they'll fight like buffalo bulls and that we'll run from them like buffalo cows, or *women,* with the accent on the latter."

Dutton eyed Dallas. "What do you think?"

"They still mean business."

"We haven't seen any of them, and evidently your Rees haven't either."

"No."

"What do you suggest?"

"It isn't too late to head south. We're not in the hills yet."

"Yes." Dutton fumbled in his dusty beard. He looked at the bare, brooding hills. "One thing for sure: We won't enter those hills tonight."

"There is a shallow stream a mile or so ahead."

"Good bivouac?"

"To the best of my knowledge, sir. The Rees said it was all right."

"That's beyond the marker though."

Dallas nodded and eyed Dutton. The man did not want to admit that he was worried by a pile of stones, two bleached skulls, and a crooked willow branch. "They won't attack at night, sir," he said.

"Yes." Dutton flung up an arm and yelled. "Forward Ho!"

They moved out, passing the curious pile in the trail, the men eyeing it as they passed it in turn. Oddly enough none of them thought to disturb it.

The Rees hung back until they were tongue-lashed on by Dallas. As they rode on, silent, dark little men hunched on the backs of their horses, he wondered how many of them would still be with the column when the dawn mists left the stream beside the bivouac. For the stream known as the Little Hatchet was well within Sioux country.

CHAPTER TWO

The October night was as soft as velvet before the rising of the hunter's moon. The wind soughed through the cottonwoods and willows that lined the banks of the Little Hatchet. Now and then a coyote howled faintly through the clinging darkness. The mess fires of the troopers glowed from their pits beneath the cutbank, and the mingled odors of roasted antelope meat and issue coffee mingled with the dry astringent aura of dead prairie flowers and sagebrush.

At one end of the bivouac was the large wall tent of General Montfort, its canvas walls aglow with yellow lamplight from within and marked by huge and grotesque shadows as the officers moved about inside. Beyond that tent was the smaller tent of Jean Ross, wherein she rested from the hard day's ride. The quiet troopers and infantrymen sat about their fires, sipping their coffee, listening to the sounds of laughter and the clinking of glasses emanating from the commanding officer's tent. Beyond the men were the white-tilted forage and supply wagons, and beyond them were the picket lines of horses and mules. The sentries had been posted and instructed by Dallas Lorimer not to skyline themselves if at all possible, to stay low on the ground, and not to move about any more than they had to. More than one sentry in Indian country had been found by his relief with his throat cut, his scalp and weapons missing, and no one ever the wiser as to how the killer had reached his goal and then escaped into the darkness without sight or sound.

A sentry stood beside the ambulance that carried the money chests of Paymaster Nares while Nares, after a long day of dozing and grumbling in that same ambulance, was now convivial and gay in the company of General Montfort, for whom he had a great admiration and respect, particularly for the commanding officer's liquor and cigars.

Dallas lighted a cigar and kept the burning end of it shielded beneath his hand as he looked out across the dull pewter trace of Little Hatchet Creek toward the dim outline of the distant hills.

A tall officer stopped beside Dallas. It was First Lieutenant George Mills, commanding officer of H Company, the infantry company that formed part of the column. Mills was one of the few officers with the command who had fought Indians and who also had a healthy respect for them and their fighting abilities. Dallas silently passed him a cigar, then lighted it from his own.

Mills drew the smoke in gratefully. "How does it look, Dallas?" he quietly asked.

Dallas shrugged. *"Feel,* rather than look," he corrected.

"So?"

Dallas shrugged again. "They're out there somewhere, George, watching us."

"Particularly that nice, large sized target over there, the noisy one," said Mills dryly.

There was no need to look in the direction in which he had inclined his head. Montfort's tent would make a splendid aiming point for any glory hungry Sioux buck who could snake his way close enough to the encampment to get a fair shot at the tent.

"It'll quiet down when the evening poker game gets started," said Mills. He eyed Dallas. "You joining them?"

"No. For one thing, I wasn't invited. For another, I live off my service pay."

"Yes. I had forgotten that. Still the old problem?"

Dallas felt no offense. He had known George Mills since '66. Mills was referring to the fact that Dallas' parents had lost their Kansas property in the hectic days of the war because of guerrilla activities. At the end of the war they had found out that they did not hold a clear title to their land. By the time the matter had gone through court it had cost a great deal of money, paid by Dallas, and then, to cap the whole miserable deal, the property had been lost as well. Dallas had been forced to take over the care of his ailing mother after his father had died, and this he had done for years until his mother, too, had passed away. An army officer's pay was hardly more than satisfactory for a man to live upon, and with heavy debts it was practically nothing at all.

It wasn't easy to buy cheap boots and second-rate uniforms, to avoid the poker games and drinking parties, to forego the pleasure of inviting ladies out for dinner. It made it worse when new shavetails would appear for duty with the command wearing the finest of English hand sewn boots, tailor-made uniforms, Castellani or Solingen dress sabers and with real bullion braid instead of cheap imitation gilt decorating their fine broadcloth blouses.

Dallas had asked for and received duty as scouting officer, associating more with Ree, Pawnee, Crow, and Ponca scouts then he did with white troops. It kept him away from the post a good part of the time. It had also gained him a nickname amongst the officers who formed Montfort's groups—The Half-breed. Only one of them had made the mistake of calling Dallas that to his face. The results had caused Dallas a month's pay, confinement to quarters, and a severe reprimand, but it had been worth it.

They could hear Nares' booming laughter emanating from the tent. Mills shook his head. "He'll be sleeping off another hangover in that ambulance of his tomorrow. I should think that riding in that blasted rattletrap would cure any man of ever doing it again."

"Not Jordan Nares, George," said Dallas quietly.

Mills glanced at Dallas. "I've noticed that you've kept away from Jean as much as possible since we left Fort Locke."

Dallas nodded. He relighted his cigar. His scouting duties made it easy to keep away from her during the day; it wasn't so easy while in bivouac.

"But you can't put her out of your mind, eh, Dallas?"

"No, I can't."

"Do you want to talk about it?"

"No."

"It might do you good, Dallas," persisted the infantryman.

"Dammit! No!"

"As you wish," said Mills quietly.

The bitter gall rose within him. He had loved Jean Ross in the days when he had first met her at Fort Laramie three years ago. She had been eighteen then, fresh from a female academy in Chicago, a vision of blue-eyed loveliness and youth at the Christmas Ball in Old Bedlam, the junior officer's quarters at Laramie. He had been nine years her senior, but he had fallen in love with her as hopelessly as a man *can* fall in love.

But the old barriers had arisen: Lack of money and the fact that his mother had been alive at that time. He had not been able to continue his suit, and a very bewildered young lady had left Fort Laramie to try and forget Dallas Lorimer. A year later he had seen her again at the home of mutual friends while on leave in Saint Louis. She had been engaged then to a young cavalry officer, but Dallas had known that Jean would have forgotten the other man in a moment if Dallas had made the right overtures. He hadn't. His mother had passed on, by then, leaving Dallas with a burden that had to be met and nothing extra for a wife, even in the Spartan quarters of a frontier outpost.

He had heard later that the young officer had been killed fighting Kiowas. When Jordan Nares had been assigned to Fort Locke he had been damned cold to Dallas, perhaps because of Jean. Dallas had never bothered to ask about it. He had little use for Nares as it was.

"Listen!" said Mills suddenly.

Dallas took his cigar from his mouth. "Quiet there!" he snapped to the men at the sunken fires.

The wind had shifted. A coyote cried. The stream chuckled against its grassy banks. The wind moaned softly through the trees.

Then Dallas heard it. A faint hallooing sound.

"That ain't no damned coyote," said a trooper.

"Stow that!" barked Mills.

The moon cast a faint light on the valley of the Little Hatchet. Something was moving out on the open prairie beyond the row of willows and cottonwoods on the far bank of the creek.

"Stray horse?" asked Mills softly.

The hallooing sound came again.

"Damnedest horse whinny I ever heard," said Dallas. He strode toward the stream and stood on a fallen log, peering at the moving object. There was a man with the horse, and, as he led the animal on, he walked with a curious staggering gait. Then he raised his head and yelled. "That the camp there? Where the hell be ye? Halloo! *Halloo!*"

"For Christ's sake," said Jack Dutton out of the darkness. "It's that gawd-damned Leathers!"

"The *scout,*" said Dallas dryly.

"Making enough noise to be heard as far as the Little Chetish," said a veteran sergeant.

"Should I go out and get him, sir?" asked Corporal Faris.

Dallas shook his head. He scanned the surrounding terrain. There wasn't a sign of Sioux, which didn't mean a damned thing, for they could become part of the land and never be seen until they wanted to be seen.

"Maybe they'll catch the bastard," said Dutton savagely.

"I hope not," said Mills in an odd voice.

"Why?" demanded Dutton.

Mills glanced at the officer. "Maybe Montfort doesn't give much for Leathers, Jack, but he wants what Leathers probably has in those bulging saddlebags."

"Such as?"

"Liquor... what else?"

Dallas turned slowly, fully conscious of the noise the drunken scout was making as he neared the far side of the creek. "You mean Montfort sent him after more liquor, George?"

"Didn't you know that?"

"He's supposed to be a scout!"

Dutton spat. "We're better off without him! Look!"

The besotted scout had fallen across a log and lay with his head and shoulders in the shallow water. His tired horse stood with spraddled legs and hanging head.

"Go get him, Faris," said Dallas.

The non-com and a trooper plunged into the thigh deep water and waded across the stream. They hauled Leathers along, leading the horse behind them.

Dallas stepped close to the sagging scout. There was no doubt the man was drunk, for the reek of liquor hung about him, rising even above the sour sweat smell of the thrummed buckskins he affected. Dallas walked to the horse. He shook his head. "Foundered, sir," he said to Dutton.

Dutton raised a gnarled fist and drew it back.

"No," said Mills. "For God's sake, Jack! You know how he rates with Montfort!"

"You gawd-damned betcha!" babbled Leathers.

Dallas passed a hand over the nigh saddlebag. It was packed with bottles all right. "I'll be damned," he said.

"Where could he have gotten them?" asked Mills.

Dallas rubbed his jaw. "DeVoto's Station, where the Little Sunflower flows into the Big Sunflower."

"Good God! That's a full thirty miles from where we bivouacked last night!"

Dallas nodded. "The horse could tell you that."

"Take him to General Montfort," said Dutton. He spun on a heel and walked away.

Faris and the trooper half carried and half dragged the scout to the headquarters tent. Dallas led the foundered bay to the tent and took off the saddlebags. He deposited them on the ground with a faint clinking of glass and was stripping the saddle when he heard the boisterous greeting given to Leathers inside the tent.

"Leathers you old horned toad! You made it!" It was the voice of Arliss Montfort.

"Never fail a mission, sir," said Leathers.

"Stout fellow!" said Jordan Nares. "Where's the spirits!"

Dallas beckoned to a trooper. "Take the bay to the picket line, Fisher," he said quietly.

A tall figure darkened the front of the tent, and Dallas turned to see Arliss Montfort staring steadily at him. "What are you doing here, Lorimer?" asked the officer.

"I brought the horse here, sir."

"I see. Well, bring the saddlebags in. You might as well have a drink."

"Thank you, sir."

"Forget it."

Dallas picked up the saddlebags and bent to enter the tent flap. The heat of the lantern and the body heat of the six men inside struck him across the face after the coolness of the outside air. The general had walked to the head of the table and now stood beside his folding seat. Jordan Nares was close to the general, staring at Dallas with liquor-bright eyes. Leathers was clinging to the rear tent pole, blinking his eyes. "Got to take a leak," he announced.

"Not in *here,* you old horned toad," cried out young Willis Cox, a shavetail and Montfort's aide-de-camp. He hiccupped.

Another of the group was dark and saturnine Captain Mark Christian, commander of B Company, a man who had served in many places and in many armies and who had met Montfort during the war. A savage and sadistic man when in his cups. More than once he had been almost brought to court-martial for his treatment of the men in his command. Montfort had always stood in the way of the court-martial. Some latrine rumors had it that Christian had something on Montfort, something deep and dark from the past. He certainly wasn't the gay type that Montfort usually liked around him when he drank. They said in the regiment that no one liked Mark Christian and that Mark Christian repaid that feeling with interest.

The last officer was First Lieutenant Chet Windolph, the very image of a subaltern of light horse, neat and immaculate, polished at all times, who drank like a gentleman most of the time, sat his fine blooded horses like a Centaur, and gave the battalion *tone* in the garrison parades, for no officer quite looked like Chet Windolph. He had only one trouble for an army officer. His professional knowledge was the exact opposite of his appearance. In short, he stuffed an officer's uniform like a military tailor's dummy. There was a saying in his command, C Company, that if you hit First-Sergeant Bert Magnus in the head you'd knock Chet Windolph's brains out.

Dallas placed the saddlebags on the table, and Nares eagerly fumbled with the straps.

"Take it easy, you drunken old coot!" cried out Willis Cox. The fact that Jordan Nares wore the oak leaf of a major and had been in the army before Cox had been born had little effect on the irrepressible and drunken shavetail.

"Got to take a leak," said Mordecai Leathers solemnly.

Dallas glanced at the scout. His dirty ragged beard, stained with tobacco juice, waggled up and down as he spoke; fully half of his teeth were either missing or were rotting snags. His hook of a nose, speckled with oily blackheads, always had a lucid drop hanging at the tip of it, and his eyes were a dirty yellow. The wonder of the man was that Arliss Montfort liked him, associated with him, and protected him.

Chet Windolph poured the drinks with a steady hand and passed them out. "What's the toast?" he asked in his silky voice.

"Mordecai Leathers, the finest scout west of the Mississippi," said Cox. "Who else could find liquor out in this hell-hole of a country?"

"Hear! Hear!" said Nares.

They raised their glasses, and even Dallas did it, for he wanted no part of any trouble with Montfort. He eyed the commanding officer as he did so. Arliss Montfort had aquiline features, gray eyes that were almost too light for his dark smooth complexion, and curling brown hair that he wore long on the neck. He was tall and lean, a perfect horseman and tireless marcher, and any man who saw him in uniform knew he was the soldier born.

"Got to take a leak," insisted Leathers. He staggered toward the door, brushed past Dallas, then fumbled with the front of his filthy trousers.

"Not here," said Dallas coldly.

"Why not?" demanded the scout.

Dallas looked at Montfort. Camp sanitation was strict, and many a trooper had found that out when dealing with Arliss Montfort. There was an odd look in Montfort's eyes, for he usually let Leathers get away with almost anything.

"Why not?" repeated Leathers.

Montfort glanced at the scout. "Get to the latrine," he said.

"Too damned far, general!"

"Get to the latrine!"

"Oh, gawd-dammit! All right! All right!" Leathers shot a look of hate at Dallas and staggered away.

A moment later there was a crashing noise followed by the spat out curses of troopers, then the hoarse yelling of a man in pain. "That drunken Leathers fell into our fire!" cried a trooper.

Dallas turned on a heel to see them dragging Leathers from the fire. He had seared his hands and knees in the embers. He slobbered and cursed in his pain. "Damn you, Lorimer," he snarled. "Hadn't been for you buttin' in I'd been all right!"

"Take him to the medical sergeant," said Dallas. "He'll live."

He returned to the tent in time to see the glasses being refilled. Windolph handed him a glass. "We don't see much of you, Dallas," he said politely.

Nares eyed Dallas. "Poker game starts later," he said thickly.

"Thanks, no," said Dallas.

Nares nodded. There was a malicious look in his small eyes.

"Jean will be in later," said the paymaster. "The General has some wine being chilled for her." He was trying to turn the knife within Dallas now, for both of them knew Montfort's reputation as a shady Don Juan. Any woman was fair game to him.

"Enchanting girl," said Willis Cox. He grinned drunkenly at Nares. "How did a baldheaded old buzzard like you ever get a niece like that?"

Mark Christian emptied his glass and refilled it. Women were not one of his failings.

Chet Windolph leaned back in his chair. "We're going to miss Jean after we leave you at Fort Edgerton, Jordan," he said quietly.

The paymaster grinned evilly. "At least she'll be away from you lechers."

Cox smiled vacuously. "Into the hands of the lechers at Fort Edgerton," he said.

"Not bad for you, Cox," said Christian sarcastically.

Cox smiled again. There wasn't any doubt about what was in his simple mind.

"I hope Miss Jean isn't husband-hunting," said the general. "It seems to me that the game isn't that far afield, Jordan."

The paymaster spat indelicately. "I want her to marry a man of substance, not some poor frontier officer."

Dallas ignored the looks some of them shot in his direction.

Nares refilled his glass. "She's a real catch," he said complacently. "Lovely. She'll breed well and be a comfort in bed to any man who wins her."

Almost as though he was talking about a brood mare, thought Dallas.

Nares stared thoughtfully at his drink. "Thirty years in the Army and hardly a sou put away. With my retirement pay and her husband's fortune, I should be well fixed for the rest of my days."

None of them spoke. Careless as they were for the most part, it seemed almost evil to sit and listen to the man.

Montfort caught Dallas' eye. "Poker later?" he asked.

"Not tonight, sir," replied Dallas.

Christian looked up. "They say you were quite a poker player at one time," he said.

"Lucky at cards, unlucky at love," said Nares. He emptied his glass and looked quickly at Chet Windolph. His meaning was plain enough. Chet Windolph had money, a great deal of money.

"Good night gentlemen," said Dallas. He left the tent. Nares laughed drunkenly.

She was standing near the bank of the stream with a scarf hanging loosely about her shapely shoulders. Dallas flushed. She must have heard every word. She turned and smiled. "Very interesting, wasn't it?" she asked quietly.

"I'm sorry," he said as he took off his hat.

"For what? You didn't say anything. It was him."

"Maybe I *should* have said something, Jean."

She shook her head. "No. It's plain enough to everyone. He has nothing and I have nothing. He's the only living relative I have left, Dallas. I had nowhere else to go."

"Perhaps it would have been better if you had tried things on your own."

She laughed. "What do I know?" She looked down at her full bust, passed her hands up and down her shapely thighs, then looked at Dallas with a tilted head. "I know nothing with which to make a living, but I have something to trade for a husband and money."

"Dammit, Jean! I can't bear to hear you talk that way."

There was a strange look in her eyes. "There was a time when you might have taken me, Dallas."

"Wait a little while, Jean. I'll make out somehow."

She smiled, but there was no mirth in her lovely eyes. "Perhaps it's too late, Dallas."

"No!"

She glanced toward the tent. "Listen to them," she said sarcastically. "Eat, drink, and be merry, for tomorrow..."

"Which one of them is it, Jean?"

"What difference does it make?"

"Windolph? Montfort? Cox?"

She looked away. "Windolph has money," she said in a low voice. "Montfort is a spendthrift. Willis Cox is a fool." She turned, touched his cheek with a soft hand, kissed him gently, then walked toward the general's tent. She did not look back.

He stood there on the bank of the Little Hatchet and listened to the far-off crying of a coyote, but that nocturnal wanderer was no more lonesome than Dallas Lorimer, officer of cavalry.

CHAPTER THREE

The Rees had been nervous all day as the column slogged on through country that was gradually rising on either side of the faint trail in low rounded humps cut deeply by coulees. But none of them had deserted as Dallas Lorimer had suspected they would. They were still on duty, and this time they all were flung out from the column, riding cautiously through the hills on either flank, probing into the coulees and shallow valleys ahead, with two of them bringing up the rear behind the cavalry squad that rode as rear guard. They were all there, led by their sub-chief Horns-In-Front: Good Face, Bull-In-The-Stream, Goose, Red-Foolish-Bear, Crooked Horn and Forked Horn, Bear-Running-In-The-Timber, Owl, and Strike-The-Lodge.

Dallas rode with them in the advance all morning, then returned to the column and changed horses, only to ride to the far right flank to scout with Owl and Good Face along the banks of the Little Hatchet. It was hardly more than a trickle now. The thin dust rising from the column mingled with a faint October haze that arose from the low hills as the day wore on.

The thing that bothered Dallas most was the fact that none of the Rees were too sure of this part of the country. Horns-In-Front, the Ree sub-chief who led his tribesmen, had been through there as a boy when the Rees and the Sioux had been on good terms, but that had been long ago, and, despite the phenomenally good memory any Indian has for any country he has passed through, even once, the Ree chief was still in doubt about some features of this country.

There was Mordecai Leathers of course. He had claimed that he had known the country well before the war, had been one of the few men who had escaped from the hard fight there in '60 when the Oglala had barred the way, then had driven two companies of regulars back to the Little Sunflower with thirty percent losses. He even claimed he had been in there hunting buffalo *during the war,* between battles in the East, of course, for the war would never have been won had it not been for Mordecai Leathers.

Dallas watched Owl ride slantways down a long ridge, then draw up his horse beside the stream to wait for Dallas. "What is it, my brother?" asked Dallas.

Owl thrust out a thin arm, pointing to a dim notch in the rougher hills ahead. *"Wicunkasotapelo,"* he said in the guttural Sioux tongue. It was the stream known to the whites as the Big Hatchet. It was known to them for other things as well, and not of pleasant memory.

Dallas nodded. He had known they must be somewhere near the Big Hatchet by this time.

"No good," said Owl.

"Be of brave heart, my brother."

"I am not afraid, my brother, but there are many young men with me. The Lakota medicine is strong in these hills. Perhaps we will not return home."

There was nothing for Dallas to say. He kneed his horse away from Owl. "Follow me, my brother," he said quietly. "Let Good Face continue on. He has a fast horse."

They rode toward the column, rising to the top of a

ridge to look down upon the dusty progress of the troopers and the wagons. There was no sign of Mordecai Leathers. In fact, Dallas had not seen him all day. Dallas and the Ree rode down toward the column. The sun was slanting to the west, and already long shadows were creeping across the rolling country.

General Montfort was at the head of the column. His hounds coursed along beside him. The man didn't look as though he had been up most of the night drinking and playing poker. Dallas saluted and Montfort drew rein.

"Well, Lorimer," he said pleasantly enough, "what news do you bring?"

"No sign of hostiles, sir."

There was a faint gleam of amusement in Montfort's eyes. "You didn't expect them to attack, did you now, Lorimer?"

"This is their country, sir."

"Their country? This is *our* country. The United States!"

"As far as we can shoot, sir."

"I never took you for a man afraid to pass through Indian country."

Dallas flushed. "There is such a thing as flaunting your courage in front of the hostiles. They like challenges, and I've never met one of them who wouldn't take up one placed before them. Another thing, sir: They outnumber us greatly."

"You place a great deal of confidence in their numbers and ability, Mister Lorimer."

"I have served on the frontier for fourteen years, sir. I think I know them better than most men."

"Including your commanding officer perhaps?"

"I didn't say that, General Montfort."

"Your meaning is clear. You place a great deal of confidence in your ability as a scout officer then?"

Dallas hesitated. "The General would not have asked for me if he had not believed in my ability as such."

Montfort's face tightened and then he smiled. "Touché, Mister Lorimer! How is the camping ahead?"

"The Big Hatchet can be reached before dusk. I'd advise no fires tonight, sir."

"The Sioux know we are here."

"Agreed, sir."

"I notice they keep away from us."

Dallas looked to the south. "Look, sir!" He pointed to a high ridge.

Montfort stood up in his stirrups. "It's a prowling wolf."

"Look closer, sir."

Montfort shot an angry glance at Dallas, then stared at the wolf. It took that moment to stand up on its hind legs, almost casually. It was a hostile scout in wolf cap and pelt.

"Damn, Lorimer! You're right! Tell Captain Dutton to bivouac on the Big Hatchet! We'll join the column there at dusk!" He turned in his saddle. "Leathers, Cox, Christian, and Windolph! Follow me! The game is in sight!"

Jean Ross cantered up, supremely attractive in blue blouse buttoned tightly across full breasts, blue riding skirt, and with an officer's forage cap tilted on her lovely head. "May I ride, too, General?"

He smiled, revealing even white teeth. "Of course! You'll be safe enough with us, Miss Jean."

Then they were gone, racing up the ridge, while the lone scout eyed them casually, then vanished as quickly as he had appeared.

Owl looked at Dallas. He swiftly drew his hand across his throat; the sign for Sioux, the throat-cutters.

Dutton rode up. "What the hell is this, Lorimer?" he demanded.

"The General has gone after a Sioux scout, sir. We're to bivouac on the Big Hatchet. He'll join us there."

"I almost hope he doesn't!"

"Take it easy, sir!"

"I don't think I have to explain to you how I feel."

"No, sir."

"Get about your business then. I'll feel safer with you up there with the Rees, but for God's sake don't take any chances!"

Dallas smiled. "Your solicitude for my health is very pleasing, sir."

Dutton spat. "Buffalo crap! I know I can depend on you to keep us from walking into an ambush. That's my chief concern, Mister Lorimer!"

Dallas grinned. You always knew how you stood with Jack Dutton. He spurred ahead of the column, followed closely by Owl.

The moon was flooding the shallow valley of the *Wicunkasotapelo,* the clear flowing stream known to the *Wasicun,* the Whites, as the Big Hatchet. Here the hills had somehow seemed to move in closer after dusk, as though curious to peer into the bivouac of the dusty men and horses who had come from the east into the country of the Oglala, known variously as Those-Who-Stand-In-The-Middle, Dirt-Throwers, or Scatter-One's-Own. There was another name for them; a grimmer name, a portent to those who now camped along the Big Hatchet —*The Throat-Cutters.*

There was a quiet, brooding quality about the camp. Jack Dutton had allowed the usual pit fires for the making of coffee, the frying of meat, and the heating of issue beans, then had ordered them to be extinguished except for the one fire that kept the guard coffee pot hot and also served to cook supper for General Montfort and his coterie of Sioux hunters, for the commanding officer had not appeared at dusk as he had said he would.

Time and time again Dallas Lorimer walked out beyond the guard perimeter with a pocket pistol in his hand to watch and listen for the missing men.

The wind swept down from the hills bringing with it the mingled odors of dried wildflowers and sage, raveling the faint scarf of smoke that hung along the creek, bringing also what seemed like a faint and indistinguishable but insistent voice of warning. *"Wah-nee-chee,"* it seemed to say. "No good." It was in the tongue of the Sioux, which was fitting, for this was a stronghold of those people. *"Wah-nee-chee.* No good."

Dallas eyed the moonlit hills. They were well into them now, but it was only a quarter of the distance they would have to go through to reach the more open country on the approaches to Fort Edgerton. The deeper they rode into that hill country, the closer the hills would crowd in on them until one day the hills would bristle with feathered bonnets and warpainted Sioux, Cheyenne, and Arapaho, with their ponies' tails tied up and the deep chested war cries echoing from the hills.

George Mills came out behind Dallas carrying his Henry rifle. "Any sign, Dallas?" he asked.

"None."

"Dutton says if they don't come back he'll pull out of this trap and head south."

"It will have to be tomorrow then. For after that we'll have no choice except to go back the way we came or push on ahead until we get out of these hills."

"Maybe it would be better if Montfort didn't come back."

"You're talking like Dutton now."

Mills shrugged. "The Rees aren't even sure of the way now. What about you?"

"They know more than I do."

"That leaves Leathers."

Dallas spat.

"Your meaning is clear enough, Dallas."

Dallas raised his head. The wind had shifted, bringing with it a faint thudding noise. He dropped to the ground and placed his ear against it. The vibrations came through clearly. "Hoofbeats," he said.

"Ours?"

Dallas grinned. "You wouldn't hear the hostiles coming, if that's what you mean."

Then they heard the faint sound of voices. No Indian would make that much noise.

"There they are," said the infantry officer.

The party had appeared on a low hill, urging their horses down toward the valley.

"Thank God the Sioux don't fight at night," said Dallas. "If they did, those men would be cut to pieces before they got off that damned moonlit hill."

They walked back toward the bivouac, and by the time they reached it the horsemen had passed the sentry perimeter. Montfort flung down from his horse. "Cassidy!" he barked. "Leathers has prime buffalo hump. Get it started on your mess fire."

"Yes, sorr," said the headquarters cook. "Ye were huntin' then, sorr? Ye had us fair worried, ye did."

Montfort slapped the dust from his clothing with his hat. "The scout evaded us but we had fine sport running down a buffalo. A man could almost get his fill of game in this country."

"Or Sioux," said George Mills in a low voice.

Montfort looked up quickly. "What was that, Mister Mills?" he demanded. The man had hearing like a dog.

"Nothing really, sir."

The angry grey eyes studied the tall infantryman. "Take care, sir! Take care what you say in my hearing unless you care to explain it!"

"My apologies, General Montfort."

The commanding officer nodded abruptly, then walked to his tent. He turned. "Mister Lorimer, pass the word to all officers that there will be an officers' meeting in one hour and a half exactly, here at my tent."

"Yes, sir."

The moon rose higher and higher, etching shadows of trees and rocks upon the light colored earth, changing the coloring of the stream so that it seemed like dancing, molten silver rushing between its banks. The odor of cooking buffalo hump rose over the bivouac. In General Montfort's tent there was merriment as the hunters had a few appetizers in the way of rye and branch water.

The clear silvery light also revealed something on the far bank of the stream where the rushing waters of the spring freshets had cut deeply into the soil, then had retreated in time to cut another bank lower down the slope. Scattered on the moonlit ground were white rounded shapes and lengths of what looked like whitened tubing. It was hard at first to distinguish what the objects were, but gradually it dawned upon the men, and the news went swiftly about the bivouac until only those men in the tent of General Montfort were ignorant of the facts. They were still busy with succulent buffalo hump and rye whiskey.

It was time for the officers' meeting, and they were all there: Montfort, Christian, Nares, Dutton, Mills, Windolph and Cox, as well as Dallas Lorimer and Mordecai Leathers. The rest of the officers sat well back, away from Montfort's coterie. Horns-In-Front, the Ree subchief, sat just behind Dallas, wrapped in his blanket; his thin dark face painted the very picture of gloom.

Montfort nodded to Willis Cox, who soberly leaned forward and tapped a fork against the water glass that had been placed atop the little field table that stood in front of General Montfort. All of the officers stood up. George Mills eyed Cox, then whispered softly to Dallas. "Well, Little Willis has done his duty for the day. Damned if it isn't the only thing he does well."

Montfort glanced angrily at Mills, then nodded. "Sit down, gentlemen. No formality here. We're in the field." The officers all sat down again.

Montfort looked from one to the other of them. "We're in the heart of hostile country according to all reports." Here he glanced at Dallas. "I agree that the hostiles are in this country, but we'll have no trouble with them I assure you. We pursued a scout today who ran like a coyote rather than the wolf he was supposed to represent."

"Oh, God," said Mills softly to Dallas. *"One* warrior."

Montfort raised his head. "We have three companies of cavalry and one of infantry, plenty of ammunition, and the ability to use it. I could march this command clear through the Sioux Nation!"

Somewhere off beyond the Big Hatchet a wolf howled. A moment later another wolf howled from the low hills to the south.

"Lakota," said Horns-In-Front. He knew those were not wolves, and so did Dallas Lorimer.

"My purpose in having this meeting is to stop the rumors that been floating about the command ever since we left the Little Sunflower. Fear has no place in this command! Our duty is to take Paymaster Nares, his niece, and his payroll through to Fort Edgerton, and this we will do at any cost! I want no more rumor peddling, no frightened looks at the hills, no more trembling at the sight of a dirty red arrow or a few skulls and stones placed in our path. They means nothing to me, gentlemen, and they will mean nothing to you. The Sioux fear us more than we fear them!"

"Hear, hear," said George Mills in a whisper to Dallas.

"Thus far we have progressed well," continued Montfort. "We have kept up our schedule of marches. We have had no trouble with the hostiles. We have eaten well, slept well, and have had good water and grazing. What more can we ask?" He eyed each officer in turn. "Morale!" he snapped. "The morale necessary in any tightly woven command of Regulars. This I want, from now on! Are there any questions?"

The wind sighed through the trees. No one spoke. Mordecai Leathers hiccupped.

Arliss Montfort didn't seem to be listening for questions. He was staring across the creek toward the white rounded shapes and the lengths of whitened tube-like material that lay on the far bank. "What is that lying over there?" he demanded.

Dallas stood up. "Skulls and bones, sir, of horses and men."

Montfort's face tightened in the moonlight. "Of *what* men, Mister Lorimer?"

"In all probability the men of the two cavalry companies who fought in this area just before the war, sir. They had thirty percent losses. They had just time to dump the bodies into a coulee over there and cover them with a little earth. The Big Hatchet evidently shifted its course in a spring freshet and uncovered the bodies, sir."

Mordecai Leathers hiccupped. Montfort looked at the scout. "Is that right, Leathers?" he asked.

"Yes, sir. I was right here in them days. Right here, fighting like a tiger. Hadn't been for me they'da never got out. Now I..."

"That's quite enough, Leathers," said the commanding officer.

There was cold fear etched on the faces of many of the officers. It was not a good place. *Wah-nee-chee*...

"This is nothing to upset us, gentlemen," said Montfort, but all the same there was an odd look on his handsome face. He knew and they knew that his brave words had been neatly cancelled out by the silent bones across the Big Hatchet.

"*Wicunkasotapelo,*" said Horns-In-Front.

"What does that mean, Leathers?" asked the general.

"I don't palaver Ree," said the scout, "only Sioux and Crow."

"Lorimer?" said the general.

Dallas looked at the officer. "It isn't Ree, sir. I thought Mister Leathers knew Sioux."

"Can't remember every gawd-damned tongue twisting word," snarled Leathers.

Dallas smiled thinly. "It isn't a word but rather a

phrase. It's Oglala for the name they have given this stream and place."

"So?" demanded Montfort testily.

The wind had picked up and was keening shrilly through the valley.

"It means The Place Where We Killed Them All," said Dallas quietly.

A cold pall seemed to drop over the group. Montfort glanced at the skulls and bones bathed in the silvery light. Just then the wind blew down the silken guidon which had been placed, butt thrust into the soft earth, just at the entrance to the headquarters tent.

Horns-In-Front slowly drew his blanket up over his loose dark hair, arose, and walked away into the shadows of the trees.

Montfort glanced angrily at the guidon. Willis Cox sprang to raise the guidon and thrust it back into the earth, but the rising wind fought with him as though for possession of it. Once again, the guidon fell down, and not until Jack Dutton gave a hand to the young aide did the guidon remain upright.

"Good night, gentlemen," said Montfort quietly.

As they walked back to their beds the officers could hear the wolves calling to each other from the low hills along the valley of the *Wicunkasotapelo*. This time there were many more of them crying out into the night, and they were much closer to the bivouac.

Dallas walked to the far end of the line of tents to look toward the distant, dreaming hills. "Dallas," she called out. He turned. She stood just within the doorway of her tent. There was no one else within sight. He walked to her, and she took him by an arm and drew him into the tent. The perfume of her body and nightgown mingled with the warm smell of the canvas and the dried grasses beneath their feet. She slid her arms about his neck and drew his face down to hers, placing a soft lingering kiss on his mouth. He rested his hands on her rounded hips. There was no need to talk; he wanted her more than he ever had before. There had been some passionate moments between them in days gone past, but this seemed different to him, almost as though she was throwing herself at him; yet she had said it was too late for him just the night before.

She kissed him again, and he looked down at her lovely face in the dimness. There was no need to say anything. He carried her to her cot and passed his hands up and down her warm body. The gown fell away from her smooth flesh. She drew him close. "Now," she said breathlessly. "Tonight, Dallas. *Tonight or never!*"

In that instant he forgot everything but his hunger for her, and they both forgot where they were for a short time, and yet seemingly such a long time.

CHAPTER FOUR

The command moved out as quietly as possible in the pre-dawn darkness, but no matter how quietly white men, other than veteran scouts, moved in Indian country, there was enough noise carried on the dawn wind to keenly listening ears just beyond bullet range to let the hostiles know what was going on.

First, the silent Rees had drifted off into the windy darkness an hour before A Company's advance party had moved out. Then A Company's remaining platoons had moved out at a walk ahead of the little headquarters detachment followed by half of B Company, ahead of the wagons and the two ambulances, with the second half closed in behind them. The infantrymen of H Company walked alongside the wagons with a steady mile eating stride, carrying their long-barreled Springfield .45/70 rifles with ease at every which way and angle. C Company closed up as rear guard, with a screen of flankers out along the sides of the column; a few Rees tailed after the long column just behind the last of the drifting dust stirred up by the moving mass of men, wagons, and horses.

Dallas Lorimer moved through the darkness between his outflung Rees and the unseen advance guard. It was chancy business, for the Rees were nervous and the troops were jittery, and over and above those possible dangers there was a greater danger, that of the hostiles who were somewhere in the darkness like great listening cats.

There had still been a chance for General Montfort to turn back. During the long night, when Dallas had prowled restlessly about the camp after leaving Jean, he had heard Jack Dutton talking to Montfort in the general's tent. The gist of the talk had been that Dutton had wanted to turn south, away from the brooding hills, to reach the safer trail to Edgerton by a forced march while there was yet time.

Dallas was no eavesdropper, but something had kept him within listening distance, and he had ears every bit as good as a Sioux scout. It hadn't really been hard to hear the discussion, if you could call it that, for both Montfort and Dutton had raised their voices in anger more than once. There were others who had heard the two men arguing. Willis Cox, Mark Christian, Chet Windolph, Mordecai Leathers, and an assorted set of enlisted men bunked not far from the headquarters tent, and they could hardly miss hearing the two men.

Dutton's arguments had been conclusive and right, as far as Dallas was concerned. But Montfort, despite his stubborn insistence on the more dangerous hill route, had really offered no valid reason for his decision other than a saving of time. It was a less than poor reason; they might save a little time and lose everything including their scalps. It wasn't like Arliss Montfort to risk life and reputation in such a move. True, the man was daring and courageous; sure of himself and proud of his past record. But there would be little glory in getting beaten by the hostiles, if the command survived. There was no concrete reason for Montfort to lead his command through those hills. Why was he doing it?

Dallas rode slowly back toward the advance party.

The weight of the lives of the one hundred and seventy-five men who formed the column was enough to make any commanding officer think twice before he flaunted them in front of the Oglala and their allies. Then, too, there was the payroll. Fifty thousand dollars was a fortune by any standard. The hostiles wouldn't touch it. They'd be more interested in the scalps, guns, and horses of the column than in the greenbacks in Nares' ambulance. And then there was Jean Ross...

There was a faint suspicion of light in the eastern sky, the coming of the false dawn. A cold wind swept through the defiles to the west of the column as it moved steadily along, deeper and deeper into the hostile country. In a little while the die would be cast, and there would be no turning back.

But the long day wore on and on, and there was no sign of the enemy. No thin thread of a smoke signal mounting against the bright blue sky. No feathered warrior watching them from the hills. No warning signs placed in their path. Nothing.

The noon halt came and passed, and the troopers settled down for the long hot afternoon, slogging on and on, leading their horses most of the time. It wasn't quite the place to be caught with a tired horse.

Dallas was here, there, and everywhere, now with the advance Rees; now with the flankers; then with the last of the Rees who followed the column. Nothing. Nothing but dust, sun glare, and the ceaseless dry wind.

By three o'clock in the afternoon they had debouched into a large oval valley, flanked on all sides by low, naked hills and peopled with racing antelope. It was too much for the blood of Arliss Montfort. He led the way in the chase, followed by Jean Ross, Willis Cox, Mordecai Leathers, Mark Christian, Chet Windolph, and the fleet greyhounds. They assumed they were safe enough. No hostile could cross that valley without being seen. They would have time to regain the column should the hostiles try to head them off.

But the chase was too exhilarating, and in twenty minutes the racing horsemen had vanished into a draw after the antelope. But the column still slogged on. Dallas Lorimer rode far out on the right flank, dripping into swales and draws, losing sight of the column now and then. The Rees were worse now. Horns-In-Front had taken out his bag of sacred red clay and had ridden from one of his men to another and another, smearing the red clay on their naked chests, tracing sacred symbols in the daubed clay. It was a bad sign, for the Rees were thus admitting that they expected battle or ambush. *Wah-nee-chee*...

The troopers eyed the hills ahead as they led their dusty horses; the infantrymen walked along in their steady swinging stride, and they, too, watched those hills. The teamsters shifted their tobacco cuds, spat, then reflectively studied those hazy hills again.

The hills closed in now, and the column filled the valley with its dust. That dust could be seen for miles. But still there was nothing to be seen beyond the dun hills and the fleeting clouds that sent their shadows ahead of them across hill and valley, then pursued those shadows in a hopeless race they could never win, allowing only the dusk to end the futility of it.

Dallas found himself hoping for dusk. The hostiles would not attack at night, and they'd hardly attack a well-planned bivouac of stockaded wagons garrisoned by troops firing breech-loading rifles and carbines. There was at least three hours of daylight left, and time and time again Dallas eyed the slanting rays of the sun, then snapped open the case of his watch and glanced at those slowly moving hands.

Montfort was gone, almost as though he had care-lessly abandoned his command to its fate. It was the Montfort Way; his luck was always with him. All Dallas had to do was to ride away from that column for ten minutes, and he'd find out that he had failed his responsibilities in one way or another. There wasn't that kind of luck in the life of Dallas Lorimer.

They had reached a raised area on the valley floor, rimmed by lower ground which in turn was rimmed by the sere hills. The head of the column was at the western end of it, with the slowly moving tail just rising to the eastern crest, when one of the Rees suddenly appeared on a ridge to the north-west, raising his rifle high overhead, then pirouetting his paint horse in tight little circles. *Enemy in sight!*

But the warning was too late for the column to shift into a sure defense. A handful of panicky Ree, lashing their racing horses savagely, turned back from the narrow defile just ahead of the company and slammed their way through A Company's advance party of two squads, raising a yellow pall of dust, and the troopers had hardly regained their seats on the plunging horses when far better horsemen debouched from an unseen draw and drove into them like a feathered battering ram.

The yelling troopers were driven back on the remainder of A Company. Jack Dutton tried to rally his company, but half of them were on foot and half of them had mounted, and in the confusion the smashing hostile charge drove them back on the little headquarters detachment. Gunshots rattled steadily as Sioux, Cheyenne, and Arapaho spread out into a crescent and closed in on A Company and the headquarters group. Then as the warriors emptied their guns they slammed their painted horses against those of the cursing troopers and went to work with pipe-axe, war-club, and lance.

It was hell and confusion, laced with screaming, wide-eyed fear, and the discipline of the troopers was riven clean through like the skull of Jack Dutton, from crown to bearded chin, even as he had opened his mouth to rally his fear crazed company. The warrior who had killed

Dutton leaped his horses over the corpse and struck into the leading squad of B Company, lashing right and left with his axe until he went down with a .45/70 slug through his sternum.

Then up from the rear came a tight knot of Cheyenne. *Ho-ta-min-tanio.* The Crazy Dog Soldiers stuck the rear guard after scattering the few Rees behind it. C Company had been almost ready for this attack, and they fought from behind their horses, striking down a quarter of the hard riding Cheyennes. The dusty infantrymen fought from behind the wagons, not realizing that there was no back and no front to this mad battle, for up from the southern rim of the raised area of the valley floor, debouching from brush-shielded draws and coulees, came a wave of slim Arapaho, whose first charge struck the infantrymen from behind, and as they turned to fight the Arapaho a wave of Sioux and Cheyenne came up from the northern side and were in amongst the wagons and the frenzied teamsters, who had no time to reach for the rifles carried behind their seats.

A dust pall rose higher and higher over the valley, laced with blossoms of red and white as guns flashed ceaselessly.

"H'gun! H'gun!" screamed the Sioux as they gave voice to their courage word.

The Crazy Dog Soldiers, wearing their distinctive three black feathers at the rear of their heads, drove through fighting C Company to reach the wagons to get at the infantry, who had already suffered heavy losses from the Arapaho. A wagon turned from the column at a run, its front wheels struck a hole, and the wagon rose slowly into the air and came down heavily, scattering its load. The screaming horses lashed out with their hoofs and killed Second Lieutenant Morgan Bellis of H Company as he staggered past, blinded with his own blood from an inch-deep scalp wound.

Dallas Lorimer was charmed, at least at the beginning

of the fight, for the screaming hostiles had passed him in a dead run for the wagons. He found himself almost a spectator, holding down his rearing horse in the swirling dust as feathered warrior after feathered warrior shot past him, some with curved coup sticks outthrust to tally glory for themselves.

An Arapaho closed in on Dallas with raised lance and went down with a pistol bullet in his chest. Dallas crouched to get beneath the sweeping blow of a pipe-axe and fired twice into the sweat-dewed belly of a burly Cheyenne. His fourth, fifth and sixth shots cleared a path through a knot of warriors so that he reached the tail end of the wagons.

He kneed his horse close to a wagon and had just time to reload his pistol when he found himself astride a dead horse. He cleared leather, alighted on his feet, and felt a bullet tear through the crown of his hat and another rip through the slack in his sweat-soaked shirt.

There was nothing to do now but to fight alone, for there was no discipline left in the column. The Johnny Raws died screaming, and the veterans died silently after tallying a buck or two. Second Lieutenant Harry Bond of C Company fought like a tiger, wrestling on the ground with a Cheyenne, only to die with a lance thrust through his kidneys. Lieutenant Julius Homer of B Company opened his mouth to yell a command and had it stopped by a chewed slug from a trade rifle, and even as he went down a scalping knife circumscribed his skull, and he lost his scalp before he hit the ground.

Quartermaster Otto Pfennig fought like a berserker, clearing a path with a reversed rifle that was little more than a bloody tube of steel with tatters of wood, hair, and flesh on it, until he went down when struck by a charging Sioux horse and died with three bullets in his head.

Horns-In-Front charged through the yellow pall to reach Dallas but died with an arrow through his shoulder-blades. The Rees had been scattered. Some of them fought. Some of them died before they could fight. Some of them ran. It was the white man's fight, not theirs. They had been paid to scout, not to fight, and they considered it no fault of theirs that the hostiles had sprung as neat a trap as had ever been seen on the Plains. The Rees had failed the column and those that didn't stay and fight or stay and die, vanished through the dust, praying hopelessly to their God that they could pass unseen through a swarm of enemy warriors.

Some of the Sioux and Cheyenne were laughing scornfully as they used their quirts on the few Rees they had trapped. It was the prime insult. The Rees begged to be killed as the quirts lashed at them viciously. Death was better than such disgrace.

"H'gun! H'gun!" screamed the Sioux. *"Hay-ay! Hay-ay!"* echoed the Elk warriors, the Crazy Heads, and the Fox warriors of the Cheyenne, who fought as well as the famed Crazy Dog Soldiers.

A yelling Sioux beat badly wounded First-Sergeant Magnus of C Company to death with an elkhorn bow, measuring his blows with his shouting, "Hownh! *Hownh! Hownh! Hownh!"*

"Brave up! Brave up!" yelled the hostiles. "Take courage! The Earth is all that lasts!"

Dallas Lorimer staggered through the mingled smoke and dust trying to rally the scattered troopers, but it was no use. The column was defeated, and it was doomed, for that was the way of the grim enemy that had trapped and defeated them. There would be no prisoners, and it was better so, for if the hostiles took prisoners to the Indian camp, the women would have their way with knife and fire, and they were more savage than the men in many ways.

A charging horse drove Dallas Lorimer to one side against an ambulance. He caught a glance of Jordan Nares, lying across the back seat, his pasty face loose and slack and the top of his bald head naked to the blood reddened bone; the warrior who had scalped him, more as a joke than anything else, had stuffed the hairless flap of skin into Nares' gaping mouth. But the money chests were still beneath him.

Already the victorious warriors were riding through the mess, thrusting their lances into the left thighs of the dead so that they could make an official count for their tribesmen. Other warriors on the outskirts of the fray were driving off captured horses or carrying loot while a handful of white men still fought here and there in the noisy confusion.

Dallas Lorimer swung up onto the seat of the paymaster's ambulance, gripped the reins in his left hand, and lashed at the mules with the long whip. They buck-jumped and broke free of the press, scattering screaming warriors. Dallas fired his six-gun dry, then snatched up a Colt that lay on the seat beside him, and emptied that, too, forcing a way through the confused mass of horsemen.

The stench of smoke, dust, death, and hot brass hung about him as he raced toward the rear of the column with the hoofs striking the dead and wounded and the wheels riding high over them. A Cheyenne drove in close, drawing back an elkhorn bow to drive a shaft into Dallas, but the whip curled out across his broad painted face, and the arrow flew off into the dusty air.

The ambulance bounced and careened on the rutted trail. Dallas looked back across the bouncing body of Jordan Nares. He wasn't being followed. There was a faint chance. It was then that the mules plunged into a coulee. The ambulance shot out into space and fell fifteen feet, coming to rest on its top while the wheels spun on. Dallas Lorimer knew nothing more.

CHAPTER FIVE

A vagrant ray of moonlight, peering through a split in the side of the overturned ambulance, awakened Dallas Lorimer to a consciousness plagued by waves of pain that shot through his twisted body. His left eye was partially gummed shut by coagulated blood, and his scalp was caked with clotted blood and dirt; his throat was slate-dry. He slowly moved his body, fearing to find splintered bones, but he had nothing to fear in that respect.

He had been battered and bruised but was still fit enough. Fit enough if he could overcome the intense weariness that had settled in his lean body.

He looked about the interior of the ambulance and settled his hazy vision on something that leered at him in the dimness. With a start of horror, he saw the set, ghastly face of Jordan Nares staring at him with wide open eyes that would never see again. Something heavy lay across one of Dallas' legs, and he cautiously moved it to one side. It was one of the wooden, metal bound money chests that had been entrusted to the grinning dead man.

He lay there for a time trying to orient his thoughts. He was alive and comparatively unharmed, but a cold feeling crept over him as he realized that the column had been doomed. How was it that *he* was still alive?

He raised his head and listened, suddenly aware of a foul stench as gas escaped from the dead mules that lay in an inextricable tangle partly beneath the vehicle. There was little sound from without: the dry whispering of the prairie wind softly sighing a dirge over the valley of death, the rustling of brush in the wind, the nearby crying of coyotes as they hovered on the moonlighted hills watching and listening for signs of life in the valley before they prowled down for the unexpected feast spread for them.

Dallas Lorimer moved quietly. The first thing he did was to feel for a weapon, and his questing fingers found a Colt, which he slowly reloaded with shaking hands. He eased himself free from the tangle within the ambulance and cautiously peered out from beneath it. There was no sign of life. Nothing but the soft movement of the dried grasses beneath the touch of the wind. He bellied out from beneath the ambulance and looked up at the lip of the coulee, half expecting to see a painted face looking down at him, sighting along an arrow or rifle barrel. But there was no human within sight.

He crawled up the steep slope of the coulee until he could lay just beneath the brim of it, his head concealed by tufts of buffalo grass. From this point he could see the area where the massacre had taken place.

He picked away the blood from about his left eye as he studied the scene. At first he was surprised to see what looked like white boulders scattered the length of the raised area in front of him, ghastly white in the moonlight, until the knowledge came harshly to him that he was looking at the stripped bodies of the dead, intermingled with the dead horses and mules of the command.

The wagons had been completely looted and then burned. Over the silent battlefield hung the stench of death, powder smoke, burnt material, and hot brass from expended cartridges, and the wind had done little to dissipate it. There were no bodies of Indians lying about the field, although many of them had died or had been wounded during the time Dallas had participated in the fighting; but that was the Indian way, to remove the dead from a battlefield if possible. There were many dead Indian horses with those of the white men.

No one would ever know how many of the hostiles had died. Dallas touched his cracked lips with the tip of his tongue. He was just high enough to see the whole length of the field. There, at the extreme western limit of the raised portion of the valley floor was where the advance detail of A Company had been turned back, mingled with the screaming Rees, and then shot down one after another as they plowed back into the rest of their company.

There had been no time to form lines and to fight as white men did; the bodies of the soldiers were scattered about as though a great hand had gathered them up and strewn them carelessly on the dry earth.

Those who had not died had probably been taken to the hostile camps. It would have been better had they died.

But the desire for survival is strong in man, and it came to the rescue of Dallas Lorimer. He raised his head and listened. He could have almost sworn he had heard something moving out on the bloody field. Perhaps there were wounded out there. If so, he must help them in any way he could, although the chances of getting any wounded to safety were almost nil.

He slid down to the ruined ambulance and peered inside. It had contained a medicine chest, carried by regulations in all ambulances. He reached inside, over the stiffening body of Jordan Nares, to pull the chest from the ambulance. The money chests lay there, stained with the dark blood of the paymaster. They had not been touched. Dallas glanced at them. Even if the hostiles had found the wrecked ambulance they would not have taken the money. It was of no use to them, perhaps even considered bad medicine. Dallas smiled thinly. In many cases it was bad medicine for white men as well. He'd have to cache the money before he left.

He hauled the medicine chest to the top of the coulee and lugged it toward the first of the fallen. It was then that he saw a faint movement at the head of the fallen troopers at the far end of the area. He stared at it. Something was moving about out there. Then a coyote lifted its voice from the silvered hills, and a ghastly thought fled through his mind. He peered at the moving object, then saw it vanish into a draw. It wouldn't be an Indian, for they wouldn't stay near the newly dead.

He placed the medicine chest on the ground. Then a soft crying sound came to him, and he saw one of the bodies lying near a burned wagon appear to move a little. He eyed it. The newly dead sometimes whisper restlessly in the cool of the night. Cold sweat worked down his sides as he stood there.

Then he saw a movement again near the draw, and a figure moved silently toward the area where the crying sound had come from. Dallas stared. His vision was still not clear. He could have sworn he heard voices. Then the moving figure raised something in its hand, and the moonlight flashed on steel as it moved down swiftly and struck hard, followed by a strangled, grunting cry. Then it was silent again.

Dallas dropped to his knees, then to his belly, and felt for the pistol he had found in the ambulance. It was gone, and he remembered then that he had placed it to one side as he had reached into the ambulance for the medicine chest. He eyed the dim figure that now moved across the field. It stopped again, peered intently at something, then struck hard with the knife. This time the cry was loud and clear. The knifer stood up and looked about the field. It was not an Indian, unless it was one who had dressed himself in trooper's clothing.

There was something unholy and eerie about the way that figure stood there peering intently from one body to another. Perhaps it was a trooper crazed from the battle. In any case, it was no place for Dallas Lorimer to be without a weapon.

Then he saw something that raised the hair on his head. One of the naked men had arisen to his feet and stood staring at the man with the bloody knife in his hand. The knifer moved toward him. The naked man turned and ran in a staggering gait, directly toward the place where Dallas lay. His face was smeared with drying blood, and he ran with a wild desperation, but the other man was too swift for him. He bounded over several bodies as he silently chased the trooper.

Dallas rolled over to the edge of the coulee. There was a strangled scream from the fleeing man, snapped short as the blade went home between the shoulder-blades. The trooper went down and lay still, and this time he would not arise from the dead as he had done before. The killer left the knife there, as though satisfied there were no other wounded left on the field for his deadly intentions. He started to walk directly toward Dallas.

Dallas dropped into the coulee and winced as his ankle twisted beneath him. He could not walk. He began to crawl toward the pistol he had left lying beside the ambulance and had almost reached it when he heard the pattering of gravel behind him. He glanced back and saw the man standing at the lip of the coulee. He could not see the face because of the low-pulled campaign hat but he saw the hand dart down to a belt gun.

Dallas clawed for the Colt he had left beside the ambulance just as the other man's pistol cracked flatly. The slug spurted dirt up into Dallas' eyes. Once again the pistol cracked, raising rolling echoes, and this time the slug ripped across the side of Dallas' skull like the blow of a white hot mallet; he lay still and unknowing for the second time that day.

For a time he lived in a place of swirling light, interspersed with periods of complete darkness; there was a dull but intense pain in the left side of his skull that never let up, a steady tom-tom like throbbing from the inside of the bony structure of his head. It seemed as though the contents of his skull swelled and swelled in an effort to burst through the casing. There were periods when his throat seemed closed by dry husking hands. His eyes throbbed, and he could see nothing except grayish light through which dim things moved. He could have sworn he heard voices now and then, but he could not distinguish what they said.

Then there were the long periods of unconsciousness from which he awoke, still seeing nothing, to know that the pain had not left him. But there was motion, and beneath him he felt a dragging and a bumping and at times the motion made him sicken so that he spewed his guts out into the colorless void that surrounded him at all times.

Perhaps it was death, but in death there was supposed to be no pain. Then where was he? Who was he? He had been a soldier for a long time. That he well knew. But how had he come to this strange place of existence? There was no recollection of that transition at all.

But still there was motion that stopped for indefinite periods of time, then began again; the world about him was dark and then light; he smelled the odors of wood smoke and cooking food, and then he was fed slowly and persistently, no matter how many times his stomach revolted.

A strange feeling came over him that this was to be his way of life forever. The odor of dried sweet grass and flowers came to him now and then, mingled with the sour stench of his vomit and the dry, astringent odor of sage. And always there was motion at regular intervals, and he knew he was being taken somewhere. But from where to where? Who was he and where was he being taken? But it proved that he was important or valuable to someone; to the mysterious, unseen being that fed him and cleaned him and talked to him in words he could not distinguish.

In time, the motions stopped, and there was the feeling that he was within walls. The vague indefinite figures that moved tantalizingly just beyond his visual perception were still taking care of him. There was nothing he could remember other than that he had been a soldier and had gone through great violence and a great bloodletting. Beyond that, nothing...

It was cold when he awoke in the middle of the night and looked up at the low ceiling above him. The moonlight streamed in through a partly open window, and the wind that crept in was cold, with a hint of coming winter.

He looked from one side to another. The room was small. The walls were of chinked logs. The fireplace was roughly made, and the hearth was thickly covered with ashes with here and there a winking red eye of ember. He lay on a rough bunk bed covered with heavy trade blankets. He closed his eyes for a moment, then opened them again. He looked down at his hands. They were thin and claw-like, and the reddish hairs seemed to stand out clearly against the white skin.

He slowly raised his hands to his face and touched a short, ragged beard. His face was gaunt, and his questing fingers felt a thick scar alongside the left of his skull. This then was the cause of the throbbing pain he remembered so well.

He pulled down the thick blankets and slid his weak legs over the side of the bunk, feeling for the floor, shivering in the stark coldness. He tried to rise, and a swirling wave of dizziness swept over him; he fought for control until the feeling was gone. Slowly he reached for the head of the bed, gripped it with weak hands, then pulled himself upright, hanging on for dear life, until he felt his balance return.

Foot by foot he made his way across the puncheon floor until he could peer from the window. The moonlight coldly silvered the bare earth between the building and a low banked stream about fifty yards away bordered by bare willows and naked cotton woods, and the moon shone on thin scum ice that sheeted the stream. It was early winter then!

It was deathly quiet. He felt himself alone in a frigid world. Then he heard a distant sound, the mournful howling of a wolf from the barren hills far beyond the icebound creek.

He made his way back to the bed and crawled into it, drawing the covers up over his shivering and emaciated body. Someone had taken care of him. Someone had brought him here from wherever he had been found. But who was it? Where was he?

He closed his eyes and tried to think, but whenever he tried too hard the dull, persistent pain came again through his head until he pressed his thin hands against it to drive away the agony. He didn't even know who he was...

When he awoke again it was daylight. A fire crackled in the fireplace. The window had been closed. The odor of cooking meat came to him through the partially opened door that led into the rest of the log building. Somewhere outside a horse whinnied and a mule brayed. It was early morning, and the sun shone brightly through the oiled paper that covered the window.

He was not aware of her at first, for he did not see her, but there was a subtle something that slowly made him turn his head to look in the direction of the doorway. Their eyes met, hard gray and soft doe brown, and something seemed to happen at that instant, even before he studied the features of the girl—for she was hardly more than that—who stood there, one slender hand resting lightly against the side of the door and her head tilted slightly to one side. She wore her dark hair in Indian style, the thick braids flowing down in front of her shoulders and rising from the swell of her breasts, and a buckskin dress, decorated with a few beads and quills, nothing more; there were moccasins on her feet. They were either Sioux or Cheyenne moccasins. She seemed to be Indian, and yet there was a difference in her as though some other breed had been mixed with Indian blood to fuse into something lovely and enchanting.

He closed his eyes as though to make sure she was not a vision from his bewildered mind. When he opened them again she was there in the room placing wood upon the crackling fire, her straight back and smoothly rounded hips plainly apparent beneath the soft flowing buckskin dress.

She turned and came slowly to the bed, looking at him with questioning eyes, as though unsure that he was really aware of the world once again.

"Hello," he said quietly.

She smiled instantaneously. "Thank God," she said fervently, clasping her slim hands in front of her almost like a little child who had achieved full happiness.

"Thank you for what you have done," he said.

She nodded. "It wasn't just me. There were others. It has been a long time."

"What month is this?"

"Late November."

He had expected such an answer, but the shock was still very great. Somewhere in the mad shuffle of time he had lost a full month.

"Where am I?" he asked.

"On the Upper *Wicunkasotapelo*. Your people know it as the Big Hatchet."

She spoke excellent English, but her pronunciation of *Wicunkasotapelo* was pure Sioux in origin. There was a mystery about this girl. The Upper *Wicunkasotapelo* was still in the heart of hostile country. More mystery, for the place in which he lay had been built by white men. No Indian could build like that. *But it was still Oglala country*.

"What is your name?" he asked.

"I am called Marie. And you?"

He half closed his eyes, trying desperately to think of it, but it was no use.

"No matter," she said encouragingly. "It will come back to you."

He eyed her. "Do you really think so?"

"You were terribly wounded. It is a wonder that you're alive. Be thankful for that at least. Your memory will return in time. So my grandfather says."

"Your grandfather is here?"

"Yes. He'll come and see you after you have eaten."

He nodded. He watched her leave the room as softly as the chinook wind blowing across the prairie in the warm spring days.

When he had finished eating she gathered the dishes and placed them on a flat wooden tray. He glanced up at her. *"Ha ho,"* he said quickly in the Sioux tongue. *Thank you,* he had said.

She smiled. "Are you testing me? Yes, I speak the tongue of my mother's people. Is that what you wanted to know?"

He flushed.

"My father was a white man," she said. Then her voice lifted a little and an almost fierce note of pride came into it. "My mother was Lakota!" She looked down at him. "She was the daughter of a chief! I am the granddaughter of a chief!" She turned suddenly and left the room with the tray of dishes, leaving behind her the subtle fragrance of dried prairie flowers. There had been a hint about the fact that a horrible tragedy had happened. But where? How? He closed his eyes. Perhaps the girl's grandfather would know more than she did.

He fell asleep in the comforting warmth of the room,

and for the first time in such a long time his dreams were not those of blood and violence, of pain and horror, but instead they had been replaced by the lovely oval face of a budding young woman: Marie, the granddaughter of a Sioux chieftain.

CHAPTER SIX

The sound of voices awakened him. It was late in the morning. Marie had returned, and with her was a man of medium height, massively broad through the shoulders. His beard was thick and shot with gray and white, and his eyes were surprisingly blue and clear, like those of a much younger man. He placed a cool hand on the forehead of the man who lay in bed. "My granddaughter says that you seem to be all right, that you have regained your senses," he said.

"I have regained my senses, but I don't know who I am."

The man nodded. "You suffered a terrible wound. It should have killed you. You have no recollection of it?"

Dallas shook his head and tried to remember, and the pain of it caused him to wince.

"I am Martin Benedict," said the man. "You know of me?"

"No."

"You are a soldier?"

"I think so."

"Rank and unit?"

"I don't know."

"Your uniform was hardly recognizable, but I think

you were a cavalryman. There were no papers upon you. Your hat was bullet-torn and coated with blood. The only thing we could find was a printed word on the sweatband: Dallas. Does that mean anything to you?"

"No."

Benedict took out a pipe and began to stuff it with rough shag. "It might mean Dallas, Texas, but I hardly think so. Perhaps it is your name?"

He smiled whimsically. "It will do."

"Do you remember from whence you came? Fort Locke? Fort Edgerton?"

"Nothing, sir. But absolutely nothing..."

Benedict lighted his pipe. "I have seen cases such as yours. In time bits of the puzzle will fit together and perhaps bring back the lost memories."

"You are sure?"

"I think so."

"You are not sure at all."

In the silence that followed the older man looked at his granddaughter. A log snapped in the fireplace.

Dallas raised his head. "I was a soldier. I have seen fighting. I can tell you that much."

Benedict looked keenly at him. "The massacre? The loss of every man in your column except you?"

Dallas shrugged. "There was fighting."

"On the Lower Wicunkasotapelo?"

"It is possible."

"Marie says you speak some Sioux. Where did you learn it?"

Dallas shrugged again and held out his thin hands.

"You know this country?"

"I seem to remember some of it."

Benedict sucked in on his pipe and blew out a cloud of smoke. "Let me tell you what *we* know and perhaps something will come back to you. In late October a column of troops from Fort Locke passed through the country south of here, escorting an army paymaster and his monies to Fort Edgerton. The column was led by a General Arliss Montfort, who, contrary to custom, did not lead his column far to the south in safer country but instead took them through the hill country in defiance of the Oglala.

"Somehow General Montfort was separated from his command. He was accompanied by a handful of officers, a young woman, and a civilian scout. While he was gone the Oglala, with their Cheyenne allies and some Arapaho, struck the column in a place where it could hardly maneuver. The fighting did not last long, and when it was over, just before sunset, *not one man of that column was left alive*. Not one man, you understand, unless perhaps, it is *you?*"

"I don't know."

"A relief column came into that country after the massacre. They counted over one hundred and seventy dead white men and some Ree scouts on the field. Most of the bodies were flyblown and badly decomposed by that time. Some of the bodies were never found." Benedict closely studied Dallas' face. "A number of men were said to have escaped, but that is pure conjecture. There is one thing that is known for certain. Close to fifty thousand dollars was in the two money chests entrusted to Paymaster Nares. Not one cent of it has been found."

"The Sioux would not touch such money. *Wah-nee-chee!* No good! Bad medicine!"

Marie's lovely eyes never left the gaunt face of the man in bed.

Benedict tamped his pipe. "It is said that someone survived that massacre and escaped with all that money. A fortune! But it has never been verified that there *was* a survivor."

A mule brayed outside. The wind scrabbled coldly along the eaves.

"Dallas, *you* may be that man," said Benedict quietly. "You were found by us wandering along the banks of the

Wicunkasotapelo, more dead than alive. We brought you here and took care of you."

"Ho, ho," said Dallas in grave Sioux.

The government wants that lost money. Scouts have been in this vicinity. Marie would not let me tell them you were here."

"Why?"

"She said that any movement would kill you. I agree." Dallas nodded.

"There is nothing you remember? Nothing at all?"

"Killing...blood...powder   smoke...dried   prairie flowers."

"That is all?"

"That is all," said Dallas wearily. He placed an arm across his aching eyes.

"You must remember!"

"Let him alone, Grandfather," said Marie.

"All right. But as soon as he regains his strength he must be taken to Fort Locke."

"The winter is coming on. He can't be moved for weeks. Once the winter is here he cannot be moved until spring."

"We can send Mitch to Fort Locke with a message that this man is here."

"No!" she said fiercely. "They'd come for him then! He stays here until he is well enough to move, no matter how long it takes, and he will *not* be moved before that time!"

Dallas opened his eyes at her tone of voice.

Martin Benedict smiled apologetically. "She is the granddaughter of a chief," he said.

Dallas studied him. "How is it that you can live in this country and not be bothered by the Sioux?" he asked.

"They do not bother us." There was something enigmatical in the tone of the voice and the expression on the bearded face. "We will call you Dallas then, for want of a better name. Agreed?"

"One name is as good as another," said Dallas, "but I will not rest until I know my real name."

Benedict nodded and stood up. He walked to the door and slid an arm about the slender waist of his grand-daughter.

Dallas raised his head. "You mentioned the fact that a General Montfort and some others were separated from the column *before* the massacre. What happened to them?"

"Rumor says some of them might have reached Fort Edgerton. Another rumor is that they were all slaughtered."

"The Sioux must know." He knew as soon as he spoke that they would tell him nothing more.

"You may be the last man alive of that column," said Benedict. They silently left the room.

Dallas closed his eyes. There was nothing he could remember beyond the fact that he had been a soldier.

———

BUT THE WEEKS FLED ON, one after the other, and *Wani-yetula,* the Winter, spread his cold robe over the country of the *Wicunkasotapelo,* freezing the streams, driving the bears into their caves and the turtles deep into the mud at the bottoms of the creeks. He mantled the hills and valleys in icy white and howled across the width and breadth of the land. He shook the thick winter lodges of the Oglala and made the coats of their ponies grow thick and wooly. The snow fell heavily in the valley of the *Wicunkasotapelo* and mounded over the many graves of the *Wasicun* soldiers, the Long Knives who had fought and died there in the late fall, and it sifted down into the crevices where the hidden dead of the Oglala, Cheyenne, and Arapaho lay covered with earth and rocks not far from the valley of massacre.

Dallas was now able to move about and take his meals

with Martin Benedict and his granddaughter, whose
Oglala name was the musical *Wica-cante-yuha-winyan,*
which meant, Captures-Everybody's-Heart-Woman, and
to the quiet, thoughtful patient no more fitting name
could have been given her.

There was another man who came and went. Mitch
Boutonne, whose father had been pureblooded Negro
and whose mother had been half white and half Oglala.
He was a man who could travel at will through that
deadly hostile country. To the Sioux he was known as
Wasicun-sapa, the Black-White Man, and to them he was
socially acceptable despite his curious blood mixture.

It was Mitch Boutonne who kept an eye on any
strangers in that vast white land, and, when they
appeared, the man known as Dallas went into hiding.

Night after night, when the house creaked in the grip
of freezing cold and the banshee winds howled down
from the distant mountains, he tried to remember his
past. Was he really the last man alive of all those soldiers?
One man out of over one hundred and seventy-five! Now
and then vague and tantalizing scenes fled through his
confused mind: smoke and flashes of light; shrieking of
men and thudding of guns; blood staining the ground and
the blue of uniforms. If he did go to Fort Locke, what
could he tell them? He did not even know his true name
or his past.

Martin Benedict was another puzzle. Seemingly he
had no means of income, and yet he was comfortable in
his sheltered valley. Mitch Boutonne hunted game for the
old man. Now and then, when the snow stopped falling
and the wind stopped howling, the old man would vanish
into the loneliness beyond the valley. He would be gone
for days and then would suddenly reappear, saying
nothing but looking very tired. But Dallas was never
alone with Marie, for Mitch Boutonne never left the
place when the old man was gone.

The weather grew more bitter after the first of the

new year. Dallas gained enough strength to ride one day with Mitch Boutonne to bring back a cow buffalo he had shot and cached. They led a mule for the meat and had bundled themselves in furs. Dallas had been given a battered but serviceable Henry rifle to carry, but it was not for defense against the hostiles. Mitch came and went as he pleased in their country, and Dallas knew he would not have been allowed to go along if there had been any danger.

It was noon when they reached the draw where Mitch had hung up the carcass in a tree, out of the way of the ravenous timber wolves that infested that country. As the horses slogged through the deep snow the sound of howling wolves drifted to the two men.

Mitch's dark face tightened. "Strange," he said. "You ever hear wolves howl at midday, my friend?"

Dallas shrugged. It was not in *his* memory. Nothing was.

"They are cowards," said the breed. He spat.

Something drifted quickly through Dallas' mind. "If they are out at midday, they are starving," he said quietly.

Mitch glanced quickly at him. "Where you learn that, eh?"

"I don't know."

"You wolf?"

"What does that mean?"

"Trap, poison wolf for fur?"

Dallas shrugged.

"Better not in this country. Wolfers use strychnine to kill wolf. They place it in buffalo carcass. Wolf eat. Indian dog eat, too, and die. Sometimes starving Indian eat meat and die. Wolf die. Dog die. Indian die. *Wah-nee-chee!* No good! If Indian catch wolfer, take long time to kill. Slow... slow...takes long time." Mitch grinned. "You scared? Want to go home?"

"No."

Mitch nodded. "It won't take long. Tonight we eat buffalo hump. You like buffalo hump, Dallas?"

Dallas closed his eyes. Somewhere in the past he had eaten succulent buffalo hump. But where? How long ago?

"I'll go on," said Mitch. "Bring on the mule. Look! The sky darkens! There will be much snow! No time to lose! *Mani! Mani!*" Mitch flogged his horse on through the snow.

But the mule was stubborn, and its knees had been cut by the cruel crust of the snow. As Dallas led him on he heard again and again the distant howling of the wolves, and it seemed as though they were a little closer each time. When he reached the lip of the draw the howling was very close. He saw Mitch standing with his back to the tree where the buffalo carcass was hanging. Mitch held his bowie knife in his hand, facing more than half a dozen of the biggest timber wolves possible to see in that country.

"Let them have the meat!" called Dallas.

"They are after me, too! My gunlock is frozen! My horse ran way in fear! I can't turn my back on them!"

Dallas stared down at the man who was ready to fight with the knife, knowing full well he didn't have a chance. Dallas looked down at his rifle. Somehow he knew he had used such a weapon before. He slid from the back of his horse and slogged down through the deep snow.

"Go back, my friend!" yelled Mitch Boutonne.

One of the wolves tore in swiftly, snapping for the throat, but knife was quicker than fang, and the steel ripped out the throat of the wolf. In an instant the rest of the pack closed in. There was no time for the man on the slope to get closer. Something from the forgotten past triggered him into action. He levered home a round, raised the rifle, and fired all in one fluid motion. The flat crack of the rifle echoed from the hills, and a wolf died instantly with a .44 slug in its head. Three times more the Henry slammed out flame and noise, awakening the rolling echoes, and each time a wolf was smashed aside by a softnosed 216 grain bullet. Dallas plunged down through the drifting powder-smoke just as Mitch went down under the rush of muscular and furry body. The knife ripped upward, but teeth and claws tore at Mitch's thick coat until the Henry rifle blasted the wolf's brain from its bony casing. A steel-shod butt broke the back of another wolf. The gaunt-faced man with the rifle struck again and again until the ground was littered with the big bodies and the snow was reddened with their blood.

Mitch Boutonne wiped the blood from his face. "How you learn to shoot like that, my brother?"

Dallas shrugged. He looked down at the hot rifle in his gloved hands. It had seemed so natural for him to use it.

"We'd better get out of here," said the breed. He came close to Dallas and gripped him about the shoulders. "We are brother-friends," he said in a quiet voice. "You know what that means, my brother?"

"No."

"We are closer than blood brothers! There is nothing we will not do for each other!"

Dallas looked at the dark and bloody face of the breed. He liked what he saw in those eyes. "Brother-friends," he said.

They worked quickly to load the buffalo carcass onto the mule. There would be no time to skin the bodies of the wolves. They had just mounted to race the storm back to the shelter of the valley when Dallas suddenly looked up to see half a dozen mounted men at the edge of the draw. Their high-cheekboned faces were grim beneath their low-pulled fur hats.

Mitch wet his thick lips. "Oglala," he said out of the side of his mouth. "They must have seen everything."

"Will they attack?"

"Not *me*. I am their friend. Wait here. *Don't move!*"

Mitch quirted his horse up the slope and for a long,

long ten minutes he talked to the hardfaced warriors, whose eyes never left the white man who sat his horse below them.

Then Mitch came sliding down the slope. *"Co-oco-o!"* he cried. "Get ready!"

Ready for what? To fight? To run?

Mitch grabbed the halter of the mule and led it up out of the timbered draw. "I told them they can have the wolf carcasses," he said. "Heads and hides are good medicine. I told them you were mind-gone-far. They have heard of you as the strange man who lives with Martin Benedict. That was old *Mato-Najin* up there—Standing Bear. He calls you *Ota Kte.*"

"Is that my real name?"

"It is to them. Means Plenty Kills. *Hoppo!* Let's go! The snow will race us to home!"

They rode as swiftly as possible, and every now and then Dallas looked back toward the timbered draw. A vague piece of the puzzle was trying to slip into place.

The first hard driven flakes of snow swirled about them, touching their faces, as they saw the welcome thread of smoke arising from the valley, marking their home.

CHAPTER SEVEN

Dallas was chopping wood when he had an uncanny feeling that he was being watched. He raised the double-bitted axe and struck it deep into the half-frozen wood before he turned his head. He glanced quickly about the area. There was no sign of human life beyond the noise Mitch Boutonne was making as he heaved steaming manure from the barn door. Dallas raised the axe, and the eerie feeling poured over him again. He turned slowly, and, though he had expected to see something, he wasn't quite prepared to see the three warriors seated on their ponies watching him from the slope behind the barn. The sun glinted from the brass tacks with which they had decorated the stocks of their repeating rifles. One of them was an older man, one was in the prime of his life while the third was hardly more than a stripling, an untried brave.

Dallas felt cold sweat stiffen his thick woolen shirt as it froze. He was alone in the open. The old man and Marie were in the house. Then Dallas recognized the oldest of the trio. It was the grim old warrior who had watched him the day he had saved the life of Mitch Boutonne. *Mato Najin.* Standing Bear. He who had named

Dallas *Ota Kte*—Plenty Kills, in grudging respect, for Mitch had said they did not give such names freely.

The youngest of the trio was playing with his rifle, and he raised it slowly until a hard look from Standing Bear made him put it down. Dallas dropped the axe, then extended both hands, palms outward, and touched his fingers to his forehead in a sign of respect. Standing Bear eyed him, then imitated the gesture. Even when Dallas made the gesture he could not remember how and when he had learned it.

Mitch Boutonne whistled softly as he came out of the barn, and the whistling died on his lips as he saw the Sioux. *"How kola, Mato Najin,"* he said easily.

"How kola, Wasicun-sapa," answered the warrior.

The visitors dismounted, and Mitch led them into the house. Troubled, Dallas turned again to his work.

The wind had a sharper edge to its teeth, and the northern sky looked ominous as he put down the axe and shrugged into his thick woolen coat. Mitch came out of the house and walked toward Dallas. "What's up, Mitch?" asked Dallas.

Mitch handed his beaded tobacco pouch to Dallas. Dallas filled his pipe, then lighted up as Mitch filled his foul smelling pipe. "Old Standing Bear is here on business," said the breed.

"Me?"

"No. Martin Benedict is a skilled healer, Dallas. I guess you know that. Standing Bear's youngest son is sick, and he wants Martin to go to the village to treat him."

"Quite an honor, Mitch."

"You have no idea," said Mitch drily. "He don't want to go. Standing Bear says yes. I think he might go."

"Who are the other two smiling ones?"

"Oldest one is Kills Alive. Standing Bear's second son and a first rate warrior. The younger one is Little Horse. He's going to be a bad one. *Wah-nee-chee!"*

"And Kills Alive?"

He didn't get his name pulling wings from flies. He's a killer. Likes to take prisoners. Plays with 'em. Knife and fire. Makes a man sick. He *likes* it, though." Mitch glanced toward the house. "Another thing. Standing Bear come to talk about Marie."

"So?"

"Kills Alive wants a squaw, Dallas."

Dallas took his pipe from his mouth. "Marie?"

Mitch nodded. "They're staying the night. You keep your eyes off Marie? Understand?"

Dallas knew now that Mitch had seen the way he looked at Marie and the way she looked at him. The man was no fool. "What do you think, Mitch?"

Mitch inspected his pipe. "Fine woman. Make good wife. Smart. Good blood."

"Go on. You're not through yet."

"No, I ain't," said Mitch slowly. "You're a long ways from where you come from, Dallas. You ain't no common soldier. You got breeding. You been with us a long time. Marie is the only woman you've seen in a long time. Man can fall in love with ugly old bitch that way. Seen it done. Some trappers would marry grandmother to have woman. Maybe you play up to that girl and take her, then leave her."

"You mean that?"

"I been around. You play with her. Sleep with her maybe."

"Take it easy, Mitch!"

"No! I don't take it easy! I know men. I know you. You mean well, you *think,* and when spring comes you no want her and leave her. Break her heart." Mitch turned on a heel and walked to the barn, then he turned. "Remember this, my brother: You break her heart and leave her, you die. Understand?" The dark eyes held Dallas' eyes, and Dallas knew that Mitch meant exactly what he said.

The wind had shifted after it grew dark, and it had become stronger. The first soft flakes of snow were already whirling across the dark hills to drop atop the older and harder snow that coated the ground. Martin Benedict had vanished into the night with the three Oglala, riding hard ahead of the storm. "The old man will be gone quite a while," Mitch Boutonne had said, "but we three ain't going nowheres. This storm will stop anyone from moving for days."

By nine o'clock that night the wind had increased into a howling frenzy. The snow was driven horizontally across the country and began to pile up in the draws and coulees and to cover the thick ice on the streams. It piled up high against the buildings until they were half buried. The wind shrieked about the low eaves. Even the roaring fires within had little power to drive back the cold.

Mitch Boutonne paced back and forth in the living room of the house, sucking at his pipe, listening to the howling of the wind. Dallas stoked the big fireplace. There was plenty of wood in the house and close by it, but it would be a hardship to go out and bring in more wood if needed, for the raging wind had the power to drive a man away from the house and within fifty yards of it he might be lost forever.

Marie sat quietly beside the fireplace beading a pair of men's moccasins. She had said little after her grandfather had left. He was past his prime, and it was unwise for any man to travel through that country, no matter his strength and youth.

"He'll get through, Marie," said Mitch.

"It is the worst storm this year," she said quietly. "Perhaps the worst in many years. *Wah-nee-chee.*"

"What about the horses and mules, Mitch?" asked Dallas.

"They have good shelter. The water trough inside might freeze though."

"I'll go and free it from the ice."

"No. You're not strong enough yet. I'll go."

"You might not get back."

Mitch shrugged. "Plenty horse blankets and sacks out there. Deep hay. Animals will keep place warm. I can take food with me and sit out storm."

But Mitch held off. He feared that storm. Perhaps more than Dallas did. His mixed blood would make him more superstitious despite his greater strength. In his mind the wind was demoniacal and more dangerous than anything human.

It was well after eleven o'clock by the waggle-tail timepiece on the wall when Mitch at last stopped his restless pacing. He filled a tow sack with food, then quickly slid a bottle of whiskey into the pocket of his thick coat. He smiled apologetically as he caught Marie's quick glance. "No, Marie," he said. "It is for the cold. No-more."

"Remember your promise to Grandfather, Mitch."

He nodded. He looked at Dallas. "I'll try to get back before daylight."

"Don't take any chances!"

The breed took a coil of rope. "Open door," he said. "I'll tie line to post, then hold on while I try for the barn. If I miss, I can always come back here. Ready?"

Dallas lifted the latch and pulled back the door. The icy wind rushed in with howling glee. Mitch made the line fast and then plunged into the drifts to vanish instantly. The wind cut into Dallas' face like tiny whetted knives, and his face tightened in the intense cold. He slammed a shoulder against the door and was losing the struggle when he felt the soft but strong body of Marie against his. Together they forced shut the door and latched it.

He turned and felt her soft, unhampered breasts against his chest. He placed his hands on her shoulders and drew her close. She did not resist as he sought her cold lips and gently kissed her, and in that instant both of them knew that this was the beginning of something even stronger than the howling storm outside.

Marie walked to her chair and picked up the moccasins she had been beading. "Kills Alive has asked for me," she said.

God knows Dallas wanted her, but who was he to speak out? He didn't know his name or who he was.

"I do not want to marry him, Dallas."

"They can make it difficult for you and your grandfather."

She looked up. "Unless I was married to someone else."

He slowly filled his pipe and lighted it. "Who are the moccasins for?" he asked at last.

"For the man I love," she said quickly.

"Who is he, Marie?"

"I am not sure yet."

"When *will* you know?"

"Only God knows," she said simply. "But I will know before too long, Dallas."

"You are sure of that?"

She smiled a little. "I think I already know," she said.

The two of them were as much alone as though they had been stranded upon a tiny islet in the wide and lonely reaches of the vast Pacific Ocean. Dallas knew that Mitch Boutonne would never make it back that night; not in that storm and with a bottle of whiskey to keep him good company.

The drifts had become deeper, insulating the house against the mad noise of the wind, but nothing could protect those within from the icy cold that would become worse during that long night.

There was nothing to do but go to bed. Dallas kissed her, and they did not speak as she went to her room. He'd have to dig a way out when the storm subsided. He hoped to God that Mitch was all right.

He entered his cold room and threw an armful of

wood upon the dying fire in the fireplace, then undressed in the flickering uncertain light of the flames. He stripped to the skin, for he had learned somewhere in his forgotten past that one slept warmer that way. He crawled under the thick pile of cold blankets and lay there watching the play of firelight on the low ceiling. The howling of the storm seemed further off now, but this was a delusion. It was there, all right, and it would be there for some time to come. Perhaps for days. He closed his eyes and drifted easily into a dreamless sleep.

There was something unholy and eerie about the way the figure stood there, peering intently from one sprawled body to another. Then a naked man staggered to his feet and began to run, pursued by the eerie figure with the bloody knife in its hand. The blood smeared face of the pursued man was plain in the silvery moon-light. Then a strangled scream ripped through the night as the killer sank the knife blade deep between the shoulders of the victim.

The watching man slid down into the coulee and winced as his ankle twisted. He began to crawl toward the pistol that lay beside the shattered ambulance. Gravel pattered behind him. He turned to see the figure standing at the lip of the coulee with a low pulled campaign hat. Then the gun cracked flatly, and the bullet struck like the blow of a white hot mallet alongside the skull. He screamed piercingly again and again, then opened his eyes...

He stared up at the dark ceiling of the room, faintly illuminated by the dying firelight, and icy sweat dewed his forehead as he thought of the horror he had seen in his nightmare.

The door swung open. "Dallas! What is it?" cried Marie.

He could not speak. She came close to the bed and placed a hand on his clammy forehead, and he trembled at the touch. "A nightmare," he said at last. "But not a nightmare. It was almost as though I were actually there!"

"What was it, Dallas?"

He looked up into her lovely face, framed in her loose dark hair. "I don't really know," he said slowly.

"Then there is nothing to fear."

He shook his head. "There *is* something to fear. Something monstrously evil. It is there, Marie. I know..."

"You were like this sometimes when you were in that awful sleep." She gently stroked the thick scar on his head.

"Don't leave me," he said hoarsely.

"I'll freeze, Dallas."

He drew her close and felt the soft warmth of her body through the thick woolen gown she wore. She shivered violently. The cold struck bitterly at his naked shoulders and chest. He threw back the blankets and drew her down beside him. "Dallas," she protested in a small voice. He closed his arms about her, feeling her luscious softness. She stroked his head. "You'll be all right," she promised.

"Stay with me," he said.

She did not answer. The firelight was almost gone now. Her long, sweet-smelling hair was against his fevered face. "I must go now," she whispered.

He kissed her and drew her tightly to him. They lay there together for a long time. "It had to happen," she said at last.

"I am no one, Marie."

"It doesn't matter!"

Her warmth seemed to soak through the thickness of her gown into her tense body, and slowly a great peacefulness came over him for the first time in many weeks. He pulled the gown from her slender, supple body, and she did not resist him. Then there was nothing between them and their hunger, and the coldness and the loneliness of the winter night were swiftly forgotten in the new wonder they experienced together.

When he opened his eyes at last, it was to see a soft,

diffused light in the room. A fire crackled on the hearth, and he turned his head to see her standing in the doorway, fully dressed, with a tray of food in her hands. She sat beside him, and when she at last arose she quietly placed the newly beaded moccasins she had been working on the previous night beside the bed.

The wind had died during the early morning, but the cold still held the country in a relentless grip. Slowly Dallas cut a way through the drifts outside of the door until daylight poured through. Mitch Boutonne plowed over the high drifts. He hiccupped as he saw Dallas through bloodshot eyes.

Dallas grinned. "You kept warm enough, I see."

Mitch hiccupped again. "Man die out there without strong waters," he growled.

As they drank coffee while Mitch ate his breakfast they both knew that *he* knew what had happened.

Dallas emptied his coffee cup and filled his pipe. "When do you think Martin will be back?" he asked Mitch.

"Who knows? A day. Two. A week. Two weeks. Hard traveling for some time. He'll be all right. They take care of him. He's almost *Wicasa-Waken* to them. Holy man."

"He has great skill in medicine," admitted Dallas.

Mitch nodded. He looked at Marie.

"Where did he learn it?"

There was no answer. The waggle-tail clock ticked on.

"Does it matter?" asked Marie after a time.

"Not really." Something was wrong.

"I am Martin Benedict," he had told Dallas. "You know of me?" Almost as though he had *expected* Dallas to know.

Mitch stood up. "Martin Benedict is a good man. Too good for some people. He saved my life some years ago when I was sick. I never forget. You saved my life, too, Dallas. This I never forget." He glanced at Marie. "Marie is like my sister. Her, I never forget." He walked to the door and looked back. "I sleep in barn from now on. It is better that way. After he comes back, who knows?" He put on his coat and left the house.

Marie looked at Dallas. "He knows," she said quietly.

"He is not afraid for himself but rather for us. If Standing Bear returns with Kills Alive what shall we do?"

"I don't know, Marie."

"We can't escape now. Even if we could, they would find us."

He stood up and drew her close. There was a hopelessness in her voice. He kissed her, and she seemed to regain some of her strength. They would have a few days of complete happiness together, for Mitch Boutonne would not interfere now, nor would he talk later on. But there would be something hanging over them and their happiness with the naked face of death. The face and hate of Kills Alive.

In the following days they were together always. Yet always in the back of Dallas' mind was the puzzle of his past life. Perhaps he would never find out who he really was. Would it matter to her? They loved each other. Wasn't that enough? He must go to Fort Locke in the spring. They would know who he was. But the thought of what he might have been, and that his past life might lose Marie to him, was something he could hardly bear.

Martin Benedict returned on a clear, cold day just before dusk accompanied only by Standing Bear. Marie had outdone herself in preparing the evening meal. But the dark eyes of Standing Bear were always watching her and Dallas.

Standing Bear had returned with Martin Benedict for one reason and one reason alone. He could have sent some of his young men to escort the old man back home, but he had come himself across that bitter country. Kills Alive still wanted a wife, and he wanted Marie Benedict.

Later that same evening Dallas walked to the barn to

see Mitch. Mitch was weaving a horsehair bridle. He looked up at Dallas. "They still at it?" he asked.

Dallas nodded. "I wasn't listening to them," he said.

"Takes time. Real formal. Big thing. Giving the virgin to the groom." He glanced sideways at Dallas.

"She won't agree, Mitch," said Dallas as he sat down.

"Maybe...maybe not...Standing Bear is big man in Oglala. Kills Alive will be big man. War chief. Plenty coups."

Mitch reached into the hay and withdrew a bottle. "Drink?"

Dallas nodded. He pulled out the cork and drank deeply. It flowed down warmly and then seemed to explode in his gut. "My God!" he said hoarsely.

Mitch grinned. "Old Creek Bottom." He took a drink and began to sing softly in guttural Sioux.

"You know a lot about the Sioux, eh, Mitch?"

"Sure. I like 'em. They don't give a damn if ol' Mitch Boutonne is white, black, or red. You think that don't matter?"

"I think it does."

"I wonder." The keen dark eyes studied Dallas. "You were gentleman. Officer maybe?"

"I don't know."

"I think so. I can tell shoulder straps when I see 'em."

"Does that make any difference to you?"

"Hell no!" He handed Dallas the bottle. "This is on ol' Mitch Boutonne, the white-black-red man. I love everybody. Don't make no difference to me. It might to Marie though."

"How so?" asked Dallas quietly as he lowered the bottle.

"You'll find out who you are. If it's an enlisted man it won't make any difference, but if you're shoulder straps..."

"I don't quite understand."

"Look, my brother! Officers in the Army are a class by

themselves. Sure, they drink, gamble, chase whores like the rest of us, but they don't *marry* out'a their class. If you *are* shoulder straps, and I'll bet my bottom dollar you *are,* you couldn't go back to the Army with a breed wife."

Dallas stared at the half drunken breed.

"We don't know nothing 'bout you. You got to go back some day. When the chinook wind comes *you got to go back!* You maybe figger you marry Marie? You don't have to answer that! I know! You goin' back with a blanket bride? A *squaw?*"

"How the hell do I know what I'll do? What I am?"

"All I know is you can't take that girl back there until you know what and who you are. Makes sense, don't it."

Dallas stood up. "What can I do?" he asked helplessly. "You know what we mean to each other. I can't let her get taken to that Sioux camp to be a bride! Sleeping in a filthy skin lodge with a greasy buck!" Dallas flushed as he saw the look on the breed's face.

Mitch took another drink. "Forget it," he said thickly. "This is *Wasicun-sapa* talking. The black-white man, or white-black man, or red, white, and blue man. Least-ways the Oglala think I am a *man!* You got a friend here, Dallas. But you cross them Oglala and you won't be worth a pinch of dried buffalo crap! You take that girl out'a here, and they'll kill you if they can. If you do get back to Fort Locke with that girl and find out you're shoulder straps, those people there will kill her as surely as the Oglala would kill you! Now get out and let me get drunk in peace!"

Dallas stood outside on the crisp snow. A wolf howled, and Dallas thought he saw movement amidst the naked trees on a hill. A wolf, or a man dressed as a wolf? The house was dark. He would go alone to bed this night. He knew that it was not a wolf crying, and that as long as he lived there, one of them would always be watching and waiting.

CHAPTER EIGHT

Snow still lay in soiled windrows in the valley, and the stream was still thick with ice, but there was a faint promise of the chinook wind in the air. Much of the ground was already firming after an early spring thaw. Mitch Boutonne and Dallas led the four heavily laden pack mules down into the valley at the end of their journey from DeVoto's Trading Post at the fork of the Little and Big Sunflower Rivers. Dallas had remained in a hidden camp while Mitch had gone for the supplies. It was not yet time for Dallas to go to Fort Locke, and DeVoto's Post was a news center for that lonely country. It would not have done for him to have been seen.

Scouts were still looking for massacre survivors and had been doing so all winter despite the bitter weather, so DeVoto had told Mitch. Evidently the government was bound and determined to find survivors, or a *survivor*.

Mitch turned in his saddle. "Weather has broken," he said quietly. "It will be soon time for you to leave, my brother."

Dallas nodded. In the weeks that had followed the

visit of Standing Bear, Marie and her grandfather had often discussed the marriage proposal of Kills Alive. By the laws of the Sioux a woman had a great deal to say about whether or not she wanted to get married and to whom. It was quite evident that Marie had no intention of marrying her suitor.

Mitch drew rein and relighted his pipe. The two of them looked down into the peaceful valley. No smoke arose from the chimneys of the low house. "Listen well, my brother," said the breed. "The old man knows about you and Marie. I guess you know that, eh?"

"Yes."

"I got advice if you want it."

"Go on, Mitch."

"You take Marie. Get to hell out'a here. Don't go to Fort Locke. Just keep going. Anywhere!"

"I have to find out who I am, Mitch."

"To hell with that! What difference does it make? You love her now. You take her. You go to Fort Locke and find out what you are, and you'll want to forget you was ever in love with a breed woman."

"You told me once I couldn't take her back to my kind of life, whatever it was, until I found who and what I was. Now you tell me to pull out with her. You don't make sense!"

Mitch kicked at his horse and rode down the slope. "I gave you good advice then; I give you better now. Marie don't give a damn who you are, just so she is with you. I don't give a damn who you are either! Just *you* give a damn!"

They crossed the stream, and while Mitch led the animals to the barn Dallas walked into the house. It was cold, and when he called out he heard nothing but the echoing of his voice. A note was lying on the table. He read it quickly, then crushed it in a big hand. Mitch came in behind him. "What is it, Dallas?" he asked.

"They've gone to the Oglala camp. Standing Bear's son had a relapse. Martin went there and took Marie with him."

Mitch rubbed his dark face. He did not look at Dallas.

"Kills Alive is behind this."

Mitch spat into the fireplace. "Hell, he can't flout Lakota law no matter how tough he is. She'll be all right."

"For how long, Mitch? *For how long?*"

Mitch shrugged. "It's a cinch you can't go after her."

Dallas turned slowly. "How much did you know about this?"

"What the hell you mean?"

"You were damned insistent that I go to DeVoto's with you."

"It was Martin's idea. He said you needed exercise."

"Sure! Sure!" sneered Dallas. "You're a liar, Mitch!"

The breed's face worked. "I swear to God I never knowed nothing about this."

Dallas strode past him and reached for the door latch.

"Where you think you're going?" asked Mitch quietly.

"To get Marie!"

The tip of a knife blade rested gently between Dallas' shoulder blades. "Now you listen to *me,* my brother," said Mitch softly. "You go after her and you won't live ten minutes after you get there. I'll go to the camp and see what is up. You stay here. I'll come back. Maybe bring her with me. I'll tell her you want her to go away with you. Agreed?"

Dallas nodded.

"Not to Fort Locke."

"No."

"Good!"

So it was. Mitch Boutonne ate a hurried meal, stuffed a couple of bottles of rye into his saddlebags, and was gone to the west, leaving a man who now knew what utter loneliness could be. That night his only company was the crackling fire, the ticking waggle-tail clock, and, from afar, hardly heard above the moaning of the night wind, the howling of wolves.

Three days crawled past, and the loneliness was worse than it had ever been. Spring was coming on apace. The days were warmer, but the nights were still very cold. The winds were slowly drying the plains. The creek was no longer ice-locked, and the patches of dirty snow lying in the hollows began to shrink.

Time and time again he rode to the highest hill west to look in vain for Mitch Boutonne. Strange thoughts fled through his mind. Maybe she had already been taken by Kills Alive, and Dallas had been left alone until he realized the truth.

He returned from his lonely vigil on the hill late on the afternoon of the fourth day. He stabled his horse and walked into the house, kneeling beside the fireplace to get a blaze started. The fire was just licking across the dry wood when he had an eerie feeling that he was not alone. He turned slowly to see a man standing in the doorway of his bedroom. The stranger was grinning a little, and he held his rifle aimed at Dallas' head. The sour odor of dirty, sweat-soaked buckskins came to Dallas. The yellowish eyes of the man studied Dallas.

"Who are you?" asked Dallas. "What do you want?"

The stranger grinned wider. "Cut it out, Lorimer," he said coldly.

"Lorimer?"

"Yuh ought'a know your own name, Mister Lorimer."

"My name is Dallas."

"Sure. Dallas Lorimer. *Mister* Dallas Lorimer. Yes, sir!"

Dallas stood up. Vague, unconnected thoughts raced through his confused mind.

"That beard ain't fooling me none," said the man.

"I'm not trying to fool anyone."

"No? You been missin' since last October, *Mister*

Lorimer. Seems to me you would'a had more sense than to hole up around here. I ain't that stupid that I didn't think of this place once the chinook came." Leathers grinned. "The last man alive. You played it cute. Where's the money, Lorimer?"

"What money?"

"The fifty thousand you made off with after the massacre."

Dallas shook his head. "I've been here all winter. I don't know anything about fifty thousand dollars."

"You think I believe that? They never found yore body. There was a rumor that one white man survived the massacre on the Big Hatchet. The money vanished and so did you. Get it?"

Dallas stared at him. "You keep calling me Lorimer," he said.

"Sure! First Lieutenant Dallas Lorimer, U.S.A. You was scout officer for Montfort's column last October."

Martin Benedict had said: *"It is said that someone survived the massacre and escaped with the paymaster's money chest."*

"You're wanted at Fort Locke, Lorimer, to face other charges beyond taking the paymaster's chest. Now, *where's the money?"*

Dallas looked about in bewilderment. The rifle stock swung up and caught him alongside the head, driving him to the floor.

"Talk!" rasped the man. "Ol' Mordecai Leathers ain't too patient, Lorimer!"

"Will you wait until Martin Benedict returns? He'll tell you about me."

"Him? Hawww! Some friend you got. Lets his son marry a squaw. Gets kicked out'a his profession. Treats the Sioux like they was as good as white folks. Maybe you split the money with him, eh?"

"I know nothing about that money," insisted Dallas.

The rifle butt rested on Dallas' crotch. "You start talkin' or I start poundin'," said Leathers coldly.

Dallas gripped the rifle and jerked it to one side, spilling Leathers, who hit the floor beside Dallas. Dallas kicked out, driving Leathers into a corner beside the fireplace. Dallas grabbed for the rifle but Leathers could move fast as well. He snatched up a thick billet of firewood and hurled it at Dallas. The end caught him on the forehead. He saw the floor speeding up at his face, and then he knew nothing more.

Fort Locke sprawled on a bluff overlooking the yellow flood of the swollen river, glutted with melting snow. Mordecai Leathers led Dallas' horse down the slope toward the post. Dallas' bound hands rested on the pommel, and his ankles were tied tightly together beneath the belly of the horse. His head had been throbbing dully during the four-days' ride across the thawing plains to a fort he could now vaguely remember. Dallas knew now who he was and what he was. The stunning blow administered by Leathers had cleared up his memory. He remembered everything now, everything except the killer who had prowled amongst the dead and wounded of the shattered column that moonlit night. He knew now that it could not have been an Indian. No Indian would have come to that place of death after daylight. It must have been a white man.

Arliss Montfort found it hard to recognize his former scout officer when Dallas stood before him with bound hands. He narrowed his eyes and studied Dallas. "By the gods," he said. He shook his head. "Cut him loose, Leathers."

"He might be dangerous, sir."

"Do as you're told!"

Montfort leaned back in his chair and watched Dallas rub his numbed wrists. "You're dismissed, Leathers," he said.

"Say! I aim to hear him confess, Ginral!"

"When will you learn to take orders, Leathers?" said Montfort. The corners of his mouth whitened.

Leathers walked to the door and turned. "I'll talk to you later, Ginral," he said coldly.

Montfort studied Dallas. "Why didn't you return before this?" he asked.

Dallas touched the scar alongside his head. "I was wounded at the Big Hatchet. Lost my memory, sir. There was nothing I could remember except that I had been a soldier and had been in hard fighting. Martin Benedict took care of me. He seemed to think I was the only survivor of the massacre on the Big Hatchet."

"Why didn't you let me know where you were?"

"I was ill and weak. They said I could not travel."

"Quite a story," said Montfort dryly. "How did you regain your memory?"

"Doctor Mordecai Leathers trepanned me with a billet of firewood. It was very efficacious." Dallas smiled wryly.

"I have heard of such phenomena. Then you claim you remember nothing of the massacre on the *Wicunkaso-tapelo* until after Leathers struck you with the billet?"

"Yes, sir."

Montfort stood up and walked to the window. "This would hardly stand up in a court of inquiry, Lorimer."

"The Benedicts and a man named Mitch Boutonne will bear witness for me, sir."

"I see. A doctor barred from his profession. A half-breed woman and a renegade like Mitch Boutonne. *Witnesses,* Lorimer?"

"You know quite a bit about them then?"

"I do."

"Then I assume you think I *have* no witnesses," Dallas said.

"That is correct, Mister Lorimer."

"Leathers said I am charged with leading the column

into a trap. Stealing the payroll money. Desertion. Is that correct, sir?"

"No man survived that massacre, Lorimer. No man but *you,* that is. The money has not been found. The hostiles would not take it. Yet, when the relief column reached the scene of the massacre there was absolutely no trace of the money."

"I know nothing of the money," said Dallas.

"Yet *you* were the only survivor, beyond my small party, and, of course, we knew nothing of the loss of the money at the time. Coupled with the fact that you were well-known to be deep in debt, Mister Lorimer, doesn't it seem coincidental to you that *you* alone survived the massacre and that the money has never been found?" Montfort turned. "There wasn't a chance for any man to survive that massacre. But one man *does* survive! He reaches the home of a man known to be a renegade from the white race and hides there for the winter and does not attempt to inform his commanding officer as to his whereabouts. You're clever, Lorimer, but not clever enough. Why did you tarry with the Benedicts? Did you think that you might come back to your post and commission, the lone survivor of the massacre, to regain your position while knowing the bloodstained money you stole would solve all your financial problems and no one would be the wiser? You overplayed your hand, Mister Lorimer!"

Dallas stared at him. The facade of lies the man had built up was magnificent indeed.

Montfort lighted a cigar. "Thank God some of us survived to tell the truth, or you might have gotten away with it."

"Very fortunate," murmured Dallas. "The commanding officer of that column was off chasing antelope when he should have been with his men. Every man in that column died fighting his best. Every man but General Montfort and his coterie and me, of course. You *knew* we were in dangerous country. The fifty thousand dollars doesn't matter in the long run, but the deaths of one hundred and seventy men do matter!"

Montfort paled. He glanced at the closed door. "I hereby place you under arrest in your quarters, incommunicado, until such time as official charges shall be placed against you."

As Dallas was escorted to his quarters he had the feeling that he had touched the quick of Arliss Montfort. He dropped onto the bunk and lay staring at the ceiling. Someone tapped at the door. "Come in," said Dallas.

Private Jonas Westerberg entered. He had once served as Dallas' orderly. "Come to make up the fire, sir," he said.

Dallas sat up. "How long has General Montfort been in command of Fort Locke?" he asked.

"I ain't supposed to talk to you, sir," said the orderly.

Dallas smiled. "Who's to know about it?" he asked.

"Since last December, sir," said the soldier. "When he got back from Fort Edgerton. That was after the massacre."

"Odd that they managed to escape from the hostiles."

Westerberg nodded. "Damned lucky they was, sir. If they hadn't a' been out lookin' for a safe passage through them hills, they would've bought it like the rest of those poor devils."

"I see. The party consisted of General Montfort, Captain Christian, Lieutenants Windolph and Cox, Miss Ross, and Mordecai Leathers?"

"Yes, sir. But it's *Captain* Windolph now, sir. Mister Cox is a first Lieutenant."

"Quick promotions," said Dallas dryly.

"They was jumped over quite a few, and I may say, sir, *better* officers, for them promotions. Miss Ross kind'a got a promotion, too. She's engaged to General Montfort." Westerberg grinned. "She was kind'a cozy with Mister

Windolph for a while, but he got transferred out'a here to Fort Edgerton damned suddenly, sir."

Westerberg's meaning was clear. Montfort wanted no local competition. What was it Jean had said to Dallas so many months ago? *"What do I know? I know nothing with which to make a living, but I have something to trade for a husband and money. Windolph has money. Montfort is a spendthrift. Cox is a fool."* What had made her change from Windolph the well-to-do to Montfort the spendthrift? That night on the *Wicunkasotapelo* she had given herself freely to Dallas, perhaps as a farewell to the man she really loved.

Recall blew brassily across the post as Westerberg closed and locked the door behind him.

"Incommunicado," said Dallas. No messages in or out. There would be little communication between isolated Fort Locke and Department Headquarters, at least for some weeks, until the plains dried. Until that time, Fort Locke, presided over by Arliss Montfort, was as isolated as though it were on the moon. Montfort had come out of the Big Hatchet mess with a clean slate; he had cleared himself of any disgrace. Perhaps he feared that Dallas might destroy that illusion.

An icy feeling came over Dallas as the room darkened. *Montfort could not afford to have Dallas speak at a court of inquiry.* One way or another he'd have to stop Dallas' mouth. He'd have to discredit Dallas; if he did not, he'd be discredited himself. There was another way. A surer, swifter way and one that Dallas would not put past Arliss Montfort. It would be so easy: a paid assassin. Montfort would not stain his own hands. Mordecai Leathers would do it without hesitation. Dallas was a prisoner, perhaps already condemned and sentenced in the devious and subtle mind of Montfort; a prisoner in the very place where he had thought to find security and the resumption of his army career.

Twice his life had seemed to collapse about him—first

at the *Wicunkasotapelo* and now here at Fort Locke, and he had lost Marie Benedict as well, for by the time Dallas found her again, if he ever escaped from Montfort, she would probably be the blanket bride of Kills Alive.

"The last man alive," he said to the darkened room. He had never felt so alone in his entire life.

CHAPTER NINE

The soft wind had shifted during the night, and in the dark hours before the dawn it became stronger and stronger, blowing with an icy searching breath across the plains from the Canadian border; just at dawn the first icy pellets of snow began to rattle steadily against the thin walls of the buildings of Fort Locke.

By noon the snow had begun to drift, and by the middle of the afternoon the countryside was a howling maelstrom of shrieking wind and whirling snow through which nothing could be seen, nor could its freezing fury be faced by man or beast. There was nothing to do but hole up and pray to God, or any other deity, that life would remain until the blizzard blew itself out.

The river was frozen a foot thick, then drifted with snow, until it showed as a mere depression between the low white bluffs. Nothing but the mantled tops of the trees were visible through the all-prevailing whiteness.

Waniyetula, the Winter, was not yet through with that country. It was his last effort before he was forced to yield to the warming chinook winds of spring. It was a good one. There would be no communication between Fort Locke and Department for some time to come.

Locke was living up to its evil reputation. "Hell in summer and the Yukon in winter," was the catch phrase for Fort Locke.

By dawn of the second day the snow storm had blown itself out. Nothing moved on the vastness of the white plains surrounding the post. The only signs of life at the post were the many drifting wraiths of smoke from the post chimneys.

Dallas Lorimer lay on his bunk, reliving, for the hundredth time, every detail of that fateful day whose violence still hung, like a black and threatening thunderhead, over his life. Suddenly a thought loomed large and clear through the mistiness in his mind. Montfort had been in the vicinity of the massacre the night of the day it had happened! Montfort, Christian, Windolph, Cox, Leathers, and Jean Ross had been there in the dark hills, quite likely the only living white people, with the exception of those badly wounded the hostiles had overlooked and Dallas Lorimer himself! Dallas was sure it was a white man who had prowled that bloody field after dark, killing off the wounded, and thinking he had killed Dallas Lorimer as well. It had to be a white man! The hostiles would not come back to that field of horror after dark, not until they were sure the spirits of the dead had gone to *Wanagi Yata,* the Sioux 'Land of the Big Shadow.' Thus, five white men and a white woman had been close enough to the battlefield to reach it easily enough to kill off the wounded, making sure all lips and eyes were sealed forever.

"Fifty thousand dollars!" said Dallas aloud.

The money had never been found, at least by the government people who had searched for it. The hostiles would not touch it. Perhaps Dallas himself had hidden the payroll chest, but, if he had done so, he had no recollection of it. Perhaps there *had* been other survivors. Perhaps the man who had returned to the scene after dark had found the money and had hidden it or made off with it. No matter who had done it, the blame was on Dallas.

Jean Ross was his only hope. She was the only one who might talk, of the six whites who had been saved from death by hiding out in the hills. None of the others would help Dallas. They knew better. There was something indescribably foul about the whole situation. If Jean was on the post, and Dallas was quite sure she was, she'd probably be living in Jordan Nares' quarters until such time as she married Montfort and moved into his quarters. Montfort would never let her get near enough for Dallas to question her. And there was so much she could tell him, if she would.

He lowered the lamp and walked across the room to the bookcase. He had remembered something he had long forgotten. He felt behind the row of dusty books and brought out a double-barreled derringer. He broke it and saw the bases of two cartridges in the chambers. It wasn't much, but it was better than nothing.

Taps had long been blown when Dallas heard the brusque challenge of the sentry. A moment later feet grated in the hallway and the key turned in the lock. Dallas put down his book and stood up. The door swung open and Arliss Montfort entered. Mordecai Leathers was behind him. He closed the door.

"Good evening, sir," said Dallas.

Montfort nodded. He took off his thick buffalo coat and cap. "Comfortable in here, Lorimer?"

"Yes, sir."

Mordecai Leathers moved over behind the stove, warming his dirty hands, but his cold looking eyes were on Dallas.

Montfort drew out a brandy bottle from his coat pocket and filled three glasses. He handed one of the glasses to Dallas and another to Leathers. "Takes the night chill out of the bones," he said with a smile. Quite charming and gracious. The 'Montfort' charm.

Dallas sipped the good brandy. Nothing would take the chill out of his bones that night. Not with Montfort and Leathers showing up like two grave robbers after the post was dark and quiet. Montfort had had all day to come and see Dallas. Why at night, after Taps, when the post was like a graveyard?

"I was restless tonight," said Montfort as he lighted a cigar. "Couldn't sleep. Thought I had better have a personal talk with you, Lorimer, before we went any further on the matter of your court-martial."

"Court of inquiry," corrected Dallas. He smiled. "That comes *first,* you know, sir."

"That is hardly necessary," said Montfort.

"But *regulation,* if I request it," said Dallas.

"Yes. You still believe you can get away with a plea of not guilty, is that it?"

"Yes."

"With no creditable witnesses?"

"None that the general agrees *are* creditable."

"I don't think they are," said Montfort. "Besides, they can hardly travel in this weather, if they agree to appear at all. Do you, as a sensible man, agree to that?"

"Possibly."

Montfort twirled his glass, then sipped at the liquor, his eyes studying Dallas over the rim of the glass. "It could likely be only your word against the testimony of myself, Christian, Windolph, Cox, Leathers, and Miss Ross. Further, it is possible, due to your wound and your subsequent loss of memory, as you claim, that you could be judged mentally incompetent."

"Possibly," said Dallas dryly.

"It could be a *certainty,* Mister Lorimer."

The fire snapped and crackled. Leathers did not take his eyes from Dallas. Montfort refilled the glasses.

"Come now, Lorimer," he said in a friendly tone. "We want no trouble. Forget about the court of inquiry. Plead guilty before the court-martial. I'll use my influence to see that you get off lightly."

Once I make a recorded statement to clear him, thought Dallas, *he'll make sure, one way or another, that I never get another chance to talk again.*

"I can't do it, sir," said Dallas.

Montfort stood up and drained his glass. He looked down at Dallas. There was icy hell in his eyes.

Dallas stood up, keeping both of them in sight. He could draw the derringer to defend himself if it came to that. He felt now like Mitch Boutonne must have felt when he faced those ravening wolves closing in on him.

Montfort put on his coat and hat, drove the cork back into the bottle, then looked coldly at Dallas. "Take care, Lorimer," he said thinly. "No man crosses me! I've smashed many a better man than you for trying it."

Dallas doused the light as the key turned in the lock, and he was alone with his thoughts. Montfort held most of the cards. He was working to save his career and reputation, and as long as Dallas was alive there was always the danger that Dallas might destroy him.

As he crept into bed he knew he had to get out of there. But how? *How indeed?*

CHAPTER TEN

The icy wind of the night seemed to be tapping softly against the frost covered window just above the cot of Dallas Lorimer. He opened his eyes. The room was in complete darkness. He closed his eyes, and the tapping came again. It was not the wind. He arose, felt for the derringer, then stood to one side of the window and tapped on it himself.

Then he heard the faint voice. *"Ota Kte! Ota Kte!"*

A strange, exhilarating thrill raced through his chilled body. No one at Fort Locke knew *that* name. *Ota Kte!* Plenty Kills! The name given to him in grudging respect by Standing Bear of the Oglala! "Mitch?" he said softly.

"Yes! Let me in for God's sake! The outside guard is gone!"

The window was hard to get open, but at last Dallas got it partway up, high enough for a formless, fur-clad body of a man to tumble in. Dallas gripped him. "Thank God!" he said.

The dark face of Mitch Boutonne broke into a grin. "You got a way of getting into trouble, *Ota Kte*. Good thing ol' *Wasicun-Sapa* is brother-friend."

Dallas forced down the window. "Did anyone see you?"

The breed laughed softly. "Hell! A buffalo bull could wander around here bellerin' all night, and no one could hear or see him!"

"Why did you come?"

Mitch looked surprised. "I said I'd come back. You wasn't at the house. I seen where there had been a fight. They was only one place you could be. Fort Locke. I come here."

"In this weather?"

"I said I'd come back to you," the breed said simply.

"What about Marie?"

Mitch looked away.

"Mitch!"

The breed rubbed his dark face. "She ain't home," he said at last. "They stayed at the camp of Standing Bear."

"And?"

"She ain't a blanket bride...yet."

"What do you mean?"

"She's been promised, Dallas."

Dallas gripped the breed by the arms and stared fiercely into his face. "Damn you! Why didn't you stop it?"

"What could Mitch Boutonne do, Dallas?"

Dallas released him. The breed was right. "My full name is Dallas Lorimer, First Lieutenant, United States Army," he said.

"I knew you was shoulder-straps."

"It makes no difference in my feelings for Marie."

Mitch looked up. "I know," he said quietly. "How come they got you locked up, under guard?"

"I have no time to tell you now. But I must get away from here, Mitch."

"That's why I come here like I did. Didn't want no one to see me. I got horses hidden a mile from here. Food and water. Plenty blankets."

Dallas dressed swiftly, putting on his warmest clothing. Now and then he walked to the door and placed his ear against it. Maybe the sentry in the hallway had heard them talking, but more than once Dallas had been told by the orderly that he was known to talk frequently in his sleep.

When he was ready he placed the derringer in his coat pocket. "How long until dawn?" he asked.

"Five hour maybe. Maybe more."

"There's one thing I have to do before I leave here."

"You want to get away, you got no time to play games!"

"There is one thing I have to do. Go on ahead and I'll follow."

Mitch shook his head. "You'd never find me, or the horses. Besides, you look like you're going to look for trouble, and you'll need Mitch Boutonne." Mitch turned to the window, then turned again, picked up the bottle from the table, shook it, grinned, and slid it inside his huge buffalo skin coat. He slid up the window, peered outside, then worked his way through. Dallas quickly made up his bed to look as though he was still in it by forming clothing beneath the thick layer of blankets and comforters. Then he left the room by the window and slid it down behind him. There was no sign of the guard.

The cold bit into him as he followed Mitch behind the low building. It was dark and frigid, but there was no sign nor sound of life about the sleeping post. The sentries were huddled within doorways, out of the wind, hardly alert to any movement in that frozen world. Even the hardy Sioux didn't travel in this kind of weather.

Smoke drifted up from chimneys and hung low over the post. The only light in the whole place was in the guardhouse near the main gate.

"Where to?" asked Mitch Boutonne.

Jordan Nares' old residence was in the row of separate quarters near the headquarters building. Dallas paused outside.

"You going in there?" asked Mitch curiously.

"Yes."

"Money in there? Guns?"

"No. A woman, I think."

"You mind-gone-far? You got a woman! Leastways you *think* you got one, eh?"

"I have to talk with her, Mitch."

The breed shrugged. "Helluva time to talk with woman."

"Keep watch for me, Mitch."

The breed nodded. He pointed to a small shed behind the quarters. "Be in there in hay or straw." He padded softly across the frozen ground, turning to look curiously at Dallas only to shrug and continue on until he vanished into the shed.

Dallas stepped up onto the rear porch and tried the door.

By a stroke of good fortune, it swung easily open, and a draft of warm air swept about him. He looked quickly to the right and left, then stepped inside, closing the door behind him. He was in the kitchen. Supposing Jean Ross did *not* live there? The thought made Dallas shiver.

He opened his coat and took it off. If he had to move in a hurry the coat would slow him down. He walked to the door that led into a hallway which, in turn, led to the living room past the bedrooms. The quarters were quiet, but he knew someone must be in there. The thought of Jean Ross snugly in bed, her soft warm flesh covered by a silken gown such as she had worn that night so many months ago when she had called out to him in the bivouac on the *Wicunkasotapelo,* brought back that night to him. But something came between those thoughts and Dallas Lorimer: the lovely face of Marie Benedict.

He passed silently through the hallway and into the living room. A red eye of ember winked from the bed of ashes on the wide hearth. He peered about the darkened room. There was no one in it. He walked to the fireplace and saw some pictures placed upon the wide mantel.

Dallas knew then that Jean Ross must be in the quarters, for the pictures on the mantel were those he had remembered from the days when Jordan Nares had lived there. Jordan Nares in his Civil War uniform, right hand thrust firmly into the unbuttoned front of his dress blouse, chin outthrust, with the look of an eagle in his little eyes. Jordan Nares, the war hero, who had never left Washington all during the war, safe in the Disbursing Office of the War Department.

There was another picture there, and even in the dimness he could see the lovely features of Jean Ross as he had first known her three years past at Fort Laramie when she had just been eighteen and when he had lost his heart completely to her. Did she still love him? Jean Ross had changed somehow in the time between his last meeting with her in Saint Louis and when he had seen her again at Fort Locke just before Montfort's ill-fated column had left for the hostile country.

But that night in the sun warmed tent upon the banks of the *Wicunkasotapelo* she had loved him, if only for a little while. A farewell perhaps to the only man she had ever loved but would never marry.

He padded into the hallway and softly eased open the door of the left hand bedroom. He peered inside. The room was cold. The single bed was empty of mattresses and covers. A faint musty odor hung in the vacant room.

He turned and walked to the next bedroom door. He stood there for a moment, gathering his courage. If she cried out... Then he gripped the doorknob and twisted it lightly. The door opened easily and he stepped inside the room. He knew she was there at once by the mingled aura of her body and her perfume. As his eyes grew accustomed to the dimness, he saw the form in the wide bed. The fire flared up a little in the draft from the door, and he saw her hair flowing over the top cover, as lovely and soft-looking as he last remembered it. She was alone. But why shouldn't she be? Then a dark thought came into his mind. The quarters of Arliss Montfort weren't too far away.

He walked softly to the side of the bed and looked down upon her tranquil face; some of the old emotion took hold of him, but only for a moment, for stern reason took the reins. This lovely woman, whom he had once loved, might have the secret to his future and perhaps his very life. *She* must know the truth.

Suddenly she opened her dark eyes and stared up at him, and then a look of cold fear raced across her face, distorting it into something less than its usual cool loveliness. "Dallas!" she said, and then his left hand closed upon her soft mouth, and he bent his head close to her. She could see the look in his fierce eyes, the crusted scar alongside his head, the etched lines of past pain and tension on his gaunt face. "Listen," he said harshly. "I must talk to you! There is something I must know! Perhaps you are the only one who can tell me! Will you be quiet and talk sensibly?"

Her eyes turned toward the doorway behind him so quickly that he turned to look himself. There was no one there.

"Jean?" he asked.

She nodded and he removed his hand. "They said you were ill," she said quietly.

"I was."

Her eyes searched his face again. "Don't hurt me, Dallas. I'll do anything you want me to."

"Such as?"

She raised her head close to his. "Do I have to tell you?"

"That is the price you'll pay for my not harming you?"

"If that is what you want."

She glanced toward the door again.

"You are sure?" he asked softly.

"Don't you *want* me, Dallas?"

The fire crackled dryly. The wind crept above the eaves of the quarters.

"Dallas?" she asked.

He was almost tempted. It was cold in that room, but there was warmth such as a man had often dreamed about in a womanless time just beneath the weak barricade of the blankets and the sheer covering of silk against a silken skin. But the temptation fled swiftly from the hard core of the man's will.

"Dallas! Don't hurt me!"

He knew then that she thought more of her loveliness than she did of her virtue. What was it she had said to him that night so long ago? It had been on the night before she had given herself to him. She had passed slim hands up and down her shapely thighs and then had said, *"I know nothing with which to make a living, but I have something to trade for a husband and money."*

"Dallas," she said softly.

"You're safe enough, Jean," he said a little bitterly.

There was a subtle look on her face as she relaxed. "What is it you want to know?"

"You've heard the story about how Arliss Montfort was supposed to have left the column to find a safer way for it through the hostile country. You know that is not true. I know that it is not true and so does Montfort and his shadows, Christian, Leathers, Cox, and Windolph. I can't ask any of *them* for the truth."

"So you're asking me?"

"Yes."

She drew him close. "Come in beside me," she pleaded.

Again he was almost tempted. Perhaps she would tell him in the swift surge of emotion coupled with the hard thrusting of their bodies together; then he saw her game. If he got in with her he'd be doomed, for she'd scream rape until the whole post was alerted. The walls of those quarters were thin. He'd never have a chance then. They'd never believe *him*.

"Dallas? Come..." She raised her head and kissed him gently at first, then hard and savagely until his lips hurt. He drew way from her. "No, Jean," he said gently. "I must leave this place."

"You won't have a chance out there in that wilderness."

"I will," he said quietly.

"They'll track you down, Dallas."

He laughed softly. "They'd never catch me, Jean."

"Then why not go? Forget about Arliss and his fabricated story." Then she realized what she had said, and she bit her full lower lip and looked quickly away.

"Then it *was* fabricated," he said coldly.

"You know it was."

"Will you testify to that?"

"I am to marry him soon, Dallas. Then I can't testify against him."

"He has nothing. You as much as told me that last summer. Why marry a man like that? Marry a man with money! The man who can give you everything you want, Jean. Why *him?* Forget him. Testify for me. For God's sake, Jean! It means my whole life!"

She shook her head. "He will have money, Dallas. He told me so."

He narrowed his eyes. It was well known throughout the Army that Montfort had had an income other than his service pay but that he had spent it as fast as he had gotten it. The man was almost as penniless as Dallas Lorimer. "You believe him, Jean?" he asked at last.

"I know he will have money!" she said fiercely.

He knew then and there that Montfort hadn't lied to her. He had no proof, *but he knew*.

"You'd let me be ruined for life because of him and his money?" he asked coldly.

"What do you want me to do? Damn you! None of

you care about me! Just yourselves! Yes, dammit, I'll marry him and be Mrs. General Montfort, and I'll spit in everyone's face who looks at me with less than respect!"

He stared at her in the dimness. She had risen up to a sitting position, and her gown had dropped, revealing one big nippled breast, as white as the crusted snow that covered the ground outside. Then she stared at the door. Dallas turned in time to see a tall figure launch itself across the room at him. He barely had time to get to his feet to meet the rush of Arliss Montfort.

Montfort was lean and solid. He hit Dallas with a driving one-two and kicked him in the groin as he fell across the wide bed. Dallas drew back his knees and kicked out with both feet, catching Montfort in the belly. The wind went out of the man with a rush and he fell back into the fireplace, cursing in agony as the embers seared through cloth and flesh.

Dallas jumped from the bed as Jean screamed like a wounded mare. She screamed again and again as the two met and locked in deadly combat in the middle of the room, slamming hard punches at each other. Dallas felt his strength ebb. He was not yet fully recovered. His left fist caught Montfort on the mouth, and he felt blood spurt across his hand. He drove a fist into the officer's belly, and, as the head came down, Dallas raised a knee to meet the downcoming chin. Montfort grunted in agony and fell heavily.

There was no time to waste. Jean was ripping the night with her screaming. Dallas darted through the doorway and into the kitchen, snatching up his coat as he fled, driving a shoulder against the rear door, and plunging across the icy porch to land in the snowy yard. Mitch Boutonne was waiting for him. "For God's sake!" he said. "What the hell you do now, you Gawd-damned idiot?"

"Mani! Mani!" said Dallas.

They plunged over the drifts past the shed. A man

yelled at them from the front of the quarters, then fired. The slug sang thinly over their heads. Lights flashed on in various buildings.

"Alarm! Alarm! Alarm!" screamed a sentry. He raised his rifle and fired.

The two fugitives cleared the last of the buildings and darted across a level area of frozen ground while the night crackled with the sounds of gunfire.

Mitch grinned as he ran. "What in hell they shootin' at, *Ota Kte?*" he yelled. "It ain't *us*. They seein' ghosts?"

Mitch was in the lead. He slid down into a draw and ran to the north while Dallas slogged along behind him, losing ground. Mitch turned and gripped Dallas under an arm, and together the two of them reached the end of the draw, then ran into a bosque of cottonwoods, stark black against the whitened ground. "Keep tryin'!" said Mitch. "It ain't too far, *Ota Kte!*"

They covered ground swiftly, and the sound of the firing died away behind them, but they could still hear faint yelling.

But there was one place where it was quiet. Deathly quiet. The bedroom of Jean Ross. She lay flat on her wide bed, her naked breasts rising and falling spasmodically, looking up into the lean, bloody face of Arliss Montfort. "I didn't tell him anything, Arliss!" she said hysterically.

"What did you tell him, Jean?" he insisted.

"Nothing!"

He looked closely at her. "You're lying," he said coldly.

"No, Arliss!" She raised her head. "I knew you were coming tonight when everything was quiet. See? I was ready for you! Look at me, Arliss! I was ready for your arms!"

"I am looking at you," he said. He held out his hands, and she half rose to meet his embrace, but his hands did not slide about her half naked body. Instead they closed firmly about the ivory column of her throat, and he closed her mouth with a vicious kiss as he tightened his hands about her throat until she suddenly was still. He released his grip, looked down at her, then stood up. "You'll never get a chance to talk again, you bitch," he said quietly.

Arliss Montfort walked to the front door of the quarters and opened it. He stepped out onto the porch. "Officer of the Guard!" he called out.

The officer leaped over a drift and ran to his commanding officer. "Yes, sir?" he said as he saluted.

"Lieutenant Dallas Lorimer has escaped from the post."

"Does the General want me to form a searching party and send them out?"

Montfort slowly shook his head. "They won't catch him, Prentiss." He looked out toward the far distant and frozen hills. "They'd never live out there and *neither will he*."

"Yes, sir."

Montfort looked down at him. "One more thing, Mister Prentiss. I have just been into Miss Ross' quarters."

"We heard her screaming, sir."

Montfort nodded. "She'll never scream again," he said softly.

"Sir!"

"*She has been murdered by Lieutenant Lorimer.* Throttled after she was raped."

"My God, sir!"

Montfort slowly touched his battered face. "I fought him, but he was like a madman. He *is* a madman. If he doesn't die out there we'll have to hunt him down like a mad dog and kill him."

The men within hearing grew quiet. They shuffled their freezing feet in the hard snow and looked away from their commanding officer. All but one man who stood in a doorway looking at Arliss Montfort. Mordecai

Leathers. And what was on his face was not belief in what Montfort had said. *Mordecai Leathers knew far better than that.*

Far to the north-west two bundled figures rode across the silent, frozen wilderness bound for the Upper *Wicunkasotapelo;* possibly no longer Mitch Boutonne and Dallas Lorimer, but rather *Wasicun-Sapa,* the Black-White Man, and *Ota Kte,* Plenty Kills, for perhaps they could never again associate with the white men of that country.

CHAPTER ELEVEN

Thin threads of smoke hung in the windless air, rising like ghosts from the thick winter lodges of the band of *Mato Najin,* Standing Bear, scattered along the banks of the frozen stream. Far up the valley was the big horse herd of the band, sheltered in amongst the cottonwoods and willows and guarded by the young men.

Dallas Lorimer lay flat on his belly feeling the cold creeping up through his thick buffalo coat and inner clothing, but he paid no attention to it, for his eyes were on the lodges of the Oglala, trying to determine in which one was *Wica-cante-yuha-winyan,* Captures-Everybody's-Heart Woman: Marie Benedict, the woman he loved beyond all else.

Somewhere in the frozen hills a wolf howled mournfully. Dallas raised his head. Mitch Boutonne had been gone a long time down in that valley. He had gone down there before the moon had arisen, and now it was on the wane. They wouldn't bother Mitch Boutonne. For all they knew he had been off hunting or on some other mission of his own instead of traveling to Fort Locke to find his brother-friend, Dallas Lorimer.

Then Dallas saw a shadowy figure leave a lodge and

drift like wind-driven smoke into the thickets along the stream. A few minutes later Dallas heard the soft crying of an owl not too far from him. It was the voice of Mitch Boutonne. He slid down the slope to meet the breed.

Mitch grinned. "She is there," he said.

"You took plenty of time," growled Dallas good-naturedly.

"Christ, man! You just don't walk in, look around, say hello, then walk out again! Them people know Mitch Boutonne. They know I get around. I tell them news. They listen, digest it, grunt, belch, and fart, then ask for more. Takes time, dammit!"

"O.K.! O.K.! How is she?"

"Lovely," said Mitch quietly. "Lovely but sad. Least-ways she was sad until I got word to her 'bout you."

"So?"

The breed shrugged. "She's in Old *Sunkele Ska*'s lodge. Spotted Horse's lodge. That's an uncle of hers. Martin is down there, too, staying with Standing Bear."

"How long will they be there?"

"Until she gets married to Kills Alive."

"No!"

He said it so fiercely that Mitch drew back a little. "*Hou! Hou!* It is so! I only bring news, *Ota Kte!*"

Dallas nodded. He gripped the shoulder of his brother-friend. "I must see her!"

"How? You mind-gone-far! You hang around here until daylight and them hunters come out and they'll find you. Gawd-damned right they will!"

"Did she have any message."

Mitch did not answer. The wolf howled again.

"Mitch?"

"She said: Go away, Dallas. They'll kill you."

"She knows I'm not afraid of them!"

"If you ain't, you ought'a be!"

"I must see her!"

The breed peered over the lip of the draw. "You see them stacks of wood?"

Dallas nodded. The Sioux had the habit of cutting their firewood in long lengths, then stacking it vertically almost like copies of the lodges.

"Man can creep inside them stacks," said Mitch thoughtfully. "Stay hidden. Maybe Mitch could get word to her and you could see her. Jesus God, but you'd take a chance! The dogs might smell you out, and they hate a white man worse than a strange dog in camp!"

"I'll take the chance."

The breed looked at him. "If they do smell you out, *Ota Kte,* you got to pretend ol' Mitch Boutonne knows nothin' 'bout you bein' there."

Dallas nodded.

"It don't make sense! I told her you was an officer in the Army; that you knew for sure who you was. That you was in trouble but you would get out of it."

Dallas eyed him. "Sure, sure," he said dryly.

Mitch did not look at him again. "She won't go with you, *Ota Kte.* She knows you'd be sorry if you done it. You can't tell a woman you won't be. She'd know no matter how you treated her."

"Why don't you let me talk to her, Mitch?" said Dallas quietly. "She'll know if *I* talk to her."

"Maybe. You know what them Oglala will do to you if they catch you?"

"They won't catch me!"

Mitch grunted. *"Wah-nee-chee."*

They crept along the bank of the stream in the darkness. Now and then Mitch raised his head; the man gave Dallas an odd feeling. It was almost as though the breed had acquired the acute senses of a wolf, the mannerisms, the whole character of the animal. No wonder the Sioux and many other Plains Tribes dressed their scouts in the body and head skins of wolves.

There were no night horses kept beside the silent

lodges. The Oglala did not expect any surprise attacks in this weather. Some of the night horses were as good as dogs when it came to giving alarms. But no dogs could be seen either. They would be asleep beside the fires in the centers of the big skin lodges. Maybe they were stirring restlessly right now, with that strange and uncanny sense a dog has when a stranger is about.

The lodges were pitched in a great circle, open to the east, as was the custom. The medicine lodge was along the western edge, directly across from the eastern gap. No smoke arose from the medicine lodge. A thought came quickly to Dallas Lorimer.

Mitch lay belly flat at the edge of the thicket. He silently pointed out the lodge of Spotted Horse, then a particularly large stack of firewood not too far from it. He glanced at Dallas. "Take courage, brother," he said softly in Oglala. "The Earth is all that lasts." Then he was gone, sliding belly-flat along the ground, and as he went Dallas knew that Mitch Boutonne had no faith that Dallas would ever live to leave that camp.

The breed was now next to the lodge. He looked back at Dallas and signaled with a hand, then he was gone.

Dallas felt icy cold but not from the frigidity of the night. The fear of death crept over him; of slow and awful death by fire and knife. But there would be no turning back now.

Dallas bellied along, taking advantage of every scrap of cover, foot by foot, until he reached the stack of firewood. He eyed the base of it. There was a space just about wide enough to slip through. He looked about. There was no sign of life about the camp. He wormed his way inside the pile, half expecting it to topple upon him.

He squatted there, wrapping his thick buffalo coat about him; then he drew out the knife Mitch had given him. A Green River knife honed to razor sharpness. He'd have to use that rather than his revolver if he was discovered.

The wind rose a little, searching through the pile of wood, chilling him to the bone. Now and then he peered through a crack, and the third time he did so his heart almost stopped, then thudded on erratically. Something was moving on the white ground. At first he thought it was a prowling wolf, but it was too small for a wolf. It was a camp dog. A lean savage animal, sniffing suspiciously at the ground; the dog raised his head and looked directly at the wood pile.

Dallas hardly dared breathe. He gripped the knife and waited. There was nothing else he could do. The dog came closer and closer. If he got a sniff of white man, he'd bark his damned head off, and then... Dallas did not like to think of that eventuality.

The dog was just beside the pile now, but still he did not seem alarmed. Then a thought came to Dallas. The thick buffalo coat he wore had been an old one of Mitch Boutonne's, left at the Benedict homestead. Many a time Mitch had worn that coat into the lodges of the Oglala using it as covering, and he himself had Indian blood. The dog smelled *Indian,* not *white* man.

Dallas moved a little. The dog drew back. Then it came close again, and Dallas could see the eyes bright and glittering. The lips drew back over the long white teeth. The damned thing was part wolf for sure.

Closer and closer came the dog until his head was a foot inside the wood stack, inches away from Dallas. There was no time to lose. Dallas darted out his left hand and gripped the beast by the muzzle, clamping down hard with a big hand while the knife snaked forward, blade up, and sank deep into the side of the throat. The dog snapped up its head even as its jugular was sliced clean through, and the hot blood steamed as it poured from the slashed throat. The hind legs scrabbled on the frozen ground for a moment, and then the dog sank to the ground.

Dallas felt his sweat congeal icily on his face, and he

closed his eyes for a moment. Then he dragged the dead dog in beside him. Now he had to make a quick decision. If he stayed there and the other dogs winded their dead comrade, Dallas Lorimer would be driven from the wood pile into the hands of the Oglala. If he left there he would not see Marie Benedict.

Even as he tried to make a decision, he saw a slim figure leave the lodge of Spotted horse and come silently and swiftly across the snow to him, and no one needed to tell Dallas Lorimer who it was. He arose from his hiding place, and she met him with lips and arms, drawing him close to her as though the two of them could blend into one forever.

He did not speak as he led her swiftly across the hard ground behind the great stacks of firewood to the medicine lodge. She drew back instinctively as she surmised his desperate intention, for the blood of her mother's people was strong in her, but her desire to be alone with him, if only for a fleeting moment or two was stronger than her superstitious fear. He opened the door of the lodge, knife ready in hand, but the lodge was empty, as he had expected it to be. No one lived in a medicine lodge. Only the custodian of the medicine bundle, wrapped in purifying sage, could enter that place, for it was *Wakan-Tanka*, Big Holy. An embered fire glowed faintly in a fire pit.

She came in close behind him, feeling swiftly for his free hand for strength. The medicine bundle hung on its tripod in the center of the lodge. Dallas turned and drew her close. She looked up into his gaunt face. "This is madness," she husked.

"No matter. I had to come. You must come with me."

Her eyes were wide with fright. "No!" she said.

"Are you afraid?"

"Not for myself, Dallas."

"Marie," he said quickly and tensely, "I am in deep trouble with the government, and it will take time, much time, to clear myself. I'll have to keep on the run, hiding from white man and red man as well, and it will be many months, perhaps, before I will have a chance to clear myself. I know you have been promised to Kills Alive. By the time I could come back for you, you'd be his woman. I couldn't stand that. That's why you are going with me. Tonight!"

"You can't escape them, Dallas."

He placed his hands, dirty and still stained with the blood of the dog he had killed, on each side of her face and tilted it up to look closely into her eyes. "I'm going to try," he said quietly. "If I fail, they'll kill me, and that's just as well, because I don't want to live without you."

"What happens to me then? Living with a man I hate, thinking only of you. I'll go with you then. But promise me one thing."

"Anything!"

She hesitated. "If there is no hope for you, there is no hope for me. They will not kill me, Dallas, but I won't want to live. If the end is coming for you, then you must kill me first."

He closed his eyes and turned his face away from her.

"Dallas?"

He raised his head and looked up and saw the sage-covered medicine bundle. It was big medicine, but there was a bigger medicine in the heart of Dallas Lorimer, and he prayed to that.

"Dallas?"

"Yes," he said. Then he turned quickly. A dog had howled and then another. He released Marie and walked to the door of the lodge to peer out. Two dogs were sniffing about the woodpile where he had left the stiffening corpse of the dog he had killed.

Then more dogs began to howl. A horse whinnied sharply somewhere behind the medicine lodge. Then the flap of a lodge was thrust aside, and a burly warrior stepped out with a repeating rifle in his hands to stare at the dogs, then to swiftly scan the village. There was still enough faint moonlight to see him walk toward the woodpile, and a moment later three more warriors joined him. There was no chance now.

He turned to her. "Slip out of here," he said. "They won't know you were with me."

"No, Dallas!"

He gently led her back behind the tripoded medicine bundle, then took off his huge buffalo coat. He had a Colt six-shooter, a double-barreled derringer, and his knife. Eight shots between him and the end. Six cartridges for the Oglala, one for Marie, one for himself.

The Oglala were thronging into the open area between the lodges. One of them set fire to a mass of wood piled in the center of the lodge circle, and by its flickering light the suspicious *akicita,* the camp police, prowled about looking for intruders. One of them had hauled the carcass of the dog from beneath the woodpile where Dallas had killed it. None of them as yet had looked toward the medicine lodge.

But Dallas Lorimer knew it was only a matter of time. They'd root him out. Already some warriors were looking close by the medicine lodge, which was painted red above and black below to represent day and night.

Dallas turned to look at her. "Please go while you still have time," he said.

"I stay!"

He shrugged. He eyed the sage-covered medicine bundle. Then a thought struck him with the impact of a Comanche lance. He took his keen-edged knife, raised it high overhead and drove it into the taut fabric at the front of the lodge, just over the door flap, then ripped down swiftly so that the front part of the lodge fell aside, forming a great door through which he and the medicine bundle could be seen. He felt the cold sweat running down his sides as some of the startled *akicita* stared at him as though he was something from *Wanagi*

Yata, the Land of the Great Shadow, a *Maiyun,* or ghost spirit.

Then almost silently, but very swiftly, the word went around the village, and the Oglala gathered not far from the central fire which was now leaping and crackling, casting fitful light about the great circle. The warriors stood there watching the tall white man who stood just within the doorway of the medicine lodge and who eyed them as silently as they did him.

Then a tall warrior came through the crowd until he stood just before the front rank. There was no mistaking old *Mato Najin.* Beyond him was Kills Alive, with his face set into a ferocious scowl as he looked at Dallas Lorimer, for he had seen the woman standing in the dimness at the rear of the lodge. Far to the right of the crowd stood a man dressed partly in Indian clothing and partly in white man's garb. It was Mitch Boutonne, and his dark eyes did not move from Dallas Lorimer; instead of awe or hatred of the white man, there was deep respect in his eyes for him.

It was quiet for a few minutes except for the crackling of the great fire; then Standing Bear spoke quietly to the young warrior who had accompanied him to the home of Martin Benedict. It was Little Horse. The young buck trotted to Mitch Boutonne and spoke quickly. The breed nodded and then walked to the side of Standing Bear who spoke in a low voice to him. Mitch nodded again. He looked at Dallas. "Standing Bear wants to know why *Ota Kte* has come into this village in the dead of night to desecrate the medicine lodge," he translated.

"Tell Standing Bear that I have come for my woman."

When Mitch translated there was a low hum of voices amongst the Oglala. The chief eyed Dallas, then spoke to Mitch.

"She is not your woman, Plenty Kills. She has been promised by her uncle Spotted Horse to the proven warrior Kills Alive," said Mitch.

The fire crackled as the wind arose and whined down from the frozen hills.

Mitch sent a message with his eyes to Dallas, something that was not clear enough yet to Dallas, but it seemed almost as though the breed was hoping a thought would occur.

Then it came to Dallas, a continuation of the thought he had had before. They were afraid to come near him as long as he was near that medicine bundle, not because they were afraid of him, for the Sioux feared no one, but because they feared what he would do to their sacred medicine bundle.

Then Marie spoke softly so that no one beyond Dallas could hear her. "The medicine bundle must never touch the ground, for this will bring incredibly bad luck to them."

"Hear me, Standing Bear," said Dallas. "If you do not let me leave this village, unharmed, and with the woman beside me, I will hurl your medicine bundle to the ground!"

"What does he say, *Wasicun-Sapa?*" asked the old chief.

When Mitch translated the piercing eyes of the chief seemed to strike out at Dallas, but there was nothing he could say. Dallas stepped back and held out a hand toward the bundle. A mournful sound came from the watching warriors.

"I am waiting," said Dallas in his crude Sioux.

They watched him silently. Once again he reached out his hand to that mystical bundle. Standing Bear raised his head. This one white man mattered little to him, alive or dead, but the medicine bundle was life itself for his people. "It shall be so, *Ota Kte,*" he said at last.

"One more thing," said Dallas.

"Nothing!" roared the old chief. "I have already given you and that woman your lives! Nothing!"

Dallas raised a hand and pointed to the sky. "Until the sun is there tomorrow, no man can follow me."

Kills Alive's lips drew back over his strong white teeth.

"Agreed!" said the chief.

Kills Alive vanished quickly into the throng.

"The grandfather of this woman shall not be harmed?" asked Dallas.

"*He* is our friend," said Standing Bear simply. "*She* is only a woman."

"We will not be tricked?" asked Dallas.

Standing Bear drew himself up. "You have the word of *Mato Najin,*" he said clearly.

Mitch caught Dallas' eye and nodded. Then he held his right hand low in front of him and made the sign language gesture for all haste.

Dallas sheathed his knife and held out his hand toward Marie, and in her haste she brushed against one of the legs of the tripod. For a fraction of a second the structure shook and it almost seemed as though it would go over. The eyes of the Oglala were riveted upon it, and a lightning swift prayer shot up to the heavens from the heart of Dallas Lorimer. The tripod settled to rest, slightly tilted, but still at rest, with the sage-covered medicine bundle swaying gently back and forth. The Oglala covered their mouths in awe.

Dallas threw his coat about Marie's slim shoulders and walked with her from the lodge straight past Standing Bear, and the dark inscrutable eyes of the chief seemed almost to hold a glint of respect for this white man who dared all.

The crowd parted, then closed behind them as they walked toward the eastern gap from the circle of lodges, and they did not look back, but the last eyes to follow them were the dark, almost blood-red ones of Kills Alive, and there was horrible death forecast in them for the white man who had taken a woman from the Oglala.

CHAPTER TWELVE

D allas Lorimer lay flat upon his lean belly, hat slanted across his eyes, watching the faint thread of dust rising on the open plain beyond the valley that was below the butte where he was hidden. The late spring sun was warm on his back. After the last hard storm of the winter, when he had outbluffed the Oglala and escaped with Marie, the spring had come on with incredible swiftness. It was time for the early hunters to be about. Time for the Army to shake off the sluggishness and boredom of the winter and begin to move out into the Indian country. The trails were already dry, and the streams were within their banks. It would be a hot and dry summer.

The young men of the Teton Sioux, the hotbloods of the Oglala, Brules, Hunkpapa, Wahpeton, Sans Arcs, Miniconjou, and Si-ha-sa-pa, would be thirsting for war. The young men of the Army would look forward eagerly to glory and battle. The generals would want to garnish the old laurels won during the Civil War, now fading little by little into history, and add new laurels in the Indian country. Settlers, ranchers, homesteaders, and buffalo hunters were poised at the borders of the country of the Sioux, Cheyenne, and Arapaho, and some of them would trickle into that country despite the warnings not only of the military, but of the grim red men themselves.

It was time of spring, and it would soon be the time of blood and death. Dallas shifted a little and glanced back over his shoulder. Behind him, down a steep slope and past a curiously mazed labyrinth of rock, was the faint trail he had found in his flight from the Oglala at a time when he had almost given up hope. Down there was the place he had brought his woman. It had been safe from the winter winds and the falling snow, hidden from prying eyes, and well supplied with small game and areas of dried grass for grazing for the horses, which Dallas had been forced to slaughter for meat.

They had been safe enough there during the latter part of the winter, but now it was spring, and he had made a practice of spending many hours at his lookout. This was the first day he had seen signs of man.

Behind the butte was a desolate area, a badlands. A place with little game and hardly any water. There were no trails in there. Marie had said that the Oglala feared the place. It was said to be the abode of evil spirits. Dallas knew that few white men would enter the place, not from fear of evil spirits but because of the lack of water and game. A good soldier may choose a citadel of defense to make his stand to the bitter end; a better soldier chooses a place to make a stand and also a way of escape.

They could run if they had to, but there was one unforeseen factor that had changed the plan of Dallas Lorimer. Marie Benedict was already bearing the child of her union with Dallas. She was in the fourth month. She would travel if she had to. Her Sioux blood would probably carry her through any hardships, but that was problematical. Dallas could not and would not expose her to anything that might cost the life of the child and possibly her life as well.

He eyed the thread of dust again. It was coming from

the east, the country of the white men, although there was no definite border between their country and the lands of the Lakota.

He looked to the west, not expecting to see anything, but a cold shaft of fear drove into him as he saw another thread of dust drifting faintly on the freshening wind. West...the stronghold of the Oglala.

He had never deluded himself that he would be safe however in the hideout. It had been a waiting battle against time. The time of spring and war; the time of the coming of their first child. But the baby would not be born until the fall, which meant that if Dallas stayed here much longer Marie would not be able to travel at all.

He walked down the slope, a lean lath of a man who walked like a jungle cat and who was just as dangerous. Perhaps those far-off travelers would pass the butte and never investigate, *unless they were looking for Dallas Lorimer.* It seemed as though every man's hand was against him.

He walked lithely down the dim trail which was hardly discernible to a stranger. It was tricky, that hidden approach, for time and time again a man would find himself up against what seemed like a blank wall of rock, only to note at the last possible moment that here was a hard turning to right or to left; a place beneath overhanging rock and fallen timber where a man could work his way through. It had not been exactly so when Dallas had arrived there leading the two horses, on one of which rode his half frozen woman. The way had been more treacherous then, and less hidden. He had turned that around. It was now less treacherous and far more hidden.

Dallas padded down the slope, passed through a thick bosque of trees, then followed a pathway hidden in a thicket until he approached a labyrinth of shattered rock and tangled brush. He entered it and followed his trail until he was within hailing distance of the cave he had made into his home. He whistled softly three times, then twice, then once. A moment later he heard the whistle signal repeated in reverse order. She was all right then.

He walked up toward the cave. He had walled the front of it with timber and covered it with earth and brush; a man would be almost upon it before he knew that it concealed something. She was waiting at the entrance for him, and he noted that she had her rifle close at hand. She could shoot very well, for Mitch Boutonne had taught her, and Dallas had warned her time and time again never to stray too far from her rifle.

She came close to him and kissed him. Beautiful as she had been when he had first known her, her approaching motherhood seemed to have worked a charm upon her that surpassed her earlier beauty. "What is it, Dallas?" she said.

"Nothing. I was hungry."

She studied him as they walked into the dimness of the cave. Beyond a turn was their home. He had formed a crude, but comfortable bed. Their cooking was done outside when the smoke could not easily be seen. "There *is* something," she said firmly.

There was no use trying to fool her. He nodded.

"White men?" she asked.

"I don't know."

"Oglala?"

"I can't say."

She tilted her head to one side. "*Both* then, Dallas?"

He told her about the faint columns of dust, one from the east and the other from the west.

"It doesn't surprise me," she said quietly. "It is that time of the year."

"Yes," he said. "We can hardly run, Marie."

She looked up at him. "You spent a great deal of time and thought on making this a hiding place. We can fight if we have to."

He placed an arm about her shoulders. That was the

spirit of her Lakota ancestors speaking from her soft mouth. "You're thinking of the child, then?" he asked.

"Yes. But there are other things, Dallas."

"Such as?"

"How long can you run away, my husband?"

He smiled ruefully. "Every man's hand seems to be against me, and I have you to think about."

"That is true, but you must still face the world. You're innocent, Dallas! This you must prove!"

"At the cost of my life and perhaps yours? Not yet, Marie. I'll prove my innocence. I've known all winter long that I must do that if we two and the little one are to have any life at all."

She was silent for a time, and then she looked into his face, searching it closely with her great eyes. "With a *half-breed* wife, Dallas?" she asked softly.

"I've told you not to talk that way!"

"The truth again, Dallas? The truth that *really* hurts? The loss of your commission? Your career? Your own people?" She quickly looked away. "For *me*, Dallas?"

He had been through this before, and there was only one way to allay her fears. He gently picked her up and carried her to the bed. He placed her upon it and knelt beside her, kissing her gently, again and again, until at last they were close together. His actions plainly told her that her fears were in her own mind, for Dallas Lorimer was willing to forego the things she had mentioned to him just to be with Captures-Everybody's-Heart-Woman and the child she would soon bear.

Once again he was at his observation post, in the late afternoon, watching the lengthening shadows and the dim trace of dust to the east. The dust from the west had vanished as mysteriously as it had come. That was what bothered Dallas. As long as he could see the tell-tale veil rising, he knew where the approaching parties were. Maybe even now they were watching his place of hiding, and the uncanny feeling fled through his mind that even at that instant there were eyes upon him.

He shifted and placed a hand on his rifle. It was then that he heard the soft crying of an owl. It startled him. It was too early for those fine, velvet-winged hunters to be about their night's business. Once again the faint cry came to him. He edged into deeper shadow and gripped the rifle. The cry came once more, then died away. The shadows grew longer as he waited, and a cool wind crept slowly around the butte. He shivered, not from the cold, but from the eeriness he felt. He half closed his eyes, and then a thought struck him. He remembered the moonlit night months ago when he had waited outside the sleeping village of Standing Bear to hear word from Mitch Boutonne.

Dallas raised his head and listened. The crying came again upon the wind. This time he hooted softly himself, then shifted his position and brought his rifle hammer to full cock. Minutes ticked past, and then he saw a misty shadow drift quickly across an open patch of ground on the slope beneath him. He leveled his rifle and sighted on the brushy area where the shadow had vanished.

"*Ota Kte!*" the call came up the darkening slope.

A feeling of intense relief flowed throughout Dallas Lorimer. "*Mitch!*" he called out. "Mitch Boutonne, my brother!"

The breed came up the slope with a wide grin splitting his dark face. They said nothing more as they met and hugged each other like two shaggy bears. Mitch stood back and stared at Dallas. "As ugly as ever," he said solemnly.

"And you stink as much as you ever did," said Dallas.

"It's *you* all right," said the breed with satisfaction. "My Oglala friends, they ain't so fussy!"

They squatted side by side. "How did you find me?" asked Dallas.

Mitch hesitated. He wet his thick lips.

"Well?"

The breed looked down the slope. "I followed someone to this area. I'da never found you else."

"Someone else? No one knew I was here!"

Mitch turned, and there was an odd look in his eyes. "You mean you ain't seen anyone around?"

"No. Who are you talking about, Mitch?"

"Kills Alive and Little Horse. They been hunting you all spring, *Ota Kte*. They never talked much about it, but they went out all the time. Never fooled anyone. They was after you and Marie. I got wise ten days ago. Followed them. They come right around here. West of here. They was there earlier this afternoon, then they went north for a time. I didn't follow. Figgered there was one place a man would go and hide with his woman." Mitch glanced up at the butte top, then stabbed a finger down onto the ground. *"Here!"*

The cold feeling returned to Dallas. "All spring?" he said slowly.

"All spring," said Mitch. He smiled faintly. "I knew they hadn't found you, and I knew I had to find you first."

"Why, Mitch?"

The dark eyes studied Dallas. "First because I figgered mebbe I let you down back there at the village when you bluffed them Oglala. Christ, but you had brassbound nerve that night! Mitch Boutonne thought he was all man until he seen you facing them Oglala!"

"You didn't let me down, Mitch. It was my fight."

Mitch shook his head and looked away. "I mind the time when *Ota Kte* fought them wolves to save ol' Mitch Boutonne, the Black-White Man. You was amongst worse than wolves back there that night in the village."

"I never blamed you for staying out of that mess," said Dallas. "You've done more than enough to repay me for saving you from those wolves."

"Man never repays a brother-friend," said the breed simply. "Can't never repay such a man for his friendship."

The sun was gone now. The wind had shifted. It was colder, too, but not to Dallas Lorimer. The strange man of three races was back at his side. "Come on," said Dallas. "Time to get warm and to eat."

"She is all right, *Ota Kte?*"

"You'll see."

Dallas led the way through his hidden trail, and now and then Mitch grunted in satisfaction. Before they reached the last part of the trail Dallas turned to his friend. "You said you had come back because you had let me down at the village. But you're holding something back, Mitch. Is it something Marie shouldn't know?"

The breed nodded. "You want to know why Kills Alive and Little Horse turned north today? I'll tell you. White men were coming from the east. Five of them. Men you know. Men looking for you, *Ota Kte.*"

Dallas stared at the breed. "Five men? Soldiers?"

"All but one. Montfort, Christian, Windolph, Cox, and Leathers."

The icy feeling came over Dallas once again.

"I was at DeVoto's Station before I come here. Ginral Montfort had been through there. Said he was on a leave of absence, with *friends,* hunting. You know damned well who he's hunting."

Dallas wet his lips. "Because of that damned money?"

Mitch nodded. "Partly. There's more. Something I don't like to tell."

"Go on, Mitch."

It was dark in the canyon, and the wind whispered quietly and insistently through the deepness of it.

Mitch came closer to Dallas. "You remember the woman you went to see the night we busted you out'a Fort Locke?"

"A man couldn't easily forget Jean Ross," said Dallas dryly.

"You can now, *Ota Kte*..."

Dallas gripped Mitch by the arm. "What do you mean?"

"She was found strangled to death after you left her, *Ota Kte*."

"Good God!" said Dallas unbelievingly.

"Strangled and raped," continued Mitch. He wiped the cold sweat from his broad face. "They say you done it, my brother."

"That's a damned lie, Mitch!"

"I know."

"You believe me, don't you?"

"You know damned well I do! You don't tell Mitch Boutonne, *Ota Kte*. When you busted out'a that house she was still screamin'. Take a damned good woman to scream after she was strangled to death, eh? But it ain't no joke! They say you done it. Lot of weight behind it, too."

"What do you mean by that?"

The breed shrugged. "Ginral Montfort says he found you with the body. Says he fought you, but you was out'a your mind. He was goin' to marry her, and they say he ain't been the same since she was done in. That's why he got leave of absence and his friends joined him on the hunt for you."

Dallas nodded. It figured all right. They had wanted to get rid of him months ago. The one man who could wreck their careers. The one man who was supposed to know what had happened to the missing money. Montfort had cleared his record and had managed to keep the mouths of Christian, Windolph, Cox, and Leathers tightly shut, although it must have cost him something to do so. Jean Ross had been the other member of the party, and she was dead. Not by the hand of Dallas Lorimer, as everyone thought. She had been alive and screaming like a fury when he had left her. Left her with Arliss Montfort.

"What do you figger on doing, *Ota Kte?*" asked Mitch.

"I fight back," said Dallas Lorimer quietly.

"You're wrong in one way. We fight back, *Ota Kte!*"

There was no need for speaking further. Dallas led the way to the cave. He turned a little. "We don't wait for them, Mitch," he said quietly. "We go after them."

Mitch grinned widely. "Spoken like *Ota Kte,*" he said.

Somewhere north beyond the towering butte, in the black, velvet darkness, a lone coyote howled. Two red men listened as they performed the *hanblake oloan,* the Sioux prayer for advance knowledge of their enemy, the white man known as *Ota Kte.* They finished the medicine pipe, thrust slender willow wands into the ground, and attached tiny offering bags of willow bark and tobacco mingled together to the wands.

To the east, almost in the towering shadow of the butte, five white men made their tireless camp, chewing on dried beef and hardtack. No prayers came from them, but they, too, wanted advance knowledge of the man they knew as Dallas Lorimer.

The coyote howled once more and then vanished into the thick darkness, for the smell of men was too strong for him that night. There was another, subtler smell in the night air: the cold aura of approaching death.

CHAPTER THIRTEEN

The moon was not yet up when Mitch Boutonne emerged from the cave to wait for Dallas outside. Dallas kissed Marie. She said nothing, nor did she shake in fear, but he knew her heart was going on the warpath with him that night. He left her, and he did not look back for fear that his heart would fail. He had gone to seek battle many times before, and he had been afraid, but now it was different because of his love for Marie.

Dallas led the way from the canyon. Now and then he stopped to listen, but there was nothing to hear beyond the soughing of the night wind, the scurrying of small nocturnal creatures through the swaying brush, and an occasional sharp squeaking as one of them met swift and bloody death in the ceaseless life of hunter and hunted.

They reached the top of the canyon and walked across to the lip of the butte, then down the faint, almost indistinguishable trail Dallas had found in his early days there. It was difficult enough during the day but perfect mental hell at night, not only from the standpoint of falling to one's death far below in the velvety darkness, but because of the fear that a falling stone would strike below and alert any listening enemies.

But they made it to the bottom without much noise, then stopped to rest. Neither of them spoke. They held their rifles ready and listened to the enveloping night. Mitch looked at Dallas. Now was the time to make the first decision: to strike the two Oglala first, or to find and deal with the five white men. There was no need for the two men to speak. The Oglala would fight or ambush, no quarter asked and none given. Even up and devil take the losers. But, with the white men it was more complicated, because there still might be a chance for Dallas to free himself from the charges against him. If there was, he could hardly go ahead and kill men with whom he had served. Surely *some* of them would listen to reason.

"Which way, *Ota Kte?*" asked Mitch impatiently.

"East."

The breed eyed him. "Get the Oglala *first, Ota Kte.*"

"They don't matter as much."

"Listen to me, my brother! They've spent months looking for you! Find them! Kill them! We two can handle the whites easily enough, but those two Oglala are different!"

"East," said Dallas Lorimer.

Mitch opened, then slowly closed his mouth. He shrugged. "Lead on," he said. He shook his head as Dallas crept off through the whispering darkness.

There was the faintest suggestion of the rising moon when Dallas came to a halt, with the towering hulk of the brooding butte behind him. There had been no warning to eye, ear, or nose of the presence of enemies, but, even so he had been warned by that honed sixth sense that a man develops on the frontier or in time of war. Mitch Boutonne had halted as well. He raised his head and sniffed the air.

"Tabac," said Mitch softly.

Dallas nodded. He had caught the faintest whiff of burning tobacco. White men, for Indians smoke only in ceremony, if young, and only in the peacefulness of the tepee, if old.

Dallas squatted, trying to skyline horse or man. It was no use. The wind was questing from the north-east, bringing the odor with it.

Mitch knelt close beside Dallas. "I go on in," he said, jerking a thumb toward the darkened tangle of rocks and trees, interlaced with brush, that lay just beneath them, enveloped in the darkness.

Dallas wet his lips. He was the leader. They were his enemies, but Mitch Boutonne was better skilled than Dallas to probe into that inkiness and pinpoint the enemy. Dallas nodded.

The breed drifted noiselessly off into the night. Minutes later a horse whinnied softly. Something clattered against a rock. Silence again.

Dallas bellied forward, raising his head now and then, conscious now that the moon was rising swifter than he had expected it would. If he was caught on naked ground he'd be a prime target for those five men, and every damned one of them, despite their other weaknesses and failings, was an expert marksman. Where the hell was Mitch Boutonne! Then a dog barked clearly.

As if in answer there was a muffled curse, the scuffling of feet, then the sharp cry of a man, and Dallas instantly recognized the voice of Mordecai Leathers. Dallas rose to his knees and full cocked his rifle, trying with staring eyes to tear the veil of darkness from the terrain.

Then he heard a thudding sound. A horse whinnied and then another. A dog barked sharply again and again. Dallas cursed beneath his breath. He might have known that Arliss Montfort, whether he was hunting game or men, would hardly move without at least one of his damned hounds.

"Got him!" cried a voice. It was that of Chet Windolph.

Dallas bellied forward, trusting that the dog wouldn't

get a snootful of his scent. Mitch Boutonne had almost been ripe enough to get ridden out of an Oglala camp on a rail.

"Who are you?" demanded Arliss Montfort.

There was no answer from Mitch Boutonne.

"Gawd dammit!" snarled Leathers. "Talk!"

"Who are you?" demanded Montfort once again.

"Ota Kte! Mani! Mani!" cried out Mitch Boutonne.

"That's his name," said the inane voice of Willis Cox.

Dallas felt sick. *Mani! Mani! Walk fast!* Get out of there!

"Is that Sioux?" asked the General.

"Yup," said Leathers.

"He sure stinks," said Christian.

"All Indians do," said Cox loftily.

"He don't look like no pureblood to me," said Leathers. "Seems like I seen him somewheres before at that."

The moon was rising; the silvery light was already flooding across the low hills to the east, and Dallas could see vague movements in the dimness before him. Montfort and his 'hunters' had holed up in a small natural fortification of rock, earth, and fallen trees.

"Where have you seen him, Leathers?" asked Montfort.

There was a pause, then Leathers spoke quickly. "This is Mitch Boutonne! The Sioux called him *Wasicun-Sapa!* Means White-Black Man."

"Black-White Man," said Mitch Boutonne sarcastically.

Leathers spat. "Yeah...one quarter dirty Oglala, one quarter white trash, one half nigger."

"And all *man,* you sonofabitch," said Mitch.

There was the sound of flesh being struck hard, and it was followed by the sound of a falling body. Then again and again came the sound of something hard hitting something soft, and a sickening memory raced back into the mind of Dallas Lorimer. The grinning sadistic face of Mordecai Leathers as he had beaten Dallas in the Benedict house so many months ago.

Dallas inched forward, and hell was in his heart for the scout. Now he could see the movements of the men in the hollow. He raised the rifle, sighting on the lean form of Mordecai Leathers as the man raised *his* rifle to beat at the prone breed. Dallas took up the trigger slack.

"Enough, Leathers!" rapped out Montfort.

"He don't talk to *me* that way!" spat out Leathers.

"I said for you to stop!"

"Go to hell!"

Chet Windolph stepped up behind Leathers. The moonlight glinted on his handgun. "You heard the General, Leathers."

"We want him to talk before you beat him to death," said Christian. "You can have him later, when we're through with him."

Leather's breath was harsh and fast. "All right," he jerked out. "Listen! This breed bastard is a good friend to Martin Benedict! He was probably around when Lorimer holed up with Benedict and his breed granddaughter. He knows plenty! How about it, Breed? Where's Dallas Lorimer?"

There was no answer from Mitch Boutonne.

"Talk, or by God, we'll make you!" grated Christian.

"He with the Oglala?" asked Leathers.

"On the *Wicunkasotapelo*?" demanded Montfort.

Nothing from Mitch Boutonne.

The moonlight flooded down into the area, and Dallas sank out of sight, rifle resting on the lip of the hollow. The wind was blowing toward him, and for a time that damned dog and those horses might not wind him.

"Give me a little time alone with him," said Leathers.

"You'd get started, and you'd kill him before you were done," said Mark Christian. There was a hard, set look on his drink-ravaged face. "Hand me your little knife, Chet."

Windolph looked at Montfort. Montfort nodded. The officer handed his knife to Christian. Christian tested the edge. He nodded, then looked down at Mitch. "I served with the Foreign Legion once," he said. "I saw the work the Touareg can do with a knife. I also served on the Border for a time. The Yaqui are better than the Touareg. Quite a study, Boutonne."

The wind shifted a little and the dog growled softly. Willis Cox giggled. "Get going, Mark," he said. "He evidently doesn't believe you."

The dark eyes of the man known as Mark Christian, soldier-of-fortune, glittered in the moonlight. "He will," he said quietly. *"He will..."*

Dallas Lorimer knew Mark Christian well enough. Every man at Fort Locke did. A man who had served as a soldier in many armies and places and had learned strange and evil things. Morose and sullen most of the time and a beast when in his cups, as many a trooper who served under him had learned well to know. There was only one man who tolerated Christian, and that man was Arliss Montfort, although no man knew why.

There was a far better man than Mark Christian lying helpless at his feet, waiting for the cruel bite of the knife. Willis Cox grinned vacantly. "Get going, Mark," he pleaded. "You've talked enough about how good you are with the knife. Show us."

Christian looked up at Montfort, and the moonlight made his dark, saturnine face look like that of a demon peering from the ajar doorway of hell itself. The General nodded. Instantly there was a rending of cloth as Christian cleared the way for his horrible, bloody work. They'd never get a thing out of Mitch Boutonne, for they'd never have a chance. Dallas took up a little more on the trigger, and the heavy rifle cracked flatly, driving smoke and flame from it just as Mark Christian bent low. The soft-nosed 216 grain bullet struck Willis Cox full in his grinning mouth, driving through to cut his spine neatly in two. His lolled sideways like a rag doll as he fell heavily against Chet Windolph, driving him to the ground. The slamming echoes of the shot reverberated through the hills.

"Run! Run!" yelled Dallas.

Mitch wasted no time. He was up on his feet and driving toward a place where he could hurdle the rocks to freedom when Mark Christian leaped forward with his knife bent and hooked in his powerful hand. The blade rose and fell, and Christian snarled like a ravening wolf as the steel sank deeply into the back of Mitch Boutonne. The breed grunted but kept going, dragging the officer behind him, held fast by the razor-edged hook of steel. "Aaah! Aaah!" cried Mitch Boutonne.

Dallas fired at Christian, and the man fell, but Dallas knew he had missed. The man bore a charmed life. The gunsmoke drifted over the rock hollow, making vision difficult. Montfort and Windolph opened fire, but the lead keened high over Dallas' head. There was no sign of Leathers; Dallas knew the scout had left the hollow and was probably trying to outflank him.

Montfort's hound leaped from the hollow and raced courageously toward Dallas only to be stopped by a heavy slug.

There was no time to waste. Dallas retreated, trying to find Mitch. He sped over the hard ground, hurdling rocks and bushes, until he saw the breed, weaving and swaying as he walked toward the butte; the moonlight glittered frostily from the silver shaft of the knife that protruded from his back like some strange and alien growth that would, in time, kill him. Dallas turned and saw fleeting figures hit the ground. He let his rifle roar into staccato life, splattering lead and shards of rock over the cursing white men. The echoes rolled and reverberated, dying away into the hills. Every hostile within miles would be alert now.

He had given himself enough time to reach Mitch,

and as he did so he heard the high-pitched voice of Arliss Montfort. "God *damn* Lorimer! Damn him to everlasting hell! He killed Brutus!" Nothing about the quick death of Willis Cox, his aide-de-camp and erstwhile drinking and wenching companion. Just the death of Brutus, his favorite hound.

Dallas bent low and hooked one of Mitch's arms over a shoulder. He looked up into the dark, contorted face, beaded with cold sweat. "Go on, *Ota Kte*," said Mitch hoarsely. "I'm heading for *Wanagi yata*."

"*H'gun! H'gun!*" said Dallas. He worked his way down a slope, fearful of hearing the white men closing in on them. He made it to a place where he could hold off a platoon, quickly reloaded his rifle, then bent to look at Mitch. His heart and belly sickened within him. The tip of the blade must have penetrated deeply. There was nothing else to do. He gripped it and pulled it free. "*Aaah!*" husked Mitch before he passed out completely to trail on toward *Wanagi Yata*, The Land of the Big Shadow.

As Dallas Lorimer carried Mitch Boutonne to safety, the blood of his friend hotly stained his neck and face and traced sticky little rivulets down his strained and sweating body. Now and then the breed would open his tortured eyes; his wide mouth would open so that the moonlight made chalk of his teeth, and then he would pass out again. But he no longer made a sound. He knew what Dallas Lorimer, *Ota Kte*, his brother-friend, was trying to do at the risk of his own life; any extra sound would bring ravening two-legged wolves slavering after him.

Even as Dallas reached the top of the butte he knew there would be little safety now. The quiet night would carry every sound. He rested and listened. To the east a wolf howled, and another answered from the north. The imitations were well-nigh perfect, but those sounds did not come from wolves, rather from the throats of Kills

Alive and Little Horse. They had a good idea now of where Dallas Lorimer and his squaw were hidden.

There were others, too, who knew. Four bitter white men. They led their horses into the thick shadows at the western base of the butte and looked up at it with searching eyes. There were other eyes looking up at the cold moonlit sky: the vacant eyes of Willis Cox. His memorial service and epitaph had been spoken by his commanding officer in one short cold sentence. "Leave the silly bastard to the wolves."

Marie Benedict keened softly in her throat as she worked on Mitch Boutonne while her man stood guard outside. She had learned native skills from her mother's people and medical practices from her grandfather.

The moon was gone when Dallas Lorimer came into the cave and looked down upon the dark face of his friend. Marie shrugged. "I've done the best I can," she said. "He may live, Dallas. But he can't be moved."

"Neither can you," he said.

She looked up at him. "What will you do?"

He passed a hand across her dark hair. He was alone now. Attrition was working. *One* of them for his ally Mitch Boutonne. That left four whites and two Oglala.

"Dallas?" she softly questioned.

"I go after them," he said.

"Hole up here! Hold them off!"

"No," he said. "I have a good many hours before dawn. They know we are up here. If I wait, they'll find us, one way or another. They'll kill me to get in. The whites will kill you, too, to keep your mouth shut. Mitch won't have a chance either. The Oglala, well, Kills Alive may still want you. If not..." He let his voice trail off.

"Can't we get help?"

He laughed harshly. "Who? First Lieutenant Dallas Lorimer, disgraced Army officer wanted for desertion and worse? *Ota Kte*, Plenty Kills? You know what the Oglala would do to me."

"There must be *someone*, Dallas!"

"I fight alone," he said. He bent and kissed her, then he was at the entrance to the cave. "If I don't come back in twenty-four hours you must make your own plans, Marie."

She nodded. Her face was impassive, but her heart was cracking.

Then he was gone as silently as a wisp of wind-driven smoke.

CHAPTER FOURTEEN

The wind was out of the west, keening softly across the country and whispering about the top of the dark butte. Chet Windolph raised his head now and then to look and listen. This manhunt was none of his choosing. Chet liked the social part of an Army officer's life or riding with a strong column on the edge of Indian country where game was plentiful and the dangers were not. He had begun to curse the day when he had been assigned to Montfort's command. He had begun to curse Arliss Montfort, too. Death seemed to dog the footsteps of men who associated with the commanding officer, but it didn't seem to bother Montfort. The curse was on those who followed Arliss Montfort, not on Montfort himself. The Montfort luck always seemed to hold.

Windolph stepped into the thick shadows of a rock ledge, not far from the sheer brink to his right. Leathers had started to lead the way up the almost invisible trail that led to the butte top until he had lost his nerve and Montfort had taken over. You had to give Montfort credit for that in any case. Montfort and Lorimer, that poor betrayed bastard, were foemen worthy of each other's steel.

Windolph shifted his position. He was dying for a smoke. Dying for a drink. Dying to get the hell out of this damned haunted country before he got what poor Willy Cox had gotten. He raised his head sharply, then turned it slowly to the left. There was no one there. Just as he thought to turn to the right he felt the cold, sharp tip of the knife rest lightly against the right side of his throat at the jugular. His guts moiled in fear.

"Don't speak, Windolph," whispered Dallas Lorimer.

The wind soughed on. An owl hooted softly far down the rocky slope. Chet felt the cold sweat trickle from his armpits and run slowly down his strained sides. Oh God, he thought, it's coming to *me* now from this silent, bitter man. The man who had raped and strangled poor lovely Jean Ross, the man who had killed poor Willy Cox. *It's me now!*

"Windolph," said Dallas softly. "The others are far beyond hearing us. We have a little time. The knife stays an inch from your throat."

"What do you want?" husked the officer.

"Information."

"Ask on, for God's sake!"

"You know damned well Montfort was away from his command, playing around in the hills, when the column was wiped out—except for me, and a few others."

Windolph blinked and digested what Dallas had said. "You were the only one left alive, Lorimer."

"No. There were others."

"Where are they?"

"Dead."

"By whose hand?"

"Not mine."

"I don't understand."

"One man came back to that field of battle that night. One man who killed the wounded the Sioux had overlooked. He was no Indian, Windolph. Even you know an

Indian would have avoided that place as if there had been plague."

Windolph nodded. "But you...*you* lived."

"He *thought* he killed me."

"What do you want to know?"

"One man came there, Windolph. A white man. To kill off the wounded and get that government money. In my opinion, that one man was from Montfort's little party of six people. It wasn't Jean Ross, God rest her troubled soul. It wasn't Willis Cox, he didn't have the guts to do it."

"*You?*" Dallas laughed softly, but the sound of it made the hairs rise on the back of Windolph's neck. "*You* didn't need money. Why should *you* come back?"

The young officer nodded again.

"That leaves Leathers, Christian, and Montfort himself."

"*What do you want to know?*"

"Which of those three men was gone from your party long enough to do the job?"

Windolph did not answer. The knife tip pierced the skin of his throat, and he felt the lazy trickle of blood.

"Talk, Windolph!"

"There is a thing called '*for the good of the service,*' Lorimer."

"Jesus God! For the good of the service? Doesn't the death of almost two hundred good men mean a thing to you? Men led into a trap by a man like Montfort? Who spoke to you of 'the good of the service'?" Dallas spat to one side, and then he knew the answer. Montfort himself had deluded this clothing dummy of an officer into thinking he had better keep his mouth shut for the good of the service.' "*Who came back,* Windolph?"

Chet Windolph wet his lips. He had signed Montfort's report of the battle. The report had been falsified. Montfort had shut his mouth by dangling the twin silver bars of a captain before his eyes. He couldn't pay Chet

Windolph any other way. Captain Chester Windolph. It sounded so good to him, and when he got his long-anticipated leave and went home to Philadelphia it would sound even better. But if he had to confess that he had signed a false report, the shame would be worse than death.

"Windolph?"

The handsome young officer moved too swiftly even for Dallas Lorimer. Windolph strode directly for the brink and then stepped off.

But Dallas Lorimer was already moving by the time Chet Windolph hit bottom three hundred feet below. The sound would carry far. Even as he moved for cover he felt a grudging feeling of respect for Chet Windolph, the military tailor's pride and joy. He had died like a man no matter the cause.

Mark Christian had heard the death of Chet Windolph, although he did not know who had died. There was one thing he did know: It hadn't been Dallas Lorimer who had plunged to his death. *That* was a certainty. He had seen a silently moving man in the darkness shortly thereafter, and he knew it was Lorimer. Christian moved softly. There was a feeling within him that he was close to something of importance. He didn't know why, but his years on arduous and perilous service with half a dozen armies had hand-honed his sixth sense.

He eyed the eastern sky. It was faint with the light of the false dawn. Montfort and Leathers had quested over to the southern side of the butte, leaving Windolph to scout the northern side and Christian to take the western slopes, but it was the eastern terrain that drew Christian, for the very reason that it looked inaccessible and impenetrable.

He had found a place that led him into a labyrinth, a maze of twisted walkways and narrow passages, that seemed to lead nowhere, when he met a blank wall, only to lead further on where least expected. The washed-out light of dawn was tipping the eastern hills when he emerged into the hidden canyon and drew in a soft, appreciative breath. He could hear the faint murmuring of the waterfall at the far end, mingled with the whispering of the wind. He scanned the walls of the canyon, but it was still too dark to distinguish anything. It was then that he heard the sudden startled flight of a bird from the maze behind him. He turned quickly, drew his bowie knife and sank down behind a rock.

Dallas Lorimer came from the maze with his rifle in his hands. "Christian!" he said. Then he stepped quickly behind a boulder.

Mark Christian rubbed his lean face. He eyed the boulder. He could have easily dropped Lorimer with a fast shot, but that was not why he had come on this manhunt. "Lorimer?" he said.

"I'm here."

"This is the place, isn't it?"

"You know it is."

"I could have killed you just then."

Dallas laughed softly. "I could have killed you as you entered the labyrinth, Christian."

A cold feeling came over the soldier-of-fortune. He had been so damned sure of himself. "Why didn't you?" he asked.

"I wanted to talk with you."

"This is no time to be sociable."

"Don't play the fool, Christian. That was for Cox and Windolph."

"You've killed both of them then? Why?"

A quirk came into Dallas' mind. "For the good of the service," he said.

"And me?"

"I want *you* to talk."

The wind died away. Christian shifted a little, trying to pinpoint Dallas, and then he realized that he had been outsmarted. His back was to the canyon, which was below a wide rock ledge, and the dawn light was coming behind *him,* not Lorimer.

"You've got something on Montfort," said Dallas. "I'm not interested in what it is."

Christian laughed. "He's paid plenty to me for it, Lorimer."

"I thought so."

The officer grinned sardonically. "Cost him damned near every cent he had, the blasted political soldier."

"He needed more?"

"What do you think?"

"I don't know. That's why I'm talking with you instead of looking down at your body."

"You talk big, Lorimer."

"You know Montfort falsified his report of that mess on the *Wicunkasotapelo.* You know he let that column go to its death. You know someone left your party to come back to the massacre for the money."

"Yes."

"It certainly wasn't Jean Ross, Willis Cox, or Chet Windolph."

Christian spat. "You fooling, Lorimer? Certainly it wasn't any of them!"

"*You?* You're good with a knife, Christian."

Christian rubbed his jaws. "You damned fool," he said quietly. "Do you think if I *had* done the job I would have come out here now? That I would have gone on to Fort Edgerton with Montfort?"

Dallas knew that he spoke the truth.

"Listen, Lorimer," said Christian. "I want to get my hands on that money. I don't give a damned sou for my record, *or* the Army. Montfort was broke and I wanted money. He said he had an idea on how to get some. Never told *me* what it was. It wasn't until we came back to Locke from Edgerton that I knew he meant to get rid of me in case I used his failure on the *Wicunkasotapelo* to screw more money out of him. I was too smart to let him get Leathers to slip a knife into me. The only reason I came along on this damned manhunt was to find out where that money was. I know you know where it is."

"I don't."

"Come on! You're talking to Mark Christian now!"

Now that Dallas was sure that it had not been Christian out there on the *Wicunkasotapelo*, there was no longer any need to keep him alive.

"Lorimer?" asked Christian eagerly. "Look! Let's work on this together! I'll help you get rid of Montfort and Leathers. We get the money, split even up, then take off, and no one the wiser!"

The man was a cold-gutted shark. The memory of what he would have done to Mitch Boutonne came back to Dallas. "All right, Christian," he said slowly.

"Good!" Christian stood up and walked toward Dallas with a smile on his face, holding out his hand for gripping.

Long ago Dallas had wondered what weakness, if any, would be that of Mark Christian. Now he knew—Money. Dallas moved his left hand quickly. He held out his right hand to solidly grip that of the mercenary and to draw him close enough so that the keen blade in Dallas' left hand slid up just under the rib cage into the man's heart. Christian's face froze in a contorted mask. "You saw the work the Touareg can do with a knife," said Dallas quietly.

Christian fell heavily. "The Yaqui are better than the Touareg. Quite a study, Christian."

Dallas wiped the knife on Christian's shirt, then hauled the man by the legs to a cleft. He rolled the body into it, dumping rocks in atop it. Then he hid the man's weapons, padded back through the labyrinth, and went to hunt for the last of them, Leathers and Montfort. It had to be one of them.

Dallas had gambled a little too long. The dawn was coming swiftly, and there were two more men waiting for him somewhere else on the butte top. Those were the dangerous ones, Montfort and Leathers. Luck had been with Dallas most of the time, except for his loss of Mitch Boutonne.

He faded into the rough tangle of brush and rocks at the entrance to his labyrinth, hoping to God that he hadn't been seen. It wasn't likely that they knew where the entrance was. Christian had been playing a game of his own when he had found it. The wind had begun to shift with the coming of the dawn.

There was one weapon Dallas had. His recollection of the fact that Leathers had tried to force the secret of the lost money from Dallas when he had found him at the Benedicts. Later, Dallas had known that if he had had the money and had given it to Leathers he would have died right then, and Mordecai Leathers would have vanished with the loot. It was one reason, perhaps the only one, why Leathers would not have killed Dallas before this time. It stood to reason that Leathers *still did not know where that money was hidden.*

He worked his way through the harsh tangle toward the southern lip of the butte that overlooked the badlands. They'd know he had not gone down there unless he was damned desperate. But they were all gambling now, and the stakes were of the highest. Suddenly the words of Jean Ross came back to him. *"He will have money, Dallas. He told me so. I know he will have money!"* The veil began to part for Dallas Lorimer. There were only two of them left to fight him, and Leathers didn't know where the money was. Neither Leathers, Jean Ross, Chet Windolph, Willis

Cox, or Mark Christian knew or had known where it was. That left one man and one man alone! *Arliss Montfort!* "Jesus God," said Dallas.

"Don't move, Lorimer," said the harsh voice behind him.

He lay still and the cold sweat broke out on his body.

"Let go that rifle! Put that six-gun out there, too! Get rid o' that knife!"

Dallas did as he was told.

"Turn around!"

He got to his feet and turned around, raising his arms, to look into the vulture face of Mordecai Leathers. Leathers grinned and spat. "Neat as sin," he said. "Yore slippin', Lorimer."

The butte top was completely lighted by the dawn. Dallas realized he had done to himself that which he had done to Christian, outlining himself against the light. Well, the odds always had been high, and he had taken his winnings; now he'd have to pay the piper. There was no sign of Montfort.

"Yuh lookin' for the Ginral? He's off somewheres. Now listen, Lorimer, and listen well. I don't give a damn about Montfort's service record and his damned glory-huntin', but I want that money."

"I don't know where it is, Leathers."

The rifle hammer came back to full cock. "Look! Yore goin' with Ol' Mordecai, and we're goin' to find that money. Now it ain't right around here, but I'll copper any bet that it is still somewheres around the *Wicunkasotapelo*, and that ain't but twenty-thirty mile from here. Right?"

"You're right about the distance. I don't know about the money, Leathers."

The man's dirty face worked, and his hands trembled on the gun. "All right! All right! Then we go look for it, and you'd wish to God you'd never been born! Once more! *Where's that money!*"

"*He* doesn't know, Leathers," broke in a silky voice from behind the scout. *"Don't turn!"*

Leathers' bottom jaw dropped, and cold fear broke across his face. "For God's sake, Ginral!" he rasped out.

"Let down the hammer of that rifle, then drop the weapon!"

Leathers did as he was told. Dallas could just see the

outline of the officer's head and shoulders beyond the scout, in a thicket. Montfort's campaign hat was drawn low. There was no insignia of rank on his shirt. Then, clearly as a flash of prairie lightning lancing into a butte came the memory of that horrible moonlit night upon the slaughter field of the *Wicunkasotapelo* when he had been crawling toward the ambulance to get his gun and had turned to see that silent and eerie figure standing on the edge of the coulee, with unseen face, watching him.

"*You,* Montfort!" said Dallas.

"I thought you might have figured it out by now, Lorimer. You were damned near as stupid as Leathers here."

"Ginral! For God's sake! I was gonna split with yuh!"

Montfort laughed softly. "You damned idiot! I know where the money is. I *alone!*"

"So now you are in the clear," said Dallas slowly. "Your record clean, all witnesses gone, the blame for the massacre on the honorable dead, and the money hidden away for when you need it."

"Exactly!"

Leathers turned his head a little. "Sure, Ginral, Lorimer will die, but I'm still around!"

Montfort's gun flashed and roared, and the slug rapped into the back of Leather's jacket, raising the dust. "You *were,*" said Montfort.

Dallas Lorimer made one last desperate cast of the dice. He raced forward past the falling body of Leathers, snatched his hat from his head, and hurled it edgewise against the face of Montfort. Montfort cursed and jumped to one side, but Dallas had picked up Leathers' pistol on the fly, and he cocked it and pulled the trigger. The gun misfired. Montfort didn't stay to fight. He hurdled a rock, fell, and lost his pistol. Dallas leaped after him and, in turn, fell. Montfort crashed through the tangled bush like a wild animal in a frantic effort to escape. Dallas re-cocked and fired the pistol until it ran dry. The echoing of the shots reverberated throughout the hills, and the gun smoke hung in a sheet over his head; Arliss Montfort was gone.

There was no time for anything else. No chance to see Marie and Mitch once more. The game was afoot. Dallas snatched up his rifle, knife, and pistol and crashed through the brush after Montfort until he realized how much noise he was making. Common sense took the place of hate and rage.

The sun was just up as he worked his way down the southern side of the huge butte, taking advantage of every minute hand and foothold, until he was at the base, looking toward the fantastically colored and shaped natural towers, walls, battlements, and escarpments of the badlands. A place of grotesque beauty and a place of death for the unwary.

He moved to the west until he reached a place where tracks led off to the southwest. The tracks of a horse. A shod horse, so it must be Montfort. Even as Dallas looked about he heard the faint whinnying of another horse. He worked his way toward it around the western side of the butte and saw the remainder of the horses left there by the men who had died upon the butte. He chose a rawboned dun, took an extra canteen, filled his pockets with cartridges, then rode off just as the sun began to flood throughout the badlands, bringing to life the fantastic coloring of salmon, rose, pink, red, and yellow.

He rode steadily, and now and then he found traces of Montfort's flight. The man was careless, but he was moving fast in as close a trail as he could make to one place, the *Wicunkasotapelo,* The Place Where We Killed Them All. And while one white man fled and another hunted him, two Oglala, alerted by the gunfire at dawn, had approached the base of the butte in time to see Dallas Lorimer ride off into the badlands, a place where *they* would not go. For a time, Kills Alive sat his horse, looking up at the butte and then at the badlands, while

Little Horse, his eyes wide because of the immense loot in horses and gear that they had found, wanted to go home to the village of Standing Bear, a hero in the eyes of the older warriors and of the maidens.

There was indecision on the painted face of Kills Alive. The woman was around somewhere. Close perhaps. It would be easy to find her, but the lost time might lose for him the quarry he really wanted. The man known to the Oglala as *Ota Kte*.

"Which way, my brother?" asked Little Horse.

Kills Alive looked up at the sky. Softly he began to sing the *heyokan-lowan*, the thunder song, for advance knowledge, and as he did so an eagle floated high above them, then suddenly flew off to the southwest, and as he did so a feather detached itself and drifted slowly downward to earth near Kills Alive.

There was no choice now. Kills Alive led the way along the very rim of the forbidden badlands toward the distant *Wicunkasotapelo*.

CHAPTER FIFTEEN

The two Oglala had caught the lone white man as he had debouched from the badlands, and they had taken him to the banks of the *Wicunkaso-tapelo*. It was not far from the place where the Oglala and their allies, the Cheyenne and the Arapaho, had been twice victorious in fifteen years over the *Wasicun* Long-knife soldiers. It was a good place. The medicine was strong. No white man could prevail against the Oglala here.

Little Horse was in his glory. They had captured horses and gear, and now they had a white prisoner to take back to the village of Standing Bear. But Kills Alive had found several bottles of *mini-waken* in the saddlebags of the captured horses, and he had drunken deeply of the stuff, so deeply that his natural hunger for cruelty and blood had overcome his desire to find the woman he wanted and his wish to return quickly to the village of his people. It hadn't taken too long to convince the stupid Little Horse that it was better to enjoy the *mini-waken* themselves than to share it with the other Oglala and that it would be far more enjoyable to work over the trussed up white man by themselves. It would be great fun to see how long they could keep the sweating white man alive.

They had stripped him and staked him down at wrists and ankles. They had already started the 'little torture fires' not far from his exposed armpits and between his thighs, not far from the crotch. They took time, the little fires, and a man could be made to suffer for many hours while he was slowly cooked to death inch by inch. It took a master hand to do the job, and Kills Alive had no peer in the fine art.

His first screams had started about the middle of the afternoon, and by the time the sun was slanting down over the western hills he had been gagged to stop his hoarse cries. Meanwhile, two bottles had been emptied, and a third was almost gone. Little Horse sat on a rock staring with double vision at the writhing man as Kills Alive went skillfully to work—his hands not affected by the liquor—with razor-edged knife. Little Horse nodded. He was learning a great deal. The sound of a distant rifle shot was the last thing he heard, for the heavy slug caught him full in the forehead, and he was dead at that instant.

The echo of the shot reverberated along the valley of the *Wicunkasotapelo* to be closely followed by another as the second shot broke the spine of Kills Alive and dumped him lifelessly across the writhing body of his victim. A thin spiral of stinking smoke arose from the breechclout of Kills Alive as one of the dead man's own 'little torture fires' started on the buckskin.

A tall man came striding down the hill with ready rifle in his hands, to splash across the shallow waters of the stream. He ran toward the staked-out man and kicked away the fires, then rolled aside the limp body of Kills Alive to look with horror on what the work of fire and knife had done. He bent and plucked out the gag and hurled it into the stream.

The victim's words were not distinguishable at first.

Then he made a little sense. "Who is it? Who saved me? Thank God you came! Who is it?"

There was no answer.

"Who is it? For God's sake! *Who is it?*" The bloody eye sockets stared up at the rescuer.

"Dallas Lorimer, General Montfort," said Dallas quietly. He turned his head away while green bile rose in his throat.

Montfort was quiet. He did not move. "What happens to me now, Lorimer?"

"That is your decision, sir."

The wind shifted, and a cold breeze blew down the valley of the *Wicunkasotapelo,* bending the spring grasses and swaying the trees and the brush. It ruffled the newly sprouted grass on the many mounded graves of the men who had been slaughtered there the previous fall. The men of Montfort's column.

"What shall I do, Lorimer? I'm blinded!"

"That is your decision, General Montfort."

Silence from the pitiful hulk of what had once been a fine looking man; a fine looking man whose soul was foulness itself. "Will you take me back, Lorimer?" he asked at last.

"If you wish."

"But you'll want the money, too?"

"Certainly, sir."

Montfort nodded. He tried to see the tall, gaunt man looking down at him, but he'd never see Dallas Lorimer or anything else again, not with *that* vision. But memory has a vision of its own, and a man cannot shut his eyes to what he sees there in the dead of the night. This ruined specimen of a man knew that, and he was afraid, deathly afraid.

Dallas went to the stream and got some water in his hat. He bathed the tortured man's face. Montfort gripped Dallas' wrist with terrifying strength for a man in his condition.

"The money chests are buried just above the field of massacre, next to a light colored boulder shaped like a man's skull. You cannot miss it."

Dallas looked up at the darkening sky. "We'll have to travel soon, sir."

"Not me, Lorimer. You understand."

"Yes." Dallas walked to Kills Alive and drew a Colt from his waistband. He spun the cylinder, then placed the weapon close beside the officer. He turned and walked back toward the stream, picking up the bottle of liquor on the way. He waded the stream and struck out for the place where he had left his horse. Dusk had just settled when he heard the distant whip like crack of the Colt. The lone echo died away in the hills. Dallas stopped, emptied the bottle, then hurled it away to hear it smash on the ground. "The last man alive," he said with a note of finality in his quiet voice. The long drawn out cry of a hunting wolf echoed near the banks of the *Wicunkasotapelo*. He'd dine well that night.

Bearded General Terry, Commandant of the Department of Dakota, looked up at Dallas Lorimer. "I am taking your word on some of your story, Lieutenant Lorimer. My investigation seems to substantiate most of your statements, and you have returned the lost money. Whether or not we can change General Montfort's report in its entirety is not the question now, but, in any case, you and Captain Dutton will be cleared of any charges implied in that report."

Terry stroked his beard. "There would be no purpose gained by staining the records of General Montfort, Captains Christian and Windolph, Lieutenant Cox, and Scout Leathers, who died gallantly fighting overwhelming numbers of the hostiles, as you reported. We must remember the good of the service, you know, Lorimer."

"The good of the service," agreed Dallas.

"There is still the question about the death of Miss Jean Ross, but you claim you have a witness to the effect that Miss Ross must have been murdered *after* you left her quarters. Is that correct?"

"It is, sir. The man named Mitch Boutonne."

"And it is your wish to leave Fort Locke to find this man and bring him back to clear you?"

"It is, sir."

The kindly eyes studied Dallas. "You will clear yourself, Mister Lorimer, of that I am sure; otherwise I would not let you go."

"Thank you, sir."

Terry leaned forward and tapped the letter of resignation that Dallas had submitted. "And you still wish this to be forwarded?"

"I do, sir."

"You will not reconsider?"

"I have made up my mind, sir."

"The woman of mixed breed, is it not?"

"Yes, sir."

Terry nodded. "She would be welcome to *my* home, Mister Lorimer, but I cannot change Army custom. However, your services can still be of value to the government. It is said that you and this man Boutonne are probably the two best scouts in this country. As such, you can serve your country. In a few weeks I leave on an expedition against the Sioux. One of my officers has specifically requested your services, either as scouting officer or as a civilian scout, whichever you choose."

"It would be difficult for me to make that decision so quickly, General Terry. I'm interested, as a civilian, in the proposition, but it is not yet time for me to go back to work. My wife, you understand."

Dallas saluted and walked toward the door. He gripped the knob and then turned. "I find it hard indeed to pass up this opportunity, sir. May I ask who the officer was who specifically asked for me?"

Terry looked up. "Custer," he said. "General George

Armstrong Custer, who will command the Seventh Cavalry on the expedition."

Dallas nodded. "I'll be sorry not to go with *him*, sir. Goodbye."

"Goodbye and good luck, Lorimer."

Dallas closed the door behind him and walked out into the bright spring sunshine. The last man alive was indeed just that, now. He swung up onto his dun and guided it toward the gateway. *Ota Kte* was riding to the north-west to be with *Wasicun-Sapa,* but most of all to be with *Wica-cante-yuha-winyan,* Captures-Everybody's-Heart-Woman, and her, as yet, unborn child.

In time, when peace came at last between Sioux and white man, Dallas Lorimer meant to make his home in the canyon where he had hidden that spring with Marie. He rode the dun up to a crested ridge, then reined him in to look back at Fort Locke. The flag snapped in the spring wind. He felt a little regret at resigning his commission, but he could yet serve his country as a scout, and perhaps it was better so. He touched the dun with his heels and rode toward the distant bluish hills of the *Wicunkasotapelo* country.

NOW HE IS LEGEND

CHAPTER ONE

The afternoon heat seemed almost molten and there was no wind to move the heavy masses of it that hung over El Corralitos, stifling life and sound like a leaden shroud. A swollen bluebottle fly buzzed lazily between the rusted iron bars of the cell window, in and out, in and out, as though waiting impatiently for the occupant of the cell to die, as the others had died several days ago against the bullet-pocked wall of the shabby old mission building that stood opposite the stinking *calabozo*.

Ross Starkey raised his head. "Get out'a here, you hungry sonofabitch," he said huskily. "I ain't ready to join the rest of them. *Viva la revolution! Viva* General Zaldivar, the liberator of Chihuahua! *Viva! Viva! Viva!*"

His voice echoed hollowly in the cell and in the filthy corridor outside of it. The echo died away and there was no other sound except that of the overfed fly. He had eaten well the past week as the barefooted, undersized, overhatted *revolucionarios* died in roped bunches against the mission wall, leaving gouts of blood on the harsh caliche and against the pocked wall of the abandoned mission. Before they had died, they had been forced to dig their own graves in the mission cemetery, for at least they had been allowed by the *Federalistas* to lie in consecrated ground, although the mission itself had not been used since the Franciscans had been expelled more than fifty years past by the new republic of Mexico. They had left a heritage; a thick wall to stop the bullets.

Ross sat up and reached for his water dish. A cockroach was feebly swimming in the tepid water, trying to scale the sides of the dish. Ross studied him. "Of all the water in El Corralitos, *cucaracha*," he said thoughtfully, "why does it have to be my dish?" He slipped a nicotine-stained finger under the insect and lifted it out, carefully placing it on the dirty floor. He watched it crawl weakly into the darkness beneath the sagging cot. "Maybe you think that was God, hey? Something huge, so huge you can't imagine *what* it is, suddenly reaches out of the blue and saves your lousy life. What kind of a god do *you* have, *cucaracha?* It can't be a man. Men can't be gods. When they line you up against a wall, my friend, the man facing you with the rifle in his hands is God." He laughed and dropped back on his bunk, covering his burning eyes with his forearms.

"There is salt in that which you say, amigo," said a dry voice from the corridor. Something tinkled musically. Something grated rustily.

Ross sat up. The cell door swung open, protesting stridently on rusted, dirt-clogged hinges. A man walked easily into the cell. His chihuahua spurs were singing softly as they struck the hard-packed earthen floor. The jailer closed and locked the door behind the newcomer. His sandals husked on the corridor floor as he returned to his siesta.

The newcomer eyed Ross from beneath the brim of his heavy felt, steeple-crowned sombrero. The sunlight streaming through the barred window glinted dully from the silver trim of the hat. His charro jacket had silver buttons and silver cord had been sewed to the sides of his soft leather trousers. From his ornate clothing to the thin, pencil-line mustache on his upper lip, he was a typical Mexican dandy, of say, perhaps, Chihuahua or Hermosillo, but hardly of El Corralitos.

Ross leaned his sweating back against the peeling wall. "I don't suppose they left you any smokin' or chewin' tobacco, caballero," he said in his cow-pen Spanish. He grinned crookedly. "By God, they at least left you your own clothes. You must have connections here in El Corralitos."

The Mexican sat down on the opposite bunk and felt in his shirt pocket. He tossed a pack of Mex ready-mades to Ross. "Keep them, amigo," he said pleasantly. He drew a match against the scabrous wall and lighted Ross' cigarette.

Ross drew in a deep breath of the sweetened tobacco and blew it out through his nostrils. "Mother of the devil," he said appreciatively. "I needed that."

"Could you use a drink?"

Ross tilted his shaggy head to one side. "Water?"

"Brandy."

Ross grinned again. "Sure, amigo," he said dryly. "Send for the waiter. I'll have a platter of *albondigas* and some *sopapillas*, too, while you're being so kind."

The Mexican reached inside his jacket and brought out a silver flask. He unsnapped the top and handed it to Ross. "Helps to drive the stink out of your nostrils," he said.

Ross took the bottle. "There *is* a God," he said fervently. As he raised the bottle to his cracked lips he looked squarely into the Mexican's eyes and an eerie feeling coursed through him along with the good *aguardiente*. He had the lightest damned gray eyes Ross had ever seen, even in an American, and they seemed downright disfiguring for a greaser. The brandy hit him hard. His senses reeled and he almost dropped the flask.

"You all right?" asked the Mexican.

Ross nodded. He held up the flask.

"Go ahead. Don't get drunk," the Mexican said.

"Fat chance," said Ross. He took another slug and took a deep drag on the cigarette. "Maybe God was kind to me because I was kind to that cockroach," he added thoughtfully.

"He won't get you out of here, amigo."

"The only thing that will get me out of here is a firing squad," said Ross. He studied the man. The Mexican was downright handsome. He seemed to have a good lick of the Spanish blood, and a little of the Indian. Maybe he got his gray eyes honestly. There were a lot of "unreconstructed" rebels still living in Chihuahua, Coahuila and Sonora. There had been a time after the war when Ross' old man had wanted to leave New Mexico instead of swearing allegiance to the United States. When he had gotten liquored up enough he would beat the subject to death until Ross' mother had to shut him up.

"Zaldivar never had a chance," said the Mexican.

Ross shrugged. "His money was good."

"How much did he pay you?"

"Twenty dollars a day in gold when there was fighting, five when there wasn't. Food and ammunition on the house. It was a good life while it lasted."

"Where's the gold?"

Ross dropped the cigarette butt to the floor and rubbed it out with his rope-soled sandals, exchanged for his good El Paso boots by the jailer, without benefit of *asking* Ross. Ross fingered a second cigarette. The Mexican tossed a packet of lucifers to him. Ross lighted up. He should have been suspicious right at the start.

"I mean the gold he paid you," added the Mexican. *"Not* his war chest."

Ross blew a smoke ring and punched a dirty finger through it. "The alcalde got his fat hands into that," he said dryly. "Three hundred in gold he said, to pay my way to the border. You can see how far I got."

"That pig would put his mother out to be a whore."

"I wasn't too bright in trusting him," admitted Ross. "My horse died just outside of town. The *Federalistas* were heading for Gran Morelos instead of here. I would have made it except for the alcalde. He held me up until some of Zaldivar's rabble came out of the hills for food and found the *Federalistas'* ambush right outside of here. By dusk that night they had executed at least twenty of them. I happen to know that at least a quarter of them had had nothing to do with Zaldivar."

"God will sort the souls," the Mexican said piously.

Ross leaned back against the wall and brushed the buzzing fly out of the way. "If they planted you in here to worm the location of his contraband guns out of me, you're wasting your time."

The Mexican smiled, revealing perfect white teeth. He lighted a cigarette. "I know nothing of Zaldivar's weapons cache and less of his gold. They say Zaldivar died bravely without revealing the cache of the weapons and the gold. It is said that he had no eyes to see his way to hell when they were through with him. A red-hot iron passed close to the eyes does not help the sight."

Ross shivered a little despite the heat.

"You are feverish perhaps?"

Ross nodded. "I haven't had food for three days."

"No money to pay the jailer, amigo?"

"Like I said: They cleaned me out, from horns to hock." Ross sipped a little of the brandy. It was really hitting him now. "So, you can go back to El Coronel Melgosa, or whoever the hell sent you, and tell 'em I don't know where the gold or the guns are, and I wouldn't tell those greasy sonsofbitches even if they do stand me up against that goddamned wall."

"There are other ways of making you talk," said the Mexican.

Ross bent forward and lifted the back slack of his dirty, sweat-soaked Mex shirt. "Like this, hombre?"

The Mexican whistled softly as he saw the welted purple lash marks. "And you did not talk even then?"

Ross airily waved a hand. He felt ten feet tall with the booze and tobacco smoke in him. "Fact is, they can't beat the truth out of me if it ain't in there in the first place."

The Mexican casually inspected his cigarette. "You're lying, mister," he said quietly in excellent English.

Ross narrowed his eyes. "Say, who the hell are you?"

The man laughed. He reached for the flask and sipped a little of the brandy. He eyed Ross in amusement. "You passed out cold when the lash began to curl about your back, mister. You couldn't have lied if you had wanted to."

Ross reddened. "Well, it had been a long ride from Gran Morelos. I had to walk damned near half the distance."

"No offense. Better men than both of us have passed out beneath the lash. At least they didn't use a red-hot iron on your eyes. Colonel Melgosa has a fancy for Yaqui trackers. When he wants to find out something he lets those Yaquis practice a little on a prisoner. Before God, amigo, they could make a dumb man talk."

Ross felt a worm of uneasiness in his pinched gut. "You didn't tell me who *you* are. You seem to know all about me."

The man thrust out a lean hand. "My folks christened me Polk Desriders. Ain't that a handle to carry through life?"

Ross grinned as he gripped the hand. It was surprisingly strong. "What do they call you for short?"

"Des," said the man. "You a Texas man, Starkey?"

Ross shook his head. "New Mexico. Canadian River country." He narrowed his eyes. "Desriders? You got a brother about your age?"

Desriders shook his head.

"A cousin maybe?"

Desriders waved a hand. "By the peck," he said.

Ross took another drink. "One of them the Tascosa Kid?"

"No."

Ross wiped his mouth with the back of a dirty hand. "Now it's you who is lying like hell."

The gray eyes became cold for a fraction of a second. The uneasiness came over Ross again. "By God," he said softly. "It can't be you? The Kid was killed along the border two years ago."

"No," said Desriders quietly.

Ross slowly took a cigarette from the limp pack and lighted it, never taking his eyes from the man. Ross had ridden the Canadian, the Pecos and the Cimarron Rivers in his cowpunching days, and although he had heard plenty about the Tascosa Kid, he had never crossed his trail; nothing but the trail of his record and reputation. They said that if the Kid had notched his gun handles, he would have whittled away the walnut to the metal frames of the butts.

Desriders stood up and walked to the window, his spurs jingling musically. "When Melgosa gets back, maybe tonight, I might end up beside you against that wall."

"What's the charge against you, Des?"

"You can call me Tascosa. I dropped the 'Kid' when I got across the border two years ago, two jumps and a holler ahead of the sheriff of Verde County."

"That was a murder charge, wasn't it?"

Desriders nodded.

Ross blew a smoke ring. "If that's what's keeping you in Mexico, you can go back," he said casually. "The charge was suddenly dropped. Seems as though you've got some friends in New Mexico."

Desriders turned slowly. "I don't like joshing," he said coldly.

Ross looked around the filthy cell. "Who'd josh in a privy like this? I'm telling you the truth, Kid."

Desriders narrowed his eyes. "By God," he said. "When did that happen?"

"Three, four months ago."

"You're sure?"

"Positive."

Desriders ground a fist into the palm of his other hand. "Cuerpo de Cristo! I never knew!" He looked at Ross. "We've got to blow this juzgado, Starkey."

Ross spat into a corner. "Sure, Kid. Sure...any time. Wake me when you're ready to go."

Desriders gripped Ross by the front of his filthy shirt. "By God," he said between his teeth. "I mean it!"

"What have they got you in here for?" said Ross.

Tascosa released Ross' shirt. He grinned. "They caught me coming out of the bedroom window of the alcalde's daughter about dawn."

"Great," murmured Ross. "With all the putas in El Corralitos you have to have your fun in the mayor's daughter's bed."

Tascosa shook his head. "I was with his wife, not his daughter."

Ross waved a hand. "Well, pardon me all to hell! That's different!"

Tascosa flipped his cigarette between the bars. "You might as well know the mayor is Colonel Melgosa's brother. The mayor hasn't got the guts to try to kill me, and besides, he's more afraid of his wife than he is of me. It's a different matter with Colonel Melgosa."

"You don't have to remind me," murmured Ross.

Tascosa sat down and lighted a cigarette. "I've got a few friends in El Corralitos." He looked at Ross over the flare of the match. "That's how I came in here with the brandy and the cigarettes and managed to keep these fancy Mex duds."

"If you're lying again," said Ross, "don't stop. You're tickling me all to hell, amigo."

Tascosa fanned out the match flame. "I knew as soon

as I saw your loving kindness to that drowning cockroach you were the kind of man I could do business with."

Ross spread out his hands. "The shop is open, Tascosa. Shoot! You shoot with the mouth or Melgosa and his boys shoot with the rolling block Remingtons. Those soft nosed .56-caliber slugs can cut a man in half and I ain't et enough in the past few days to have much of a middle. I'm open for any kind of proposition, Kid."

Tascosa walked to the door and listened for a while. He came close to Ross, wrinkling his nose. "Jesus," he murmured. "They ought to bury you right now."

Ross took a slug of brandy. "Be careful. I'm downright sensitive about such matters."

Tascosa placed his lips close to Ross' left ear. "Like I said: I've got friends. I know too much for them to let me start talking if Melgosa gets to work on me. You feel well enough to make a break?"

"You can try me," said Ross.

"I wouldn't leave a sick pup in this privy," said Tascosa. "Escuche! There won't be a moon tonight. The jailer will be occupied." Tascosa felt inside his left boot and drew out a file. "Those bars are too tough to break and this file ought to cut through them like a hot knife through butter."

"Great," murmured Ross. "What do we do then? Carry each other by turns piggyback two hundred miles to the border?"

"You open your mouth and just say anything, don't you? No thinking, no sense, just words, words, words!"

"It's a failing amongst my many virtues," said Ross modestly. He nipped at the flask again. The world was a little more pleasant.

"Lay off the aguardiente for a while! Look, I'm giving you a break. Melgosa might let you live one more night. You know as well as I do, he won't fool with you when he gets back."

Ross was suddenly fully sober. He closed the flask cap.

"My friends have hidden a horse for me in an arroyo north of town. I can see to it that they put another one with it. Water, food, rifles and six-guns. I'll tell you one thing, hombre: You'd better be able to keep up, for this boy is heading for the border faster than lightning and eleven claps of thunder. If you can't keep up..."

Ross nodded. He looked up into the handsome face of the gunman. "Why bother with me at all?"

"I said I wouldn't leave a sick pup in here, didn't I?"

Ross nodded. "It's more than that," he said. "All right! All right! Two gunfighters are better than one. Two good gunfighters can stand off a score of these greasers. Besides, we've got Apache country to pass through."

"What do you know about me?"

Tascosa smiled. "Zaldivar didn't hire you to talk gunfighting. I knew Zaldivar. Are you in on this, or do I go alone?"

"Try to get out of here without me," said Ross.

Tascosa nodded. He walked to the window and whistled softly. In a moment the admiring face of a young Mexican boy was at the window. "Juanito," said Tascosa with a winning smile. "Go to my friend and tell him he must have another horse placed with the one that is waiting. There must be another rifle and a pistol, with plenty of cartridges. You understand?"

The boy vanished as quickly as he had appeared.

"Can you trust him?" said Ross.

Tascosa grinned. "He loves me," he said.

"I wonder why?"

The Kid opened and then closed his mouth. "Tell me what you know about the country north of here," he said.

Later, when dusk came, Ross stayed near the cell door, listening to the sound of voices coming from the guardroom, while Tascosa worked on the rusted bars. There was a woman with the jailer. Another of Tascosa's friends, no doubt. She was keeping the jailer busy, from the sounds of drunken laughter. There was enough noise to cover the steady wheet-wheet-wheet of the sharp file as it bit into the iron. There were no other prisoners in the calabozo. Melgosa didn't throw his ordinary prisoners in there. The mission wall was too handy, and as Tascosa had said: "God will sort the souls."

It was very dark, both outside and in the guardroom, when Tascosa cut through the last bar. The jailer was either too busy with the woman to bother with his prisoners, or else he was dead drunk.

It was getting late, very close to midnight. The town was quiet except for the faint sound of guitar music coming from one of the cantinas on the placita.

Tascosa stood up on the cell stool and dropped a long leg outside, cursing softly as a bar stub gored his crotch. He slid to the ground and looked both ways. He whistled softly.

Ross looked around the dark hole of a cell for the last time, or so he hoped, then clambered outside. Tascosa handed him the flask. Ross drank deeply to gain temporary strength. His legs felt weak.

Tascosa bent and removed his chihuahua spurs, stuffing them into a pocket. He walked swiftly toward the dark bulk of the mission. Ross hurried after him, staggering now and then in his weakness. He remembered all too well what Tascosa had said: "I'll tell you one thing, hombre: You'd better be able to keep up, for this boy is heading for the border faster than lightning and eleven claps of thunder. If you can't keep up..."

Tascosa paused in the shelter of the mission wall. Ross leaned against the wall. He could vaguely see the dark marks where blood from shattered bodies had stained the scabrous wall.

"We'll cut through the cemetery," said Tascosa. He grinned. "You ain't afraid of ghosts, are you, hombre?"

Ross shook his head. "I'm more afraid of being made into one than of seeing one."

Tascosa slipped between the half-open rusted gates that led into the long-abandoned cemetery. Ross felt the night breeze sweeping from the north, drying the cold sweat on his face. The breeze smelled of freedom; of the border; of the United States. God, how good it felt!

The mission bell murmured softly as the breeze crept through the bell tower. The last time Ross had heard that ancient bell ring had been when a bullet had ricocheted from the wall below, after missing one of the *revolutionaries,* and had glanced from the bell high above the slaughter.

Tascosa was far ahead, striding toward the far gate that opened onto the edge of the desert that crept close to El Corralitos from the north. He turned to look back.

"Halt!" grated a harsh voice from beyond the wall. A gun hammer snicked back.

Tascosa turned slowly, raising his lean hands.

Ross faded back between the freshly mounded graves of his former comrades in the forces of Liberty. He darted clumsily into the thicker shadows of the wall, then slid between the rusted gates. There was no one in the area between him and the jail. He ran toward the west end of the mission. There was a chance they did not know he had been with Tascosa. There was a chance he could find the horses, food and water, and the guns, and head north by himself. He knew he'd rather die than go back to that privy of a jail.

He rounded the rear of the mission, stumbling over fallen tiles, cursing himself for his clumsiness. He faded into the thick cluster of thorny brush that had taken seed in a wall angle and had snuggled up along the old wall, stretching almost to the gate where Tascosa had been captured. Ross could hear the faint sound of voices, carried to him on the desert wind.

He leaned against the wall and fumbled for the flask.

He drank deeply, draining the good brandy to get strength into his shaking legs, and as he did so, he seemed to see the handsome face of Tascosa looking at him from the darkness, although he knew the man was fifty yards away, facing a cocked rifle. If the sentry cried out, or fired, he'd waken the whole town, and gone would be Ross Starkey's precious dream of freedom.

"I wouldn't leave a sick pup in this privy," the Kid had said.

Ross knew it was now or never. Any minute Tascosa would be marched back to the jail and that would be the end of him when Melgosa got back. Maybe Melgosa *was* back. God help Tascosa if that was so.

"Look," Tascosa had said. "I'm giving you a break. Melgosa might let you live one more night. You know as well as I do, he won't fool with you when he gets back."

The breeze rustled the brush. Freedom, thought Ross. Freedom in a five-minute walk to that arroyo and those horses.

"I said I wouldn't leave a sick pup in here, didn't I?" Tascosa had said.

Ross slipped the flask inside his shirt. He picked up a fallen broken tile and padded along the wall, as silent as a cat. He saw the big hat of the soldier, and his narrow shoulders. He was facing Tascosa. The breeze picked up, rustling the brush. Ross raised the tile and struck heavily. The sentry grunted and went down, while Tascosa neatly plucked the long-barreled Remington from his nerveless hands. He turned to look toward the town. The rifle struck the wall and the hammer sear slipped. The big .56-caliber cartridge exploded. The muzzle flash lighted the taut face of the sentry and his staring eyes. His neck was twisted at an unnatural angle. The roaring echo of the shot fled along the mission wall and rolled out into the desert.

"*Vámonos!*" cried Tascosa. He ran out into the desert, trailing the rifle.

The game was up, thought Ross as he staggered weakly after Tascosa. He made it five hundred yards from the mission and then went down. He looked back at El Corralitos. Lights were flashing on in the buildings. Lights bobbed about as men ran with lanterns in their hands. Horses whinnied in the corrals. Dogs barked.

He looked north. There was no sight or sound of Tascosa.

Serves me right, thought Ross. I had freedom in my dirty hands, and I had to let my head get soft. Now it's Tascosa riding north and me lying here waiting for Melgosa. When they find that dead sentry it'll be worse than a death sentence for me. Death would be preferable to what they will do.

CHAPTER TWO

The hunters were getting closer. Some of them were riding, while others led their horses as they searched through the thorny brush and in the shallow draws.

Ross bellied into a hollow. No gun, no horse; not even a shot of brandy to keep up his fast-waning courage.

Something hard struck a rock fifty feet from Ross. He turned, feeling for a weapon. He gripped a wedge-shaped rock.

A man whistled. "Hombre?" he called.

Ross closed his eyes. Weakness poured through him. It was Tascosa. "Here, Kid!" he said.

Tascosa came quickly through the darkness. He bent and picked up Ross, slinging him over his surprisingly broad shoulders. A hundred yards away a group of horsemen moved toward the two Americans. Tascosa walked steadily to the north, keeping the scant brush between him and the searching Mexicans.

It seemed like an hour before Ross smelled the horses. One of them whinnied. Tascosa heaved Ross up into the saddle. "Hang on," he said.

Ross felt a rifle in the saddle scabbard. A gun belt, the

loops full of cartridges and the holster heavy with a six-gun, hung around the big pie-plate pommel of the Mex saddle.

"I can't ride for you, hombre," said Tascosa.

"Lead out," said Ross. They'd never get him alive, and he'd take a few with him, if he could see them through his onrushing fever. He looked back over his shoulder. A pinpoint of light showed as a soldier lighted a cigarette, the flare of the match revealing his bronzed face and thick mustache.

Tascosa led the way, deeper into the arroyo, cursing softly as hoofs struck rocks embedded in the harsh ground. The wind moaned over the top of the arroyo.

Tascosa urged his horse up the arroyo side and waited for Ross. He pulled a bottle from a saddlebag and handed it to Ross. Ross pulled the cork with his teeth and swilled the booze. It was a shock. He had expected brandy. It was pulque, bitter and biting, but he felt strength pour into him. "*Salud,*" he said gaily to Tascosa as he drove the cork back into the bottle.

"Nothing like a damned fool for a *compañero* on a ride like this," said Tascosa.

They rode on into the windy darkness.

Farther and farther behind them the sounds of the searchers died away.

There was little other sound than the creak and rustle of leather and the steady thudding of the hoofs on the harsh desert surface. Now and then, there was the soft pop of a cork to add to the other sounds.

Ross Starkey opened his eyes and instantly regretted it. The bright sunlight lanced into his eyes and penetrated deep into his brain, sickening him. He was half in and half out of the booze, with a fever added to it. He lay on a blanket within ten feet of a shallow *tinaja*. The dry wind made little ripples on the surface of the water in the rock pan. Ross closed his eyes, oblivious to everything else. The faint, tinkling sound of the water was all he could hear, or *wanted* to hear. He crawled from the blanket, wincing as the heat of the naked rock burned up through his thin trousers and shirt. He bellied inch by inch across the torturing surface of the ground until he could plunge his burning head into the water.

He raised his head, licking at the water that ran down his face, then plunged his head again into the cooling waters. At last, he backed off and lay quietly, throbbing head resting on his wet forearms. He was sick, as deathly sick as he had ever been in his whole life. The sun swiftly dried the damp clothing and began to burn through the thin shirt, searing into the half-healed welts on his back. He was too weak to move.

The world seemed to reel and whirl about him. He didn't know where he was, and he really didn't care. The last thing he remembered was forking a horse in the darkness of night and riding north, with the night wind fanning his fevered face. There had been a bottle. He vaguely remembered emptying it and then heaving it as far as he could, hearing it crash on the hard ground, laughing uproariously while someone tried to stop him.

Ross raised his head. "Tascosa!" he said hoarsely.

"You called?" the polite voice said from above him.

Ross looked up. Tascosa was squatting on a rock ledge twenty feet above him, a rifle across his thighs, a cigarette dangling from his lips, a faint wraith of smoke about his lean, bronzed face.

Ross sat up, wincing in agony. *"Por amor de Dios,"* he groaned.

Tascosa spat. "There's another bottle beside your blanket," he said coldly. "You look as though you need some of it. *Some,* I said, hombre!" There was a quiet warning in his voice.

Ross crawled like a whipped hound to the bottle, pulled the cork with his teeth and drank deeply. He wiped his cracked lips with the back of a dirty hand and looked up at Tascosa with a sickly grin. "Least you could'a done," he said, "was keep it out'a the sun. Burns like cougar piss."

Tascosa flipped away the cigarette and began to roll another. "I'll have a bucket of cracked ice sent down," he said dryly.

Ross tipped the bottle up again. He drank deeply again and then once more, than placed the cork in the bottle. For a few minutes the harsh booze hurt like the devil and then the alcohol set to work, and a dullness came over the throbbing pain in his head. "Where are we?" he said.

"Just north of the Rio de Haros."

Ross digested that. "A little far west, ain't we?"

Tascosa lighted his fresh cigarette. "Maybe. Eat some grub. I don't want to sit here all day. It's late enough as it is."

"I ain't hungry."

Tascosa looked down at the older man. "The grub is in that saddlebag," he said flatly. "Eat, gawddammit! You're weak enough as it is!"

Ross stood up, his eyes blazing. "You can pull leather out'a here any time you like," he said.

Their eyes clashed and neither man looked away. Tascosa blew smoke out of his nostrils. "Forget it," he said quietly. "We're both on edge. It wasn't no picnic riding all last night with you, hombre. Between the fever and the booze, you were out of this world, I tell you."

Ross nodded. "I guess you're right," he said quietly. "I apologize, amigo."

"Forget it, I said! If it hadn't been for you back at the mission I'd likely be dead by now. I don't forget those things, Ross."

Ross ate quickly, forcing down the dry food, but admitting to himself that Tascosa was right. Between the water, the booze and the food he felt a little better, but his legs were rubbery, and he knew he had a day or two of hell in front of him. He'd have to make it. There was no going back now or waiting for the *Federalistas* to catch up.

"How does it look?" said Ross.

Tascosa shrugged. "Saw a little dust a while back. Couldn't tell if it was a dust devil or not. You ready?"

"Any time."

Ross got the horses. He filled the canteens and drank deeply once more from the *tinaja*. He nipped at the bottle before Tascosa reached the flat ground, then slid the bottle into one of his saddlebags. The booze headache was sufficiently dulled to enable him to ride.

Tascosa led the way through a shallow, winding canyon. The area was as deserted as though they were riding on the moon. It was deathly hot, and the thin dust rose from the harsh ground to coat both horse and man. Now and then Tascosa looked back at Ross, riding with bent head, one hand gripping the pie-plate pommel. If they had to move in a hurry Ross would never make it. Tascosa prayed for darkness. There would be a new moon that night. They could rest in the pre-moon darkness, then ride all night toward the border.

Both of them slept like the dead, heedless of anyone approaching their camp through the thick darkness, until the first faint rays of the moon appeared over the mountains far west of the distant Chihuahua Road. Ross felt better as they rode under the light of the rising moon. Now and then he looked about him. Tascosa was leading the way, as he had done ever since they had left El Corralitos, but he was riding too far west, slanting away from the easier ground east of the Sierra Vallecillos. Ross didn't give a damn. All he wanted to do was reach the border and sleep for a week. Still...Ross wondered about Tascosa. They should be making a beeline for the border, not slanting off the trail.

The moon was fully up when Tascosa turned in his saddle. "How far is it from here?" he said quietly.

"How far is what?" asked Ross.

"The spring."

"What spring?"

Tascosa leaned forward in his saddle. "The Eye of God," he said.

Ross rubbed his bristly jaws. "I've heard of the place," he said. "We're too far west for it."

Tascosa felt for the makings. He rolled a cigarette, watching Ross all the while. He tossed the makings to Ross.

"We're wasting time sitting here," said Ross.

"No, we ain't," corrected Tascosa.

"There's no profit in riding all this way, then sitting here waiting for them to catch up."

Tascosa snapped a lucifer on his thumbnail and lighted up, his amused eyes on Ross. "There is a profit near The Eye of God," he said quietly.

Ross' hands stopped in the act of rolling a cigarette. "Meaning?" he said.

"Five thousand in gold," said Tascosa.

Ross casually finished rolling the cigarette. He lighted it, fanned out the match, then looked at his companion. "Now it's you that has the fever," he said.

"Zaldivar's gold cache," said Tascosa. "You see, hombre, you did a helluva lot of talking last night. Too much maybe. You lied beautifully back in that calabozo. You almost had me convinced."

Ross grinned. "No gold cached at The Eye of God," he said. "Just repeating rifles. Henrys and Spencers. Too heavy to haul away."

Tascosa blew a smoke ring. "Well, anyways, we'll take a look-see," he said.

Ross shrugged. "Keno."

"Come ride up here beside me, hombre. It gets lonely."

Ross touched the sorrel with his heels and rode up beside the younger man. "Waste of time," he growled.

"Just show me the way, hombre." Tascosa smiled sweetly. "We have to water the *caballos* anyway."

Ross led the way up the twisted canyon that branched east of the mountains to end in a jumbled tangle of rock and thorny brush. He looked back at Tascosa. "The 'Paches like to lie around here waiting for white men who come to water their horses," he said.

"Do tell," said Tascosa politely.

Ross held out his hands, palms upward. He slid his rifle from its scabbard and placed it across his thighs.

The moonlight shone down into the canyon, glinting from the silvery surface of the spring that welled out from beneath a huge overhanging rock face, whiskered with thorny brush and scrub trees that clung tenaciously to the rock face, their roots buried in shallow soil pockets.

Ross watered his sorrel, watching Tascosa out of the corners of his eyes. Tascosa was completely at ease. He sang softly in Spanish as he watered his black.

"Take it easy," said Ross. "You're making too much noise. Damned 'Paches and Yaquis can hear like dogs."

Tascosa leaned against his horse and rolled a cigarette. "No problem," he said. "They won't come near this place."

"Why?"

"It's taboo for them. Some kind of curse because of the dead men buried here who are said to walk on moonlit nights."

"You know a helluva lot, don't you?" sneered Ross.

"Sí," said Tascosa complacently.

"Where'd you learn that whopper?"

Tascosa ran the cigarette paper along his tongue tip and folded it over. He thrust it into his mouth and felt for a match. "Why," he said, "friend of mine told me."

"He didn't know from nothing."

Tascosa smiled as he lighted the cigarette. "I wouldn't put it that way."

"Who told you?" demanded Ross.

Tascosa blew out a cloud of smoke. "You did," he said. "Like I told you: You did a lot of talking last night."

Ross grinned. "Keno," he said. "You hold all the aces."

"Where's the gold?"

Ross tethered the sorrel to a scrub tree and took his rifle. He walked up the rock-littered slope until he reached a level area, ringed by upright boulders. "Here," he said.

"Show me," said Tascosa.

Ross leaned his rifle against a rock and began to pull brush away from a crevice. He looked carefully for rattlesnake sign and then he dragged out a heavy wooden box which he placed on a flat rock. Weakness poured through him as he exerted himself.

"Open it," said Tascosa.

Ross turned, his mouth opening in defiance. He closed his mouth. Tascosa held a cocked six-gun in his hand and his cold gray eyes probed into Ross' eyes. Ross worked at the thumbscrews. He pulled off the lid of the box. The moonlight shone dully on the coins.

"Dios en cielo!" gasped Tascosa. "Is that all of it?"

Ross shook his head. "Three more like it are hidden all around here."

"Get 'em!" snapped Tascosa.

Ross folded his arms. "Find 'em yourself," he said quietly. "No use in waving that cutter. You kill me and you won't ever find any of them. This was the easy one, hombre."

"Find 'em, damn you!"

Ross grinned. "Look behind you," he said. "Down in the canyon."

"You think I'm a kid to be taken in like that?"

"Look, you bastard!" said Ross.

Tascosa turned and shot a glance down into the

canyon, then he turned again to Ross. He opened, then closed his mouth, then turned again to look down into the canyon. "Jesus Christ!" he said.

Ross laughed softly. "Hellsfire, Kid! There are only a round dozen of them. 'Course, there's no telling how many of 'em are still down in the canyon."

Tascosa turned and his face was as set and taut as a death mask, and for the first time Ross felt the cold chill of murder emanating from the man. "You bastard," he said thinly. "You said they wouldn't come here! That it had a curse on it. You lied even in your delirium!"

Ross nodded. "I'm ashamed of myself," he said. "Mother always said I'd come to no good end."

"What can we do!" Tascosa's voice rose to a high pitch. He would have faced a dozen Mexicans or Americans, one man against them all, but a dozen Apaches can unnerve even the toughest of hardcases.

Ross picked up the box and dropped it into the crevice. He pushed the brush back atop it, then looked at Tascosa. "They won't touch it," he said.

"What about us?"

Ross picked up his rifle. The Apaches were out of sight, hidden behind broken ground. "They like to ambush," he said quietly. "They don't like to be ambushed. They figure on two white men sitting down at The Eye of God, filling their dry guts with water, only we ain't going to be there. Get your rifle. Jump!"

Tascosa wasted no time in sliding down to his horse, with Ross laughing softly as he came down behind him. Despite Ross' own icy fear, he couldn't help but laugh at the change in Tascosa.

They led the horses into a dead-end gully, then padded, Tascosa spurless, through the brush until they reached a ledge that ran along the canyon wall. Ross dropped to his belly and peered between two rocks. "Take a look," he whispered.

Tascosa crawled up beside Ross. He could see eight of

the warriors riding slowly toward the spring, and yet their horses made no sound.

"Rawhide boots on the caballos," said Ross. He levered a round of .44/40 into the chamber of the repeater. He looked at Tascosa. "I'll start from the rear, and you start from the front. I'll try to meet you in the middle."

Tascosa grinned. "First one to get five gets first crack at the other three, wherever the hell they are."

Two rifle barrels poked between rocks. The moonlight made the night almost as bright as day. One of the horses at the spring whinnied. The first Apache drew in his paint pony and leaned forward, holding up a hand to stop his companions. At that instant, Tascosa fired, to be instantly echoed by Ross' first shot. The canyon became a hell of crashing explosions, intermingled with the roaring echoes slamming back and forth between the canyon walls, overpowering the screams of the Apaches. In three minutes, thirty murderous rounds of soft nosed .44/40 slugs had ripped all life from the bucks and had killed three horses, while the others galloped madly off in all directions, crashing through the thorny brush.

Acrid gun smoke mingled with the smell of hot brass. Ross wiped his sweating face as he fed bright brass cartridges into the magazine of the hot, smoking Winchester. "Let's get to hell out'a here," he said. "Those four who are left won't bother us—for a time at least. But I'll guarantee you, if there are any more of them within fifty miles of here, they'll be on our asses by dawn tomorrow."

They scrambled back to their horses. "What about the gold?" said Tascosa as he swung up on his black.

Ross grinned. "You want to go back for it, hombre? Go ahead. I'll see you in Lordsburg when you get there. You can stake me to a meal, a bottle, a poker game and a woman."

Tascosa cursed bitterly as Ross led the way through the pathless tangle. Ross grinned again and again, and it wasn't the occasional shot of red-eye he took to keep him going that made him grin. At that, it had been a near thing...

CHAPTER THREE

You pay a price for everything. Maybe at the time of purchase, or perhaps years later, when you least expect it. But you always pay the price. The thought was Ross Starkey's as he felt the sorrel stagger under him. The sorrel was weakening fast, but not much faster than his rider. Fear, booze and desperation had driven Ross from the place where he had been awaiting execution. There had been no hope for him there. But he had left one desperate situation for another. They had outdistanced or lost the *Federalistas,* but both of them knew they had not outdistanced or lost the Apaches. There was no sight nor sound of them in the two days that had passed since they had ambushed the party at The Eye of God, but that meant nothing. An Apache is not seen unless he *wants* to be seen.

Ross' last great effort had been the killing of the bucks and the swift ride on tired horses out of the canyon, heading into the malpais country north of the Sierra Vallecillos. There was likely no water there, and there was none in the canteens. The wind came fitfully and when it did come it did nothing but stir up the bitter dust that scoured the throat and burned the eyes.

"We had to kill them," said Ross.

"Sure, sure," said Tascosa bitterly. "We kill eight of them and bring down half a hundred. By God, you tricked me! I'd never have gone to The Eye of God if it hadn't been for you!"

Ross spat dryly. He swayed in the saddle. Fever, heat and lack of water were slowly destroying him.

"Five thousand in gold lying there!" said Tascosa. "Five thousand! And we can't get at it."

We, thought Ross. He remembered all too well the look on Tascosa's face and the cocked pistol in his hand when he had seen Ross pull out the first box of gold.

There was a low line of hills ahead of them, shimmering and moving in the heat haze. Beyond them showed the humped shapes of leaden-colored, hairless mountains. Beyond those mountains should be the border, but that wouldn't make any difference to the Apaches. They owed allegiance to no country; to no one but themselves.

Ross turned in his saddle. Here and there dust devils swirled lazily across the baking plain.

"Serve you right if I left you behind for those bushy-headed devils," said Tascosa.

Ross rode on. He did not look up. The hills always seemed to recede like waves on a shore every time he looked at them.

The sun was low in the west when they reached the hills. The country behind them was still empty of life and yet there was an uneasiness in the leaden air. A hostile, alien feeling came from the land.

They found the shallow tinaja in a silent, brooding canyon that slashed through the hills like an open saber wound. They pushed aside the floating scum and pinkish bladders and strained the gamey water through their dirty scarves. There was enough to water the horses, fill their own bellies and the canteens, but hardly a drop more.

Tascosa rolled a cigarette. "That sorrel is about done," he said.

Ross nodded. He wiped his cracked lips. The sun was almost gone but the heat of it hung over the windless land, enervating and weakening, waiting for its insensate chance to kill. The black was tired, but it had reserves of strength the sorrel had lacked.

"We can rest here awhile," said Tascosa.

Ross did not answer. He picked up his rifle and staggered a little as he climbed a slope. He looked south, then west and east.

"What is it?" called Tascosa.

Ross did not answer. He pointed with his rifle. A thin streamer of smoke seemed pasted against the clear western sky like coarse hair on pale blue cloth. It was about five miles off.

"Ranch burning?" said Tascosa.

Ross shook his head.

"Campfire?"

Ross leaned on his rifle, almost utterly spent. "They're gathering over there," he said. "By moonrise they'll have bucks ahead of us, between us and the border."

"We can head east."

Ross shook his head. "They'll have scouts that way. If we get spotted, those scouts will signal the main party. Besides, even if we could get past them, we could run into the Federalistas."

Tascosa blew a smoke ring. "We can't go south."

"We can't stay here."

Tascosa looked at the brown sorrel. The horse stood with spraddled legs, head hanging, yellowish foam drying on its gummy lips, its sides heaving erratically.

Tascosa didn't have to say what he was thinking. The black was in good condition. Good for fifty more miles at least.

Ross clambered down the rocks and felt for the makings. He rolled and lighted a cigarette.

"We can't hole up here," said Tascosa. "No water."

"The Apaches will have every water hole north of here covered by dawn."

Tascosa looked sideways at Ross. "Hell of a note, ain't it?"

Ross nodded. His head was throbbing from the exertion of climbing. If the sorrel died Ross could hardly walk five miles, maybe less.

"Let's go," said Tascosa. He mounted the black and rode away from the dry tinaja.

A gecko lizard looked at Ross with bright eyes, then scuttled away, diving into cover in a slit of rock so narrow it seemed impossible for him to fit in it.

"Little ol' lizard," said Ross, as he mounted, "you got us humans beat three ways from Sunday."

The sun died in a welter of rose and gold and a faint dry breeze came whispering across the darkened desert and crept into the broken hills.

The sorrel went down for good just at the edge of the looming mountains. Ross just cleared the leather as the horse fell. He drew his rifle from the scabbard and unhooked the big canteen. He took the last bottle from the saddlebag and thrust it inside his filthy shirt. He looked about. The darkness was soft and velvety, but it had a menacing quality to it. There was no sign nor sound of Tascosa and the black. A faint wash of moonlight stained the eastern sky. By moonrise they'll have bucks ahead of us, between us and the border. Those were Ross' own words.

He walked unsteadily through the clinging darkness, feeling the hot rock burn up through his worn rope sandals. All he wanted was a chance to put the rifle muzzle into his mouth and pull the trigger before the swift, silent rush of the bucks.

The eastern mountains etched their craggy tops against the rising moonlight. The wind shifted, rustling the dry brush, making dust eddies that swirled up about the plodding man and stung his eyes. He coughed.

The moonlight touched the dull mountains ahead of Ross and began to work its alchemy on the colorless slopes. The higher elevations began to stand out in the silvery light, but it only served to deeply accentuate the pools of shadow on the rough slopes. What was hiding in those stygian shadows?

There was a foreboding silence about the night. Memories came back to Ross Starkey as he plodded along, one aching foot in front of the other, on and on, and there was no ending. He remembered the little ranchita on the Canadian where he had been born. His brother still owned it, although none of the Starkeys now lived on it. Lloyd Starkey had gone and got himself educated for the law and now practiced in Santa Fe. Last rumor Ross had heard of him, he had been working his way into Territory politics. Maybe if Ross got out of this scrape, he'd con Lloyd into letting him run the ranchita. He laughed shortly. There was enough gold back at The Eye of God to buy the ranchita and a couple more like it.

He stumbled and went down on one knee, wincing in pain. When he got to his feet and started walking again, he had to limp, favoring the badly bruised knee. "Damned near thirty years old," he said to the night, "and not enough sense to come in out'a the rain." He felt his cracked lips, then sipped a little water, spitting it back into the canteen. "I wonder where Mary Ellen Spragg is now?" He grinned. "Probably fatter than she was and got a brood of kids." He shook his head. "She was sure sweet on ol' Ross." He pulled out the almost empty bottle of booze. "Might'a made a good wife at that. How about that, booze bottle? You got any answers in that glass belly of yourn?"

He emptied the bottle, gathering temporary strength from the biting, pungent pulque. He carefully placed the bottle on a rock and walked on, looking back to see the moonlight glistening on it, standing there like a fat-bellied knight in armor. Just another dead soldier. "I wonder how many of them I've killed in the past ten years?" said Ross. "Damned near thirty years old and not a damned bit of sense."

His leg throbbed and each step became agonizing, while each time he slid on a glazed pebble, or hit a shallow dip in the ground, a lance of sheer torture shot through it.

The moon was fully up when he reached the canyon mouth. The wind whispered through it. He had no desire to walk into it, but he'd never be able to walk around it. Apaches knew the white man's ways. Apaches kept to the heights, never the low ground unless it was absolutely unavoidable. White men as a rule kept to the low ground. Ross had no choice this night of hell.

He entered the brooding silence of the canyon, walking as softly as possible, but even so, his slightest noise brought an answering echo. The place was like a rock sound box.

The moon was grinning expectantly down into the canyon when Ross went down as the sorrel had gone down. He gripped his rifle with almost nerveless hands. If he wasn't seen in the moonlight, they'd find him in the darkness. They could hardly miss his ripe scent. Dawn would bring death in the form of thick-haired men walking silently on thick-soled desert moccasins, liquid eyes staring at him through masks of white bottom clay. There would be no expression on their faces as they slowly tortured him, keeping him alive as long as possible.

A horse blowed in the shadows.

Can't blame him, thought Ross. I'd blow too if I smelled me. He grinned, wincing as a new crack opened at the side of his mouth. He rested his head on the warm rock.

Feet husked on the harsh ground. They stopped.

Ross looked up into the set face of Tascosa. "I never thought you'd get this far," said Tascosa.

"Hitched me a ride on a moonbeam," cracked Ross. He closed his eyes.

"I can't leave you here...alive," said Tascosa.

Ross rested his pounding head on his forearms. "You can't shoot," he said. "The sound would carry for miles."

"I wasn't thinking of shooting."

"You've been down here long enough to know how to use a knife."

There was a long pause. Ross looked up. Tascosa was still standing there. "You silly sonofabitch," said Tascosa. "Don't you know when you're licked?" Ross shook his head.

Tascosa squatted beside Ross and placed a hard hand on Ross' forehead. "Am I alright?" said Ross.

Tascosa picked up the rifle. "You won't need this," he said. "You got the six-gun."

"Take that too," said Ross. "You can hock it for ten bucks in Lordsburg."

Tascosa rubbed his whiskered face. He looked up at the moonlit sky, then down the long stretch of the empty canyon. "This place should be crotch-deep in Apaches by now," he said, almost as though to himself.

Ross couldn't help it. "Maybe they got a taboo on this place too. Hawww!"

"You sound just like a jackass I once knew," said Tascosa. "Relative of yours?"

Tascosa turned on a heel and vanished into the darkness. Ross slowly eased out the Colt. He opened the loading gate and turned the cylinder. It was fully loaded.

Hoofs rang dully on the rock. Tascosa reappeared, leading the tired black. He bent down and lifted Ross, staggering a little with the load. He dumped Ross unceremoniously over the saddle. He carried the rifle in his hand as he led the black north up the empty canyon.

Ross awoke in thick darkness. He lay on a dusty

blanket in a rocky area. He raised his head. The night was as quiet as a tomb. "Tascosa?" he said. There was no answer, not even a whinny from the black. Ross' feet were bare. The pistol lay on the blanket beside him, and the rifle leaned against a rock. Ross forced himself to sit up. Why had Tascosa taken the worn rope sandals? His questing hand struck a boot and then another. He pulled them close. They were Tascosa's finely figured Mex boots. Ross rubbed his shaggy, dusty head. "Beats the hell out'a me," he said.

He crawled about the area, sensing rather than seeing that he was high on a slope that slanted down toward the east. The moon was fully gone.

Ross leaned back against a rock. His right knee was painfully swollen. He could go no further, and even if the knee had not been injured, he knew well enough his strength was almost gone. There was just enough left to press trigger. Tascosa at least had left him that insurance against the slow, agonizing death meted out by Apaches.

He remembered the Sangre de Cristo Mountains and the cool, swift-rushing streams, as different from this lifeless land of baked rock as heaven is from hell. He remembered the timbered heights of the Capitans and the Sierra Blanca. He remembered a little placita there and a girl named Serafina. No, it had been Filomena. He might have married her except for his cursed Anglo-Saxon superiority. But then she would have started to become shapeless by now. Just as loving and dutiful as ever, but fat. How old had she been? Seventeen? No, it had been fifteen, marriageable age enough in that country. He might have married her at that except for her three brothers, tough as boots, who had ridden with the Seven Rivers corrida in those days, when Ross had been riding with the San Patricio corrida. There could have been no peace between them. That had been a long time ago. No, only seven years.

Now and then he peered down the dark slopes, seeing

nothing, but listening well. He had to be ready with the pistol before the swift rush of painted death.

He slept. He didn't know how long. It had been a dreamless sleep, but it had refreshed him.

Something moved down the slope. Ross cocked the Colt. His cold sweat greased the gun butt. His breath came short and fast, and he was certain it could be heard a good distance away.

A shadow moved. No, it was a man! Ross raised the pistol. Better to take along a few for honorary pallbearers before he used the last round on himself. Show them how a white man can die.

A soft, low whistle came up the slope.

Ross wet his cracked lips, darting his burning eyes back and forth, looking back over his shoulder for a sudden rush.

The whistle came again. "Ross?" called Tascosa.

Jesus God! Ross slumped against warm rock. He was completely unnerved. For a minute he thought he was going to faint.

Tascosa came up the slope leading three horses. One of them was the black. "You got guts enough to ride, hombre?" he said.

Ross looked down at Tascosa's feet. He was wearing Ross' thin rope sandals. As Tascosa led a horse to Ross, Ross thought the younger man was wearing black gloves. "Where'd you get them caballos?" asked Ross hoarsely.

Tascosa grinned. "The only place I could," he said.

"The Apaches?" said Ross incredulously.

Tascosa nodded. "Keno," he said.

"Impossible!" said Ross.

Tascosa looked at him wearily. "There were only two of them. One was a boy, an untried warrior, with the drinking tube and head-scratching stick hanging about his dirty neck. He was no problem. The buck was an old man, but he fought well enough, for a buck."

Ross looked at Tascosa's hands. He knew now what made them look so black.

Tascosa mounted one of the captured horses. "Mex Army saddles," he said casually. "The Apaches must have hit one of their patrols." He grinned. "Maybe one of the patrols looking for us. Dog eat dog."

"I still don't believe it," said Ross. He picked up his rifle and pulled himself weakly into the saddle, his breath coming harshly in his raw throat.

Tascosa looked at Ross from under the brim of his big Mex hat. "You said I had been down here long enough to learn how to use a knife. You were right, hombre." He touched the horse with his heels and rode down the slope, leading the worn black.

It was still a long way from the border.

CHAPTER FOUR

Ross Starkey sat on a chair, tilted back against the adobe wall behind him, in the shade of the *ramada* that had been built against the ranch house. A warm breeze swept across the open country and swung the water olla back and forth in its hangings. He slowly rolled a cigarette, watching the lone horseman pick his way across the broken ground north of the isolated ranch. A Winchester rested beside Ross' chair. Ross lighted the cigarette and watched the smoke swirl out into the slanting sunlight. It had been a week since Tascosa had left for Deming, leaving Ross in the care of Bass Orcutt and his Mexican wife. Tascosa had rested for some weeks before that, seemingly reluctant to leave the place, but at last he had gone, to find out if Ross had been right about Tascosa having been cleared of the murder charge held against him in Verde County. Somehow or other Ross had the idea that Tascosa didn't quite trust him. He grinned as he remembered the look on Tascosa's face when he had seen the Apaches closing in on The Eye of God.

Ross got to his feet. His knee was still a little sore, but it was healing fast. He must have gained five or six pounds in the past six weeks, with Consuelo Orcutt's good cooking in him. Consuelo was quite a dish herself, a long way from her native town in Sonora. Ross had never quite figured out how a spavined, weather-beaten old boss like Orcutt had gotten himself such a wife, and how he managed to keep her on his isolated ranch on the edge of Apache country, miles from any other people.

Ross picked up the rifle. It was a white man, and not a Mexican by the look of his clothing. They weren't so far over the border that a party of *Federalistas* couldn't slip over in the dark of the moon and snap up a couple of fugitives, then be gone by dawn. Ross levered a round into the rifle.

The horseman waved as he reached the sagging fence. "Put down that damned repeater!" he yelled. It was Tascosa all right.

Ross leaned the rifle against the wall. He watched Tascosa ride toward the house. He had done himself proud in his new rig-out. Dark gray hat and coat, white shirt and string tie. "You look like a circuit-riding preacher," said Ross. "Got a Bible in them saddlebags?"

Tascosa shook his head. "Better than that," he said. "Got some clothes for you and a bottle of rye or two."

"Christmas comes but once a year," said Ross.

Tascosa swung down and slapped the dust from his clothing.

"How was Deming?" said Ross.

Tascosa shrugged. "I went all the way to Las Cruces," he said.

"That's damned close to Verde County, Kid."

Tascosa looked about. "Dammit," he snapped. "I told you to call me Polk around here!"

Ross smiled. "They ain't here. Old Bass took his bride over to Columbus. She deviled him into it. Wanted a new dress and some other odds and ends. Seems like she's taking a new interest in life around here, now that you got a job with old Bass."

Tascosa spat. "Had," he said. "You were right about me being cleared, Ross. I can go back home now."

"Where?" said Ross dryly.

Tascosa took the saddlebags from the black. "I got nothing against Verde County," he said.

Ross flipped away his cigarette butt and began to roll a fresh smoke. "Funny thing," he said slowly. "A dead man most always has relatives and friends."

"I said I was cleared!"

"Yeah," said Ross. He lighted the cigarette.

Tascosa looked at him, little white lines radiating from the corners of his mouth. "Sometimes you talk too much," he said coldly.

"Sometimes I don't talk enough," said Ross.

"That'll be the day!"

Ross shrugged. "I was doing some listening to old Bass the other night. Might be to your advantage to listen to him, instead of talking to his wife all the time."

"Go on."

"Hand me one of them bottles first."

Tascosa handed Ross a bottle of the rye. Ross took a drink. He wiped his mouth. "Begod," he said. He gasped. "After old Bass' kill-or-cure booze, this is like manna."

Tascosa handed Ross a second bottle. "You mean nectar," he said. "Manna is a food."

"You been reading books again," said Ross. "Anyway, old Bass was doing a lot of talking while you were gone. Seems like you didn't fool him none with that Polk name of yours, even if it is right. He had a damned good idea who you were. Maybe he saw you working on his wife."

"You always run off at the mouth with a shot of booze in you," said Tascosa disgustedly.

"I'm making sense," said Ross. "Things ain't the same back in Verde County, Kid. Bass says they're choosing up sides again."

"Helluva lot that scrawny old torn turkey knows."

"He knows enough. Used to live thereabouts. Come out here because it was peaceful."

Tascosa laughed. "Peaceful? With Apaches looking over the next rise and bandidos riding over the border in the dark for a crack at the nearest Americano ranch?"

"He meant it was peaceful compared to Verde County. Here you can kill an Apache or a bandido and no one says anything except good riddance. But back in Verde County it's a feud, man! One killing follows another and you ain't exactly innocent, Kid."

Tascosa placed the saddlebags on the chair and pulled out some clothing which he tossed to Ross. He handed him a nice pair of secondhand boots. "Couldn't get any new ones your size, hombre. These'll do until we get someplace civilized."

"Like where?" said Ross.

Tascosa looked at him. "El Paso?"

"Fair enough. But I've got a job here."

Tascosa looked out over the barren land. "Here? You make me laugh. My old wounds hurt when I laugh like that."

"It'll do for a time," said Ross.

"Punching a handful of cows?"

"You got any better offers?" Ross quickly raised a hand. "Don't answer that!"

Tascosa rolled a smoke, leaning against a post, eyeing Ross from beneath the brim of his low-pulled hat. "I was figuring on heading north for a time. Maybe Albuquerque or Vegas."

"We'll need money."

"We can get it."

"How?" said Ross quietly.

The wind shifted and the rattlely-bang windmill began to whirr stridently into life.

"Punching cows?" prodded Ross.

Tascosa shot a hard look at him. "That ain't my line."

"It's good enough for me."

"You weren't exactly punching cows with Zaldivar," said Tascosa.

Ross sipped a little rye. "Only by the grace of God did I get out of that mess."

"And me," said Tascosa. "You'da never made it without me, hombre."

"Granted," said Ross. "But I'm damned near thirty years old. I don't aim to end up being a broken-down cowpoke sitting in a cantina talking about the 'old days' while I'm cadging drinks, and I don't want to die with my boots on."

"Like me, maybe?"

Ross lowered the bottle. "You don't have to go back to Verde County," he said quietly. "Or maybe you do have to."

"You don't make sense, as usual."

"They pay a lot for good gunfighters there. Enough to stake a man for a while, if he lives through it. I never did know if they guaranteed a real funeral, with candles and all that."

"Look, Ross," said the younger man, "throw in with me. We can go to El Paso, or Albuquerque, or anywhere you like, for a time anyway. Then we can mosey quiet like into Verde County and get the feel of things. You can side me. I need a good partner. You and me could make a real team."

Ross carefully corked the bottle. He looked steadily at Tascosa. "You're a loner," he said. "Like me. Only I don't want to be a loner anymore. You want a reputation and I want one too, only they ain't quite the same."

"You're going respectable?" said Tascosa with a faint smile.

"I'm going to try."

"I can get you in with some big men in Verde County."

"I'll try it on my own," said Ross. "Somewheres else."

"This is goodbye then?"

"For a time, Kid. We'll meet again someday."

Tascosa nodded. He thrust out a hard hand. "I want to make it to Las Cruces by tomorrow morning," he said.

Ross took the proffered hand. "You can go in the morning," he said.

Tascosa did not answer. He walked into the bunkhouse and in a few minutes he was back with his gear, stuffed into a warbag. He slung the warbag over the rump of the black. "Keep the saddlebags," he said over his shoulder.

"I owe you something," said Ross.

Tascosa mounted and spurred the black. He rode toward the gate. "You don't owe me a damned thing," he said back over his shoulder.

Ross watched him ride to the northeast, raising a trailing wreath of thin dust, shot through with the dying light of the sun. A feeling of utter loneliness struck through Ross.

It wasn't until he was halfway through the first bottle of rye that he suddenly realized that Tascosa must be a helluva lot lonelier than he was, but there was a difference. Tascosa would never have admitted it to Christ himself.

He was still sitting there in the velvety darkness, looking up at the glittering ice-chip stars, when he heard the rattling of the ancient buckboard and the thudding of hoofs on the hard-packed road.

The buckboard was halted in front of the ramada and a lean, rawboned man swung awkwardly down to the ground. "Gawddammit, Ross," he said. "You could'a lit a lamp, or a candle or somethin'. Man comin' clear from them hills and not a light. Struck me maybe the 'Paches had come. You shouldn't ought'a done that, Ross."

"Bass," said Ross from the thick shadows. "Get lost!" He hiccupped.

Orcutt helped Consuelo down from the buckboard.

The odor of cheap perfume, mingled with the bitter smell of the dust, drifted to Ross.

"You get some grub cookin', Connie," said Bass.

She looked toward Ross. "How many eating, Ross?" she said.

"Polk ain't here," said Ross.

"Not back yet?" demanded Bass. "If he's goin' to work for me, he's got to be here! I got a good mind to send you after him!"

"Save the time and trouble," said Ross. He lighted the cigarette he had just rolled, and the flare of the match revealed his lean hawk's face and bitter eyes. "He ain't never coming back."

"How do you know this?" said Consuelo swiftly.

Ross fanned out the match. "He came back and left again."

Bass lifted a sack out of the buckboard. "Verde County, hey?"

"Quién sabe?" said Ross.

"They'll kill him yet. You mark my words."

"He can do a little killing himself, Bass. Don't never forget that."

Ross got up and limped to the buckboard, watching Consuelo switch her rounded little outraged tail into the dark house. Ross took a box of groceries from the buckboard. "What's bothering Connie?" said Ross.

Bass grinned. "Well, we wasn't goin' to tell anybody... yet." He shifted his chew and spat accurately at a post. He wiped his juicy lips and grinned again, looking sideways at Ross.

Ross had an uneasy feeling. Damn that Tascosa anyway!

Bass hefted the sack across his narrow shoulders. "By God," he said, almost breathlessly. "Here I was about to think she wasn't goin' to breed. Did my damnedest, I tell you, Ross, and I was quite a rooster with the ladies back in Verde County, I tell you."

"Muy hombre," said Ross.

"Well, the doc says there ain't any doubt now. You and Tascosa brought me luck, I tell you."

Ross started for the house. "Brought you more than just luck," he said in a low voice.

"What's that, amigo?" said Bass.

"I'm glad we brought you luck," said Ross. He shrugged. You needed it, he thought, but not quite the way you figured it.

Later, at supper, with the guttering lamplight playing on the faded and yellowing plaster of the walls, Bass Orcutt couldn't stop eating and talking at the same time, half of his words losing their meaning by being strained through the beans, fat pork and hard bread.

Ross was hard put to keep looking at his plate. He didn't dare look at Consuelo.

"Yessir," said Bass proudly as he speared another slab of dripping pork and plopped it on his plate. "Times is changin' for good ol' Bass Orcutt. Not that I'm too old so's I can't keep up with you younger bucks." He leered suggestively at Consuelo and then at Ross. "Man can use plenty of strong sons on a place like this. They tell me the railroad may run a branch line through here. Soon as I can get me a real good water diviner I'll find water, sure as you're sittin' there, amigo. With water, more cows, two or three sons and maybe a daughter or two to help Connie in the hacienda here, I'll be in the chips, I tell you."

Oh my God, thought Ross. There was no reason for the railroad to run a branch line down thataway, and water was a scarce item anywhere south of Deming, west of the Rio Grande and east of the Animas Valley. Further, if Tascosa had planted his seed in Consuelo, it would likely be the last of the Orcutts in that area, unless another wayfaring stranger with good looks and the qualities of a good stud came drifting through to stop at Bass Orcutt's 'hacienda'.

Bass waved his fork. "Yessir, Ross. You stick with me and soon's as I get things organized, you can ramrod for me. Take a few years and I can't give you no more than twenty a month and found, and mighty good found it is too!" He speared another slab of bread. He looked fondly at Connie. "Great cook! Good wife. Fine little woman! Begod, Ross, she'll make a fine mother, too."

Ross shoved back his plate and felt for the makings. He looked politely at Consuelo whose face had taken on the wooden aspect of her part-Indian ancestry. She nodded, but there was murder in her liquid eyes. By God, she wasn't blaming Tascosa, the smooth sonofabitch! She was blaming Ross for letting Tascosa leave! Ross rolled a cigarette and lighted it at the smoking Rayo table lamp, direct from Montgomery Ward. He leaned back in his seat. Bass had been talking all the time. He had not noticed that Consuelo had left the room after placing the coffee pot on the table. Maybe she was hunting a cuchillo in the kitchen, sharp enough to cut Ross' heart out.

Bass looked up from his plate. "Beats the hell out'a me why Polk left," he said. "Fine fella. Good man with horses. Not the cowman you are, Ross, but you can't have everythin'. Where'd he go, you say?"

"I didn't say," said Ross cautiously. He filled his coffee cup. Connie's coffee was as strong as buffalo tea, as a rule. This night she had outdone herself. It would have been better than soda for cleaning an old, rusted rifle barrel.

"Verde County likely," said Bass. He flourished his fork. "They wanted me to stay there and work for them, bein' a good gun, good man with stock and a fighter from whom laid the chunk, as the locals used to say. Tough enough to hunt bears with a switch, they used to say about me in them days. 'Course I was younger then. Not settled. Got a wife now and a hacienda, and no time for them goin's-on."

Ross sipped his coffee. "What goings-on?" he said.

"All that trouble between that foreigner and old

Hardy Newcomb. Newcomb ran that county like it was his private preserve until that foreigner come along. Englishman name of Fitzgerald."

"More likely Irish," said Ross.

Bass shrugged. "Six of one and half a dozen of the other. Never liked him. Wore white collars into town and tweed suits. Begod, they say he et by candlelight when he had good mail-order lamps all over the casa! Took a bath every day, too, they do say."

"Shocking," said Ross dryly. It was a good thing Bass Orcutt didn't require more water for washing himself at that. He rarely used it, except to water his rotten booze.

"Anyways," continued Bass, "all the trouble started because of property sold by Hardy Newcomb to that Englishman or whatever the hell he was. Newcomb is nobody's fool, I tell you! Sold that foreigner a lot of land, a sawmill and other odds and ends, then the foreigner finds out he bought the land and the mill and suchlike, but ol' Hardy had chivvied him out'a the water rights! Hawwww!"

Ross emptied his coffee cup and looked toward the kitchen. It was dark. He had the uneasy feeling she was watching him from the shadows like a hunting cat. The hair crawled on the back of his neck.

Bass shoved back his plate, looked thoughtfully at the fly-specked ceiling and then belched deeply. "That's the ticket," he said in deep satisfaction. "Got room for coffee now."

"You were talking about Verde County," reminded Ross.

Bass filled his cup. He noisily sucked in half of the coffee. "Well, like I said, Fitzgerald was a dude, but he wasn't any coward. Some of them foreigners got guts too, they say, just like us Americans."

"Do tell?" said Ross in astonishment.

Bass nodded wisely. "Sure as you're sittin' there! Fitzgerald went into court, but he was dealin' with a fox,

I tell you. Besides, the judge was a cousin of Newcomb's, and the sheriff was his amigo in the war, fought all through it with Hardy, he did. Half that county seems related to ol' Hardy, or friendly to him anyways. Hardy always pays for a funeral when the Mex folks ain't got the money, and you know Verde County is about seventy-five percent Mex. You pay for a funeral for them, and you got a friend for life, no matter what else you do. Some of them Mex gunfighters is hardcase, I tell you." He shook his head. "Some of them can fight durned near as good as Americans."

"I'd never have known that," said Ross wisely.

"Things quietened down for a time, after the governor put his foot down, but then the governor was changed, and the new man was an old amigo of Newcomb's."

"I might have guessed that," said Ross. He lighted a cigarette, glancing toward that dark kitchen. Supposing old Bass got wise? Maybe Consuelo would hang the blame on ol' Ross Starkey and let him take the punishment. It was a cinch she'd never tell on Tascosa. Maybe the damned fool thought Tascosa would come riding back like Lochinvar, or whoever the hell that waddie's name was in the poem.

"So Newcomb and Fitzgerald begins to go round and round again. Newcomb had most of the old Seven Rivers corrida ridin' with him by then and Fitzgerald had to recruit some gunslingers, so he lines up some of the old San Patricio bunch. You've heard of them?"

Ross rolled his eyes upward. "Some," he said. It was his old outfit. A good many of them had been shot to doll rags by the Seven Rivers boys years ago and Ross had lit a shuck for parts unknown, leaving no forwarding address.

"Anyways, it has been hell to pay and no pitch hot in Verde County. Killin's and beatin's, and suchlike, and the governor sittin' on his hands, waitin' for the outcome. Hell, it's like a separate country down there,

Ross! You got to choose sides. There ain't no walkin' the fence."

"And Tascosa went back into that!" said Ross, half to himself.

Bass slapped a hand on the table, jingling the tableware and tin plates. "I knew it was him all the time! Couldn't fool old Bass, I tell you. Funny thing, he didn't remember me in my gunfightin' days in Verde County. But then I was never one to blow my horn, notch my guns, or nothin' like that."

"Modesty is a virtue," said Ross.

"Exactly!"

Ross blew a smoke ring. "Who was Tascosa fighting for in them days?"

Bass reached for Ross' makings and deftly rolled a cigarette. "May surprise you. It wa'n't Newcomb at all."

Ross narrowed his eyes. "Fitzgerald?"

Bass nodded like a gooney bird. "Tascosa was just a kid when he first met Fitzgerald. Fitzgerald was a gentleman, like I told you. He treated his cowpokes like they was gentlemen, too. Waste of time on most of them, but they say the Kid liked it. Maybe he wanted to be like Fitzgerald. Quién sabe?"

Ross nodded. It was the first bright thing Bass Orcutt had said in the weeks Ross had known him.

"Well, Fitzgerald can use the Kid, from what I heard in Columbus. Newcomb has got Fitzgerald up against the wall, I tell you. Folks say they figure Newcomb wants to drive that foreigner out'a business, keep him from gettin' the water he needs, chouse his men and rustle his cattle, then buy back the land he sold him at a quarter the price Fitzgerald paid for it. Nice profit, too! Sharp as a Barlow knife, that Newcomb."

Ross yawned. "Time for the hotroll," he said. "What's on the docket for tomorrow?"

Bass looked up importantly. "Fence fixin'," he said. "I brought back some rolls of wire and some staples. Got to get this hacienda area lookin' like somethin' first, before we go ahead on the big plans, eh, Ross?"

"Sure thing, boss."

Bass seemed to swell a little. "Take care of that leg," he said. "Maybe Connie ought'a rub some liniment on it like she done on Tascosa's sore back some weeks ago. Good nurse she would'a made."

Ross shook his head. "I'll take a little walk to settle this good grub," he said.

Ross walked outside. He went into the shabby, sagging bunkhouse and gathered his gear. He stuffed it into a sack and then crawled out a back window. He went to the corral and got his horse. He saddled it, slung the warbag over its rump, then tethered in a draw beyond the barn. Ross walked back to the 'hacienda'.

Bass, happy as a clam at high tide, was helping Consuelo with the dishes. Ross got the saddlebags, making sure the rye bottle was all right, then took them to the bunkhouse. He changed into the good clothing Tascosa had given him. He sat for a while in the dusty darkness of the bunkhouse, nipping at the first bottle of rye, and smoking half a dozen cigarettes. When the lights had winked out in the casa, Ross slipped out the back window again. He limped to the horse and led it a quarter of a mile from the ranch buildings, then mounted and rode toward the dim northern end of the West Potrillos.

He looked back through the darkness. God help Consuelo if her firstborn was the spitting image of Tascosa. Maybe then Bass Orcutt would realize just exactly what kind of luck the Kid had brought him.

CHAPTER FIVE

Ross turned over in his sleep, then suddenly raised himself on one elbow. He tried to blink the sleep out of his eyes. The moon was almost gone, and a mournful wind crept through the canyon rustling the trees and swaying the brush. The faint rush of the creek water came to him. The wind had shifted since dusk, bringing with it the faint suggestion of rain. Ross shivered. He pulled on his boots and clapped his hat on his head, then felt for his Winchester. He was too far north for Apache trouble, but even then, the Mescaleros had been tagged and put on a reservation for some years.

Far down the canyon a horse whinnied shrilly, and the sound carried clearly to Ross. His own horse was picketed up a small box canyon behind him. An eye of fire showed in the ashes of his campfire, like a ruby on velvet. He kicked dirt over it, shoved his blanket and tarp under a bush, then padded down the slope until he found cover in a nest of rocks.

Deep shadows had formed along the west wall of the canyon, but the creek bed was still lighted by the dying rays of the moon.

Something moved up the canyon and then Ross saw a lone horseman, riding fast, rifle across his thighs, looking to right and to left, and then ahead again. He looked up the slope, almost directly at Ross, then away again.

A steer bawled. Hoofs thudded on the soft ground. A bunch of cows appeared through the swaying brush, running as fast as they could go, with a trio of horsemen driving them, one on either flank, and one behind.

"Sticky loopers," said Ross. He sank a little lower. Rustling was good business in Verde County, or at least it had been.

The place was thick with tangled canyons, many of which led down to the lower country south, east and west, so a rustler could pick and choose his way to bedevil his pursuers. They were moving fast. They thudded past Ross' position, not more than a hundred yards away, lashing at the flanks of the steers with their quirts, looking back from where they had come. In five minutes, they were out of sight, leaving behind them the churned track, wide enough for a blind man to see, and the acrid odor of fresh droppings.

Ross felt the cold sweat break out on his forehead. "This ain't no place for Mrs. Starkey's second son," he said. He scuttled up the slope and hastily threw his gear together. Hot haste was in him. Hang first and ask questions afterwards was the current style of thought in Verde County.

He carried his gear to the horse, saddled it, threw his gear aboard and mounted the clay bank. He slapped it on the rump with the butt of his Winchester and rode out of the box canyon, looking back in the direction from which the rustlers had come. Something was moving there in the darkness beyond the light of the moon. "Chihuahua," said Ross. He galloped the clay bank, heading along the line of tracks. The ground was soft after a recent rain, and he had no desire to break his tracks away from those of the rustlers; not yet anyways.

He crossed a wide patch of moonlight. A rifle flatted off and the slug whispered a foot past Ross' head. The rifleman had eyes like an Apache. Ross wrenched the clay bank to one side and clattered over some loose rock, looking back over his shoulder. Something flashed and a fraction of a second later the rifle sounded off. The slug sang eerily from a rock.

Ross plunged into a wide draw. The clay bank had hard going on the loose rock. Once he almost went down. Men yelled down in the canyon as Ross set the horse at a steep slope, riding like a monkey on the back of the animal.

A shot cracked out and Ross' hat was plucked from his head. Thank God it had had a high crown. He turned into a side canyon and let the clay bank full out. The ground was rocky, but a good tracker could trail him in better light. He turned into an arm of the canyon, hoping to God it wasn't a box. There was no one behind him, close enough to see him anyway. He plunged through a branch of the creek, followed the far bank, then went back into the shallow waters, driving the clay bank full out, showering the water in crystal sheets to each side.

A wide canyon opened to his right, still lighted by the moon. He had no choice. He slammed down it, looking back over his shoulder, the thudding hoofs echoing from the high walls. He could be heard for half a mile. The ground was hard. He knew the clay bank couldn't last much longer at this pace.

Ross slid from the saddle and led the clay bank up a slope and into the shelter of some pinnacles of rock. He slogged on, his weak knee bothering the devil out of him, but there was no time to take it easy. Not with those shooting fools coming after him, and begod, he didn't have any real reason for being in that country other than being a wayfaring stranger, and that was tantamount to looking for a free hanging, if he was caught near a sticky looping job such as he was sure he had just witnessed.

The moon was long gone when he stumbled out on a rude wagon track that led down to broken ground through scrub timber. The bittersweet odor of woodsmoke hung in the now windless air. Far down the slope a yellow eye of light stood out like the orb of a cat. Ross wiped the sweat from his face. He sheathed the Winchester and then sat down on a rock to rub and flex his bad knee. He looked back now and then, but the darkness was quiet. He had come through an unknown maze of rock and timber and by the grace of God he had not gotten thoroughly lost in the back canyons.

A faint invisible finger of wind teased his damp hair. A drop of rain struck his nose. Ross rolled a cigarette and lighted it behind the shelter of the rock. He shielded the quirly in a cupped hand as he mounted the clay bank and rode slowly down the track. By the time he reached the more open ground he had to stop to put on his worn slicker.

He used the light as his temporary goal and saw that it was coming from a small ranch house. Must be getting close to dawn. The rain slanted down in a silvery veil. He had the urge to keep going, all the way out of Verde County. He wasn't sure in the first place why he had come there after a couple of weeks of drifting after he had left Bass Orcutt's 'hacienda'. He had started twice for Santa Fe to see his elder brother, once getting as far north as old Fort Craig, but then he had let himself drift easterly, across the Jornado del Muerto to the Jicarillas. Lloyd would have to wait to spout his: "I *told* you so, Ross. Never would listen to me. Isn't respectable, or profitable to drift all the time." And so on and so on...

Ross looked back over his shoulder at the dim mountains. "A man could get hung or shot fooling around here, hoss," he said.

The rain was still slanting down when he saw the *placita* beyond the rushing creek. He knew the country to the east much better than this area. Years past there had been many such *placitas* stippling the flanks of the mountains, guarded by their crumbling *torreones,* but during the war, when Unionists and Texas Confederates had been beating each other over the head from El Paso plumb up to Santa Fe, there had been no Regulars left to hold the Apaches in check and the Jicarillas and Mescaleros had ravaged that country until there was hardly a living white man, American or New Mexican, outside of outposts of the contending military forces, from the Rio Grande to the Pecos, and from Signal Peak to Cougar Mountain. Only after the war had some of the New Mexicans crept back to their ravaged little *placitas* to try and take up the old ways. They hadn't reckoned on the Americans who had flooded into that fine cattle country after the war, ex-rebel and Unionist alike.

Ross rode across the creaking bridge. The rising water was inches below the bridge flooring. The single, winding street of the *placita* was empty of life although it was already early afternoon. Woodsmoke hung pungently in the wet air and smoke hung low over the old adobes, while muddy water the color of chocolate poured from the roof spouts into the street. Most of the adobes had a thick thatch of natural growths on top of them, so old were they. There was a strong odor of decay about the place. At the end of the street the church sagged against the nearest house. The old *torreon,* built to repel Apaches in days long past, had completely collapsed, partially blocking the muddy street. A mangy dog, soaked to the hide, slunk into cover when he saw the hatless gringo ride into town.

Mist hung over the nearby mountain, hardly distinguishable from the drifting rain. It would be an early winter.

Ross dismounted stiffly. His guts tightened within him. He felt for the makings and found them soaked. He pulled out a bottle from the nearest saddlebag and found it almost empty. He emptied it and tossed it atop the nearest roof, wondering if the extra weight would collapse the rain-soaked roof. He tethered the patient clay bank under a dripping *ramada*. The rich odor of chili beans drifted to him from across the street. He squelched across the mud, avoiding the deeper puddles, feeling the cold water leak into his boots. A wide, low building had *Santo Tomas Cantina* printed across the front of it, although sun and rain had long ago erased most of the paint.

Ross opened the door and walked in. Half a dozen candles guttered in front of makeshift tin reflectors, as the draft from the door caught them. Ross sniffed the thick air. He had found the right place.

A short, thickset man looked up from a table where he was spooning food into his mouth. "Please to close the door," he said in good English.

Ross nodded. "There is food?" he said in Spanish.

"You are welcome to some of mine, senor. There is too much for one man."

"Gracias," said Ross.

"Por nada."

Ross was served, at the long zinc-topped bar, a thick-walled bowl deep with beans and oily rich chili sauce, with good bread to side it, and a bottle of beer for a wash.

The man studied Ross. "You have lost your hat?"

"Wind blew it into the crick," said Ross. He scraped his spoon along the bottom of the bowl, chasing the last elusive bean. "Can you reload this bowl?"

"A pleasure!"

Ross reached across the bar and plucked a sack of Dime Durham from the rack. He rolled a quirly while the proprietor refilled the bowl. The man looked at him. "There is a hat here," he said. "Left long ago by a man who wanted credit against his hat. It is a good hat. To you, two dollars."

"Maybe he'll be back."

The proprietor placed the filled bowl in front of Ross, withdrew his thick thumb from the hot chili and thrust it into his mouth to lick it. "No," he said around his thumb. "He will not be back. There was a matter of some cows found in, how do you say it, his poss..."

"Possession?"

"Sí! That is it! They were not his cows."

"So he doesn't need his hat?"

The man smiled, extended both greasy hands, palms upward, and shrugged eloquently. "In a casket!" he said.

Ross shoved two damp dollars across the bar. "It's a deal."

"You are not superstitious?"

Ross shook his head.

The hat was a little small, but Ross figured he could wet it and loosen it, when he had time. It would likely be wet enough by the time he got out of those hills and headed for Santa Fe. He had had a bellyful of Verde County. He placed the hat on the back of his wet head and began to punish the beans again.

"You are passing through this country?" asked the cantina owner.

Ross nodded. He sipped the beer. He didn't want to waste too much time around this placita. A sort of unholy haste was building up in him; an uneasiness that would not leave until he was far north, heading up the Rio Grande Valley once again.

"This is not a good country for strangers."

Ross looked up. "I ain't a stranger," he said. "Just a traveling man."

"Santo Tomas is a long way off of the regular roads."

Ross gnawed a piece of bread, watching the man with cold eyes. "I like the scenery," he said.

"I am not being nosey, as you Americans say, but there is much trouble in Verde County. A man must choose one side or the other."

"Which side is yours?"

Again, the extended hands, palms upward, and the eloquent shoulder shrug. "I am not a fighting man. My cousin Orlando rides with the Newcomb corrida and my cousin Gaspar rides with the Fitzgerald corrida. My brother Pamfilo died some years ago in this very place because he rode with the Seven Riders corrida and was in here when the San Patricio vaqueros came into town looking for booze and women, as they said." He pointed to a bullet hole in the ceiling and another in the dingy wooden frame of the cracked, gold-flecked bar mirror. "Pamfilo was very brave. Muy hombre. But there were too many of them. Pamfilo did not go alone."

Ross finished the meal and allowed himself a gentle belch. He rolled a second cigarette. "Give me half a dozen Dime Durham. You got any chewin'?"

"Rock Candy, Winesap or Henry Clay?"

"Winesap. Two plugs."

Ross stretched his stiffened muscles. He had a long ride ahead of him, taking it easy on the clay bank until he got out of these damned hills that seemed to move in on you all the time. He stowed away the smoking and chewing tobacco and paid his tab. He turned on a heel and heard voices outside of the cantina, and the faint jingling of spurs.

"Business," said the proprietor. He smiled widely.

Ross felt his heart catch. Like the man had said: "This is not a good country for strangers."

"There is a back door," said the man.

Ross nodded. He started along the front of the bar when he heard the front door bang open behind him. It was too late. He stopped in mid-stride. "Give me another bottle of beer," he said. He blew a puff of smoke toward the back bar, glancing in the mirror as he did so, the smoke shielding his look. A big man stood framed in the doorway, rain running down his yellow slicker and dripping from his hat brim. He was looking directly at Ross. Ross lifted the beer bottle and took a good slug of it. He might need it before the day was out.

"Señor Cassidy!" said the cantina owner. "It has been

a long time. You do not often come over to this side of the hills. Luz Avita has been wondering where you have been."

There was no answer from Cassidy. Ross could hear other men talking outside of the cantina. "Come on, Cassidy!" said one of them. "Least we can get a drink or two before we go on!"

"Maybe we won't have to go on," said Cassidy. He walked to the end of the bar and looked down at Ross' empty chili bowl. "You servin' meals here now, Fedro?"

The proprietor shook his head. "I shared the chili with this man. He was hungry and wet. It was the Christian thing to do."

"For a price," said Cassidy dryly.

Spurs jingled in the doorway and a tall man bent his head to get inside. Water poured from his turned-up hat brim. He grinned. "Hey, Fedro! Get a mop! I brung the water!"

Fedro laughed. "That Señor Slim, always with the jokes!"

"Rustle a bottle," said Slim. "Rye all right with you, Ben?"

A short, bench-legged cowpoke came in. He nodded, his hard eyes flicking back and forth about the low-ceilinged room. He centered his flat eyes on Ross. "Rye is OK with me," he said in an expressionless voice. He never took his eyes from Ross.

"Shut that goddamned door," said Cassidy over his shoulder.

Slim kicked it shut. A lump of wet adobe fell heavily from the damp, sagging ceiling and struck a table. Slim grinned. "We better get that likker in a hurry," he said.

Fedro placed bottle and glasses on the bar. "This place is old," he said. "My cousin Ignacio promised to fix the roof, but, as you can see, it is raining now."

Slim filled the glasses. "Sure, Fedro," he said soothingly. "And when it's dry, what's the use of fixing it? But then, winter always comes, don't it? When we want a drink here, we'll have to dig down through the roof to find it. Well, it'll save you buyin' a coffin, Fedro, eh?"

Fedro quickly crossed himself. "Do not talk like that," he said. He picked up a battered pan and placed it under the place where the adobe had left a hole in the ceiling. Muddy water began to drip rapidly into the pan.

"You got inside plumbin' now," said Slim.

Ross studied his beer bottle as though he had never seen one before, but he knew without looking that all three men were studying him.

"That your hoss outside, mister?" said Cassidy at last.

"The clay bank," said Ross.

"Looks tired, and muddy..."

Ross sipped at his beer. "He is," he admitted.

"Come a long way, eh?"

"Some," said Ross. His beer was getting flat.

"Fast, too, eh?"

Ross looked at Cassidy. "No," he said.

"Which way did you come?"

Ross turned slowly. "Who are you?" he asked.

Cassidy looked at Slim. "He wants to know who I am," he said.

"Tell him," said Slim. He downed his shot.

Ben downed his shot and refilled his glass. His flat eyes never left Ross. "His hat don't seem to fit very well," he said in his expressionless voice.

Cassidy's blue eyes flicked toward the hat. "Put it on square, mister," he said.

"I don't wear it that way," said Ross.

"In the rain?" said Slim.

"It ain't wet," said Ben.

"Put it on square," repeated Cassidy.

Ross picked up the makings and began to fashion a cigarette.

"Go get the hat, Slim," said Cassidy.

Slim opened the door and walked outside.

Ross wet the cigarette paper and placed the cigarette in his mouth.

Slim walked in, carrying Ross' bullet-punctured hat, thoroughly soaked. He threw it on the bar in front of Cassidy.

"Once more," said Cassidy. "Put that hat on square!"

Ross snapped a match on his thumbnail and raised it to the cigarette tip. Cassidy took two steps forward and slapped the cigarette from Ross' lips. "You hear what I said?" he demanded.

Ross fanned out the match and looked squarely at Cassidy. "If you were alone," he said, "I'd knock your gawd-damned teeth out'a your big mouth."

Cassidy smiled. He reached over and pulled Ross' new hat down on his forehead. "It doesn't fit, boys," he said.

"Figures," said Ben. "Because it ain't his hat." He looked at Fedro. "Where's that hat that was left here by that sticky looper?"

Fedro paled. He swallowed. "It's gone," he said.

Ben nodded. "Figures. That's it, ain't it?" he jerked a thumb toward Ross.

Fedro looked at Ross, with misery in his eyes. "Yes," he blurted out.

"Take it off," said Cassidy.

Ross took off the hat and placed it on the bar. Cassidy picked it up and turned over the dry sweatband. "What's your brand?" he said.

"Starkey. Ross Starkey."

Slim narrowed his eyes.

"The initials in this hat are J.C.N.," said Cassidy. He picked up Ross' bedraggled hat and looked inside. "R. S.," he said.

The cantina was very quiet except for the dripping of the muddy water into the pan.

"We found this hat in Boca Grande Canyon," said Cassidy. "Left by someone who cut off from a group of rustlers to lead our bunch astray. You denying this is your hat?"

Ross shook his head. They wouldn't have believed anything else anyway. "I don't know anything about any rustlers," he said. "I was camping along the crick back there. I saw the rustlers go by and figured I'd better high-tail out'a there in case I might get picked up by mistake."

"Oh, there ain't no mistake," said Slim. He leaned on the bar. "Ross Starkey," he added. "I've heard of you. You used to ride with the San Patricio bunch some years past, eh?"

"I won't deny that," said Ross. "I've been in Mexico since then."

"In Mexico? Do tell!" said Cassidy. He looked at his two partners. "He was in Mexico, companeros."

Ross wet his lips. He wanted a smoke, but if Cassidy slapped the quirly from his mouth he knew he'd tangle with the man and that would be a damned fool stunt.

"He doesn't seem to know who we are," said Slim.

"We ride for Hardy Newcomb," said Ben, like it was being a member of the Round Table or something.

Ross couldn't help it. "Congratulations," he said.

Cassidy leaned forward. "How long you been riding for that damned Irishman Fitzgerald?"

"I ain't," said Ross. "Never have been."

"Fitz has been hirin' gunfighters, they say," said Slim. "You a gunfighter, Starkey?"

"He looks more like a mangy hound dog," said Ben.

Ross looked at Ben. "You don't talk much," he said. "Whyn't we keep it that way?" His six-gun was trapped beneath his slicker. He'd never have a chance of drawing, and if these hardcases rode for Hardy Newcomb, he had an evil feeling they'd all be faster than he was anyways.

Ben shoved back his glass. "You've had your fun, Cassidy," he said sourly. "Now let's get down to business."

"I want no trouble in here," protested Fedro.

"Go get the marshal," said Ross.

Slim laughed. "Marshal? Here? They can't even afford a watchdog."

"You goin' to talk or not, Starkey?" asked Cassidy.

"I don't know anything about rustlers," said Ross.

Cassidy reached over and ripped at the front of Ross' slicker. The buttons scattered over the bar. Cassidy plucked Ross' six-gun from its holster and placed it on the bar. "Come on, hombre," he said.

Ross walked toward the door. He might have a better chance in the open at that. Slim opened the door. Ben thrust out a foot and Cassidy shoved Ross. He was catapulted through the doorway into the thick mud. He lay belly-flat, listening to Slim laugh, and sheer hate poured through his soul.

CHAPTER SIX

R oss slowly raised a muddy hand and wiped the thickest of the mud from his face. He could feel the cold water penetrating his trousers. The odor of fresh manure filled his nostrils. He pushed himself up on his hands and saw that he had targeted in on a pile of fresh droppings from one of the three horses tethered to the hitching rail. He closed his hands on the thick mud.

"Get up," said Cassidy shortly.

Ross got up slowly. He turned and the mud was in startling contrast to the drawn whiteness of his face. For a clear moment he saw the grinning face of Slim, the cynical look on the face of Cassidy, the flat, expressionless look of the man named Ben, and it seemed as though time stood still for that fraction of it.

It was madness, but the hate in him had burned away all fear and restraint. He hurled a gob of the filthy mud into Slim's grinning face and another toward Ben. They leaped back, cursing and clawing at their bespattered faces. Cassidy had made his mistake in not covering Ross with a gun, for Ross plunged forward, stiff-legged, muddy fists already driving at the thin air before they made contact with Cassidy, and when they did, the big man was driven back against Ben, knocking him down in the reeking mud underfoot. Slim yelled explosively, dabbing at his blinded eyes, dancing around like an angry stork on his long legs.

Ross sank a smashing left into Cassidy's lean gut, just above the gun belt buckle, and as Cassidy bent forward, a muddy fist rose to meet his chin, snapping back his head, while a looping left, with no style whatsoever, burned against his right ear, driving him sideways where he tripped over Ben and fell flat on his face in the mud.

Slim could just manage to see now. He clawed under his slicker, and thereby undid himself, for a right glanced from his lean jaw while a left stoppered his open mouth, and he felt teeth crack. He raised his right, but it was too late to stop a slamming one-two in his belly. He smashed back against the cantina wall.

Ben struggled halfway to his feet and a hard boot heel caught him just below the throat, driving him back over Cassidy. Slim bounced from the wall and roared in, throwing rights and lefts at thin air as Ross waited for him, then stepped in between the long arms and butted the long man in the chest, driving him back once again.

Ben rolled over in the mud, coughing and gasping. A boot heel hit him on the back of the head and nearly knocked him senseless. Cassidy got to his feet and swung a wild left that caught Ross over the left eye, shaking him, and a right poked into his nose, stinging it and drawing forth a flood of blood.

Slim leaped forward, shoving Cassidy to one side in his mad haste to get at Ross. Ross met him with three soft punches, trying to get footing in the thick mud. The long leverage of the tall man gave him the power to hit Ross back over a horse trough. He rolled over to avoid Slim's stamping boots. He gripped the tall man by one leg and stood up, upending him into the flooded gutter.

Cassidy threw an arm about Ross' head from behind, working the muddy surface of his slicker sleeve into Ross' eyes, while hammering at his kidneys with a hard right fist. Ross went down on one knee and a boot heel, unseen to him, cracked alongside his jaw. He rolled over, almost blinded, blood pouring from his nose, trying to avoid the booting he knew he was going to get.

One boot landed on his back and another boot caught him in the side and then he was free of them. He tried to get up and fell heavily, but no more blows came.

"I could smell the blood and guts all the way at the end of the street," a familiar voice said. "Now supposing you three gentlemen let the man get up and take you on one at a time. By God, I think he could do it!"

Ross wiped the mud from his eyes and looked up, the rain slanting against his bloody, battered face. "Hello, Kid," he said around a broken tooth and a mouth full of salty blood.

The Tascosa Kid sat a fine gray in the middle of the street, the rain slanting down on him, dripping from his hat brim and glistening from his slicker. It also glistened from the cocked Winchester he held across his left forearm, the unmoving muzzle covering the three Newcomb waddies. He looked at Ross in astonishment. Then he grinned. "I'll be dipped in sheep shit!" he said. "Begod, my old riding partner from El Corralitos! You haven't changed much. How's Consuelo?"

Ross got slowly to his feet. His breathing hurt his side. He blew the blood from his nose. "You ought'a know," he said. "You dirty bastard, I'll swear you left me there to face ol' Bass when he found out the truth."

"I wouldn't do a thing like that!" said Tascosa in mock astonishment. "What's the trouble here?"

Ross felt his sore jaw. "These three hombres said I was mixed up in a rustling in Boca Grande Canyon last night. I told them I wasn't. They didn't believe me. I don't know where they was aiming to take me, but I didn't think it would be a healthy place for Mrs. Starkey's second son Ross."

"Don't get mixed up in this, Kid," said Cassidy.

Tascosa smiled thinly. "Only three against one? Whyn't you go back and get the rest of the corrida?"

"Newcomb won't like this, Kid," said Slim. He picked a loose tooth from his mouth. "That bastard hits like a mule."

Tascosa suddenly touched his gray with the spurs, dancing it to one side while he raised the rifle a little. "Watch it, Ben!" he snapped.

Ben slowly withdrew his hand from the muddy front of his slicker while his flat eyes never left Tascosa.

"You got no call to get mixed up in this, Kid," said Cassidy. "You ain't ridin' for Fitz anymore." Tascosa smiled winningly. "I ain't?"

Cassidy and Slim paled beneath the mud and blood, but Ben stood there like a block of wood, his eyes still on Tascosa like a snake trying to hypnotize a chicken. Some snake and some chicken, thought Ross.

The rifle seemed to have taken on new meaning now. Slim glanced up and down the deserted street. Every Mexican in town knew what was going on by now, but they weren't coming out into that street for fear it would turn into a bowling alley for wild bullets.

"Get on them horses and ride," said Tascosa pleasantly.

Cassidy looked at Ross. "We want him," he said.

Tascosa leaned on his saddle horn. "Toss your gun into the mud," he suggested, "then you go try to take him, Cass. I'll sort'a officiate like, with the powers invested in me by the Winchester Repeating Arms Company."

Ben raised his head. "Get off that hoss," he said flatly. "You got a big mouth with that rifle in your hands. Get off that hoss and meet me in the middle of the street, Kid."

The challenge hung in the wet air and four men stood there waiting to see what the Kid would do.

Tascosa shook his head. "I've got a royal flush, Ben," he said. "Now you three git!"

Cassidy held up a hand. "Hardy Newcomb will want this man," he said.

"Is Hardy Newcomb the law in Verde County?" asked Tascosa.

"Fitz ain't," said Slim quietly.

Tascosa patted the wet stock of the Winchester. "Right now, we got Winchester law," he said.

The three Newcomb men untethered and mounted their horses. They rode out into the middle of the street. Cassidy turned in his saddle. "You ridin' for Fitz again then, Kid?" he asked.

Tascosa nodded.

"That's all I want to know," said the big man.

Their horses' hoofs squelched in the pasty mud. The only one who looked back was Ben, first at Tascosa and then at Ross, and if Ross Starkey had ever felt the foul breath of death in a man's look, he saw it now.

Tascosa waited until the three men were out of sight. "Get inside," he said.

"They might come back," said Ross.

"No, they won't. The news is more important to Hardy Newcomb right now than a shooting is."

"Meaning you?"

"Meaning me." Tascosa dropped from the gray and led it into the ramada beside Ross' clay bank. "Christ! You ridin' plow-horses now?"

"He got me out'a that mess in Boca Grande Canyon last night."

"He didn't get you out far enough," said Tascosa dryly.

Ross walked inside and leaned against the bar. Fedro's head appeared above the bar. "Madre de Dios!" he gasped.

"Glasses," said Tascosa. "Pronto!"

Ross sipped at the strong liquor. Weakness poured through him. "You timed it just right," he said.

"Another minute would have been far too much for me."

"You were doing all right," said Tascosa. He downed his shot and refilled the glass.

Ross tilted his head to one side and studied him. "Just how long was you watching, Kid?" he asked quietly.

Tascosa grinned. "I saw the opening act," he said.

"Gawddamn you! I could'a got booted to a pulp out there!"

"You didn't," said the Kid casually. "Wipe that horn of yourn, killer. You're getting blood in your drinking likker."

Ross shook his head. "Beats the hell out'a me why I come here at all," he said. He rolled a cigarette.

Tascosa snapped a match on his thumbnail and lighted the cigarette. He smiled. "Maybe you was looking for your old riding partner," he suggested.

"Fat chance," said Ross. He blew out a cloud of smoke.

Tascosa knew. He had an insight into such matters, but he was smart enough not to press the point. "I'm heading back to the ranch," he said. "We can make it by nightfall if we leave now."

Ross refilled his glass and downed the liquor. His side hurt. His nose and mouth hurt. His eyes stung. His fists were lacerated. He was cold and wet, far from home and fully fed up.

Tascosa picked up Ross' pistol. "Jesus God," he said wonderingly. "This yours?"

Ross nodded. "It's the one you had me supplied with back at El Corralitos."

"What do you use it for? Cracking walnuts?"

"Heads," said Ross. "Now shut up, will you?"

"You can't carry a beat-up old cutter like this if you want to ride with me for Fitz."

"I ain't riding with nobody for nobody," said Ross sourly.

"You'd better come with me anyway. You'll be safe there. No rough boys to take away your toys."

Ross slid the bottle into his coat pocket. He sheathed the Colt and walked to the door.

"Serafina Padilla has been asking for you, Señor Kid," said Fedro.

Tascosa turned. "She's married now, ain't she?"

"That shouldn't stop you," growled Ross.

Fedro smiled. "Her husband is working along the Sacramento," he said.

Tascosa smiled. "Where does she live?"

"The last adobe south of town."

"Gracias," said Tascosa.

They mounted and rode out of town in the opposite direction from that taken by the three Newcomb riders.

Ross looked at Tascosa. "Who choused those cows last night?" he said.

Tascosa grinned. "Some of my boys."

"I didn't see you with them."

"I had other business."

Ross snapped his cigarette butt from his thumb and first finger and began to roll another. "Does Fitzgerald know about it?" he asked.

Tascosa shook his head. "He needs help. He was fighting a losing war with Hardy Newcomb. You got to hit back hard, amigo. You got to hit back harder than they do!"

"So you're taking over Fitzgerald's war? By egging on Newcomb? That ain't too bright, Kid."

Tascosa looked at him. "He's the only man in my life ever gave me a real square deal and treated me right. He got me cleared of that murder charge that drove me out of this country. Fitz can't win his way. If I can get Newcomb riled enough to start a real shooting war, then we can make up the odds. We can't win this way, like I said."

Ross lighted his cigarette and looked sideways at the

Kid. "And you think the Tascosa Kid can make up the odds? Just like that?"

Tascosa smiled coldly. "You seen what I done back there, didn't you?"

Ross rolled his eyes upwards. "Oh, Jesus," he said. He looked at the Kid. "I can't figger it out. You fighting on the losing side of a range war."

Tascosa's hand tightened on his reins. "It won't be the losing side much longer," he said. "I got the ball rolling now. It's Newcomb's next move."

"He's made it already," said Ross dryly. "I damned near had to pay the bill for you egging on Newcomb."

Ross was cold and wet, but an even colder feeling came over him as he thought of the implications of Tascosa's words and the hard-edged tone of his voice. He remembered something else, too: the killing look on the face of the man named Ben.

"Fitz will hire you on my say-so," said Tascosa casually. "You'll likely find some of your old San Patricio bunch riding for Fitz."

"I finished riding with them years ago. When the Seven Rivers corrida got through with us there wasn't enough of us left for pallbearers. I left this county fanned by their bullets. Besides, those three coyotes back there know I used to ride with the San Patricio corrida. It was Slim that knew about it. Bass Orcutt told me that Hardy Newcomb was hiring Seven Rivers boys and Fitz was hiring San Patricio boys."

"You know all about the feud then. Ol' Bass gave you all the dirt, hey?"

Ross nodded. "I told you that you should'a listened to him instead of bracing up to his wife all the time. By Jesus, you should'a seen the look on her face when she found out you had lit a shuck out'a there. Man, oh man! She was fit to kill, I tell you!"

Tascosa laughed. He slapped his thigh and laughed so hard the tears came into his eyes. Ross looked sideways at him, still surly as a bee-stung bear. "It ain't quite that funny," he snarled.

Tascosa stared at him, gray eyes swimming with tears. "It ain't?" he demanded.

Ross couldn't help it. He remembered the look on Consuelo's face and the twitching of her outraged little strumpet's rump as she had gone into the house, and then he began to laugh, too, as they rode along a tree-bordered road, which was hardly more than a cow trail, with the rain slanting down in a silvery veil.

Ross took out the bottle and handed it to Tascosa. "Well," he admitted, "it's worth a drink." He rubbed his sore jaw. "Come to think of it, I never paid Fedro for this bottle."

Tascosa spewed out a spray of pure rye. He stared at Ross.

"You didn't? By godfrey! That's the first time in the history of Verde County anyone ever beat Fedro out'a a drink."

Ross grinned, his face aching. It was good to be riding leg to leg with the Kid.

Tascosa took another drink and wiped his mouth. "I'll get a job for you with Fitz."

"No," said Ross flatly.

"You got any dinero?"

Ross shook his head.

"Then you can work for him. You don't have to do any fighting, amigo. Fitz has a great spread. He's breeding the best damned blooded cattle in the Territory. He can use a good stockman."

"I ain't no gawddamned stockman," grunted Ross. "I'm a cowpuncher. A waddie. By godfrey, if I could cook, I'd get me a job as cocinero so I wouldn't have to get mixed up in no shooting scrapes. I got a bellyful, I tell you, riding with the San Patricio bunch, and then with Zaldivar, the 'Champion of Liberty'."

Tascosa did not answer. He knew Ross better than

Ross thought he did. Besides, he had seen Ross in action at The Eye of God and in the muddy street of Santo Tomas, taking on three of the toughest boots in Verde County, one man against three, and the hardheaded bastard hadn't known he was going to get licked, and maybe maimed or crippled for life back there. It was food for thought, and Tascosa had taken it on himself to champion Sean Fitzgerald. He'd need every fighting man he could get, for although Tascosa would not admit it to anyone but himself, he knew the odds were high against Fitzgerald, with a stacked deck to boot.

"Maureen can take care of that face of yours," said Tascosa.

"Maureen? Another one of your friendly fillies? That's a helluva name for a Mexican gal."

"She's no filly! She ain't no Mexican! She's Fitzgerald's sister!"

Ross looked curiously at the Kid. He saw the tight white lines radiating from the corners of the Kid's mouth. He whistled softly.

"What does that mean?" snapped the Kid.

Ross raised a hand. "Peace," he said. "I didn't know you was soft in the cabeza for her."

"Who says I am? How could you tell? You ain't never seen her!"

Ross smiled. He took out the comforting bottle and belted a good one. He wiped his mouth and offered the bottle to the Kid. The Kid shook his head. "I don't want to ride through this country with a belly full of tangle-foot," he said. "You didn't answer my question," he added.

Ross deliberately drove the cork into the bottle. He deliberately slid it into his coat pocket and patted it gently. "Stay nice and warm, friend," he said to the bottle.

"Well?" demanded the Kid.

Ross felt for the makings. "In all the years I've known you," he said quietly, "since we was snotty-nosed kids back on the Cimarron, I never knowed you to talk so nicely about a lady."

"I never knowed you until a couple of months ago! You getting drunk again?"

Ross rolled a cigarette. "Why not?" he asked. "I wish to hell now I'd never crossed the Rio Grande. The only way to look at this county is through the bottom of a whiskey glass, pretty as it is."

The rain slashed down. Tascosa withdrew into himself as he led the way through dripping underbrush, following almost indistinguishable trails, fording rushing streams, guiding his gray through seemingly impassable natural passages that cut through rugged outcroppings of the basic structure of the mountain flank. He was like a Mescalero Apache in these mountains, thought Ross. Ross had known this country well in the old days, but he was thoroughly lost now, for the peaks and landmarks were shrouded in drifting mist above the thin, silver veil of the rain.

There was something else, too. Despite Tascosa's thorough confidence in himself and his fighting ability, and despite his defiantly hurling the gauntlet down in front of Hardy Newcomb's imperious nose, to egg the hardcase rancher into a shooting war, there was something else. A shadow was riding his wet back; the shadow of death speaking in the flat tone of a rifle from ambush.

CHAPTER SEVEN

The rain had stopped, and a cold-looking moon had slid out from behind drifting clouds, to shed a clear light down into the valley of the Rio Dulces. Across the wide, rushing river, shielded by swaying cottonwoods, blinked the yellow lights of a large house.

Tascosa turned in his saddle. "There it is," he said. "The 'Shamrock' spread. The best spread on this side of the mountains."

Ross nodded numbly. The cold and the long ride had taken a heavy toll of him, and he realized now that he had never fully recovered from his sojourn down in Mexico. The battle in the street of Santo Tomas had not helped any. Even the booze had not helped much. He swayed a little in the saddle.

"You all right, amigo?" said Tascosa.

"I'll be all right. Begod, is there any heat left in this world?"

They clattered across the creaking bridge. The rio was rushing along just below the thick floor planking. Tascosa spat into the water. "This'll help turn that ol' sawmill wheel," he said.

Ross looked at him. "Bass Orcutt said Fitzgerald had bought a sawmill from Hardy Newcomb," he said. "But he said Newcomb had chivvied him out'a the water rights."

"He did," said Tascosa. "Dammed up the Little Bonita and wouldn't let a shot glass full of water through, claiming he needed all the water for his cows. Hell! There's enough water on Newcomb's land to flood this whole damned valley."

"So, how did Fitzgerald get around the lack of water?"

Tascosa grinned. "He hired a real sawmill man. Fella by the name of Buck Ellwood, from Michigan, who knows more about lumbering than Paul Bunyan. Ellwood takes the sawmill machinery apart and has the whole thing hauled down to a fork of the Rio Dulces, gets it set up and is ready to do business. Ol' Hardy Newcomb don't know about it...yet."

"What happens when he does?"

Tascosa shrugged. "We can wait and see. Newcomb has a sawmill on the Burrito and used to have a monopoly on all the sawmilling around this county. That's why he sold the old mill to Fitz, then cut off the water for it. Made a nice profit, the bastard!"

"Supposin' he don't like the new location of the sawmill?"

"What can he do? He can't stop the Rio Dulces and its forks, because they run plumb through the center of the 'Shamrock' and even Hardy Newcomb couldn't hardly dam the Dulces."

Tascosa stood up in his stirrups and whistled sharply three times, paused, then whistled twice. He drew rein and waited. The wind brought a faint whistle from the darkness of a motte that lay between the rio and the ranch buildings. Twice, then three times. The moonlight glinted from something polished. A rifle barrel, thought Ross.

Tascosa rode up the slope road. He glanced toward the motte. "Everything quiet, Pardy?" he called out.

"So far, Kid," answered the unseen rifleman. "Fitz has been askin' for you. Where you been? Chasin' fillies down to Santo Tomas?" He laughed at his own joke.

Tascosa swung down and opened the Texas gate, waving Ross through. He closed the gate and then led the gray toward the long, low stables. Ross whistled softly. The place reminded him of the fine haciendas he had seen down in Mexico.

Tascosa looked back. "Ain't this the best?" he said. "Makes Hardy Newcomb's spread look cheap by comparison, I tell you. This is all practically new, Ross. Built around the old place that used to be here."

"No wonder Fitzgerald wants to stick it out," said Ross.

Tascosa gave him a hand down from the saddle. Ross staggered. Tascosa led the horses into the stables. Ross leaned against a tree. He heard footsteps squelching in the thin mud. "Is that you, Tascosa?" a cultured voice called out, in a soft, pleasing Irish accent.

"No," said Ross. "I come with him. He's in the stables."

"Who are you, sir?"

"Ross Starkey. I knew the Kid down in Mexico."

"I've heard him talk about you."

Ross grinned. "Nice-like, I hope."

The Irishman laughed. "You two must have had quite a time down there. I envy you."

"You didn't miss nothing, Mister Fitzgerald."

"You know me?"

"I guessed it was you."

The rancher came closer, and the moonlight shone on his face. He was a good-looking man, with clear blue eyes and a neatly trimmed blond mustache, but there was a tinge of sadness on his face. He lowered a rifle and grounded it. "You must excuse me for carrying this," he said.

"I understand, sir."

"Who you talking to?" demanded Tascosa from the stable.

"It's me, Kid," said Fitzgerald.

Tascosa came from the stable. He smiled with genuine pleasure. "This is my riding partner from Mexico," he said. "He's been hurt, Mister Fitzgerald."

"So?" Fitzgerald looked at Ross' swollen face. "Thrown by your horse?"

Ross shook his head.

"Thrown by three of Newcomb's boys," said Tascosa quietly. "He done a little throwing himself. By godfrey, Mister Fitzgerald, you should'a seen Ross here taking on all three of them."

"Three of them?" said Fitzgerald.

"Art Cassidy, Slim Bellew and Ben Miller."

"My God," said the Irishman. "And he came out of it alive?"

Ross shoved back his hat and passed a tired hand across his battered face. "If it hadn't been for Tascosa here, I wouldn't be standing here now."

"Come into the house then!" said the rancher. "I've had some experience in medicine. Was a pre-medical student at Belfast, but never finished. Had some experience in Africa as well, and Maureen is a born nurse."

Ross limped toward the big casa. His leg was deviling him again. Tascosa looked at him. "They said he had been chousing steers in Boca Grande Canyon last night," he said.

"Whose steers?" said Fitzgerald.

Ross looked back at him. "Newcomb's," he said. "I was camped in the canyon when the rustlers come through there. When they passed I knew they was being chased. I figured it was no place for a stranger. I lit out and the guys doing the chasing saw me. I just got away from them by the skin of my teeth. I made the mistake of stopping too soon in Santo Tomas. They caught up with me there."

"But you had nothing to do with it!" said the rancher.

Ross laughed dryly. "Correct," he said. "But they meant to hammer something out of me, lies or anything else I could think up. Good thing I didn't know at the time who choused those steers."

It was suddenly very quiet. Ross looked back over his shoulder into the set face of the Irishman. "Who was rustling those cattle, Mister Starkey?" said Fitzgerald.

Tascosa's look was deadly in the moonlight.

Ross covered his bobble. "I thought I recognized some of the boys I used to know in this country some years ago. Couldn't be sure, of course. I had to get out of there in a hurry, I tell you!"

Tascosa went ahead and opened a heavy door set deeply into a thick adobe wall. Soft lamplight flooded out onto the wet gravel of the path and a drift of heat caressed Ross like a welcoming hand. He stood aside to let the rancher pass.

"No," said Fitzgerald. "Please go in." He looked at Ross' face, clear in the lamplight. "Good God," he added.

Ross pulled his soaked hat from his head. He was standing on thick carpeting with his muddy boots. He suddenly felt completely out of place in this great house.

"Let me show the way," said the rancher. He walked down the long hallway. He looked back over his shoulder. "The study will be best."

"Study?" said Ross, rather stupidly. He looked at Tascosa.

"Where one reads books and thinks," said Tascosa wisely. He grinned as Fitzgerald turned to open a door. "Stupid bastard like you wouldn't know what it was for."

"When did you learn how to read?" grunted Ross.

"I been studying the labels on horse liniment bottles," answered the Kid.

Ross limped into the room. He looked around in astonishment. Two of the walls were lined with bookshelves, floor to corbeled ceiling, so high that a ladder, running on a brass track, reached up to the upper rows of books. Firelight from a large beehive fireplace in the corner shone on the rich leather bindings of the books. The floors were covered with rugs which he recognized as being from the Chimayo country up north. He had never seen any as big as this. The furniture was almost massive, with deep, rich leather padding. A large table, thick enough to stop a .44/40 slug or maybe a stampede of cows, stood to one side, with a big Rochester lamp on it.

"I'll get water, liniment and bandages," said the rancher. He left the room.

"Classy, eh?" said the Kid. "You ever seen anything like this before?"

"Only in a high-class bawdy house," said Ross.

"How'd you ever get in one?"

"I had a letter of introduction," said Ross.

Tascosa leaned against a wall. "The whole casa is like this. I been in every room except Maureen's."

"What's been holding you back?" said Ross.

Tascosa did not answer. He was looking past Ross.

Ross turned slowly and his battered face turned red. A young woman was standing in the doorway looking at him, and he had no doubt about who she was. She looked much like her brother, except that her dark brown hair had a tinge of redness to it. She wore a dark, wine-colored dress that matched her hair, and stood out in contrast to her creamy skin.

Tascosa straightened up. "Miss Maureen," he said. "This is my riding partner from Mexico, Ross Starkey."

She smiled softly. "Pleased to meet you, Mister Starkey," she said in a voice that sent a thrill right into the deepest inner being of Ross Starkey. He was suddenly acutely aware of the rising odor of horse manure coming from his clothing, brought out by the heat of the room. He hadn't shaved for five or six days and hadn't combed his hair in two.

"My brother said you had been beaten by some men in Santo Tomas," she said.

"He was doing a little beating himself, ma'am," said Tascosa.

"Help him off with his outer clothing, Tascosa," she said.

"All of it?" blurted the Kid.

She laughed softly. "Sometimes I think you're kidding me, Tascosa."

"Who? Me? Not me, ma'am!" said Tascosa.

Ross looked sideways at the Kid. Begod, he had never seen him like this before! He remembered then the sudden anger of the Kid when Ross had shot off his boca about Maureen back on the trail. No wonder.

Tascosa gave Ross a hand with the ripped, filthy slicker. He pawed clumsily at the wet coat and as he peeled it off, the rye bottle fell from one pocket, and a half-chewed plug of Winesap fell from the other. The bottle smashed on the polished floor, luckily halfway between two of the Chimayo rugs. The rich, fruity odor of the rye drifted up to add to the overpowering smell of manure and horses that hung about Ross like a shroud. The look that Ross gave the Kid made even him wince a little.

Sean Fitzgerald came into the room with a pan of water and a tray covered with medicines and bandages. "Off with the shirt," he said. He looked down at the smashed bottle. "First time I ever saw a partly full bottle around you, Tascosa."

"Sir!" said Tascosa. "You know I don't drink that much."

"It's mine, Mister Fitzgerald," said Ross. "A little protection against the cold, and Tascosa here."

Fitzgerald nodded. "I think I know what you mean."

Tascosa worked at Ross' shirt. He peeled it off, revealing Ross in all his glory in a dingy, yellowed, patched and torn undershirt. Tascosa discreetly moved beyond the big table.

Sean Fitzgerald unbuttoned the undershirt and dropped it about Ross' lean hips. He looked at the bruised side, reddish-purple from hipbone up beyond the lower ribs. "God in Heaven!" he said. "You must have ribs like steel." He led Ross to a chair. "Maureen, bathe his face. I'll have to put plaster on that side."

Oh my God, thought Ross. She'll have to stand next to me now. "The street was pretty mucky," he blurted out.

"I imagine the Newcomb boys don't smell any better," said Sean Fitzgerald.

Maureen began to bathe Ross' face, and drifting through his own rank odor came the faint touch of lilac perfume and the sweetness of young woman flesh. He did not dare look at Tascosa. She looked down at Ross. "The Newcomb boys?" she questioned. "Were you fighting with some of them?"

"Three of 'em, ma'am," answered Ross.

She smiled. "I'd like to see them," she said.

Tascosa laughed. "I thought he was going to take all three of them," he said.

She turned slowly. "Where were you when all this was going on?"

Tascosa opened and then closed his mouth.

Go on, you bastard, thought Ross grimly. *Tell the lady!*

Sean Fitzgerald walked to a sideboard. He looked at Ross. "Bourbon, wine or rye? Perhaps a touch of Scotch?"

"Rye is fine," said Ross. He winced as she touched a tender spot on his face, staring steadfastly at her bosom, just inches from his eyes, trying to keep his mind on what was going on.

Maureen finished the job and stepped back to look at him. "There," she said. "You look better now, Mister Starkey."

"Go get him some fresh clothing," said the rancher to Tascosa.

When Tascosa had gone, Maureen left the room with the basin and extra bandages. Fitzgerald placed a whiskey glass on the table beside Ross and filled it, placing a cigar box beside the glass. Ross selected a cigar and accepted a light from the rancher. He drew in the rich smoke and sighed in satisfaction. "Prime," he said.

Fitzgerald lighted a cigar and sat down opposite Ross. "Tell me about it," he suggested.

Ross blew out a puff of smoke. This was chancy ground.

Fitzgerald inspected his cigar. "You mentioned the fact that the rustlers could have been men you had known some years ago. Tascosa once said you had ridden with the San Patricio bunch. The remnants of that bunch now work for me. It's possible you might have seen some of them last night."

Ross sipped the rye. It was the best grade and proof he had ever tasted. This was living, sore side, battered phiz and all.

"Mister Starkey?" gently reminded Fitzgerald.

"Are you asking me, or telling me, sir?" said Ross.

A log snapped in the fireplace, sending a shower of sparks up the chimney.

"I'm asking you," said Fitzgerald quietly.

Ross emptied the glass and pulled his undershirt up about his body, thrusting his arms into the sleeves. He got up. "I thank you for your kindness," he said, just as quietly as Fitzgerald had spoken.

For a long moment they looked eye to eye, then

Fitzgerald waved his cigar. "Sit down," he said. "I had no right to question you that way. Please forgive me."

"Why?" blurted Ross. "You ain't done nothing but be kind to me, a stranger in your house."

Fitzgerald waved a hand. "We've come upon hard times here. I suppose you know something about it?"

"I've heard some things," admitted Ross.

"What do you think?"

Ross inspected his cigar. He did not speak for a few minutes, and when he did, it was in a low voice of measured words. "A man's land is his to protect. As I understand it, Hardy Newcomb is chousing you. Well, if it was my land and my living, I'd fight him to the bitter end."

"You're a fighting man, Mister Starkey. I can see that. I have been a soldier, fighting in Africa, and I am not unused to violence, but I did not come to this country to fight for my property, and perhaps my life. I came here because there is a future here."

"And yet you can't go on like this," said Ross. "You're damned if you do and damned if you don't!"

"You've phrased it very well," said the rancher. He got up and paced back and forth, his hands clasped behind him, and a line of worry and tension drawn on his high forehead. "I didn't realize the power Mister Newcomb has in this county."

"He runs it, Mister Fitzgerald, and don't you ever forget it. I should'a known better than to come back here."

"You've had trouble with him before?"

Ross grinned wryly. "Well, there was some question about some of his cattle being missing one time. The Seven Rivers corrida wasn't riding for him at the time, but he had some hardcases that was just as bad. Newcomb paid off the Seven Rivers boys and they ambushed the San Patricio corrida." He looked directly at the Irishman. "The

'Paches couldn't have done no better. I lost some of my best friends in that fracas. There was nowheres else for me to go but plumb out'a Verde County, I tell you, with the devil setting on my coattails. 'Course it was never proved Newcomb had paid the Seven Rivers corrida to take care of us, but we had been getting along with them fairly well for a time, for our mutual benefit, like they say. It was that what done us in. We never suspected they'd turn on us."

"Dog eat dog, if you'll pardon the expression."

Ross waved a hand. "You're right. The thing was, we didn't have nothing to do with rustling Newcomb's cows, not that we was innocent of borrowing a few strays here and there from other spreads."

"I see. You're not working now?"

Ross shook his head.

"Would you like to work for me?"

Tascosa walked into the room with clothing draped over his arm just as the rancher spoke. He looked expectantly at Ross and nodded his head a little.

"No," said Ross.

"May I ask why?" said Fitzgerald.

Ross stood up. "I'm tired of fighting; leastways that kind of fighting."

"Damned fool," said Tascosa under his breath.

Fitzgerald warmed his lean hands at the fire. "Get dressed," he said quietly.

Ross nodded to Tascosa and looked at the door.

"You getting modest in your advancing age, Ross?" said the Kid with a grin.

"Something you wouldn't know about," said Ross. He peeled off his wet, filthy clothing and then dressed in the new outfit the Kid had brought.

"Ross is a top stockman," said the Kid.

"I'm a cowpoke! A waddie! A wrangler! But I ain't no stockman! I told you that before!" rasped Ross at the Kid.

Fitzgerald turned. "Try us for a week or two, Starkey," he said. "All you have to do is work on the ranch."

"Sure," said the Kid. "Ol' Tascosa will do your fighting for you."

Ross relighted the cigar and blew out a puff of smoke. "You nor anybody else don't have to do my fighting for me," he said quietly. "That is, when it's my fight."

"You make me sick!" snapped the Kid.

Ross fanned out the match. "You can say the same thing for me, regarding you, Kid," he said. "Don't chouse me tonight. I ain't in the mood."

Fitzgerald smiled. "Get a good night's rest," he said. "I can have the Kid corralled for the night if you like, so that he doesn't bother you."

Ross shook his head. "Maybe the Kid is the only amigo I got. Not much choice, but he's all mine."

"Come and see me in the morning," said the rancher. "We can ride together over the ranch and see the possibilities. Perhaps then you'll change your mind."

"Perhaps," said Ross. He picked up the wet clothing and followed the Kid from the house.

The moon had slid behind the low-hanging clouds as they walked toward the bunkhouse.

"How do you like him?" said the Kid.

"He's all right," said Ross absentmindedly. He was thinking of someone by the name of Fitzgerald all right, but it was Maureen, not her brother. Ross felt as though he had left a piece of himself back in that big casa. He had left pieces of himself here and there in his life, and quite a lot of blood, when it was pooled, but this time it was something different. Something he didn't quite understand, for, you see, it had never really happened to him before, although many a time he had been sure it was the real thing. It was crazy. It was loco. It didn't make any sense. But he liked it.

"The best there is," said the Kid. He looked back at the house.

"She sure is," said Ross.

"I mean him!" snapped the Kid.

"Yeah... How bad is this thing really, Kid?"

The Kid looked directly at him. "Damned bad," he said quietly, "and it's going to get a lot worse before it gets better."

Somewhere in the soft darkness a dog howled at the sky.

CHAPTER EIGHT

oss had roped and saddled a horse for himself after breakfast, eaten while the gray light of the dawn had given way to the brighter light of early morning. Sometime during the night Tascosa had left the bunkhouse with several of the men. Ross had not met any of them, for they had all been asleep when he and Tascosa had arrived at the bunkhouse. There had only been three men at the breakfast table, an elderly horse wrangler with a limp called Greener, a younger pimply-faced man named Marvel who did odd jobs about the ranch, and the man named Pardy who had been on guard all night. All three of them had been remarkably close-mouthed with Ross. It seemed part of the atmosphere of the rancho. Rancho de la Rio Dulces was the name of the place, but Ross had given to understand that the locals all called the place the "Shamrock" spread. He liked that better anyway. Spic names had never appealed to him as being fitting for an American ranch, and yet Fitzgerald was hardly different from being a spic, for he was a foreigner, too.

Ross had had his last cup of coffee and cigarette alone. He felt stiff and sore from the previous day's events, but more than that he felt at odds-ends, as though he had no business being in the Rio Dulces country, and worse than that, in Verde County. Verde County had been like a suburb of hell for him in past years. It hadn't exactly welcomed him back, either.

The sun warmed his back as he led the horse from the corral. The horse whinnied softly. A horseman cantered from the rear of the cluster of ranch buildings. Ross stared wonderingly for a moment, shoving back his hat, and then he remembered where he was, and that he was a guest on the "Shamrock".

It was Sean Fitzgerald, riding a fine, clean-limbed bay. He rode an English saddle, wearing funny-looking pants that bunched at his thighs like bloomers, and then tapered down to fit his legs snugly. Above the funny-looking pants he had on a tweedy coat, with a soft yellow scarf, like a cavalry scarf at his throat. One thing he had done, he bad gotten himself a decent hat anyways, thought Ross. A soft brown Stetson.

Ross touched the brim of his hat. "I took the liberty of taking a horse," he said.

"I expected you to," said the rancher.

"I wasn't sure whether or not you really wanted to go," said Ross.

"I usually mean what I say, Starkey," said the rancher.

Ross hesitated.

"Is there anything wrong?"

"Ain't you packing a gun of some kind?" said Ross.

"To wear a gun is to look for trouble," said Fitzgerald quietly.

Ross shook his head. "Go back and get one then," he said. "You might never need it, but if you do need it, you might need it in one helluva hurry!"

Fitzgerald smiled. "I see you are well armed," he said.

"I'd rather go naked in this country than go without my guns," said Ross.

"I thought you said you weren't a fighting man."

"Let's call my guns my insurance." Ross swung up on

the sorrel he had saddled. "If I had any damn sense at all, I'd just head this cayuse due north and keep going until I hit the Canadian."

They rode toward the river. Ross opened the Texas gate and closed it behind the horses. He looked toward the motte, now fresh and green in the growing sunlight. There was no one to be seen, but he had been too long along the border not to feel things, and he knew someone was within that motte, with half-cocked rifle, likely watching the both of them. The place was almost like an armed camp. Come to think of it, reasoned Ross, it was.

Sean Fitzgerald didn't talk much during the morning, but pride was in his blue eyes as he showed Ross over the spread. If it hadn't been for the threat of Hardy Newcomb and his ex-Seven Rivers corrida looming over the Shamrock, Ross couldn't have thought of a more ideal layout for a man in the cattle business. The Shamrock had everything—grazing, water, timber and shelter, coupled with a natural beauty a man couldn't cash in on, but which was an asset just the same.

Just before noon they rode out upon a saddle-backed ridge that overlooked the rolling country to the east, drifting down in undulating fashion toward a distant watercourse that sparkled in the sun between grassy banks. "We can water the horses there," said Ross as he rolled a cigarette.

"No," said Fitzgerald. He looked sideways at Ross. "That is the Little Bonita."

Ross lighted the cigarette. "So, it's still good water," he said. Then something came to him. "I thought Hardy Newcomb had dammed the Little Bonita."

"Further down, closer to my land," said the rancher. "At the foot of this ridge my land ends. It follows the line of the ridge to that grove of trees there, where the Little Bonita bends west. The dam is in there. If you look closely, you can see the sun reflecting from the water backed up behind the dam. It's a natural spot for a dam."

"Seem to me that Newcomb needs that water like he needs a hole in the head."

The rancher nodded. He took out a silver cigar case and selected a cigar. The sun flashed from the cigar case. Ross narrowed his eyes. Something had moved at the edge of the woods. A crow flew off to the east, cawing loudly. "Get off that hoss!" said Ross sharply. "Why?" said Fitzgerald.

Ross threw himself from the sorrel and his weight drove the lighter man from the saddle. Just as they hit the ground a rifle flatted off near the grove and a faint puff of smoke drifted downwind while the echo of the shot rebounded from the ridge and then died away.

"Roll down the slope!" said Ross. "Pronto!" The rancher did as he was told. Ross took the reins of both horses, keeping them in between himself and the hidden rifleman. He led the horses down the reverse slope out of sight of the rifleman.

Fitzgerald got slowly to his feet and brushed himself off. "Ruined my cigar," he said quietly.

Ross picked up the cigar case. "That was good shooting," he said. "Even if he did miss."

The rancher shook his head. "He didn't miss. It was a warning. It wasn't meant for you."

"How do you know?"

"It has happened before," said Fitzgerald. He selected another cigar and lighted it.

"We weren't on Newcomb land," said Ross.

Fitzgerald blew out a puff of smoke. "No," he said, "but it's evidently part of his campaign to harass me. Chousing, as you call it. By either name it is a dirty business." He looked at Ross. "You seem to have a sixth sense. I would have never known anyone was planning to shoot at us. How did you know?"

Ross shrugged. "The wind was blowing east. The bushes moved west. That crow took off in a hurry."

Fitzgerald nodded. "Why can't I do things like that?"

Ross rolled another cigarette. "You wasn't born out here," he said. "Even when I was a kid, we had trouble with Indian raiders. Jicarillas mostly. Then Texans would drift over the line and run off some of our stock. Had to chase them for miles sometimes, and they had a nasty little habit of raising the dust with the cows, whilst you was hot after them, then leaving a rifleman or two, like that one back there, to dust you up a bit. My cousin Gil was killed that way. Fifteen years old."

"I have a lot to learn," said the rancher.

Ross raised his head. "You got men working this side of the range?" he asked.

"Not that I know of."

"Someone is," said Ross.

"There you go again," said the rancher with a smile. "How do you know?"

Ross pulled his hat low over his eyes. "Look," he said quietly.

Five horsemen had topped a flat-topped hill a quarter of a mile away. They rode slowly down the slope and along the little fork of the creek that stemmed onto "Shamrock" land. They were evidently looking for something.

Ross blew a smoke ring. He had an uncomfortable feeling.

Boca Grande Canyon was just to the north. It was where he had camped the night before and where the rustled cattle had been driven as well.

"Those are not my men," said Fitzgerald.

Ross walked over to the sorrel and pulled his Winchester from its sheath.

"No," said the rancher. "I want no trouble."

"Maybe you want to die talking peace," said Ross. "Happens I don't." He looked at the horsemen. "I seem to remember two of those horses. They were ridden into Santo Tomas yesterday morning by two of the three Newcomb men that worked me over."

Fitzgerald studied the approaching men. "We don't have to worry," he said. "One of those men is Sheriff Hurley."

"Yeah," said Ross. "Dan Hurley. Him and Hardy Newcomb was in the war together. I've heard it said that Newcomb put Hurley into office. Very handy for both of them, I'd say."

Fitzgerald looked quickly at Ross. "That's dangerous talk," he said.

"All the more dangerous because it's true," said Ross. He ground out his cigarette and rolled another. He wished to God he had pulled leather out of there that morning instead of joyriding with this loco foreigner. He still didn't know what had kept him from leaving.

"Mister Fitzgerald!" called the sheriff as they reached the bottom of the slope. "A word with you!"

The lawman and the man who rode beside him came up the slope, while the other three riders dropped a little behind. Ross vaguely remembered Hurley. In Ross' time in Verde County Hurley had been a civilian employee of the army, in some capacity or other, going by his old title of Major Hurley. Rumor had had it in those days that Hurley had been suspect by the government for some time in the matter of perfectly good government property that had been condemned and sold at a cheap price by Hurley to contractors for the Mexican Army. It hadn't been long after that that Hurley had bought extensive property in Verde County, with the advice and cooperation of his old army pal, Hardy Newcomb.

Ross forgot about Hurley and the other three riders, as he looked at the man who rode solidly beside the lawman. There was no mistaking Hardy Newcomb. His hat was set straight on his block of a head. His big cigar was stuck at an angle from his wide mouth, jutting out from his powerful chin. His salt-and-pepper dragoon mustache had been trimmed straight across. Everything about Hardy Newcomb was straight across. Hat, eyebrows, mouth, shoulders and big hands. Everything, that is, except his conscience. It was said that the devil himself couldn't have straightened out Hardy Newcomb's conscience, or his tangled machinations in Verde County business and politics. He ran Verde County; he was Verde County.

Newcomb's frosty blue eyes held Fitzgerald's, although once they flicked appraisingly at Ross Starkey, and Ross Starkey, despite his calm expression, couldn't help but feel uneasy. There was a primeval power and aggressiveness about the man that could set almost anyone ill at ease.

"Gentlemen," said Fitzgerald with a smile.

Ross looked past Hurley into the bruised face of Art Cassidy and the empurpled face of Slim. He felt some satisfaction at the sight. Begod, he had put the Starkey brand on both of them, at least. Ben was missing, but Ross knew it wasn't because he wasn't able to ride or anything like that. Ross was more concerned about him than the other three. Few men would challenge Tascosa to meet them face to face in the street, with holstered six-guns quick to the ready hands.

"Ross Starkey," said Newcomb, as though he was mouthing a dirty word.

"Howdy," said Ross with a smile.

Newcomb ignored him. He looked at Hurley. "He was likely in on the deal," he said. "He ain't changed much since he left Verde County some years past. He's ridin' with Fitzgerald, as you can see."

"The gentleman is my guest," said Fitzgerald.

Newcomb grunted deep in his thick chest.

Hurley smiled a bland smile. "Twenty head of Mister Newcomb's cattle were driven off night before last," he said. "They were trailed to Boca Grande Canyon, Mister Fitzgerald."

"I know nothing about that," said Fitzgerald.

"One of your men was trailed into Santo Tomas yesterday morning," continued the law officer, just as though the rancher had not spoken. "Another of your men held a rifle on three of Mister Newcomb's men, allowing your man to beat Mister Newcomb's three men."

"I'll be damned," said Ross.

"Shut up," said Newcomb flatly.

Ross shut his mouth. There was no real issue as yet. Besides that, he wanted no part or parcel of Hardy Newcomb. The old bastard never forgot or forgave.

"Have you seen those cattle?" asked the sheriff.

"I have not," said Fitzgerald.

Hurley looked at Ross. "Have you?"

Ross nodded.

"Where are they?"

"Quién sabe?" said Ross. "I was camped in Boca Grande. I heard the steers being driven up the crick. I got to hell out'a there, I tell you!"

"Why?" said Hurley.

"Why? Hellsfire! If them Newcomb riders had caught me they'da strung me up for sure."

"They tried to stop you."

Ross grinned. "Yeah, with .44/40 slugs."

"You deny that you work for Mister Fitzgerald?"

"That's right."

"He's lyin'," said Newcomb flatly. He worked the unlit cigar over to the far side of his mouth.

"He does not work for me," said Fitzgerald flatly. "I do not know whose men those were who rustled your cattle, Mister Newcomb, or if they were anyone's men at all. I don't know where those cattle are."

"He's lyin', too," said Newcomb.

"Sir!" said Fitzgerald. His face whitened. "I give you my word!"

Newcomb took the cigar from his mouth and spat at the rancher's feet. "That's about the value of your word, you damned foreigner!"

Fitzgerald's face went white beneath the tan. His hands opened and closed but he managed to gain control of himself.

Newcomb shifted in his saddle. "Take Starkey along, Dan," he said, almost as though he was issuing an order.

Hurley smiled, a little unctuously. "Come on then, Mister Starkey."

"Where to?" said Ross.

"Just for a little questioning. No need to be alarmed."

"Where?" insisted Ross.

Newcomb fixed Ross with his basilisk stare, and Ross found it difficult to look into those icy, almost inhuman blue eyes. He could almost see the layer of hard ice beneath the surface. "You goin' to argue with the sheriff?" said Newcomb. It wasn't really a question, as he put it.

"I'll take you into Las Piedras," said the sheriff.

Ross looked past the officer, into the impassive faces of the three Newcomb riders. He knew his chances of getting safely to Las Piedras were pretty poor. Las Piedras was Newcomb country; in fact, the very heart of his "domain". He owned half of the town and the other half of the town likely owed him money, or worked for him, anyway.

"Are you coming?" said Hurley.

"You askin' him?" said Newcomb. He touched his horse with his heels and moved it a little closer to Ross.

"Have you a warrant for his arrest?" said Fitzgerald.

"Listen to him," said Newcomb.

"No," said Hurley. He seemed to be getting a little nervous. "I'm taking him in under suspicion."

"I'll vouch for him, Sheriff Hurley," said the rancher. "When do you want him in town?"

"Now!" said Newcomb. His three riders had moved

forward, as he had done, as though drawn by invisible wires, or an unspoken command.

"Get on that hoss, Starkey," said Newcomb flatly.

Ross wet his dry lips. There was no way out of this one. He had grounded the rifle beside him, but he did not dare raise it. He'd have a belly full of slugs before he got off one clean shot.

Hurley looked at Newcomb. "I'm inclined to take Mister Fitzgerald's word," he suggested.

"You'd take crap from him," said the big rancher.

Hurley flushed. "Now, Hardy!"

"Now, Dan!" mimicked the rancher.

Hurley looked uncertainly at Ross.

"You got your orders, Hurley," said Ross.

The wind shifted a little. It blew the horses' tails and manes and fluttered loose clothing. It brought something else, too. The soft sound of hoofs thudding on the ground southwest of where the stand-off was between Ross and the law.

Cassidy shifted in his saddle. "'Shamrock' riders, Mister Newcomb," he said.

Newcomb looked toward the newcomers. There was no expression on his face. "It's that baby-faced killer," he said.

"He's got eight men with him," said Slim.

"I can count!" snapped Newcomb.

Hurley rubbed his smooth, rounded jaw. He looked at Fitzgerald. "Bring him into Las Piedras tomorrow," he said.

Newcomb spat again. He shifted his cigar to the other side of his mouth. He looked at Ross and then at Fitzgerald. "You heard the man," he said. He turned his horse, then looked at Ross again. "If Dan lets you go, Starkey, you just keep on goin'. You hear?"

Ross nodded. He knew well enough what Newcomb meant.

The Newcomb party rode toward the ridge. They

stopped at the top of it and looked back as Tascosa and the "Shamrock" riders loped up to Fitzgerald and Ross, rifles across their thighs. Tascosa waved his hat at the Newcomb party. "The ranch line is due west!" he called out. He grinned.

When Ross looked again the Newcomb party was gone, but they had left something behind them; a cold, hostile feeling that had settled about Ross and the "Shamrock" men like a chilling, miasmic mist from some long-forgotten swamp.

Ross felt for the makings. "You reached here just in time, Kid," he said.

"Lucky for you," one of the riders said. He grinned. "Hello, Starkey!"

Ross nodded. "Hello, Mac," he said. "You been all the time in Verde County since I last saw you?"

Mac McArthur grinned again. "Well, not always. Got to admit the Seven Rivers boys dusted us a little too much some years past."

"Yeah," said Ross dryly. "You can say that again."

"Hola, Ross," said a pleasant-faced Mexican.

Ross narrowed his eyes. "Do I know you?"

"I think so. I am Francisco Ochoa."

Ross lighted his cigarette. "Ochoa? I knew a Diego Ochoa in the old days." His voice trailed off. He remembered all too well what had happened to Diego Ochoa.

"Mi hermano," said Francisco with a proud smile.

Ross nodded. "You were just a kid then, Francisco, and now you are a man. Muy hombre!"

"My brother always spoke well of you. Now it is I who rides with Ross Starkey, and the Tascosa Kid!" His white teeth shone beneath his thin mustache as he looked proudly at Tascosa.

Ross blew out a puff of smoke to hide the feeling reflected on his face. Diego Ochoa had had his back broken by a slug in the ambush so many years ago. Writhing and twisting on the dusty ground, calling for his

God and his mother until a soft nosed slug had smashed into his screaming mouth.

"My brother died well," said the young Ochoa.

"Muy hombre," agreed Ross. Perhaps you will die well, too, little brother, he thought.

Tascosa swung down from his horse. "Joe Bacon spotted you two, Mister Fitzgerald," he said. "Lucky we was working along the fork at the time."

Fitzgerald nodded. There was a deeply thoughtful look on his face. "I don't like this," he said, almost to himself.

"You got to fight fire with fire," said the Kid.

Fitzgerald looked angrily at him. "Do I? This is no way to live! Armed men patrolling either side of the boundary. Waiting for a chance to shoot and kill! Why, Ross and me were shot at from that grove near the dam pond not more than an hour ago."

"You were?" said the Kid thoughtfully. He looked at Mac McArthur. McArthur turned his horse and rode along the bottom of the ridge.

"I want no trouble," said Fitzgerald.

"There won't be any, sir," said the Kid cheerfully.

Fitzgerald mounted. Ross slid the Winchester into its saddle scabbard and mounted the sorrel.

"Was you aiming to do some rabbit shooting?" said the Kid.

"Skunk," said Ross dryly. He looked at Tascosa. The Kid knew well enough what he meant.

Ross and the rancher rode down the slope back toward the distant ranch buildings on the far side of the Rio Dulces. When they reached the first line of timber, Ross looked back. Seven men were riding north. The Tascosa Kid was missing. Ross had a damned good idea where he had gone.

CHAPTER NINE

D usk had filled the valley of the Rio Dulces and a cold wind whispered through the trees and brush, moaning softly about the ranch buildings and whining from the tops of the broken hills behind the river valley. It was very quiet about the ranch as Ross saddled his clay bank. The bunkhouse was empty. The only sound of man about the area was the rattling of pots and pans in the cookhouse. Ross closed his saddlebags and led the clay bank from the stable. He looked up at the night sky. It would rain before morning if the wind kept coming from the northeast. He looked over toward the big casa. He wanted to say goodbye to Sean Fitzgerald and Maureen as well, although he had not seen her since the time she had helped minister to his wounds. He had not forgotten that. The memory was acute. More than ever he now realized that there was a wide gap in his life, and it was widening day by day. Maybe there was something after all in a man settling down with a wife, raising a few kids. How long could he be a lobo, riding the owl-hoot trails, with no roof over his head. "The son of man has no home," he said as he led the clay bank toward the gate.

A shadowy figure moved in amongst the trees that

were between Ross and the big casa. Ross dropped his hand to his Colt.

"Is that you, Starkey?" said Sean Fitzgerald.

"Yes, sir, Mister Fitzgerald," said Ross. Damn it! He hadn't wanted to face the rancher, leaving like this in the dark of the moon.

"Where are you going?"

Ross took his hand from his Colt as the rancher walked toward him. The wind carried the faint sound of voices from the river bottoms.

"Starkey?" said the rancher.

Ross wet his lips. Maybe Fitzgerald had been waiting for him.

"You're planning to leave, permanently. Is that it, Starkey?"

"Yes," admitted Ross.

"Have you forgotten that I agreed to bring you to Las Piedras tomorrow?"

"It was your idea, not mine."

"I more or less gave my word on it."

Hoofs thudded on the road beyond the fence line.

"Then you can forget about it," said Ross.

"I can't do that," the rancher said quietly.

"You don't know who you're dealing with!"

"I think I know you."

"Listen," said Ross impatiently. "They won't bother you. They know about me from the past. They won't ever forget that fracas in Santo Tomas. They only got one way of taking care of such debts and it ain't by being peace-able-like."

"I agreed to take you there," said Fitzgerald.

The horsemen were at the gate. It creaked open.

Ross swung up on the clay bank. "Leave that gate open!" he called out.

"That you, Ross?" called Tascosa.

"It is."

"Where are you going?"

Ross touched the clay bank with his spurs. He looked at the rancher. "I'm sorry," he said, "but it's got to be this way. Say goodbye to Miss Maureen for me and thank her for me."

"I thought better of you than this," said Fitzgerald.

Ross had no answer. He rode toward Tascosa. The Kid leaned forward in his saddle. "What's the trouble, Ross?" he said.

"There isn't any. I'm just leaving."

The Kid looked at Fitzgerald. "What's going on here?" he asked.

Fitzgerald shrugged. "Ask your friend Mister Starkey," he said.

"Well, Ross?" said the Kid.

Ross felt his temper rise a little. "I'm heading out," he said. "Mister Fitzgerald took it on himself to promise to deliver me into Sheriff Hurley's hands tomorrow in Las Piedras."

"That don't make sense," said the Kid.

The rancher shook his head. "They would have taken him before you got there this afternoon," he said. "It was the only way I could get him out of their hands."

"And you still aim to take him there tomorrow?"

"I gave my word on it."

"His word," said Ross, "not mine."

"Your word ain't worth crap," said the Kid.

Ross looked closely at the Kid. Tascosa's face was set, and the danger lines showed at the corners of his mouth.

The Kid looked back at his two companions. "Go on to the bunkhouse," he said.

They rode wordlessly away, looking back over their shoulders. One of them was the man McArthur Ross had known in the old days on the San Patricio.

"Get off that hoss," said the Kid to Ross.

"I ain't taking orders from you," said Ross.

Tascosa smiled, but there was no mirth in his cold eyes. "You ain't? Mister Fitzgerald said he was going to take you into Las Piedras tomorrow. You are going to go with him."

It was very quiet now, except for the soft whispering of the wind along the river bottoms and the faint creaking of swaying branches.

"Get out of the way, Kid," said Ross.

"Let him go, Tascosa," said Fitzgerald. "I don't want any more trouble."

"You said you was going to take him into Las Piedras. That's good enough for me. He's going," said the Kid flatly.

A cold anger filled Ross. He wanted no part or parcel of the Kid, and he didn't want to back down in front of him.

"Get off that hoss," said the Kid.

Ross wet his dry lips. "I ain't taking orders from you, nor anybody else around here," he said. "I don't work here."

"Listen," said the Kid thinly. "Mister Fitzgerald give his word. That's something you wouldn't know about, and me neither. He's a gentleman. Them things mean a lot to him."

"They don't mean nothing to me," said Ross. "All I know is that Hardy Newcomb will take any chance he can to get at me. Nobody crosses him and gets away with it. He thinks I had something to do with stealing those cows. He believes it. Christ hisself couldn't bear witness for me that I didn't do it and you know it. You trying to get me killed? Maybe Mister Fitzgerald will be, too, for all we know."

The Kid shook his head. "Nobody is going to get killed. I'll make sure of that."

"I want no armed guards," said the rancher. "You know better than that. A mob of armed men riding into Las Piedras will be the gauntlet flung down, the open challenge. No, Tascosa, I won't have it!"

The Kid smiled. "It'll be all right," he said. "I'll ride along with you two."

"Gee," said Ross, "that'll make it just jim-dandy!"

The Kid nodded. "Take that hoss back," he said pleasantly.

It was no use. Ross had been bluffed out. He knew the Kid wouldn't hesitate to draw and shoot. Fitzgerald was like a chieftain to him, or perhaps a god. Nothing else mattered. Ross was nothing, if Fitzgerald's desires were to be frustrated by him. He carried no guns. With the Kid around he didn't have to. It wouldn't always be that way.

Ross dismounted and led the clay bank toward the corral. The Kid said something in a low voice to Fitzgerald and then rode after Ross. "What's for grub tonight?" he said.

Ross did not answer. He stopped at the corral and opened the gate, with the Kid sitting his horse, one forearm resting across his saddle horn. "You ain't talking to me, hey?" said. the Kid.

"You got the general idea," said Ross.

"It'll be all right tomorrow with me there."

"Sure, sure," said Ross. "Little Jesus walks the streets of Las Piedras."

"That ain't funny!"

Ross unsaddled the clay bank and slapped him on the rump. He slung the saddle over the top corral rail and looked at the Kid. "No," he said quietly. "It ain't funny. It ain't funny at all. I ain't forgetting this, Kid." He walked out of the corral and walked toward the bunkhouse, feeling for the makings.

"Don't get any ideas of slipping out of here tonight," said the Kid.

This time it was hate that poured through Ross' soul, but he was too good a poker player to make his bid now. The Kid had all the aces.

Ross walked into the bunkhouse. McArthur lay on his

bunk, lean hands clasped behind his head, his amused eyes on Ross. The other man was seated at the table, cleaning his revolver. "You're Starkey, hey?" he said. He looked at Ross with his one eye. The other was a glassie, and the color of it didn't quite match the other. "I'm Joe Bacon. I've heard of you from the Kid."

"Howdy," said Ross. He shoved back his hat and began to roll a cigarette.

"You workin' for Fitz now?" said the one-eyed man.

"No."

"Then how come you take orders from the Kid?"

Ross ran the cigarette paper across his lip and twirled the paper cylinder. He lighted it from the table lamp.

"I ast you a question," said Bacon.

"I heard you," said Ross.

McArthur looked at the ceiling. "The Kid likes to give orders," he said.

"What does that mean?" said Bacon.

McArthur looked at Ross. "Somebody's got to give them around here. Fitz is a nice hombre, but man, he don't know from nothing about runnin' a spread like this. The Kid is practically boss here now."

"It's that filly up to the casa," said Joe Bacon. He lovingly wiped the cylinder and barrel of his Colt and then began to feed shiny cartridges into it.

"Crap," said McArthur. "It's Fitz he works for, not her."

Joe closed the loading gate of the Colt. "Maybe he's workin' for the whole spread, and her. The Kid don't worry about such matters as loyalty and suchlike."

"Like you," said the lean man in the bunk. He grinned.

Joe looked at him and the glass eye seemed to move of its own accord. "I ride for whoever pays me the most," he said. "Fitz pays me better than Newcomb did, and he has better grub."

"You got a simple philosophy," said Mac.

"What the hell is that?" asked Bacon.

"You wouldn't know," said Mac.

The glass eye swiveled. Joe looked in Ross' general direction. "You never answered me about the Kid," he said.

"Lay off, Joe," said McArthur.

"I want to know."

Ross sat down on a chair and rested his arms on the back of it. He blew a smoke ring and moodily watched it waver in the heat of the lamp, rise, and then drift toward a partly open window.

"You hear me?" said Joe.

Ross looked at him. It was disconcerting as hell, trying to look into the one good eye with that glassie wobbling around. "It ain't none of your damned business," he said flatly.

Joe's face went white beneath the tan. His hand tightened about the butt of his Colt. "Ain't nobody can talk to me like that!" he snarled.

"Except the Kid," said Mac. He grinned again.

Ross knew there was something loose in Joe Bacon besides the glass eye. "Sit down," he said quietly. "I don't want any trouble and I don't feel like answering questions."

Joe walked toward him, the polished Colt swinging back and forth, reflecting the lamplight. He stopped five feet from Ross. "I'm the big rooster in this corrida," he said. "You'd better know that, Starkey."

For the first time Ross felt a twinge of fear. The man wasn't quite right, or he wouldn't have pressed his senseless question.

Joe raised the Colt and the smell of the fresh oil drifted to Ross. The hammer snicked back to half cock. "I ast a question," he said softly.

The door opened and the Kid walked in. He flicked his eyes about the smoky room. "Mac, go out and relieve Francisco at the gate."

The lean puncher dropped his long legs to the floor, but he didn't move from the bunk, watching the play between Ross and Joe.

The Kid looked at Joe. "Put up that cutter," he said.

Joe swiveled his one good eye. "He won't answer a question of mine," he said.

The Kid smiled. "My amigo is a stubborn man, Joe."

The gun muzzle centered on the Kid's gun belt buckle. "All I wanted was an answer," said Joe.

The Kid studied the older man. "Put that damned gun where it belongs," he said. He didn't have a chance of drawing if Joe's unstable mind let slip its gear.

For a long moment Joe stood there. His glass eye moved.

"I said: Put that damned gun where it belongs," said the Kid.

Joe's one good eye looked away. The glassie did a little dance of its own. The Colt was slid into its shaped holster. "All I did was ast a question," he said defensively. He turned and walked to his bunk.

"What's holding you back?" said the Kid to McArthur. "I told you to get out to that gate!"

The tall man flushed. He picked up his rifle and walked out of the bunkhouse.

Ross dropped his cigarette into the butts can and began to roll another. Whatever else the Kid had, or didn't have, there was one thing sure; he could give orders to older men, tough hardcases that maybe even Hardy Newcomb might have had a little trouble handling, and Hardy Newcomb was at least thirty years older than the Tascosa Kid.

The Kid looked at Ross. "Time for grub," he said.

"I ain't hungry."

Joe Bacon put on his hat and left the bunkhouse.

"Nice fella," said Ross as he lighted up.

"He's a fighting man," said the Kid. "Ain't afraid of nothing."

"Except you," said Ross, looking sideways up at the Kid. "He ain't that loco."

The Kid took the makings from Ross' pocket and began to roll a quirly. "There's a bottle in my warbag," he said.

"I ain't thirsty."

"That's a switch." The Kid lighted the cigarette and blew a puff of smoke toward the lamp. "You're still waspy, hey?"

"I got a low boiling point," said Ross.

The Kid shrugged. "I'll get some grub," he said. "If Francisco comes in tell him to come over and get some grub. I got something to tell him."

"Is that an invitation or an order?"

The Kid took the cigarette from his mouth. "You know," he said conversationally, "you're beginning to annoy me."

Ross slowly stood up. "You been annoying me for a long time," he said. "There's ways we can settle it."

The Kid smiled. "Not with guns, hombre."

"I can't outdraw you, Kid. I wasn't thinking of a shooting scrape."

The Kid shrugged again. "Maybe you're thinking of going out behind the stables, bare knuckles to a finish, hey?"

Ross unbuckled his gun belt and hung it over the chair.

Tascosa dropped his cigarette into the butts can. "You know," he said quietly, "you got an idea you're the big augur with them fists of yours. Somebody just ought'a take that idea out of you, maybe through the hide."

"Like you?"

The Kid smiled. "You were wide open most of the time in that street picnic in Santo Tomas."

Ross walked toward the door. "Come on," he said. "Put your fists where that big mouth is."

The Kid did not move.

Ross turned. "You yella without that gun?" he said. He knew the Kid would never take that one.

The Kid's face went white. He opened and closed his mouth. For a fraction of a moment his lean hands lingered just over his gun belt buckle and then he moved them to his sides. "I got plans," he said. "I can't afford to get tangled in a fight with a damned hotheaded fool like you."

"Hear, hear," said Ross sarcastically.

"Grub pile!" yelled Baldy the cook from the cookhouse.

The Kid began to fashion a smoke. He placed it between his lips and lighted it. He walked to the door, right past Ross. He looked squarely into Ross' eyes and Ross knew it wasn't fear that had held the Kid back from a bare-knuckled jamboree atop the old manure behind the stables.

Ross put on his gun belt after the Kid had left. He was still sitting at the table when Francisco Ochoa walked in. "Hola, amigo," said the kid.

Ross nodded. "Little Jesus wants to see you over at the dining hall," he said.

Ochoa narrowed his eyes. "Little Jesus?"

"The Kid."

Francisco leaned against the wall. "You do not like him?"

"I can live without him," said Ross dryly.

"He is one of the great ones," said Ochoa. "Fast like the striking viboras cascabeles with the six-gun."

Ross spat. "A rattlesnake has got more morals," he said.

"You had better not let him hear you say that!" said Ochoa angrily.

"Who? The rattlesnake? I'd be ashamed to say it to one of them."

Ochoa felt for the makings. He began to roll a cigarette. "He always talked highly of you," he observed.

"Because he could use me."

"Is it not true that without him you would have died in Mexico, up against a wall, or perhaps in the desert north of the prison from which he helped you to escape? Did he not save you from the Apaches? Did he not save you from those men in the street of Santo Tomas? Are you not grateful?"

Ross shook his head. "He didn't miss much, did he?"

"He is the greatest of them all," said Ochoa. "There is not one in the Southwest who is faster on the draw, or more deadly with his aim."

"I've heard that before," said Ross. "Somewhere, there is a man who is faster and deadlier, and beyond him there is another who is still more faster and more deadly, and so on and so on..."

"He will save this ranch from Newcomb. He will protect Senor Fitzgerald and his sister. He will face down and defeat Hardy Newcomb."

"All that leaves is the devil himself," said Ross. He looked up at the kid. "The viboras cascabeles is stuffing his gut. He says you should come over there. He wants to talk with you."

The young man smiled. "At once!" he said. He left the bunkhouse.

"Jesus God," said Ross, rolling his eyes upward. "Now we got the Tascosa Kid as Sir Galahad in New Mexico. First thing you know they'll have him in a nursery rhyme, for the little ones who haven't learned to read yet!"

He was still sitting there when he heard Ochoa's voice outside the bunkhouse, and later that of Joe Bacon and another waddie, the older man named Greener. In a few minutes, Ochoa came into the bunkhouse and got his rifle. He did not speak to Ross as he left. In a little while, Ross heard the beating of hoofs, heading for the gate.

Ross walked to the door and leaned against the side of it. "I wonder if Don Fitzgerald really knows what is going on around here?" he said aloud.

"He will," said a quiet female voice.

Ross turned quickly to look into the face of Maureen Fitzgerald. He snatched off his hat. "I'm sorry," he said.

"I wanted to see how you were," she said.

"I'm fine, ma'am," said Ross hastily.

"Come over to the house with me," she said. "I'd like to clean those wounds. Infection sets in easily."

"No need for that!" said Ross. He remembered too well the odor of sweat and manure that had hung about him the time she had dressed those wounds.

She smiled. "It's an order," she said.

"I don't work here," he said.

"Then come for my sake," she said.

There was no further argument after that. As they walked toward the big casa, they did not see the Tascosa Kid step from the shadows near the cookhouse and look after them. He snatched the cigarette from his lips and stamped on it, then walked toward the stables. Deep in his eyes there was a new and fiercely forbidding light.

CHAPTER TEN

Her hands were soft, deft and gentle. Ross again had the problem of keeping his mind on other things while looking directly at her bosom. Begod, he had never had that trouble with Mary Ellen Spragg when he had been courting her in the old days. The intent and the action had been the same thing in those days.

She passed a cool hand along his flushed cheek. "There," she said, "you seem to heal quickly."

"Maybe it's all in the mind," he said.

She smiled. "It's an interesting thought."

"It don't help much when a cow steps on your foot, or a bullet gets poked into your hide," he said.

She shook her head. The firelight brought out the highlights of her hair and seemed to accentuate the creaminess of her complexion. "You are riding into Las Piedras with Sean, are you not?" she said.

He grinned wryly. "I don't have much choice," he said.

"Sean would not order you to go," she said.

"He didn't. It was something else. He give his word. I can't welsh on that," he lied bravely.

There was a faint amused look on her face. "Would you like sherry or Tokay?" she said.

"I don't go for that foreign booze," said Ross. He flushed. "I didn't mean it the way I said it," he added.

She laughed. "It's wine."

"Brandy will do me fine," he said. "I shouldn't ought'a be drinking in the presence of a lady. My mom told me that when I was a kid. It didn't stop my pa though. He was always boozing it up around Mom, and she was a lady, I tell you, ma'am!"

She filled a glass for him from a cut-glass decanter and placed it on the table. "It was Tascosa that really made you decide to go to Las Piedras, wasn't it, Ross?"

"He can't make me do nothing!" said Ross angrily.

"But it's true, isn't it?"

He nodded. "I don't want no trouble with the Kid," he said.

"No one seems to want trouble with him."

"He's a good man for the job your brother gave him. I'll say that for him."

She looked into the fireplace, as though she could see pictures in the dancing flames. "I wonder," she mused. "Hardy Newcomb is a hard man. He brooks no interference with his way."

"You can say that again," said Ross. He sipped the brandy.

"Are you afraid of him, too?"

Ross shrugged. "I'd feel better with a couple of counties between me and him."

"What will happen tomorrow?"

"Your guess is as good as mine, ma'am. I don't have much choice."

"You can still refuse to go."

He shook his head. "I've changed my mind."

"Because of Sean? Or Tascosa?"

"Neither one. I'm sorry I got mixed up in this war, but I ain't going to let Hardy Newcomb hammer his damned law into me, begging your pardon, ma'am."

She sat down and looked at this lean hawk of a man,

with the battered face, and the simple, but forthright, ideas. He was almost, but not quite, homely. He had a way of looking directly at one, and she knew he was hard beneath his simple manner; hard enough to kill if he had to, and yet there was something else within him. Something she could not quite define, and yet she knew this hidden quality was something entirely alien to Tascosa. There was more. She felt herself drawn to this lean lobo of a man, and yet she knew there could be nothing between them. They were planets apart. She had assured herself of that a number of times in the darkness of her room, staring up at the ceiling, surrounded by many men, yet utterly alone amongst them.

"You're not in the same room with me, ma'am," he chided gently.

She started. "I'm sorry! I meant to ask you why you had come back to Verde County."

"Quién sabe? I was heading north anyways."

"You came from the Columbus area. That's almost due west, isn't it?"

He flushed. "Not quite."

She smiled. "You came to see Tascosa, didn't you?"

He raised his eyes, and the hard light came into them. "Supposing I did? It was the biggest mistake I've made in the past few years, and I've made quite a passel of them. I should'a kept going north!"

"Where, and to what, Ross?"

He emptied the brandy glass. "My brother has the old family place on the Canadian. I can run it."

"Is that what you really want to do?"

He looked directly at her, and something passed between them; something perhaps that neither of them really wanted, or thought they didn't want, but it was there between them for the taking. "Ain't much else," he said quietly. He could not bear to look into those eyes, for he had the eerie feeling he would fall into them, deep, deep, and never find his way out of them again. "I'm tired of drifting, fighting, eating a Spanish supper and sleeping in a Spanish bed." He looked quickly at her with that whimsical sideways smile of his. "That last don't quite mean the same like it sounds."

"What does it mean, Ross?"

"A Spanish supper is to tighten your belt a notch and a Spanish bed is to lie face down on the hard ground and pull your back over you for a cover."

She nodded. "You're tired of the old ways; the sowing of wild oats."

"That's it exactly."

She looked into the flames of the fireplace. "You're sure about that?" she asked softly.

It was a picture that would stay in his memory for the rest of his life, but he didn't know it then. She could read his mind. He was sure of it now. "Yes," he lied.

"Then you should have gone directly north to the Canadian, Ross. No, Ross, you are not through with the old ways. Not quite yet. Otherwise, you would not have come back to Verde County." She looked directly at him. "It is Tascosa, is it not?"

"I ain't smart enough to figger that one out," he said defensively.

"He is," she said simply.

"Maybe so," he said hotly.

"Where will all this end?"

He looked directly at her. "You know the answer as well as I do, ma'am," he said. He emptied his glass and stood up. "Thanks for your kindness."

She walked with him to the door. She looked up at him in the darkness of the hall. "Please call me Maureen," she said.

"I ain't got that right, ma'am."

For a moment she stood there looking at him and then she touched his battered face with the tips of her fingers. "I'm giving you that right, Ross," she said softly.

The impulse to draw her close swept through him so

quickly he almost acted before he thought, and when he did think, it seemed as though his knees were going to betray him. He actually felt as though he was swaying a little on his feet. "Thank you, Maureen," he said huskily.

Something passed between them again, and Ross knew that whatever happened to her present frame of mind, his would never change, and the swiftness and the wonder of it shook him throughout his body and soul.

She had seemed to be waiting for something and when it did not come, she touched his arm. "Take care of my brother tomorrow," she said.

"He's supposed to be taking care of me," he said with a smile.

"Please take care of Tascosa, too," she said.

He looked back at the closed door as he walked toward the bunkhouse. "Well, I'll be damned," he said to himself. "She ain't worried about ol' Ross Starkey and his bashed-in phiz. She's just worried about her brother and that damned Tascosa! Man, maybe I ain't too bright at that! She dealt out them cards so fast I never did see her doctor up the deck! Tascosa!" He mimicked her voice. "Please take care of Tascosa, too," he simpered. "Bull crap! Like taking a half-grown grizzly bear to bed with you. Me? I'd sooner have the grizzly at that!"

The ranch area was very quiet. The wind swayed the trees and the brush and it brought the faint music of the river to Ross. The brandy was warm in his lean gut. He lighted a cigarette and looked back at the house. There was one lighted window in the second story. It was her room. He saw the outline of her figure dark against the soft lamplight and once again he was badly shaken. No one had heard his last bitter words, but he knew deep within his heart that it was not so. It couldn't be so!

He lighted the cigarette. The flare of the match revealed his hawk's face and then it was gone. For a moment she stood there and then she drew the drapes across the window. Ross walked slowly toward the bunkhouse. He was too old a hand with the fillies to let any of them break him up. Sure, he knew women!

He walked into the empty bunkhouse. He had never seen a corrida that spent more time in the saddle than the "Shamrock" riders, and usually at night, too. He hunted down Tascosa's bottle and helped himself. By bedtime he was half-seas over and he didn't give a tinker's damn for Tascosa, Hardy Newcomb and the whole of Verde County, but he could not erase Maureen Fitzgerald from his mind.

There had been a lot of comings and goings during the night, with muttered conversations outside of the bunkhouse, none of which had been intelligible to Ross. At dawn his head felt like it was going to burst. After breakfast, as he rode with Sean Fitzgerald and Tascosa along the river road, his face must have revealed how he felt, for the other two were careful not to say anything to him.

When the sun came up the world seemed to silently explode into the dreamlike quality of a New Mexico autumn. The hills had begun to be mantled in scarlet, purple and gold. Green clouds of cottonwoods seemed to float above bronze-red hills. The wind was soft and the air dry and winey, after the rains. White puffs of clouds were conjured up out of thin air by some unseen master magician and they drifted from east to west, increasing in number as the day grew warmer and warmer, while their shadows followed the flow of the rolling land.

It was almost noon when they reached the outskirts of Las Piedras, riding slowly along a winding road, tree-shaded, where adobe after adobe, like beads on a string, lined both sides of the road. Bare-legged children scuttled for cover as los gringos rode by. They knew these cold-eyed men who rode with careless ease and with death hidden in their holsters and saddle scabbards. Many of their families' friends and relatives had died or been crippled in the periodic and deadly warfare that swept Verde County in cycles.

Older eyes peered from the secretive windows and from the tilled fields about the wide valley. They knew two of those men. It was a partisan country; there was no in-between. Two of the riding trio were not Newcomb men. One was the leader of the "Shamrock" corrida, and the young man who rode beside him was almost a Verde County legend. The third man they did not know, but he had the stamp of the gunfighter on him.

The pinnacled rocks that half encircled Las Piedras, and which had given it its name, were sun-soaked that day, warm and bronzed in the bright, clear light. Beyond them a faint bluish haze was already forming on the mountains. The adobes and jacales of Las Piedras slept in the warm sunlight, with scarlet ristras of peppers like coagulated blood hanging against the yellow-brown walls. The doors and windows had been painted blue for the most part and here and there on the walls the sun glinted brightly from shining stones set into the adobe when it was wet, in the form of the Cross.

The horses clattered over a bridge that spanned an acequia madre, bringing fresh, clear water to the irrigated fields beyond the town. Cottonwoods and willows waved beside the acequias, while long-tailed magpies flitted about, at peace with clouds of smaller birds that seemed to prefer the vicinity of the houses to the waving trees. The clear, bell-like sound of meadowlarks came out on the soft wind.

There were other eyes on the three riders as they approached the center of the town. Indolent women looked sideways from liquid eyes, and it was at the tallest of the riders they looked, while their men folk peered warily from beneath their wide hat brims, brown hands feeling for knife hilts. The object of the looks from both sexes rode loose and easy in the saddle, cigarette hanging from the side of his mouth, as though he was not in enemy country. The Kid was drinking it all in.

They rode into the placita and tethered their horses in front of the sheriff's office, beside the adobe calabozo. Eyes peered between the rusted bars of the cell windows and narrowed as they saw Tascosa. Here and there about the sun-soaked plaza men shifted their positions. Others looked through the windows of the saloons. There was an unusual absence of women and children about the plaza, but there were many horses, most of them with the Newcomb Box HN brand on them, tethered to the hitching racks.

Sean Fitzgerald dismounted. He looked about. "I don't like the looks of this," he said.

Tascosa dismounted and fashioned a cigarette, watching the lounging men across the placita. "Everything will be all right," he said. He looked at Ross. "There are your three sparring partners from Santo Tomas."

Ross nodded. He had already seen the three of them standing beneath the wooden awning of a saloon three doors down from the sheriff's office. He looked back the way he and the others had just come. There had been no Newcomb men in sight as they had approached the center of Las Piedras; now he could see four men leaning against adobes on either side of the street mouth. He mentally cursed himself for not pulling leather the night before. "Time for a drink," he said. "My cabeza is killing me."

Sean Fitzgerald shook his head. "Not yet," he said.

Tascosa opened the door of the sheriff's office and bowed a little as he ushered the others in. Ross looked sideways at the Kid; the sonofabitch was as cool as a brass monkey's butt in the wintertime. Ross had to give him credit for that, at least.

Dan Hurley looked up from his desk. Hardy Newcomb straddled a chair backward, his thick forearms resting on the chair back, his hat level above his level brows, his thick mustache level above the narrow line of his level mouth. He looked like a damned heathen Chinee joss idol sitting there, thought Ross.

"I see you kept your word," said Hurley with his usual smooth smile. Everything about Dan Hurley was smooth, except, perhaps, his conscience, but only he and God would know about that.

Fitzgerald nodded. "Mister Starkey kept his word as well."

"He did?" said Newcomb. "I could have sworn he'd be crossin' the Tres Cerros by now."

Ross felt for the makings. The old coot was right at that—Ross would be, if Tascosa hadn't outsmarted—or out-bluffed—Ross, whichever way you looked at it.

Newcomb and Tascosa looked at each other and neither of them looked away, and neither of them would, as though the older bull of the herd, still powerful and still in command, were taking the measure of his possible successor. Ross wondered idly what kind of a young man Hardy Newcomb had been. He had a pretty good idea. He had one advantage on Tascosa; he had lived a good part of his allotted span.

Fitzgerald took off his hat and brushed back his fine blond hair. "All you have against Mister Starkey is circumstantial evidence, Sheriff Hurley, and none of it very good at that."

"We'll be the judge of that," said Newcomb.

"I'll just bet you will," said Tascosa.

"As I see it," said Fitzgerald. "Mister Starkey was in Boca Grande when the stolen cattle were driven through it. He left the canyon, pursued by some of Mister Newcomb's riders, leaving his hat behind."

"He sure did," said Newcomb. It was about as close as he'd come to a joke.

"You have no proof he was with the men who took the cattle. You don't even know who they were. You have no case at all against Mister Starkey," said the rancher.

"The sheriff is going to hold him under suspicion," said Newcomb.

Ross felt cold inside. He remembered all too well how many of the Newcomb corrida were lounging about the placita, waiting, just waiting.

Tascosa rolled a fresh smoke. He leaned indolently against the wall, watching the others, now and then looking through the dusty glass of the window.

"I protest," said Fitzgerald.

"You crap," said Newcomb heavily. He stood up.

Hurley flushed. He was too much of the politician to stand for all of Newcomb's blunt, undiplomatic ways. "I'll have to keep him, Mister Fitzgerald," he said.

"I'll put up his bail," said the rancher.

Hurley waved a smooth hand. "He is held without bail. Incommunicado," he said.

Tascosa smiled. "What's that? Without toilet privileges?"

Hurley looked at the Kid. "Sometimes you annoy me," he said.

"The feeling is mutual."

"You're a long way from your manure pile, Kid," said Newcomb. "Whyn't you go and strut in front of the hens? You're damned good at that, they tell me."

Boots popped on the boardwalk in front of the office and the door swung open. An elderly man looked at Newcomb. "Damnedest thing, boss," he said breathlessly. "Them cows that was run off out'a Boca Grande Canyon is right back there, grazin' as peaceful as you please."

"You sure, Marty?" said Newcomb.

"Positive, boss. You know me."

Newcomb nodded. He looked at Ross. "That still don't clear you in my book," he said.

Ross felt a chill. His boot heels felt like they wanted to sprout wings.

"Then you have no reason to hold Mister Starkey?" said Fitzgerald.

Hurley looked at Newcomb. Newcomb shook his head. Hurley turned, like a puppet, and smiled. "No," he said.

Tascosa walked to the door and opened it. Sean Fitzgerald had a puzzled look on his face as he walked outside into the bright sunlight. Ross looked curiously at Tascosa. The Kid's face was a blank. Tascosa shut the door behind him. "You want that drink now, amigo?" he said.

Ross felt for the makings. He could see the Newcomb men still idling about the placita. His three sparring partners, as Tascosa had called them were still standing there, looking directly at the three "Shamrock" men. "I think we ought to get the hell out'a here, if we can," he said.

"They won't start anything," said Fitzgerald. "You're freed of those charges, Ross."

"Yeah," said Ross. "We know that, but do they?"

The door opened behind them, and Hardy Newcomb came out. He was lighting a cigar. He looked over the flare of the match directly into Ross' eyes. "You can leave," he said dryly.

"Gracias," said the Kid. "God has spoken. Everything is all right now."

Newcomb fanned out the match, never taking his eyes from the Kid. He worked the cigar from one side of his mouth to the other. It was as though he was measuring Tascosa in infinite detail, leaving nothing to chance or hearsay, as though he were impressing every feature of the man on an indelible page in his mental files.

Ross mounted and waited for the others.

Tascosa looked up at Ross. "How about that drink?" he said.

"Suddenly I ain't thirsty," said Ross.

Sean Fitzgerald untethered his horse. "I think we had better leave," he said.

Tascosa shrugged. He mounted and the three of them

rode slowly from the placita, under the cold, level eyes of Newcomb's men.

It wasn't until they were well clear of the town that Ross turned in his saddle and looked back. They were not being followed, but it was still a long way to the Rio Dulces.

Sean Fitzgerald took out his cigar case and passed it first to Tascosa and then to Ross. After all three of them lighted up, he looked back toward Las Piedras as Ross had done. "You know," he said thoughtfully, "it was almost as though Hardy Newcomb expected that to happen."

Ross blew out a puff of smoke. The thought had occurred to him, too. "He plays a deep game," he said.

Tascosa blew a smoke ring and punched a finger through it. "He ain't so damned smart as he thinks he is," he said. He grinned secretively.

"What do you mean by that?" asked Fitzgerald.

Tascosa shook his head. "Nothing, sir, absolutely nothing."

Fitzgerald flushed. "You go out of your way to antagonize that man," he said quietly. "I won't stand for much more of it, Tascosa. I have too much to take into consideration. I have written to the new governor for help in this harassment I have been suffering from Newcomb. Let's do this thing my way."

"And get a bullet in the back?" sneered Tascosa. "The new governor won't do anything about it. He knows who runs Verde County. He knows where the votes come from."

"He's appointed by the federal government, isn't he?" said the rancher.

"Sure, sure, but most of the rest of the territorial officials are elected. They control most of the money in this territory and don't you ever forget it, and they can put pressure on Washington to make or break a governor.

They won't buck up against Hardy Newcomb. That was a fool thing to do, writing to Santa Fe."

"It's my way," said Fitzgerald defensively. "What do you think, Ross?"

Ross took the cigar from his mouth. "I say a man should fight for his land. It don't have to be with bullets, though."

"Hear, hear," jeered Tascosa.

Ross jammed the cigar back into his mouth. Tascosa had a great way of rubbing salt into a person's feeling, the egotistical sonofabitch. "Please take care of Tascosa, too," she had said. Ross would like to take care of him all right, but not the way she had meant him to.

Ross glanced at the Kid, riding jauntily, cigar poked up at an angle like a bow-staff on a river steamer, satisfied with himself of course, but not quite satisfied with the world—although, of course, he meant to change all that. Sure, Hardy Newcomb had seemed to know that those cattle had been returned, but there also had seemed to be something else up his sleeve besides his arm. Something that neither of the "Shamrock" men suspected, but Ross had an uncanny, uneasy feeling, and he wouldn't rest well until he found out what it was, although he wasn't sure he really wanted to know.

They reached the valley of the Rio Dulces in the middle of the afternoon. Fitzgerald smiled. "It's beautiful," he said. He looked at Ross. "You're sure you won't stay with us?"

Ross shook his head. "Hardy Newcomb ain't forgave me," he said. "He ain't about to, neither. He don't ever forget a man once he's done something Hardy Newcomb don't like. He's got his sights on me. I make one false move in this county and he'll get me one way or another."

Tascosa laughed. "You going to let that old hellion scare you away?"

Ross looked at him. "Yes," he said simply. "I got no war with him."

Tascosa yawned. "You called me yella last night," he said.

Fitzgerald looked at Ross and then at Tascosa. "Maybe it is best that you leave, Ross," he said.

"I'm going," said Ross. "Ain't no question about that."

They rode down the long slope. Shadows were gathering on the eastern slopes of the broken hills. A cool wind picked its way up the valley of the Rio Dulces. It was quiet and peaceful, and yet there was something haunting the oncoming dusk. Something that had not yet shown its ugly mask.

CHAPTER ELEVEN

The weather had changed, driving away the mild sunny days with their cool, dry winds, to replace them with an intense heat that filled even the otherwise cool valleys. The sun beat down on the range, ravaging it once more before the start of the true fall weather.

Ross Starkey broke his simple camp on a fork of the Rio Dulces. He had left the "Shamrock" ranch two days before, after making his goodbyes to the Fitzgeralds. Tascosa had vanished, riding forth with half a dozen of the hardcases that had drifted to the Rio Dulces country to ride under the Tascosa Kid. Ross had intended to ride to the western slopes of the mountains and then strike across the Jornada del Muerto to the Rio Grande and then take it by easy stages north to Albuquerque and eventually to Santa Fe. He wanted to see his brother Lloyd. Lloyd had always been the cool head in his family, the steadfast reliable type who had left the ranch on the Canadian to work for his law degree, taking care of his aging mother as well, while Ross had drifted through the years, always looking for the pot at the end of the rainbow. So far it had cost him some of the best years of his life, and the future didn't look much better from where Ross sat his horse. Maybe Lloyd would have the answers.

Still, it wasn't easy to leave the Rio Dulces country. He had grown to like and respect Sean Fitzgerald, as Tascosa had done. The Irishman was everything that Ross wasn't, and the same thing could be said about the Kid, except that the Kid had an intense, though perhaps warped, loyalty to the rancher, which might have in it the seeds of doom for Sean Fitzgerald.

He had said goodbye to Maureen, with her brother standing close by and Tascosa in the offing, so there was nothing that could be said openly. After he had left her, he had thought of wonderful things he could have said, that would have painted a masterpiece of his feeling toward her, but the words had not come at the right time. Once again, the hag of loneliness had returned to Ross Starkey, and this time it was more bitter than gall.

A man leaves a part of himself wherever he goes. Bit by bit his body and soul are invisibly chipped at and eroded by life, and many times a man leaves something behind that years later comes back to haunt him. For some reason or another, there are scales before his eyes at the time. There is one thing sure: in almost every case, he can never return to that distant time. This time Ross had experienced something and had known at the time it was something he had never experienced before. He had left part of himself, perhaps the greatest part of himself, in the cool deft hands and deep eyes of Maureen Fitzgerald. The rest was a husk. Just dross. A mechanical man.

The sun beat down into the windless canyons, filling them with a heat and glare that seemed to bounce from the drying ground, to strike into a man's face even beneath his low-pulled hat brim and strike deep into his eyes. Ross couldn't hurry, despite the desire to escape the heat and the glare. Each stride of the clay bank was carrying him farther and farther away from the Rio

Dulces and Maureen Fitzgerald. He couldn't hurry, and yet he knew he had to go.

The late afternoon heat caught him as he crossed a ridge in the full light of the sun. He wiped the sweat from his face and urged the clay bank down toward the shade of the trees. He began to fashion a smoke as he reached the trees. Here and there, further up the canyon he could see scattered clumps of "Shamrock" cattle. The mouth of the canyon debouched onto sloping land that led down toward Newcomb's Box HN range. A stout fence had been built across the mouth of the canyon and he could just see it from where he sat his horse.

He lighted the cigarette and flipped the match into the fork. As he did so he saw black shapes silhouetted against the startling blue of the cloudless sky. They were wheeling lower and lower and every now and then one of them would drop out of sight just beyond the fence. Ross blew a puff of smoke. Likely a dead cow over there, or maybe a dead jackrabbit. He leaned on his saddle horn and watched the wheeling buzzards. One good thing about the ugly devils, they sure cleaned up the range in a hurry.

One by one the buzzards landed, but one of them still swung about against the blue, like a charred newspaper being lifted by the wind, only there wasn't any wind. Maybe they kept a guard up, thought Ross. It's a cinch no man was about, for those buzzards would rise like a filthy cloud and circle patiently, somehow knowing the exact range of the man's rifle, and hovering just beyond it.

Ross rode along the fork. He didn't want to go near Newcomb's Box HN range, but he had to follow the fence line or cross those damned heat-blasted hills, and even Hardy Newcomb couldn't panic Ross into doing that, not this day at any rate.

He saw the buzzards in a mass just beyond the fence line, waddling in, poking their ugly naked necks into the carrion they had found, ripping and tearing with beaks as strong as a blacksmith's pincers. He eyed with disgust their dusty black feathers. Christ, but they were really at it!

He saw part of the carrion as he reached the fence. It was a steer, a small one from his sight of it. Maybe a yearling. It wasn't much bigger than a man. The buzzards hadn't caught Ross' scent as yet although the lone one in the sky was swinging over, with motionless pinions, rising and falling easily on the hot updraft from the naked hills.

Ross kneed the clay bank away from the fence. He had caught the sweet-rotten odor of decaying flesh. He threw away his cigarette in disgust. Even the weed seemed to smell and taste of the carrion. He felt for the full bottle of rye in a saddlebag, parting gift of Sean Fitzgerald. Maybe a slug would take the taste out of his dry mouth and throat. He drank deeply and drove the cork back into the bottle. As he did so the buzzards caught wind of him. Squawking and protesting, they waddled along the dusty ground, rising heavily and sluggishly into the air, flapping off toward the hills, leaving behind the torn and dusty carrion.

Ross glanced once more at the carrion and drew rein sharply. He narrowed his eyes. It was the damnedest-looking fallen hide he had ever seen. No legs, just a long sort of dusty, ripped cylinder, with the dusty head in plain view.

Ross leaned forward in the saddle and stared at it. The damned booze was working fast, for it seemed as though the head was looking back at him!

Ross wiped the sweat from his face. He shook his head. It must be the enervating heat and the booze. He looked at the carrion again and a ghastly feeling came over him. Slowly he slid from the saddle and walked to the fence, staring at the carrion. He pushed up a strand of the cruel barbed wire and shoved down on the one below it with his foot, working his way through, heedless of a barb that raked his broad back. He walked slowly toward the carrion, his spurs ringing softly in the dust.

Ross stopped and put his hand to his mouth. Suddenly he spun about and heaved his liquor, followed by his last meal, then followed by pure bile. His strength drained from him, and he stood there, spraddle-legged, head bent low, chest and gut heaving, with strings of slimy green hanging from his widespread mouth. "Jesus, oh Jesus," he gasped. He passed a hard hand across his streaming eyes. The smell of the carrion seemed to drift around him, but his gut was empty.

He turned slowly and looked about. The range was empty, heat shimmering in the sun, seeming to rise and fall. The buzzards were high up now, so high it hurt to look up at them in that bright sky, swinging in great, lazy circles, waiting for the live man-smell to stop spoiling their meal.

Ross looked at the head that protruded from the ripped green hide, but the eyes were gone and the tongue that had protruded from the blackened mouth had been eaten away to the roots. The white teeth were shown in a perpetual grin, for the soft puffed lips had also been eaten away, while harsh beaks had already torn into the flesh of the cheeks. The booted feet, the spurs red-scaled with fresh rust, were tied at the ankles, protruding from the shrunken hide like the twin flippers of a seal.

Ross wiped his mouth. He had heard of such things but had never seen anything like it. The Comanches practiced such an agonizing method of execution, lashing the victim in a fresh buffalo hide, head and feet protruding from it, then placing the screaming, half-mad victim under the blazing sun. The sun would slowly constrict the green hide like the coils of a python, until the eyes protruded, and the swollen tongue was pushed through the outthrust, blackened lips. Sometimes the buzzards got there before the victim was dead...

Ross looked about again. There was no sign of life

except for the buzzards, now almost indistinguishable against the glare of the sun. He forced himself to walk to the side of the victim. The man had been slight of build, dark-haired and -mustached. A queer feeling came over Ross. He drew out his clasp knife and opened the big blade. He gathered all his will power and began to slit the rawhide lashings that bound the dead man inside the green hide. He forced himself to push a shaking hand inside and feel for the man's wallet. He withdrew it. He opened the stinking thing, trying to keep his internal organs inside his gut, for he knew they'd be next if he heaved again. There was nothing else left to heave.

He opened the wallet in the full light of the sun. A picture fluttered to the ground. He picked it up and looked at it, seeing the rather rounded and stupid face of a young woman, hardly more than a girl. He turned it over. "To Francisco with all my love," he said in Spanish. A horrible feeling came over him again. He now suspected the truth, but he didn't want to face it. He poked through the few papers in the wallet. He closed it and placed it inside his shirt. There wasn't any doubt about it now. The carrion was all that was left of Francisco Ochoa. In following his idol, the Tascosa Kid, he had followed the last trail out.

Ross got a blanket from his horse. He rolled the stiffened corpse, green hide and all, into it, then carried it to the horse. The clay bank shied and blowed repeatedly, backing away from the stench until Ross belted him once or twice atop the head. Ross lashed the corpse on the clay bank.

He rolled and lighted a cigarette, looking back across the Box HN range. It was as deserted as before. The buzzards were gone in search of another meal. Ross looked at a distant motte. There was a bright flash, as though the sun had reflected on polished metal, and for a second or two his hair rose on the back of his neck, as he awaited a rifle bullet. He trotted toward the woods along the fork and led the clay bank into the hot shade.

Maybe he hadn't been destined to leave the "Shamrock" and the Rio Dulces country; not quite yet anyway.

The sun was gone when he topped the last broken hill that lay between him and the Rio Dulces Valley. Far down below him he could see the ranch buildings within their screen of dark greenery. A streamer of smoke rose high above the buildings in the windless air. There was a faint stirring and movement of the atmosphere as the heat of the day began to be dissipated by the cool of the evening.

He limped a little as he led the clay bank down the darkening slopes. He had gotten accustomed to the stench of the swollen, mutilated corpse, but it had cost him half the bottle of rye and two sacks of Dime Durham to do it. It was a helluva gift he was bringing back to the ranch. He remembered all too well, almost as though it was yesterday, seeing the older Ochoa, Diego by name, writhing and screaming in the bloody dust until a bullet in the gaping mouth had stopped his screaming forever. He had been a good man to ride the rio with, a boon companion and a fighter from whom had laid the chunk, but the Seven Rivers corrida had wiped the slate almost clean in their ambush, and Diego Ochoa had been one of those who had helped pay the butcher's bill. Somehow or another, Francisco seemed also to have died in the same cause, if one could call it that. To Ross, both killings had been senseless.

He tethered the clay bank to a rear fence, out of scent of the house. He limped through the darkness, cigarette hanging from his mouth.

"Stand where you are!" a hard voice said.

"It's Starkey," said another voice. It was Mac McArthur.

Ross shoved back his sweat-damp hat. "Where's the Kid?" he said.

"In the bunkhouse," said Mac.

"Tell him I want to see him."

The other man laughed. "You go see him, Starkey. I ain't about to tell him to come see you." He spat to one side. "He ain't feelin' too kindly toward you, anyways."

"The feeling is mutual, Nelson," said Ross dryly.

"Don't rile him," said Mac. "He's been like a boogered grizzly all day. Been looking for Francisco."

"I found him," said Ross.

"Where is he?"

"Go get the Kid," said Ross.

Charley Nelson walked to the bunkhouse and called inside. In a moment the broad shoulders of the Kid filled the lamp-lighted doorway of the bunkhouse. "That you, Ross?" he called out in a cold voice. "They say you found Francisco. Is he all right?"

"Come and see."

"Dammit! Don't play cute with me! Where is he?"

Ross turned on a heel and walked to the clay bank. He led the tired horse through a narrow gateway and then toward the three men.

"God's sake, Starkey," said Nelson. "You ought to change them drawers of yourn once in a while, anyways."

"That ain't Starkey," said Mac in a faraway voice. He looked sideways at the Kid.

Tascosa walked forward. "What the hell is this?" he said.

Ross took out his clasp knife and cut loose the lashings, heedless of the fine reata he was completely ruining. He forced himself to take the stiffened body from the horse and carry it toward the light streaming from the bunkhouse doorway. He placed it on the hard-packed earth and then looked at the Kid. "Take a look," he said in an expressionless voice.

Someone came through the darkness from the casa. "Who is it, Tascosa?" called out Sean Fitzgerald.

Tascosa stood looking down at the blanket-shrouded form.

"It's Ross Starkey, Mister Fitzgerald," said Nelson.

"I thought you had left," said Fitzgerald.

"I had to come back," said Ross.

Tascosa pulled back the blanket from the horrible head of the young New Mexican. "Jesus God!" he said. He slapped a hand over his mouth and nose and staggered backward.

"It's Francisco Ochoa," said Ross. "I found him near the east mouth of Boca Grande, just beyond your ranch line, Mister Fitzgerald." He looked at the rancher. "Somebody'd lashed him inside a green hide and left him under the sun a coupla days. The buzzards got to him before I found him..."

"Why? Why?" said Fitzgerald.

"Ask Tascosa," said Ross quietly.

Tascosa turned. "What the hell do you mean, Starkey?"

"You know as well as I do what some men do to rustlers, Kid. You haven't forgotten Print Olive, have you? Seems to me you said you had ridden for him once, or was that some more of your bullshit?"

"Don't you talk to me that way!"

"Somebody has to," said Ross. "It looks like it's up to me."

"Who's Print Olive?" said Fitzgerald in a puzzled tone.

"Toughest old boot in the Southwest," said Mac. "If he caught a man on his range, fooling with his cows, he'd kill the nearest cow and strip the hide from it, then lash the rustler into it, leaving him out in the sun. Sometimes they lasted a coupla days, but not often."

"I can't believe it!" said the rancher.

Ross turned. "Dammit!" he snapped. "You're looking at it!"

"Don't talk to Mister Fitzgerald like that!" warned the Kid.

Ross turned toward him. "You had them cows run off

from the Box HN," he said quietly. "But you wasn't there. You sent Francisco and some of the others to drive them cows back onto the Box HN to make Hardy Newcomb look like a damned fool. Well, you only think you done it. You ain't smart enough to beat Newcomb at his own game. He knew those cows had come back. He also knew what had happened to Francisco. You stood there in Hurley's office matching looks with Newcomb and acting like you was king of the manure pile. Well you was and you are, you shortsighted, conceited, lying sonofabitch!"

Tascosa dropped his hand to his Colt, but he was a mite too late, for once in his life. Ross hit him with a long, stabbing left and followed through with a right hook that sent the tall man reeling into Nelson and McArthur.

"Keep your hands from that gun!" snapped Fitzgerald to the Kid.

For one white-hot second Ross thought he was going to get a soft nosed .44/40 in his empty gut, and then the Kid shook his head to get the blood-glare out of his eyes. He slowly wiped the blood from his mouth and smiled over his hand at Ross. Then he unbuckled his gun belt and handed the finely tooled leather, heavy with the engraved Colt and bright brass cartridges, to Nelson.

Ross unbuckled his gun belt and dropped the gear on the hard ground, careless of the Colt. He raised his fists. The Kid came forward on cat feet, stabbing out with a long left, gauging Ross, and when he threw his right, it went clean over Ross' left forearm and hit just below his left eye, stinging like a nettle. The right struck his chin and rocked him backward. The Kid laughed, forcing the fight, throwing smooth punches that stabbed and rocked Ross like a perfectly timed pile driver. Then out of nowhere a right caught the Kid on the button and a left smashed into his lean gut, followed by a short right uppercut that drove him back against the bunkhouse wall. Something fell to the floor inside the building.

Ross took two stinging punches to get in between the Kid's flailing arms. He kept bouncing the Kid from the wall, meeting him with thudding blows, until the Kid squirmed free, gasping for air, dancing about, blowing blood from his handsome nose. He grinned through the blood and sweat, but Ross knew he had shaken the Kid.

"Time!" said Fitzgerald.

"Time, shit!" said Ross. He rushed the taller man.

They stood toe to toe, driving in unscientific punches, neither of them giving or taking an inch until Ross drove the Kid back.

"Stay away from him, Kid!" yelled Baldy the cook from the cookhouse. He ran out waving a skillet.

The Kid did stay away from Ross, bobbing and weaving, but in so doing, he couldn't quite get the range of the bloody-faced man who stalked him like a lobo wolf, taking soft punches to drive those rock-hard fists into gut and jaw, until the Kid went down hard, lying flat on his back looking up into Ross' bloody face with pure hell in his eyes.

"Enough," said the rancher.

"Enough, hell!" said the Kid. He got slowly to his feet but hadn't set himself when that damned drifter bored in again, smashing and slamming, ramming his head against the Kid's jaw while he hammered at the Kid's ribs. A lucky uppercut snapped Ross' head back and a knee in the crotch bent him forward. The Kid coupled his hands and smashed them down on the back of Ross' neck as he fell, Ross seeing the hard ground coming up to meet his battered face and unable to do a damned thing about it. The impact was even worse than he had expected.

The Kid booted Ross twice before he could roll free.

"Unfair! Unfair!" cried out the rancher.

Ross gripped one of Tascosa's kicking legs and set himself and came up on his feet, spraddle-legged, and upended the Kid against the rancher. The Kid cursed but a vicious boot took some of the fight out of him and a hard, hooked heel caught him on the side of the jaw. He tried twice to get up and then he lay flat, eyes glazed, dark blood leaking from his gasping mouth.

Ross wiped the blood from his face. He licked his abraded knuckles, looking down at the Kid with dullness in his eyes. The left eye was almost shut by now.

The Kid rolled over and heaved. He pushed his bloody hands against the ground and then fell heavily. The second try worked, and he came slowly to his feet, turning quickly with a double-barreled derringer in his right hand, the twin muzzles not three feet from Ross' gut. Ross felt his stomach draw tight, expectant of two soft nosed .41 slugs that would rip him wide open to the backbone. For a long, long moment the Kid stood there and then he slowly lowered the skimpy gun. He wiped the blood from his mouth with his free hand. "I guess I owed you that," he said.

"You won't bring that kid back," said Ross.

They stood there, face to face, and somehow Ross remembered another scene, fraught with emotion, not too many weeks ago, when Ross had lain on the ground, horseless, weak to the point of utter defeat, waiting for the Kid to kill him for his own benefit so that the Apaches would not get him. He remembered all too well that if Tascosa had not taken him out of that moonlit canyon of impending death he would not be facing the Kid now.

"Shake hands, men," said Fitzgerald.

They still stood there looking at each other, and then Tascosa turned and walked toward the cookhouse.

Ross picked up his gun belt and swung it about his lean waist with practiced ease. He looked at the rancher. "You'd better bury the kid," he said. "He won't keep in this weather." He limped toward the clay bank.

"Well, I'll be damned," said Charley Nelson.

Sean Fitzgerald walked to Ross. He placed a hand on

his shoulder. "Don't leave now," he said. "I want to talk with you."

Ross rested his head on the sweat-damp saddle. His bones seemed too soft and pliable to carry him on. His belly felt like mush.

"Just tonight," said the rancher.

Ross nodded. He had lost something again; something he could not name, but it was something he had found in a stinking cell in El Corralitos so many weeks past, and had followed all the way to the Rio Dulces, only to find it turn to ashes in his dry mouth.

CHAPTER TWELVE

The weather had stayed hot just long enough to help in the horrible death of Francisco Ochoa, but the very night of the day he was laid to rest a storm broke across the mountains. The Thunder People thudded their mad drums in the canyons and across the dark mountains, while eerie sheet lightning flickered bluish tongues of light across the black sky. A wind came up some time before the dawn and brought with it sheets of rain that swept the country with a liquid broom from the Pecos westward across the mountains to the Rio Grande in successive blinding sheets that filled the watercourses brim-full and then flowed over their banks.

In the watery light of dawn, under a lowering sky that seemed to pour forth an unlimited and endless stream of rain, the Rio Dulces swirled over its banks, flooding the bottoms, carrying on its roaring waters the carcasses of drowned cattle, coyotes, rabbits and the writhing bodies of half-drowned snakes, all intermingled with brush and tree trunks, while from beneath the roaring, silty waters came the rumbling of the rocks and stones being carried in the liquid grip of the powerful current, deeply scouring the bed of the river.

Just before noon a thoroughly drenched rider, mud-splashed from head to foot, brought the news that Hardy Newcomb's dam on the Little Bonita had broken during the night. It was a little late to help Fitzgerald's sawmill, for it had been moved to a fork of the Rio Dulces, but the rider also said that the sawmill had more than enough water to turn the heavy machinery, and that Buck Ellwood had sent word that he was ready to try out the new set-up and was only waiting for the ranch owner to come and see it.

Ross Starkey rode with the rancher. He wanted no part of the ranch, and less of Tascosa, but Fitzgerald was deeply worried, uncertain of himself, and seemed to want someone to talk with besides his ranch hands and his sister.

They rode through the dripping woods on the narrow road that followed the course of the Rio Dulces. Ross was hard put to see out of his left eye. He hadn't seen the Kid since the fight, but he was willing to bet the Kid didn't look any better than Ross did, and maybe worse.

"That was a close thing when the Kid drew on you," said the rancher. "I didn't know he carried a hideout gun, as you Americans call it."

Ross nodded. "Most of them do. It's a handy thing as a last resort."

"Do you carry one?"

"Used to. They took it away from me at El Corralitos. There have been a few times since then that I wished I still had it."

"I wonder what stopped him," mused Fitzgerald.

"You did."

"I didn't say a word."

"No, but you were there."

Fitzgerald turned in his saddle and looked directly at Ross. "You mean that if I hadn't been there, he would have killed you in cold blood?"

"Quién sabe? Anyways, it wasn't exactly cold blood."

"It's hard to believe."

Ross shifted in his saddle. "No man can make the Kid lose face. It's part of his very life, Mister Fitzgerald. No one can do it, and I mean absolutely no one, excepting maybe you. I wouldn't be too sure about that either."

"You're a strange pair. You seem to need each other for some unfathomable reason. Maybe because you're much alike and yet so much unlike each other."

"That's a plain statement," said Ross dryly. "Now tell me what it means."

Fitzgerald shrugged. "Opposites attract, it is said. Maybe that's why he likes me and will do almost anything for me."

"Where does that put me? Like you? That's the best one I've heard in a long time."

"You might have hit it on the head without knowing it, Ross. The Kid admires you for something. Something he lacks. It's pretty obvious why he likes me. He thinks of me as being the sort of gentleman he'd like to be, I suppose. Strangely enough, I admire him for his skill with weapons and horses and as a leader of men, and for his cool courage and his devil-may-care attitude."

"Bravo," said Ross. "Those are fine words for the best killer in Verde County, and maybe all New Mexico Territory."

Fitzgerald nodded. "I've written another letter to the new governor," he said. He looked at Ross. "I want someone to deliver it for me. Someone who can give the governor the additional information he needs on the situation here in Verde County."

"Like me?"

"Like you," agreed the rancher. "Will you do it?"

"Why me?"

Fitzgerald turned in his saddle and looked back through the dripping woods. "I know of no one else I can trust."

"What about Tascosa?"

The rancher shook his head. "The Kid has brought his own fight here to the Rio Dulces. I needed his help several years ago and without it I would have been driven from Verde County. It was peaceful for a time until Newcomb got his hackles up again. The Kid seemed to have been sent by a guardian angel to help me, but this time it is different. I want his help, and yet I am afraid to accept it."

"You've done that already," said Ross.

"Maybe I ought to get rid of him?"

Ross glanced sideways at Fitzgerald. "You going to tell him that?"

"I'm not afraid of him," said Fitzgerald.

"Maybe not, but I wouldn't ever take a bet, at high odds, which way the Kid was going to jump. They say love can easily turn to hate, and the dividing line ain't much."

"You talk like a philosopher."

Ross grinned. "I don't know whether that's a compliment or an insult. What the hell is a philosopher, anyways?"

"A lover of wisdom," said the rancher quietly.

"Bueno! I thought maybe it was one of them hombres that made up prescriptions in a drugstore."

The mill appeared through the trees, on a cleared area on the fork of the Rio Dulces, set high enough to be above flood waters, but with the overshot wheel set beneath a solid-looking masonry dam that was overflowing. The great wheel was practically spinning on its axis.

"Wonder that durned wheel don't go flying off," said Ross.

"Buck Ellwood knows his business," said the rancher. He looked at Ross. "Will you take the letter?"

Ross felt for the makings. He began to fashion a cigarette.

Fitzgerald moved closer to Ross. "If anything should

happen to me, Maureen would lose everything. I have to think of her now, not of myself. Would you do it for her?"

Ross lighted the cigarette. "Ain't nothing going to happen to you," he said.

"I have a premonition, Ross. There is information in that letter that can thoroughly incriminate Hardy Newcomb and Dan Hurley. It's only fair to warn you that they'd do anything to keep that information from reaching the hands of the governor."

"I had a feeling it wasn't just going to be a joyride," said Ross dryly.

"If anything happens to me, Maureen will give you the letter."

"Ain't nothing going to happen to you!" said Ross hotly.

They crossed the rude bridge. Water was flowing a foot deep over it, and they could feel it shaking in the grip of the current.

A slightly built man stood under the dripping eaves of the porch that had been in front of the mill door. He wore a faded blue caped army overcoat. He smiled when he saw the rancher. "I'm glad you came, sir," he said. "Can't do any work in this downpour but it's a good chance to run the machinery. I can make any final adjustments, and as soon as the roads dry out, we'll be cutting timber."

They dismounted. "This is Ross Starkey," said the rancher. "Ross, meet Buck Ellwood."

The millman thrust out a left hand. He smiled. "Sorry, I left my right arm at Chickamauga, Starkey," he said.

"Your left feels strong enough for two hands," said Ross.

"The loss of one makes the other compensate, or so they say. Me, I'd rather have two weak ones than one strong one, but the Lord didn't see fit to make it that way." There was nothing sanctimonious in the way he said it. It was simply the statement of a deeply religious man.

Ross led the horses to the shed behind the mill. The rain had finally stopped. Ross peeled off his slicker and hung it over his saddle. He walked back into the mill and listened to Ellwood as he explained the changes and adjustments he had made in the somewhat aging machinery. Sean Fitzgerald seemed to be fascinated by it. Ross listened for a time, then made himself comfortable in the back of the mill on some baled hay. Fitzgerald had a great future in the Valley of the Rio Dulces, if he could settle his war with Hardy Newcomb, but Newcomb was kingpin in that country. He had liked Fitzgerald's money, but as soon as he had realized that the Irishman might rise to a position of wealth and power in the county, he had set his sights on him to bring him down. There could be only one major figure in Verde County, and the position was already taken. There was no room for competitors or usurpers.

Ross had dozed off. Something made him open his eyes. The millman and the rancher were at the back of the mill, beneath some of the machinery. Ross could just hear their voices, but he could not make out any of the words. He yawned and rolled over. He felt for the makings and realized he had used up the last sack. He had a couple of sacks of Dime Durham in one of his saddlebags. He walked toward a side door and opened it. Suddenly he stopped. He heard voices again, but they weren't coming from within the mill. Ross stepped outside and stood against the wall beneath the porch roof that rounded the front of the mill and continued along the back to butt onto the shed. He peered around the corner. Half a dozen horses stood in a group and a slickered man stood there holding the reins, a wreath of cigarette smoke rising about his head.

Ross looked further along the bank of the fork. Five men stood beside the dam, their backs toward him, looking at the overflowing dam and the whirling wheel, talking and pointing to the dam and the wheel. Ross studied them. He couldn't tell who they were, but as far as he knew no "Shamrock" men were supposed to be around the mill. One of the men turned and looked at the mill and Ross felt a cold feeling in his gut. It was Art Cassidy. The tall man next to him must be Slim and beyond them, right at the edge of the racing flood, was Ben Miller.

Ross looked back over his shoulder. His Winchester was on his saddle, but to get into the shed he'd pass into view of the horse-holder. He looked back at the mill's side door. Fitzgerald didn't carry a gun and he had seen no belt gun on Ellwood, and with his one arm he could hardly be of much value with a rifle.

He saw one of the men place a blasting powder can beside the dam. He knew well enough what they planned. It would be mighty slick to blow the dam and to ruin the wheel, putting the blame on the storm and the high water. They had missed one thing: they evidently thought there was no one at the mill in this weather; both "Shamrock" horses were in the shed.

Ross had to take a chance. He stepped out toward the shed, turning in his stride, and as he did so he heard a cold, flat voice. "Where you goin', hombre?"

Ross turned. A broad-shouldered man had turned the corner of the mill and stood with leveled rifle, the muzzle two feet from Ross' shrinking gut.

"March," said the man.

Ross raised his hands, glancing once more at the mill. He knew well enough what would happen to him. They'd want no witnesses.

"Got a visitor, Cassidy!" said Ross' escort.

Cassidy turned as Ross approached. He grinned coldly. "Well, well," he said. "Lookit, Ben. We got company."

The look in Ben's eyes was like a blow across the face.

"I thought he left the county," he said in a low voice. "Broke my heart it did. I ain't forgot Santo Tomas."

"You alone?" said Cassidy.

Ross nodded. Cassidy picked Ross' Colt from its holster and looked at it. "Junk," he said. "I wouldn't poke a fire with this." He tossed it into the stream.

"Where's your hoss?" said Slim.

Ross jerked his head. "Back in the woods," he said.

"We can get it later," said Cassidy. "Sid, you ready with that powder?"

The man nodded. "I can place it here," he said, thrusting a hand into a gap between the masonry, just above the level of the water.

"What about the explosion?" said another man.

Cassidy spat into the stream. "The wind is blowing toward us," he said. "There's two ridges between us and the ranch buildings. Besides, they'll likely think it was thunder. It's been thundering off and on all this morning."

"What about him?" said Sid. He looked at Ross.

"Yeah," repeated Ben. "What about him?"

"I was pulling out," said Ross quickly. He wet his dry lips. "Look, fellas, I ain't in on this war. I was heading north out of this country."

"You was?" said Slim. He raised his eyebrows. "And here we thought you was nice and cozy with Fitz. What'd you do? Make a pass at his sister or steal some of his cows?"

"Like you stole from the Box HN," said Ben.

Ross knew his death sentence had been passed, although none of them had said so.

Sid looked up. "Go get some more powder cans," he said. "We might as well make a good job out'a this."

The front door of the mill swung open, and Sean Fitzgerald appeared. He walked toward the Box HN men. "What are you doing here on my property?" he said.

"He wants to know what we're doin' here," said Ben.

Cassidy looked sideways. "This makes a mess out'a the whole thing," he said. "Damn you, Walt! I told you to check that damned mill!"

Fitzgerald looked down at the powder can and then at the man who was bringing two more from the horses. His face went white. "You've gone quite far enough," he said. "I'll have you brought up on charges for this!"

Cassidy spat at the rancher's feet. "We ain't done nothing," he said.

Slim shoved back his hat. "This makes it awkward," he said.

"It's our word against his," said Ben.

Ross felt a little better. They would have killed him, for he was a nobody, a drifter who could vanish and be forgotten in a short time, but to kill Sean Fitzgerald would be quite another matter. This wasn't the kind of war Hardy Newcomb wanted, perhaps not out of any softness on his part, but rather because it was not good business.

The mill door banged open, and Buck Ellwood appeared, his overcoat cape thrown back and an old Spencer repeating carbine in his left hand. "Get away from that dam!" he commanded.

Cassidy stared at him. "Christ," he said. "How many more of 'em is in that damned mill?"

"It's that Bible-readin' Yankee," said Ben Miller.

Sid looked up at Cassidy and then down at the powder. "Dammit," he growled. "You want me to place this stuff or not? I'm gettin' nervous with all this fight talk goin' on."

"Put it where you want it," said Cassidy. "We got orders to blow the dam, didn't we?"

"You'll face charges," warned Fitzgerald.

Cassidy hesitated.

"Don't be afraid of that one-armed bastard," said Ben. "We can take care of him."

Sid placed the first of the powder cans in the cavity.

The Spencer cracked flatly and a soft nosed .56/56 slug caught Sid squarely in the head. He pitched sideways into the rushing stream without a sound.

The shot triggered swift action. The man with the horses grabbed for a scabbarded rifle on one of the saddles. Ross dropped flat on the ground. Buck Ellwood flung the Spencer upward, twisting it sideways, opening the lever, then banged his cheek against the stock to close it, all in a matter of seconds, like a juggler on a stage. He leveled and fired just as Walt, the man who had been guarding Ross, fired his rifle. Ellwood jerked spasmodically. Walt fell sideways, rolled over twice and lay still. Ross grabbed for the rifle, but Ben stomped on Ross' hand and kicked the side of his head as he drew his Colt with lightning speed and fired. Ellwood slammed back against the mill wall and reloaded.

Slim, who was guarding Fitzgerald, raised his Colt, but Ellwood ran forward and fired, staggering the tall man, then reloaded and fired again just as Ben drove two more slugs into the one-armed man. Ellwood reloaded even as he fell. He fired at the man who had been guarding the horse, just as the man fired at him. The Box HN hand smashed back against the nearest horse and went down on his knees, dropping his smoking rifle.

Ross rolled free of Ben and ran for the trees. A slug ripped through his left coat sleeve, and another tore the heel from his left boot. He staggered sideways, saving his life, for Cassidy slammed two rounds just where Ross had been standing. Ross whirled and plunged toward the river fork. He dived cleanly, half obscured by the swirling gun smoke, and gasped as he hit the cold water. He went down deep, then fought upward, striking his left hand against the cruel masonry of the dam. The water picked him up and dropped him over the dam into the roiling current below and he missed the iron-shod blades of the mill wheel by inches.

He looked up as the current swirled him toward the

far side of the river. A bullet spat water into his face. The last thing he saw was Ben Miller firing at Sean Fitzgerald who stood there with his hands up, and the slug smashing full into the rancher's pale face.

Ross went around a bend, fighting to keep his head out of the water, his boots and soaked clothing trying to drag him down. He clawed at a tree trunk that thrust itself into the water, missed it, went down deeply, then was flung halfway over another log. He gripped the slippery trunk and pulled himself ashore. He dropped in the thick mud of the bank, choking and gasping.

The rain slashed down suddenly, veiling the woods. A cold wind swept across the fork and shook the trees. There seemed to be more than just the coldness of the fall in the wind; it felt as though it had the coldness of death.

Ross pulled himself to his feet. He staggered through the woods, stopping every now and then to listen, but he heard nothing. He reached a water-logged trail and then heard several more shots. He waited awhile, then padded through the dripping woods with squelching boots. He peered across the fork toward the rain-soaked mill. There was no sign of life. The horses were gone and so were the Box HN men, the living and the dead.

Ross waded across the shaking bridge and walked through the streaming rain toward the mill. Buck Ellwood lay face downward in the mud, still holding the repeater with which he had done such execution. Ross picked it up and levered the next round into the rifle. It was the last round of the seven carried in the magazine. Six bright brass hulls lay scattered about the dead millman.

Sean Fitzgerald lay crumpled against the stone foundation of the mill, huddled closely against it as though he had sought protection. Ross limped over to him. His gut roiled as he saw the back of the skull, smashed by a slug. The gray tweed coat back was black with blood. Ross rolled the rancher over on his back. His left arm flung outward as though in a gesture of asking for mercy. It had been smashed at the elbow. The face was gone. More than one soft nosed .44/40 at close range had obliterated the man's features.

Ross turned away. The rain sluiced down, pattering on the mill, stippling the gray surface of the rushing stream, and soaking into the clothing of the two dead men. Ross looked at the mill. It was unharmed. The wheel still whirled at high speed, smoothly and efficiently, perfectly adjusted, the last handiwork of Buck Ellwood, who had loved the mill more than his own life.

CHAPTER THIRTEEN

Once again, a weary, limping man approached the ranch buildings on the Rio Dulces, this time leading two horses instead of one, and with two dead men instead of one. The sky was dark, almost like dusk, with rain slanting down from the lowering clouds. The roaring of the Rio Dulces filled the valley with low thunder.

Ross Starkey stopped within eyeshot of the big casa. She would be there in the great house, unaware of the gruesome burden Ross was bringing back from the mill.

Mac McArthur walked hurriedly from the barn, water streaming from his slicker. He stopped and looked at Ross, pushing back his slicker to get at his Colt. "That you, Starkey?" he called out.

Ross nodded. "Where is Miss Fitzgerald?" he called.

"In the casa with Tascosa. I saw her an hour ago. What's up?"

"Get another man," said Ross.

"Greener is here. I'll get him." Mac looked back over his shoulder as he walked to the bunkhouse.

The rain pattered steadily on the canvas-wrapped bodies. Ross mechanically rolled a cigarette and lighted it. He fanned out the match and blew a puff of smoke, watching the rain beat it downward.

Mac and Greener hurried through the rain toward Ross. "Who are they, Starkey?" said Greener.

Ross looked toward the house. "Keep your voice low," he warned. "It's Mister Fitzgerald and Buck Ellwood."

"Jesus God!" said Mac. "Wait until Tascosa hears this! Who done it, Ross?"

"Never mind. Help me get them under cover."

"The shed behind the bunkhouse will do," said Greener.

They led the horses behind the bunkhouse and unloaded the stiffened bodies. Greener began to unwrap Fitzgerald's body.

"Let be!" said Ross. "You don't want to look at it."

"Is it that bad?" said Mac.

Ross nodded. He blew smoke through his nose. He seemed far away.

"You all right, Starkey?" asked Greener.

"Yeah," said Ross.

"Who's going to tell her?" said Mac. He jerked his head toward the casa.

"A good question," said Ross.

"It'll have to be you," said Greener nervously. "I don't want to be around the Kid when he hears about it."

Ross flipped his cigarette out into the rain. "He don't matter," he said quietly. He walked out into the rain, slicker flapping wide open.

"He looks like he seen a ghost," said Greener.

McArthur looked at the two bodies. "Likely he seen worse."

Ross walked toward the big house. The smoke from the chimney beat downward, carrying the bittersweet odor of burning firewood. Winter was on the way. He knocked on the side door. Minutes passed before he heard movement inside the house. The door swung open and Tascosa stood there. "You," he said coldly.

"Where is she?" said Ross.

"I'll tell her what you want," said the Kid.

"You taking over now?" said Ross.

"Never mind."

"Who is it?" called Maureen.

Ross felt, rather than saw her, and when he did see her, she was more lovely than ever.

"You're soaked to the skin, Ross," she said. "Where is my brother?"

The words stuck in his throat.

"Ross?" she said.

Tascosa narrowed his eyes. "Answer the lady," he snapped.

She came closer to Ross. "What's wrong, Ross? You look so strange."

He passed a hand across his mouth. "It couldn't be helped," he blurted out.

"Is he hurt? Where is he?" she almost screamed.

Tascosa opened, then closed his mouth. He knew.

"He's dead, isn't he?" she said.

Tascosa pushed past Ross. He walked with stiff-legged strides toward the bunkhouse. Maureen tried to follow him, but Ross held her back. "No," he husked. "Not yet, anyways."

She pressed her head against his wet chest and sobbed softly.

Boots squelched in the mud. Ross turned. Tascosa was walking swiftly toward the house. "Who done it?" he called out.

Ross turned. "Take it easy," he said.

"I asked you a question! I want an answer, by God!"

"Wait," said Ross. "You can't settle this thing now. You never could. It was wrong from the start. It's out of your hands now."

"Who done it?" grated Tascosa.

Ross stared at him. The killing blood was up. "Let me go and tell Hurley," he said. "He can't cover this thing up. He doesn't dare. He'll have to do something about it."

"Who done it?" said Tascosa.

Ross wet his dry lips. The Kid would find out anyway. Maybe the thought of facing those bloody-handed Box HN hardcases would slow him down long enough for Ross to get to the law. "There were six of them," he said slowly. "Box HN men. Art Cassidy, Ben Miller, Slim Bellew, a man named Sid, another named Walt, and some other hombre whose name I don't know."

"Where are they now?"

"Sid, Walt and the other man are all dead, as far as I know. Slim Bellew was wounded. As far as I know Cassidy and Miller were untouched. They all took off."

"Who killed the three?"

"Buck Ellwood."

"Fitz never carried a gun. Where were you all this time?"

Ross shrugged. "I wasn't in any position to do anything about it but save my own life."

"That figures!" jeered Tascosa.

Ross was utterly sick of the whole business. The only thing that was of any importance to him now was the young woman who clung to him. He knew now she would always be the only thing that would ever matter to him, no matter what she thought of him.

Tascosa turned on a heel and strode toward the stables.

"Don't go, Tascosa!" cried Maureen. "They'll kill you, too!"

He paid no attention to her. In a few moments he was outside of the stable, leading his gray. He swung up into the saddle with a smash of leather and spurred the gray toward the gate. In a moment the rain and the swaying trees hid him from sight.

"There goes death on a gray horse," said Greener.

"It's not the way," said Ross. He helped Maureen

toward the house. "It's better that you do not see your brother, Maureen."

"You'll stay with me?" she half asked and half pleaded.

He wanted to. God, how he wanted to stay with her! "I'll have to go to Las Piedras," he said. "I'll have to tell Hurley."

"They'll kill you, too!"

He opened the door and helped her inside. "I'll have to chance that," he said. He closed the door and they stood in the dimness of the hallway, close together. Her body shook with sobs. She raised her tear-stained face to his. There was nothing he could say, and precious little he could do. He cupped her wet face in his lean, hard hands and gently kissed her. "Wait for me," he said. Then he was gone.

He helped himself to fresh clothing in the bunkhouse and took a six-gun from a spare holster, checking the loads. He helped himself to a bottle of aguardiente and then went to get his clay bank. He mounted and rode off in the rain, as Tascosa had done. No matter how hard he tried he did not seem to be able to shake the mud of Verde County from his boots. He was doomed to run out the string; to play to the last turn of a card.

The rain died out as he left the valley. The road was heavy with mud and the ditches were brim-full. A cold wind swept from the east and moved the heavy, lowering clouds toward the mountains, hiding their peaks in the thick, gray wool. It grew lighter for a time, but as Ross rode the adobe-lined road just outside of Las Piedras, it grew dark again, although the rain did not start up again.

No one bothered with the lone horseman who rode into the muddy placita, hat pulled low, and cigarette pasted in a corner of his thin mouth. He dismounted stiffly in front of the sheriff's office. Yellow lamplight shone in the store windows, reflected in the many puddles. A heavily laden ranch wagon ground through the ruts, the heavy hoofs of the horses splashing mud and water high into the damp air.

Ross unbuttoned his slicker and eased the Colt in his holster. Fat lot of good six rounds would do him in Las Piedras if the Newcomb corrida come looking for him. He opened the door of the sheriff's office and walked in. Dan Hurley looked up from his desk and his plump face went pale. "I thought you left Verde County," he said.

Ross shook his head. "There's been a double killing on the 'Shamrock'," he said quietly.

"Who was killed?"

"Sean Fitzgerald and Buck Ellwood."

Hurley narrowed his eyes and stood up. "Who did it?"

"Box HN men," said Ross.

"Do you know who they were?"

Ross nodded. "Art Cassidy, Slim Bellew, Ben Miller, and some others was mixed up in it, too. Man by the name of Sid, another by the name of Walt. I don't know who the other one was. As far as I know, Walt, Sid and the other man are dead. I think Slim was wounded."

"Who killed them?"

"Buck Ellwood."

Hurley stared in disbelief. "Him? I don't believe it! It must have been an ambush! You saw all this? You must have been mixed up in it."

Ross began to roll a cigarette. "I'm the only living witness." He grinned crookedly. "You'd better watch me well, Sheriff, because those three Box HN waddies won't want me to talk."

Hurley wiped the cold sweat from his round face. "Wait until Newcomb hears this. Gawdamighty! He didn't want anything like this. No! Never in a thousand years."

"Well, he's got it," said Ross dryly. "God, how he's got it!" He lighted the cigarette. "Another thing: the Tascosa Kid knows about the killings. He's out looking for Cassidy, Bellew and Miller right now. Maybe here."

Hurley jammed on his hat. He jerked his slicker from a hook. "I'll have to get Newcomb," he said.

Ross stood in the way. "Why?" he said. "This is your job. You can't stay in office forever always taking orders from him. This is bigger than Hardy Newcomb now, Hurley. You either settle this on your own, or you won't be wearing that star long, and maybe you'll end up in the Territorial Prison."

"They've got nothing on me," blustered the lawman.

"No?" said Ross quietly.

Hurley read something in Ross' eyes that he did not like. This battered, slow-spoken drifter knew something; something that boded no good for Dan Hurley. "You'd better come with me," he said. "You won't be bothered as long as you're with me."

"Can I count on that?"

There was a different air about the officer. "Yes," he said decisively. "You're right, Starkey. This is my job, and by God, I'm going to handle it myself!"

"Bueno," said Ross dryly.

They walked out into the muddy street. "Newcomb is at the hotel," said the sheriff. "I'd better warn him anyway. Don't worry, Starkey. I'll see to it that no trouble starts here."

A tall man rounded the corner, running awkwardly through the mud, looking back over his shoulder, his right arm in a sling. "No!" he yelled. He saw Hurley. "For Christ's sake, Hurley! Help me! It's the Kid! He's goin' to kill me!" It was Slim Bellew.

The Kid walked swiftly around the corner, slickerless, his lean hands hanging by his sides, the right fingertips brushing the low-slung, tied-down holster.

"Stand back!" yelled Hurley.

Ross slammed a shoulder against Hurley, driving him back just as Tascosa drew and fired. Slim spun about and staggered sideways. Two more slugs rapped into him, and he was flung backward by the impact of the soft, heavy slugs. He splashed into the mud.

Boots thudded on a wet boardwalk and spurs chimed as a broad-shouldered man ran toward Tascosa. "He got Slim, Ben!" he yelled.

"Stay out of this, Cassidy!" yelled Hurley.

Cassidy drew and fired, and Tascosa's shot was like an echo. Cassidy went down on his knees. He looked at the Kid. "No more," he pleaded, then he fell face forward in the mud.

Ben Miller came from between two buildings. He looked at the two Box HN men in the street and then at Tascosa. He walked toward him. Doors burst open up and down the street. Boots thudded on boardwalks or squelched in the pasty whitish mud. Ben Miller stepped over the sprawled body of Slim. "You ain't dealin' with them two now," he said.

Tascosa slid his smoking gun into its sheath. "No?" he said softly. "Who am I dealin' with?"

"Ben Miller!" rasped the Box HN man. He slapped his hand down for a draw. Tascosa's slug hit the short man in the chest. He turned about and then fired again, driving forward, firing his Colt. Tascosa fired his last round. Ben jerked with the impact. He fired once more, went down on his knees and emptied his gun into the mud, game to the last.

Tascosa ran forward and picked up Cassidy's muddy six-gun. "Stand back!" he cried out.

Hurley's face was fish-belly white. "Wait, Kid," he said. "Throw down that gun! This is the law talking!"

"Law, shit," said the Kid coldly. "Where's Newcomb?"

"Put down that gun," said Hurley. He walked forward. Ten feet from the Kid he dropped his outstretched hand to his side and in so doing, he signed his death sentence. Tascosa fired from hip level. Hurley fell sideways and then doubled over.

Ross looked at the Kid's face through the smoke. It

didn't seem real, as though it was made of two halves that didn't quite fit together; almost as though one side was moving up while the other was moving down, and the eyes did not blink. "Where's Newcomb?" said the Kid in a strange voice.

"You'd better beat it, Kid!" yelled a man from the crowd.

The Kid still stared at Ross, Colt at hip level, a thin wisp of smoke rising from the hot muzzle, and if Ross Starkey had ever looked at death, he was looking at it now.

Slowly, ever so slowly, the Kid backed away, swinging the Colt from side to side, until he reached the corner, and then he darted around it.

"Go get him!" yelled Hardy Newcomb from the back of the crowd as he began to force his way through.

"Go get him yourself, Newcomb!" yelled someone. "You started all this!"

"Who said that?" roared the rancher.

Ross leaned against an awning post. He slowly began to fashion a cigarette. He heard the thudding of hoofs in a side street, and it seemed far, far away.

Newcomb looked at Ross. "What did you have to do with this, Starkey?" he demanded.

Ross looked at him as he lighted the cigarette. "Nothing," he said quietly. "But I aim to have something to do about it."

"Such as?"

Ross blew a smoke ring. "Wait and see," he said. He walked to his horse and untethered it.

Newcomb came up behind him. "Why did he come to Las Piedras?" he said.

Ross turned. "Your boys killed Fitzgerald and Buck Ellwood at the mill," he said.

"You're lyin'!"

Ross looked past the tough old boot into the cold faces of half a dozen Newcomb hardcases. "No, I ain't," he said. "I come into town to tell Hurley. For once Hurley was going to handle the law without your advice."

"You can't talk to me like that!" snapped Newcomb.

"Oh, yes I can," said Ross. "I'm doing just that. The Kid must'a gone loco. He come looking for them three, and you, too. Lucky you was out of sight. Dan Hurley's luck run out."

Newcomb narrowed his hard eyes. A look of respect came into them. "My men killed Fitzgerald and Ellwood?" he asked.

Ross nodded.

"I had nothin' to do with it."

"You sent them to blow the mill dam, didn't you?"

Newcomb hesitated. He looked back at the silent crowd.

"You don't have to say anything," said Ross.

"There was to be no shootin'!"

"No? Well, damn you, you started that avalanche, and you couldn't stop it. By God, Newcomb, you're going to reap the storm that's going to hit this damned bloody county!" Ross swung up on the clay bank and rode toward the street that led to the Rio Dulces Road.

"Where are you goin'?" called out Newcomb.

Ross turned in the saddle. "To deliver a letter," he said. He turned and rode on. The rain began to fall steadily, pocking the churned mud, streaming from the roof eaves, slowly washing the blood from the faces of the stiffening dead.

CHAPTER FOURTEEN

Ross Starkey tethered his horse outside of his brother's house in Santa Fe. It had been a fine fall day on the ride up from Galisteo, but with the coming of the swift dusk had come a cold wind that swept down from the Sangre de Cristos, blowing dust and fallen leaves through the narrow, winding streets, rattling and banging the shutters, moaning across the flat-topped roofs of the ancient city.

He walked to the door and dropped the heavy knocker several times. It had been a long and lonely ride up from Las Piedras, with plenty of time for thought.

"Quién es?" called a feminine voice from beyond the door.

"It is Señor Ross Starkey," he said in Spanish, "brother to Señor Starkey."

"Wait one moment," she said.

In a little while, chains rattled, and the door swung open. Lloyd Starkey stood there in the yellow lamplight, a warm smile on his face. His hair and mustache had grayed and there were more lines on his face, but his eyes were still young. "The Prodigal Son," said Lloyd. "I was just thinking about you today."

"Nice thoughts?" said Ross.

"Why not?"

Ross grinned. "I'm relieved," he said.

"Come on in!"

Ross jerked his head. "My horse is out there."

"Manuel will get him," said Lloyd. He led the way into the big casa.

Ross looked about as they crossed a wide patio, complete with shade trees and a fountain. Lloyd was doing well for himself.

Lloyd looked back. "The house comes with the job," he said.

"Such as?"

Lloyd opened a door and ushered Ross into a sitting room. "Legal aide to the new governor," he said.

"You're getting up in the world."

"I'm doing the best I can. Sit down. Warm yourself. Have you eaten?"

"Not since leaving Galisteo this morning."

"Galisteo? You've come a long way from the Rio Dulces."

Ross listened to his brother give orders to his woman servant. He looked about the low-ceilinged room. The firelight and lamplight glistened from the heavy, waxed furniture and the paintings on the walls.

Lloyd walked to a sideboard. "Wine before dining?" he said.

"Any time," said Ross. "Before, during and after."

"You haven't changed much."

"How did you know I came from the Rio Dulces?"

Lloyd placed the wine glass on the table beside Ross and then sat down opposite him, studying him with appraising gray eyes. "We have been interested in Verde County for quite some time," he said. He sipped at his wine. "We knew when you arrived there. We knew about your fight in Santo Tomas. We knew about the horrible killing of Francisco Ochoa. We've been investigating this so-called 'Verde County war', and we don't like it. The new governor has given me carte blanche to clean it up in any way I see fit."

Ross nodded. He felt inside his shabby coat and withdrew the thick, sealed envelope Maureen Fitzgerald had given him. "Do you know the latest from Verde County?"

"We had information some days ago."

"About the latest killings?"

Lloyd narrowed his eyes. "The last we had heard was about the man named Ochoa."

Ross emptied his glass. "Drink up," he said. "Refill the glasses. You're going to need it."

Lloyd listened silently while Ross filled in the bloody details he had witnessed during the killings at the mill and in the muddy placita of Las Piedras. The woman came in silently and placed the food on the table and refilled the wineglasses. The fire crackled as she placed fresh wood on it and then she left as silently as she had come, and all the time Ross spoke in a low voice, missing no details.

Lloyd emptied his glass and stood up. He paced back and forth while Ross ate, a cigar clenched between his teeth, leaving a trail of bluish smoke behind him as he read the long letter written by Sean Fitzgerald. He finished it as Ross finished his meal. Ross refilled his wineglass, eased off his boots and lighted a cigar. He felt somewhat pleased with himself. He had escaped the blood bath of Verde County.

Lloyd stood by the fire, looking into the flickering flames. "Who will succeed Dan Hurley as sheriff?" he asked.

Ross shrugged. "He's got a deputy. Fella by the name of Grant Orris, or something like that. Not much more than a process server, they say. Anyway, Hardy Newcomb will have his say-so on who takes over."

"Not anymore," said Lloyd firmly.

"Do you know him?"

"We've met," said Lloyd grimly. "When the Territorial

Legislation was in session last year. He bulled through half a dozen bills of his own, without ever opening his mouth in the Legislature."

"That's him," said Ross dryly.

"The new governor has written to him. Hardy Newcomb may have met his match in the governor. The governor's orders are to clean up Verde County."

"Good luck," said Ross. He blew a cloud of smoke toward the nearest lamp and watched the smoke swirl upward.

"This Tascosa Kid—he must have left the county by now?"

"Quién sabe?"

Lloyd nodded. "I'll know in a few days. Meanwhile I'll talk to the governor. What are your plans?"

Ross rubbed his bristly jaw. He looked up at his brother. "I need something from you to work them out."

"Such as?" Lloyd studied his younger brother. "By God, there's something different about you! Maybe you want to study law? You can clerk for me. You're sharp enough to catch on. A little hard work and a burning of the midnight oil, and you can pass the bar examination. I can use a partner."

Ross shook his head. "It's not that, Lloyd. Thanks anyway."

Lloyd relighted his cigar. "It's the old ranch, isn't it?"

"You've hit on it."

"It's yours. You can pay off my share when you get around to it." Lloyd fanned out the match. He tilted his head to one side. "There's something else, isn't there?"

Ross grinned. "I never could lie to you."

Lloyd stared at him. "A woman? By God, I mean a lady? With you?"

Ross looked into the fireplace. "I know it's hard to believe," he said awkwardly.

"Who is she, Ross?"

Ross looked up. "Maureen Fitzgerald," he said.

Lloyd worked his cigar over to the other side of his mouth. "You always were full of surprises. Have you asked her yet? I've heard she is a beauty."

Ross blew a smoke ring. "No, to your question. Yes, to your statement. Of course, I ain't sure she'd marry an old warhorse like me, but I aim to ask her as soon as I get back there."

Lloyd grinned. "Old warhorse? Hell, you won't be thirty for another year and a half! She couldn't find herself a better man, providing he gets some sense in his thick head and sticks to ranching on the Canadian."

"I aim to," said Ross.

Lloyd looked serious. "Is she all right, now that her brother is gone?"

Ross looked up quickly. "No man in Verde County would be loco enough to bother her," he said.

Lloyd nodded. "Not with the Tascosa Kid riding guard on her." He was startled at the look on Ross' lean face. "Did I say something wrong?"

Ross flipped his cigarette butt into the fireplace. "No," he said. "You didn't know. The Kid and I met in Mexico some time ago. I won't say how, or why. We were amigos until a little while ago."

"What happened?"

Ross rolled a cigarette and lighted it. He looked at his brother over the flare of the match. "If I go back, he'll likely try to kill me."

"Then don't go back."

Ross stood up and walked to the fireplace. He looked into the dancing flames. "I got no choice, Lloyd," he said quietly. "I got to go back."

In the days that followed Ross Starkey's arrival in Santa Fe, news drifted up from Verde County that the Tascosa Kid had killed another Box HN man and had escaped into the hills. There was more; something that had an ominous ring to it. The Spanish-speaking New Mexicans of Verde County, those of the old stock, were, for the most part, deeply sympathetic to the Kid. They were hiding him, protecting him, making a hero out of him. The Robin Hood of Verde County. Of such is legend made.

Lloyd asked Ross to come with him for an interview with the new governor. There was a curious feeling of foreboding in Ross when he met the Territorial chief executive, a straight-backed, level-eyed, bearded ex-soldier of the Civil War. Ross was almost convinced during the preliminaries of conversation that Hardy Newcomb might indeed have met his match.

"The Tascosa Kid is still on the loose," said the governor as he shoved a cigar box across his desk toward the two brothers. "Still in Verde County. Still as elusive as a ghost. He can't be caught by ordinary means. The Box HN men won't go into the hills after him. The other ranchers want no part of him, and he doesn't bother them anyway. The Spanish-speaking New Mexicans look up to him as a sort of hero. As long as they do so, he is safe from being arrested."

Ross lighted his cigar. "He's only one man," he said quietly.

Lloyd and the governor exchanged glances. Lloyd leaned toward his brother. "There isn't any law-abiding American in Verde County who doesn't want to see the Kid brought in to justice. We agree there was provocation for the Kid in the first part, but not to the bloody extent that he has taken his revenge. He has many friends. It will be difficult to capture him. But we must get him, or the Verde County war will not end! The governor is prepared to go easy on him if he agrees to give himself up. Perhaps a long jail sentence. Certainly not the death penalty."

Ross blew a smoke ring. "A jail sentence would be worse than the death penalty for the Kid," he said quietly. "You don't know him like I do."

There was a moment's silence. The governor suddenly

became deeply interested in the end of his cigar. "Exactly," he said. "Apparently there isn't anyone who knows him as well as you do."

Ross slowly took his cigar from his mouth. He looked at his brother. "What's on your mind, Lloyd? You didn't bring me here for a social visit with the governor."

Lloyd stood up and paced back and forth. "The governor is prepared to pardon the Kid, with the stipulation that he must serve a term in the Territorial Prison. The problem we have is in contacting the Kid. Someone whom the Kid trusts will have to find him and deliver the governor's message."

Ross got the idea. "Like me," he said dryly.

"I can commission you as a special officer of the Territory of New Mexico," said the governor.

"That won't cut any ice with the Kid," said Ross. "By this time, he has no more use for me than he does for the Box HN men."

"Would he believe you if you offered him the governor's amnesty?" said Lloyd.

"If I was covered by a company of cavalry and a Gatling gun," said Ross. "He'll never let me get within pistol range."

"We haven't anyone else to do the job," said the governor.

Ross blew a smoke ring and watched it drift slowly toward an open window. "I ain't too popular with Hardy Newcomb down Verde County way," he said.

"I have telegraphed to him," said the governor. "I have his assurance by return wire he will not interfere with you."

"I'd rather trust a diamondback," said Ross. He looked into the governor's eyes and knew right then and there that Hardy Newcomb had at last met his match.

"What about it, Ross?" said Lloyd. "You have to go back there anyway. You must consider the position of Maureen Fitzgerald."

Ross quickly looked at him. "What do you mean?"

"We have information by telegraph that the Kid has taken it on himself to 'protect' her, with the result that she lives virtually alone on the Rio Dulces ranch. Any trespassers, innocent or not, have to deal with the Kid. It's said she is deathly afraid of him. It's also said he won't harm her. But she's like a princess guarded by a two-headed ogre or a ferocious dragon."

"Two-gun," the governor said.

Ross slowly snubbed out the cigar. "Write out the commission," he said quietly. "I always knew I'd have to face the Kid again someday."

The governor quickly opened a drawer and withdrew a legal-looking paper, stamped with the Territorial seal. He signed it swiftly. "Stand up and raise your right hand," he said.

Ross grinned wryly. "Well, I'll be double-damned," he said. Later, with the governor's final instructions still ringing in his ears, Ross walked across the plaza toward La Fonda with his brother. "This might easily be my death sentence," said Ross. He looked at his brother. "But, like I said back there, I always knew I'd have to face the Kid again someday. One way or another I'll have to face him. My life seems bound up with that of the Kid —win, lose or draw." "Do you think you can get him?"

Ross stopped in mid-stride. "What do you mean by that?" Lloyd shrugged. "You don't have to bring him in alive," he said. "That commission covers you all the way, Ross. All the way..."

"Like a hunting license, eh?"

"Exactly."

Ross began to fashion a smoke. He looked up at the blue, cloud-dotted sky and inhaled the fresh, winey air. "Suddenly I feel cold all over," he said.

"You're doing a service to the Territory, Ross. To Maureen Fitzgerald. To all men."

Ross lighted the cigarette. "It ain't that easy," he said.

"I've hunted men and I've been hunted by men. This feels different somehow. I ain't sure that I'm going to like it at all."

"You won't do it then?"

There was a pause, then Ross looked directly into his brother's eyes, and Lloyd Starkey knew then and there he was no longer looking at a "kid" brother, but rather at a fully grown man, skilled with weapons, equally dangerous on either side of the law. "I didn't say that," said Ross at last.

"Come on. I owe you one drink at least."

Ross shook his head. "The day is young. The road is long. I'd better be on my way."

Lloyd thrust out his hand. "The ranch will be waiting for you and your bride," he said heartily.

Ross nodded. "Yes," he said in a faraway voice. He turned on a heel and walked away, followed by the thoughtful eyes of his older brother.

In an hour he was on the Galisteo Road, south of Santa Fe, riding steadily toward Verde County and his destiny, as well as that of the Tascosa Kid.

CHAPTER FIFTEEN

T he wind had shifted during the long sunny afternoon, and as Ross Starkey threaded a narrow, high-walled pass west of the Rio Dulces, he heard the faint, intermittent ringing of a bell from the high country to his left. He shifted in his saddle and looked up at the broken-toothed peaks, still tipped with the bright light of the sinking sun. The bell had stopped, or had he heard a bell at all? No one lived up there, or at least no one had lived up there to his knowledge. It was a trick of the wind, or perhaps of his imagination.

The clay bank's hoofs struck chiming music from the rocky bed of the pass and echoed from the high walls. The wind moaned softly from the east. He cleared the mouth of the pass and drew rein to look down upon the vast panorama of the Rio Dulces country. He could see the oases made by men on the open land. Where there was water, there would be a house, and around the house would rise the waving greenery that protected it from the hot suns of the summer and the cold, thin winter air of those altitudes. Rising above the waving trees were thin wraiths of wispy, bluish smoke. Far across the rolling stretches of the lower ground he could see dust rising beyond a ridge. That would likely be on the road to Las Piedras.

He looked to the south, expecting to see the rooftop of the great casa of the "Shamrock" spread, but couldn't distinguish it at that distance. No smoke arose from it. He touched the tired clay bank with his heels and rode down the twisting road, and as he did so he heard again the faint, insistent ringing of a bell. He turned again in his saddle and looked up at the higher country. No one lived up there, or at least there would be no church or chapel up there. He had heard vague stories of a lost village in this country, but the Mexes were always thinking up such stories. It was a trick of the wind, and yet he was sure he had heard something.

The sun was gone when he reached the Rio Dulces Valley. It grew colder after the warm day. He buttoned up his coat and rolled a cigarette. The wind moaned along the darkened valley. He looked toward the higher ground west of the river, expecting to see the lights of the Fitzgerald casa, but they were not to be seen.

He crossed the rushing river on the old bridge and looked toward the thick motte where Tascosa had always posted a rifleman. Ross whistled sharply, three times and then twice, but he heard nothing but the faint echoing of the signal. Maybe it had been changed by the "Shamrock" corrida.

He rode gingerly toward the motte, but there was no one there. The gate creaked loudly as he opened it, but the noise brought no response, no sharp challenge from the darkness, coupled with the sound of a rifle lever being worked. No dog barked. No lights showed. He swung down from the clay bank and drew his rifle from its scabbard. He ground out the cigarette beneath a boot and padded quietly toward the ranch buildings, the horse's reins looped about his left arm.

He halted between the big bunkhouse and the casa. Still no lights and no sound. He dropped the reins of the clay bank and walked toward the bunkhouse. He tried the door and it swung open easily. Ross walked inside and snapped a match on a thumbnail. The faint, flickering light showed that the place was empty of life. The bunks were stripped. Dust rose about his feet as he walked from one end of the echoing building to the other. The foreman's room was empty. A broken rye bottle lay in a corner.

Ross walked outside and checked the cookhouse. The stove had long been cold and the mess table in the dining room was thick with dust and the tiny tracks of mice.

He walked outside and looked toward the great casa. Not a light showed. He walked toward it, looking back toward the corrals. They, too, were empty. The place was like a ghost ranch. He called out as he reached the house but there was no answer. He tried two doors and found them locked. A weak window lock allowed him to enter the big kitchen. He rooted about and found a bullseye lantern which he lighted.

In twenty minutes, he had covered the house from kitchen up to the topmost rooms, and not a sign of life did he find, except a bright-eyed mouse that vanished beneath a bed as he entered one of the dusty rooms. No one had been in the casa for weeks, from the evidence.

He walked downstairs and into the dark study. He lighted a lamp and looked about. The place was undisturbed. He helped himself to a stiff drink from the sideboard and sat down in a chair. Where were Maureen Fitzgerald and her employees? The curious thing about the whole mystery was that the place was undisturbed. There had been no vandalism and no looting. News traveled fast in that country and if some of the people had learned that the great rancho and its hacienda on the Rio Dulces had been deserted, it would have been stripped of anything of value in a few days.

Ross poked about and found a half-empty box of cigars. He bit the end off one and lighted it. It was dry but satisfying. Maybe she had left the country and gone back to her people in Ireland or had moved into one of the towns nearby. There was one thing that stuck in his mind. Something his brother Lloyd had said. "The Kid has taken it on himself to *'protect'* her, with the result that she lives virtually alone on the Rio Dulces ranch. Any trespassers, innocent or not, have to deal with the Kid. It's said that she's deathly afraid of him. Oh, he won't harm her. Not the way one might think. But it's like she's living in isolation, like a princess guarded by a ferocious dragon or a two-headed ogre."

Ross looked about at the gathering dust. The fireplace had long been cold. Suddenly he had an eerie feeling that he was being watched. He looked quickly about, then laughed. The place was getting on his nerves. He slid a full bottle into each pocket and put out the lamp. He had no desire to stay the night anywhere near the place, and he had to know where Maureen was, and then try to get a line on Tascosa.

He walked through the echoing hall and into the kitchen. He blew out the bullseye lamp and placed it on the table. He looked back along the dark hallway, shivered again, then walked outside into the faint moonlight. The whole damned place gave him the creeps. He felt for one of the bottles, pulled out the cork and raised it to his lips. Something flashed amidst the shrubbery beyond the walled yard and a gun crack followed at the instant the rye bottle was shattered at Ross' lips, spraying his face with broken glass and good rye. Half blinded, he threw the bottle neck aside and dropped flat on the flags, feeling for his Colt.

It was very quiet after the echo of the shot died away. Ross slowly wiped the blood and whiskey from his burning face.

"What are you doing here, Starkey?" said the cold voice from the shrubbery.

"Kid?" said Ross.

There was no answer, nothing but the faint sound of the shrubbery moving in the night wind. Ross shifted and the broken glass tinkled beneath him. He eased out his Colt.

The voice came from the right beyond the wall. "I can see every move you make, Starkey," said the Kid.

Ross felt cold sweat break out on his body. The bastard moved like a ghost!

"It's a good thing for you I recognized you," said the Kid.

"Why?" said Ross dryly. "We didn't part amigos."

"I haven't forgotten El Corralitos. You saved my life there. I don't forget things like that."

Ross wiped away a sticky trickle of blood from his cheek. "Where is Miss Maureen?" he asked.

"What's it to you?"

"I've got a message for her."

"You can give it to me."

"Where is she?"

There was a long pause and when the Kid spoke again it was from a different spot, and yet Ross hadn't seen or heard a thing. Only an Apache could move like that. "Give me the message," said the Kid.

"I have to deliver it personally."

"Who is it from?"

Ross took a long chance. "The governor," he said.

The Kid laughed.

"You think I'm lying?" said Ross.

"You're too stupid to lie well."

"Gracias."

"I thought you went back to see Consuelo Orcutt," said the Kid. "Where have you been all this time?"

Ross spat. "Listen," he said. "The governor is out to get you, one way or another, Kid. I was sent down here to talk with you. I didn't think it would be this easy to find you."

"I found you," said the Kid. "Looting."

"For God's sake listen to me! The governor has had enough of this damned Verde County feud! He knows everything that is happening down here. My brother is his legal aide. Between the two of them they commissioned me to talk with you."

"They must be hard up for help."

"That's neither here nor there!"

"What's the deal?" said the Kid.

"You'll get a pardon."

"What's the price?"

Ross hesitated.

"There is a price, isn't there?" said the Kid. His voice came from another place, almost as though he was throwing it where he willed. An eerie feeling came over Ross. If he could only see the Kid!

"Well?" said the Kid.

"A prison term," said Ross at last.

The Kid laughed. "Big deal! Let 'em come and get me!"

"They will," said Ross. "The whole county is against you and the governor means to get you. If you don't listen to me, and take the governor's proposition, the ranchers will hunt you down. Hardy Newcomb alone can do it with his corrida."

The Kid laughed again. "Hardy Newcomb!" he jeered. "He won't ever bother Miss Maureen or me again."

Ross narrowed his eyes. He couldn't even see a thickening of the shadows where the Kid stood. "Did you kill him, too?" asked Ross.

"No. Something worse for Hardy Newcomb."

"Such as?"

"Go and see. It's worth the ride to Las Piedras." The Kid laughed. "Take the other bottle with you. Compliments of the house. Hardy Newcomb could do with a drink."

Ross peered into the shadows. "Kid?" he said.

There was no answer. The wind swayed the brush.

Minutes dragged past and Ross got slowly to his feet, half expecting another bullet. He wiped his face with his scarf and took out the second bottle. This time he got his drink. He drove the cork in with the heel of his hand and walked to the wall. The moonlight was sufficient for him to see that the shrubbery was not occupied. He dropped over the wall and looked about. There wasn't a mark on the soft earth. Not a boot print. An eerie feeling came over him again.

He walked to the clay bank and sheathed his rifle. Once more he looked about. The place was thoroughly deserted.

He rode toward the bridge. The moonlight showed on the cleared area where the ranch graveyard was situated on a rise overlooking the river bottoms. Each headboard and gravestone stood out. He kneed the clay bank close to the wall to look at the mounded graves. All of them were empty of flowers except the freshest grave, set off by itself on slightly higher ground. The moonlight shone on the carved headstone. It was the grave of Sean Fitzgerald, and those fall flowers had been put there that very day, perhaps that very night.

Ross crossed the bridge, the hairs prickling on the back of his neck, not daring to look back for fear of seeing a ghostly horseman on a gray horse following him through the patches of moonlight and the dark stretches of shadows.

CHAPTER SIXTEEN

The desk clerk looked up as Ross Starkey opened the front door of the Las Piedras House. He frowned a little as he saw the dusty, lean-looking man wearing a faded hat. Ross crossed the carpeted lobby, ignoring the looks of the people seated about the lobby. His spurs chimed softly until he stopped in front of the desk. "I want to see Hardy Newcomb," he said.

"Mister Newcomb?" said the clerk. He moved back a little as though to avoid the faint mingled aromas of sweat, trail dust, horseflesh, stale tobacco smoke and pungent rye.

"That's him," said Ross.

"Have you an appointment?"

Ross smiled faintly. "In a way," he said.

"He isn't receiving visitors tonight."

Ross looked past the clerk to the pigeonholes. One of them had a neatly lettered script above it. "Room four," said Ross. He walked toward the carpeted stairs.

"You can't just go up there like that!" cried the clerk.

Ross kept on climbing the wide staircase.

"Besides, it's not a room, it's a suite!" said the clerk.

Ross tapped on the suite door. It swung open and a

professional-looking man stood there, a leather case under his arm and his hat in his hand. "Yes?" he said.

"My name is Starkey," said Ross. "Ross Starkey. I want to see Hardy Newcomb."

"I'm Doctor Daily. I don't think Mister Newcomb is receiving visitors."

"Who is it, Doc?" cried out a familiar voice.

"A man named Ross Starkey," said the doctor over his shoulder.

There was a long pause. "Let him in, Doc," said Newcomb.

"I don't want him here too long," said the doctor. "A few minutes," said Ross. "What's the matter with the old man?"

Daily stood aside. "See for yourself," he said. He walked past Ross and closed the door behind him.

Ross took off his hat, glanced down at his holstered Colt, then walked into the sitting room. A white head showed above the back of a wing chair standing in front of a window that gave a clear view of the distant mountains to the west, dreaming under the soft light of the fall moon.

"Come around this way," said the rancher. "You're safe, Starkey."

"I wasn't worried," said Ross.

"The hell you ain't!"

Ross grinned. Whatever else was the matter with the old bastard, he still had his teeth.

He walked around the chair and looked down at the old man and a shock came through him. Just weeks ago, Hardy Newcomb had been as tough-looking as an old boot, but he had aged and there was a physical weakness showing on his lined face.

The rancher waved a thin hand. "Set," he said. "I look like hell. You don't have to say it."

"I wasn't going to."

Newcomb shifted a little, wincing in sudden pain. His

legs were swathed in a thick blanket from the waist down. "I heard from the governor," he said. "You took your time gettin' here."

"I didn't know I was supposed to report to you."

Newcomb shrugged. "It wasn't that. I wanted to warn you about the Kid. He's gone loco in my opinion." He looked down at his legs. "He made me pay a price."

"What do you mean?"

"Drygulched me when I went over to the Rio Dulces, my pride in my hand, to see what I could do for Miss Maureen. I never got beyond the bridge, Starkey. Another half an inch and the bullet would have cut my spine in half. The bullet is still in there." He wiped cold sweat from his forehead. "I'll never walk again. Damn me if I don't believe he did it on purpose."

Ross felt for the makings. "I saw him tonight, or at least I heard him tonight."

"You talk in riddles."

Ross told him of his experience at the casa.

Newcomb nodded. "It's his style," he said quietly. "The Mexes are startin' to call him El Espectro." He laughed. "Maybe it's what he always wanted."

"Where is Maureen Fitzgerald?"

Newcomb shrugged. "Quién sabe? No one can get near the ranch. All the hands pulled out weeks ago. The 'Shamrock' corrida is gone. They won't be back."

"And the Box HN?"

Newcomb looked up at him. "I lost my three best men that night out in the street. I'm through with this fightin', Starkey."

Ross leaned against the wall and lighted his cigarette. "About time," he said.

"I can get you help," said the old man.

"Box HN waddies? Hell no! I'd never get near the Kid with them riding with me."

"What makes you think you can get near him any other way?"

Ross looked out toward the silvered mountains. The Kid was somewhere up there most likely. "I don't know," he said.

"I'll tell my boys to stay away from his haunts."

Ross nodded. "You know about the pardon the governor is offering?"

"Yes. Do you think he'll accept it?"

Ross shook his head.

"Neither do I. Go back to Santa Fe and forget the whole thing. As long as the local Mexes are with him, and he's in those damned hills and mountains, a battalion of Texas Rangers couldn't get to him."

"Somebody has to do it."

"Why you?"

"Who else is there?"

"Is it that young woman?"

Ross turned and looked down at him. "Yes," he said. "I love her, and I think she loves me."

"You ain't too bright, Starkey. I always said that."

"Gracias," said Ross dryly.

Newcomb winced in pain. "Somebody has to get him," he said, almost as though to himself. "Maybe you're the one. By God, I wouldn't want the job! He's as slick as an Apache, as cruel as a Comanche, and deadlier with guns than any man I've ever seen or heard about. You're no match for him, Starkey. You go up in those mountains and you won't ever come out again."

Ross blew a smoke ring. "I have to go," he said.

Newcomb shrugged. "Anythin' you need?"

"My horse is wore out."

"Go down to the livery stable. Tell Max Gifford to give you any horse you want. Anythin' else? A room for the night? Money? You name it, Starkey."

Ross smiled. "I'll take the hoss and your good wishes," he said.

The rancher nodded. He twisted around to watch Ross walk to the door. "Vaya con Dios," he said.

Ross did not speak. He closed the door behind him. His spurs chimed softly as he walked toward the head of the stairs.

Hardy Newcomb wiped the cold sweat from his face. He looked toward the dreaming mountains to the west. "By God," he said quietly. "He's on a high lonesome if any man ever was." He grimaced in pain. "At that, it would be worth seein' those two face each other for the final showdown!"

There was no sleep in Ross that night, tired as he was. He traded off his worn-out clay bank for a blocky dun and left Las Piedras. He wanted no part of that town. He looked back as he crossed the bridge, toward the tallest building in town, the Las Piedras House, owned, of course by Hardy Newcomb. Well, it was his prison now, just as much as though there were bars on the windows and guards at the doors. Hardy Newcomb would probably never leave that hotel alive.

The moon swung upward in its course, flooding the Valley of the Rio Dulces. There was no sign of life except the lone horseman who rode steadily westward, avoiding the deserted ranch, to strike into the hills. Ross had followed this hidden trail, just once, heading the other way, guided by Tascosa after Ross' epic fight in the streets of Santo Tomas with Art Cassidy, Slim Bellew and Ben Miller. They were all dead now, and this time Ross was guided only by the sheer instinct he had for remembering any trail he had ever taken, though it might have been years past. The faculty had kept him alive more than once.

The moon was long gone when he emerged from the tortuous passages and saw Santo Tomas far below him, marked by a few faint lights and the fainter odor of burning wood.

The door of the Santo Tomas Cantina opened as Ross rode slowly toward it. Three men staggered out and walked the other way, laughing and talking, not seeing the horseman behind them. In a little while they were gone. Ross dismounted and tethered the dun in the same ramada he had used the last time he had graced Santo Tomas with his presence. He rapped on the cantina door when he found it locked.

"Quién es?" called out Fedro. "It is late. I am closed."

"It is the Señor Starkey," said Ross.

"Go away! He is dead, they say."

Ross clinked two silver dollars together. There was a short wait and then the bars rattled, and the door swung open to reveal Fedro holding a lantern high in his hand, peering at Ross. "Madre de Dios!" he said. "It is you! Come in! Come in!" He closed and barred the door behind Ross.

Ross walked to the bar and leaned wearily on it. "Any chance for a drink?"

Fedro nodded. "First you owe me for the bottle you took from here the day you fought those men in the street. Such a fight! Already Pablo Diaz, our village poet, has written a cancion about it. It is very good."

Ross paid for the long-empty bottle, and another was shoved toward him. Ross filled his glass. "Will you drink with me?" he said.

Fedro smiled, the lamplight flashing on his white teeth. "It is a pleasure! What brings you back to Santo Tomas?"

Ross downed the good brandy. He winced in pleasure. "I'm looking for the Tascosa Kid," he said.

Fedro stared at him. "Madre de diablo! Surely you jest!"

Ross reached across the bar and helped himself to a cigar. He bit off the end and lighted it. "No," he said. "Where is he?"

Fedro spread out his fat hands, palms upward, then shrugged with his whole back and shoulders. "Quién sabe?"

"He can't just vanish into thin air, amigo."

"Perhaps he can."

Ross blew a smoke ring and eyed the cantina owner. "You saying he's a ghost?"

Fedro sketchily crossed himself. "Some say he is dead. That it is a ghost they see riding the hills. El Espectro!"

"What hills?"

Fedro shook his head. "Everywhere. It is said he is seen one night near here, and the next a hundred miles away. He has vanished on the trail within plain eyesight of men who are known for their honesty. He has been seen riding the streets of Santo Tomas at midnight under the full moon, and one can see right through him! There are those who have seen him at the Rancho de la Rio Dulces. None of my people will go there, Señor Starkey. It is haunted."

"Listen," said Ross patiently. "He ain't no ghost. He's alive! I talked with him this very night."

Fedro crossed himself again. "You saw him?"

Ross took the cigar from his mouth. "Well, not exactly."

"You see! Perhaps you heard his voice?"

Ross nodded.

"Ah! But you did not see him, eh?"

"No."

"You see!" said Fedro triumphantly.

Ross touched the glass wounds on his face. "These came from glass splinters from a bottle smashed by a bullet fired by the Tascosa Kid. Begod, amigo, that was no ghost bullet!"

"It is said some ghosts can do such things."

"Bull crap! So, you won't tell me where he has gone?"

"I don't know."

"The woman? Señorita Fitzgerald. Where is she?"

Fedro looked toward the door and lowered his voice. "She was here in Santo Tomas not too long ago. She rented a house from my cousin Ferdinand. One night there were no lights in that house. The next day Rafaela

Perez went there to do the house cleaning. The Señorita Fitzgerald was gone. Her clothing and everything. Gone!" He shivered. "No one knows where she is."

Ross emptied his glass and refilled it. "She's likely with the Kid," he said.

"It is said that she is madly in love with him, but so it is with many of the women of Verde County. Men fear him and women love him. I am not at all sure I would want to be in his boots though."

Ross nodded. "Who lives in the mountains north of here?"

"No one."

"Someone must live up there," said Ross.

"Why are you so sure? It is true that some of my people lived there many years ago, but the Apaches wiped many of them out, and then the war was hard on them. The padres who lived up there were all killed by the Apaches. Then the people left, although no one saw them go, or knows of where they went. It is said that none of them left there alive."

Ross relighted his cigar. "I heard a bell ringing from up there," he said. He waited for Fedro's reply and then looked at him. The man was pasty-faced beneath his brown skin. "What's wrong?" added Ross.

Fedro drained his glass and refilled it. "It is the ghost bell," he said. "What time of the day was it?"

"Late afternoon. Almost dusk."

"Por Dios! It was the ghost bell."

"Bull crap! Someone had to ring it."

"It is from the old placita somewhere up there."

"Where is this placita?"

"Quién sabe? No one living knows. My people know those mountains are haunted and the Apaches will not go near them."

"So no one knows if there is a placita at all then?"

Fedro shrugged. "Now and then, someone hears the bell. If they hear it once it is a first warning. If they hear it twice it is the second warning. If they hear it the third time..." His voice trailed off.

"Go on!" snapped Ross.

Fedro swallowed hard. "If it is heard the third time, the one who hears it is doomed. He will never come out of those mountains."

Ross laughed. "What do they call that place?"

"Puerta de Luna."

"The Door of the Moon? A loco name."

Fedro shook his head. "There is a narrow pass up there. One that cannot be seen by day, but at the time of the full moon, just about midnight, the rays of the sinking moon fall upon it long enough for one to find it, if he wants to find it."

"And if he does?"

Fedro refilled the glasses. "He can go in. He will never come out...alive."

"You been drinking too much of your own cheap booze," said Ross.

Fedro shrugged. "It is late. I have a bed for you."

Ross emptied his glass. The thought of a bed sounded good.

Fedro put out the lamp and led the way into the back of the cantina. He watched Ross sit down on the sagging cot. He grinned. "Your old amigo, the Kid, has known many women on that cot."

"Figures," said Ross.

Fedro hesitated. He wet his full lips. "You are a good man, Señor Starkey," he said hesitantly. "If one was to find the Kid, he would do well to ride through the Door of the Moon." He hastily shut the door behind him.

CHAPTER SEVENTEEN

The late afternoon sun drove its hot rays against the steep western escarpment of the mountains. A heat haze, more common in summer than in the late fall, shimmered up from the heated rock and gave an unreal appearance to the jagged, fissured heights. The lowest slopes were marked by great fan-shaped playas of detritus washed down from the eroding rock high above. Above that the green belt of high timber stretched as far as the eye could see both to the north and to the south. Above that in turn was the naked rock above the timberline.

Ross Starkey sat in the hot shade of the lowest slopes. For three days he had probed the western approaches to the mountains with no results. "Puerta de Luna?" had said a young shepherd. "There is no such place!" An old, old man, whose sight had long been gone, had sat in the morning sun, facing the great rampart of the mountains, as though he could indeed see such a place as Puerta de Luna, and insisted that such a place did exist. He had been there as a boy, but that had been long before the time of the war between the Estados Unidos and Mexico.

A young cowpoke, hunting for strays, had told him that if a cow strayed into that country, it was never found again. It was the last thing he had said, over a drink of Ross' good rye, that had interested Ross. He had wiped his mouth and had looked up toward a jagged notch, just north of the pass by which Ross had entered the Rio Dulces Valley less than a week ago. "If there is such a place," he had said thoughtfully, "it is somewhere up near that notch. Funny thing, my brother said he heard a bell there one day just about dusk. I was with him that time. A week later he heard it again. Coupla days later, I was with him in that pass. We was huntin' a mountain lion with the dogs. Jerry claimed he heard that bell again. Nothin' for it but what he had to go up there the very next day and find out where it was comin' from." The cowpoke had stopped and looked at Ross. "We never saw him again."

Ross rolled a cigarette and lighted it. It was likely that somewhere up there was a place where a man could hide, and where he could have easy access to hidden trails to west and east. A place where there was good shelter, grazing, water and game. A place where one man could stand off a hundred. A man like the Tascosa Kid...

The afternoon slowly died. When the dark came Ross slept. The first rays of the full moon tipped the escarpment and shone on his face. He ate his dry food and sat there, while the slow progress of the moon changed lights and shadows on the rugged walls of rock.

He roped and then saddled the dun. He gathered his simple gear and mounted the horse, riding out of the timber into the full light of the moon. In an hour he was in amongst the slope timber and an hour later he had cleared the timberline. Now and then he looked back over his shoulder to gauge the downward progress of the moon, and as he did so he could see far across the great country to the west, over the lower mountains just east of the Jornado del Muerto. Beyond the Jornado was the Rio Grande. The night was almost as bright as daylight.

He found the road an hour before midnight, followed

it for half a mile, lost it, then found it again, but this time it ended at a sheer drop, as though thousands of tons of rock, loosened by frost and trickling water, had plunged, long ago, hundreds of feet below, taking the rest of the road with it. Still, it indicated that someone had traveled along the face of the escarpment. Perhaps there *was* something in the legend of Puerta de Luna.

It was close on to midnight when he stopped and slid from the saddle, fashioning a smoke as he scanned the heights above him. Foot by foot he scanned the rough face of the escarpment. He looked back at the dying moon, then back again at the escarpment, and his gaze became fixed on one spot, where the rock seemed different. He looked below it, and there, against the moonlit rock, he saw the faint thread of the road. It had switch-backed somewhere north of where he stood, to gain altitude, and the rock fall had wiped out much of it that had been at Ross' level.

He led the dun up the steep slope, slipping and sliding on the loose rock, making enough noise to awaken the dead. The thought sent a shiver through him. He didn't believe in ghosts and in haunts, but all this talk about a lost village, ghost bells, and vanishing people was enough to set a man's teeth on edge.

The moon was almost gone when he reached the place he had spotted. Begod! There was an opening, at least partway into the living rock. He led the dun into it and in minutes he had lost the light of the moon, although high overhead it still lighted some of the peaks.

By the time the moon was gone, he was floundering through clinging brush and slipping on broken rock, his progress echoing from the high walls on either hand. But now and then he would stumble in ruts on ground that had not yet been covered by rock falls or sliding earth.

The night was pitch dark when at last he felt a strong cold draft on his sweating face. He stopped and peered into the thick darkness ahead of him. He had no idea of what was ahead of him and yet he did not dare light up the lantern he carried on his saddle.

Ross felt for his canteen and tipped it back to drink, and as he did so a cold hand of wind passed over his heated face and the soft, almost indistinguishable ring of a bell came to him. He slowly lowered the canteen and listened, but the sound did not come again. "*If it is heard the third time, the one who hears it is doomed. He will never come out of those mountains,*" Fedro had warned.

"Bull crap," said Ross.

"Bull crap...bull crap...bull crap..." echoed the pass.

He felt for a rock and sat down, nipping now and then at his bottle, chewing on a chunk of cut plug. For some reason or another he did not want to show a light in Puerta de Luna.

The dawn wind crept slowly through the pass. Ross awoke with a start. The false dawn was tinging the patch of eastern sky he could see from where he had spent the night. He stood up stiffly and rubbed his bad knee. Some of his old wounds ached and his bones felt brittle and unyielding. "Jesus, I'm getting old," he grumbled.

"Jesus I'm getting old...Jesus I'm getting old...Jesus I'm getting old," echoed the pass.

Ross grinned. "Shut up, you bastard," he said.

"Shut up you bastard...shut up you bastard...shut up you bastard..." repeated the pass.

"Right back at me," said Ross in a low voice. "Serves me right."

Breakfast was a slug of rye and a fresh cut of Winesap. By that time the pass was sufficiently lighted by the coming of the dawn for him to be able to pick his way further east, by way of due north, then due south, and once he was downright sure he was heading due west.

The eastern mouth of the pass appeared when he least expected it, as he rounded a sharp bend in the widening pass. He dropped the reins of the dun and took his rifle from the scabbard. The morning sun struck against his face as he walked toward the pass mouth. He stopped and took off his spurs, stuffing them in his pocket. He slanted his hat lower over his face. He crouched behind a rock ledge and studied the lower ground beyond the pass. The road wound across the level ground and disappeared behind a castellated rock formation. There was no sign of life.

Ross led the tired dun across the level ground and left him beside the castellated rocks as Ross scouted on ahead. The ground sloped steadily down toward the east and he walked out upon a wide shelf. Far to his right he could see the dark line that indicated the pass he had taken the day he had first heard the ringing of the bell.

Timber dotted the slopes. The wind shifted, murmuring through the trees, bringing a sharp, winey odor with it. A line of broken rock cut off further view to the east.

He again led the dun forward until he rounded a shoulder of broken rock. He stopped short. A stone building showed on a level area. Part of the roof had collapsed, and the door hung on one hinge. Ross walked toward it, looking about for signs of life, but there were none to be seen except for an eagle drifting high against the blue with motionless wings, hunting for his breakfast.

Ross pushed the sagging door to one side and walked inside the building. He started as he saw a grinning skull looking at him with sightless sockets. He walked to the broken bed upon which a dusty blanket covered the bony remains. He drew it back. The man had died fully clothed. A ray of sunlight showing through a window picked out the initials on the big left buckle. J.S. The boots had been removed and the left trouser leg had been slit by a knife. The bones of the upper leg had been cruelly snapped. Ross felt for the makings and rolled a cigarette. Likely the poor bastard had busted his leg up there and had had just enough strength left to get into the old building, but no further.

Maybe gangrene had set in. Maybe he had died of hunger and thirst. J.S. The cowpoke who had been hunting for strays had said his brother Jerry had gone up toward Puerta de Luna.

Ross covered the grinning skull and walked outside. He led the dun through the timber and turned to look back, and as he did so, the clear, unmistakable sound of a bell came to him. He dropped the reins and walked quickly forward to the edge of the timber. He narrowed his eyes. "Well, I'll be double-damned!" he said. He took the cigarette from his mouth.

A village stood on level ground, cupped by low hills and knolls. The sun sparkled on a stream that ran past the decaying buildings. Many roofs had fallen in and those that hadn't had sprouted thick green and brown mats of grasses and weeds. At the far end of the street stood a little church, and high in the bell tower he saw a bell. The wind shifted and as it did, the bell rang faintly. "So much for legend," said Ross with a grin.

He left the dun picketed in the thick woods and encircled the deserted village. There wasn't a sign of life about it. The graveyard was unkempt, covered with weeds and drying grass. The footbridge across the stream had long ago collapsed, and the remains had become waterlogged, lying beneath the clear waters.

He walked to the church and entered it through a broken rear door. The place had long ago been stripped of holy pictures and furnishings. He climbed the crumbling bell tower stairs and looked at the ancient bell, greening with age and neglect. The bell rope hung below it. He pushed the heavy rope and the clapper touched the bell, ringing sweetly. The wind had taken over the job of the bell ringer.

Ross shoved back his hat and peered from the bell tower openings. He could see far beyond the eastern edge of the mountains. That must be Las Piedras where the drift of smoke hung against the clear sky. Far, far to the right and very low he saw the sun sparkling on the Rio Dulces.

Ross went down the stairs and walked out the front door of the church. The street was deserted, but it seemed as though the secretive windows were hollow eyes watching this trespasser.

The sun was slanting westward when he started back for the dun. The horse was gone. Strayed, thought Ross. Damn! It would be a helluva long walk down to civilization, either east or west.

He felt for the makings, and as he did so he clearly saw a boot print in the softer ground. He studied it. It was too small for his print. He knelt and examined it. The grass was slowly springing back into position... He looked up and studied the quiet woods. Whoever had made that print had been here just a short time ago.

Ross walked toward the edge of the woods. A stone lay with the darker, heavier side upward. He touched it. The dark surface was still damp to the touch and the stone lay in a pool of warm sunlight.

He reached the edge of the woods and looked toward the dreaming village. There was no one there. He walked toward it, wading the shallow stream, and as he reached the far side, he saw a pile of droppings at the edge of the street. Steam was still rising from them. Ross picked up a stick and stirred the fresh droppings. There was no trace of oats, but there was grass seed in them. Begod, it wasn't likely his horse that had dropped the pile!

Ross faded back between two buildings. He rubbed his bristly jaws. He reached for the makings and dropped them and as he bent to pick them up a rifle crashed somewhere along the street and a slug smashed against the stone wall just about where Ross' head had been. It screamed eerily off into space. Ross dropped flat and rolled over against a wall, shoving his rifle forward. A faint wisp of gun smoke drifted along the sunlit street. Begod, there was someone in this ghost town!

He studied the silent street. Fifty yards down the street he saw the sun glint on something bright. It took him a moment to realize it was the expended hull of the shot that had been fired at him, then ejected to clear the chamber for the next cartridge. Ross wet his dry lips. He inched backward like a crayfish and crawled behind the next building. A bullet skinned the ground a yard from where he lay.

"Kid?" yelled Ross. He immediately rolled over against the building, expecting another bullet.

The village was very quiet after the echoing shots. Ross inched forward and peered around the building. The rifle flatted off from behind him. He scuttled around the corner like an ungainly crab and bellied to the front of the building. As he did so he heard someone laughing. "There's a hole in the seat of your jeans, Starkey!" yelled the Kid. "You want me to patch it with a .44/40?"

Cold sweat broke from Ross. Damn him! Where was he! He couldn't possibly move that fast and still keep Ross in sight. Something else struck him; the Kid could have killed him with any of those shots. Ross took the last dregs of his courage in hand and stood up, leaning the rifle against the wall.

"That's a good boy," said the Kid.

"I've got to talk with you," said Ross.

"Why?"

"We went over that the night at the ranch."

"The deal from the governor? Does he really mean it?"

"I've got the papers right here in my pocket."

Minutes ticked past. Ross scanned the roofs of the decaying buildings with narrowed eyes, but there was no sight nor sound of the Kid. If he wasn't a ghost, he was the next thing to it.

"You can lower your hands," said the Kid from behind Ross.

Ross turned quickly. The Kid stood there, a rifle at

hip level, his cold eyes studying Ross. "I could have killed you half a dozen times since you came poking in here."

"Why didn't you?"

"I was curious."

"Where is Miss Maureen?"

"Cross the street. Pass between those two buildings. Keep walking. I'll bring your rifle. I'll be right behind you. Don't make a break, Starkey."

Ross crossed the street and passed between the two buildings. He kept walking toward a motte of timber. He passed into it and then beyond it, then crossed a swale and a low ridge. A large low building of the mission type, but much smaller than those he had seen in other parts of the Southwest and in Mexico, stood beside the stream. Three horses and a pack mule stood in a rude corral. One of them was Ross' dun.

She came to the door as he crossed toward the building. She had changed. She was thinner, seemingly older than when he had last seen her, but as lovely as she had ever been. There was fright in her eyes, as well as relief. Fright for his predicament; relief that the Kid had not killed him...yet.

"Are you all right?" he asked.

"Yes," she said quietly. "He hasn't bothered me. He thinks I'm safer up here than at the ranch."

Ross turned and looked at the Kid. There was something different about him, too. The Kid jerked his head. "Get into the mission," he said. He grinned. "There aren't any ghosts in there."

The dusty rooms echoed as Ross walked through them with the quiet young woman at his side. They had made their camp in one of the bigger rooms. Saddlebags and a pair of mule aparejos lay against a wall. Cooking gear lay on the wide hearth of a beehive fireplace. A bed had been made in one corner. Maureen looked at Ross. "He has let me have my own room," she said.

"That was nice of him," said Ross.

"Make a meal," said the Kid to the young woman. He took Ross' pistol from its holster and tossed it on top of the bed in the corner. "Set," he said to Ross.

Ross sat down and felt for the makings. He'd never be able to make a break and the Kid knew it. Ross lighted up. He watched the Kid start a fire in the beehive fireplace. "How long do you think you can keep this up, Kid?" he said.

The Kid turned. "They can't get at us up here," he said. "I know every inch of this plateau. I know every hidden trail. Trails that haven't been used for fifty years. I've got guns and ammunition cached in half a dozen places, and extra horses wherever I might need them. Most of the Mexes are my friends. They warn me if anyone is searching for me. I knew you'd eventually find me up here. I could have killed you yesterday or last night, or half a dozen times this morning."

"Why didn't you?"

"Like I said: I was curious. Let me see those papers."

Ross handed the Kid the thick manila envelope. He watched the Kid study the contents. At last, the Kid looked up. "Not too bad at that. What do you want me to do?"

"Go back to Santa Fe with me."

The Kid nodded. "That's all, eh?"

"That's it."

"We'll eat first. There will be a fine moon tonight. We can find our way out of here."

Ross studied the Kid. This was too damned easy. The Kid had a poker face. He fashioned a smoke and lighted it. "There's a bottle over there," he said.

"I ain't thirsty."

"That's a switch. You reforming?"

Ross shrugged. "Maybe."

"I'll bet," said the Kid dryly.

They ate silently. Now and then she would look at Ross with a hidden warning in her eyes, but the Kid at times seemed like his old self. They were drinking their coffee when the sun went down, and a cold wind blew across the plateau and moaned through the empty rooms.

The Kid emptied his cup and walked to a window. "Moon will be up before too long," he said.

"We'd better get ready then," said Ross. "We'll need all the time we can get."

The Kid turned. "Why?" he said. "We ain't going anywhere."

"What do you mean?" said Ross.

The Kid walked toward the fireplace. He turned. "You damned, conniving liar," he said coldly. "You and your big talk and your phony papers from the governor. Damn you! You think I don't know why you came here?"

Ross stood up. "It's the God's honest truth, Kid!" he said.

"So?" The candlelight shone on the Kid's icy eyes. "What deal did you make with Hardy Newcomb?"

"None! I swear to that!"

"Then how come you're riding a horse with a Box HN brand on him?"

Oh, Jesus, thought Ross. I never thought of that.

"You see?" said the Kid slowly. "You can't talk your way out of that one. You'd get me and Miss Maureen out of here and lead us right into a trap like you did her brother."

"You're a damned liar!"

"Yeah?" The Kid laughed softly. "Strange, ain't it, with all them bullets flying, and three of Newcomb's toughest boots there at the mill, plus a few other good guns, you happen to be the only one to walk out'a there, untouched."

"He had nothing to do with it, Tascosa," said Maureen.

He looked at her. "Forgive me, Miss Maureen, but you don't know this man. He betrayed your brother and he's betraying me like Judas betrayed Christ."

Ross felt a cold finger of fear trace the length of his spine. The Kid had gone over the edge all right. This was no longer a rational man. Hardy Newcomb, an excellent judge of stock and of men, had hit it right on the nose. "He's gone loco in my opinion," the crippled rancher had said.

The Kid lighted a cigarette and fanned out the match. "I ain't forgot you once saved my life," he said quietly. "I ain't one to kill in cold blood, but I can judge you and condemn you. I'm going to give you your Colt and let you go, with half an hour's start. Then I'm coming to look for you. You can run or you can make a stand, but you might as well know you can't get away."

"Be reasonable, Kid," said Ross.

The Kid took three steps forward and slashed Ross across the mouth with the back of his left hand, drawing blood from Ross' lips. "Git!" he said.

Ross wiped the blood from his mouth. He walked to the bed and got his Colt, knowing better than to turn on the Kid. He walked to the door and turned. "If anything happens to her," he said quietly, "I'll kill you, begod, if I have to come back from the grave!" He left the building, his boots grating on the hard ground in front of the mission, and in a little while the sound died away.

Maureen placed a hand on the Kid's forearm. "Let him go," she said.

The Kid raised his head. "He has to die," he said. "He's in my way. He betrayed me."

"You're betraying yourself," she said. "Tascosa, I love him. Don't you understand?"

He smiled at her. "You just don't understand, do you?"

She shook her head. "No, and I never will." She walked into her dark room and closed the door behind her.

The Kid blew out the candles and sat in the dark, his cold, set face illuminated now and then by the flare of his cigarette tip.

CHAPTER EIGHTEEN

H e started to run and then thought better of it. The fact that the Kid had said he'd give him a half-hour start didn't mean a thing. He might be cat footing through the darkness not fifty feet behind Ross.

He walked quickly through the motte, looking back now and then, trying to distinguish the silhouette of the Kid, but he saw nothing other than the dim façade of the old mission and the dark boles of the trees.

He crossed to the first buildings and looked up and down the street. To hole up would be worse than to run free, and yet if he kept moving the Kid would see or hear him. He'd have no chance with the Kid in a draw-and-shoot affair. With a rifle he might even the odds, but the Kid had the rifles. Supposing the Kid used a rifle instead of a Colt? He could shoot just as well with the long gun as he could with the short.

The thought came to him to make for the pass, but the moon would be up before he could reach the mouth of it, and the Kid might already be heading that way to wait for Ross. Or he might hole up in it and let Ross walk into the trap.

He could head east toward the lower ground that led

eventually to the Rio Dulces, but he didn't know the lay of that land at all, and the Kid would know it like the palms of his hands.

He crossed the street and looked at the church. It had a front door and a back door, so he wouldn't be trapped in there, but he'd have to leave either door in the full light of the moon. He looked up at the bell tower. He could see the whole village and the approach to it from the timber from up there, but if the Kid had already started after him, he'd likely see or hear Ross enter the church.

Cold sweat broke from Ross. He looked back over his shoulder. There was no sign nor sound of the Kid, but the man could walk like a hunting cat and shoot in the dark better than most men could shoot in broad daylight.

He stopped between two buildings and tried to think, but the thoughts were a jumbled mess, and panic hovered in amidst them, waiting to take over. "That's just what he wants," said Ross. He looked quickly about. It was almost as though someone else had said it.

He circled around behind the church. The sound of the stream drowned out all other sounds. He bent low and entered the cold water, wading across to the far side. He took cover in the brush while he emptied his boots. He crawled deeper into the brush and beyond it, belly flat, his breathing sounding loud enough to be heard fifty yards away, or so he thought.

He saw the western side of the mission beyond a screen of thin timber. More than half an hour had gone past. He could not see the Kid. Foot by foot he worked his way back toward the mission. The wind rose a little, stirring the trees and swaying the dark brush. The faint smell of bittersweet woodsmoke hung in the air. The odor of the horses and the mule came to him.

Ross lay flat, studying the mission. He could get a rifle in there, or at least get a horse, but then again the

Kid might have them covered. Damn him! He thought like an Indian.

There was a faint touch of light in the eastern sky. Ross remembered all too well how bright the moonlight was on the plateau. It would be like daylight in less than an hour.

He bellied closer and closer to the mission and at last stood up flat against the eroded wall between two rough buttresses. Gradually he noted that the buttresses were stepped, as though built of successive layers of crude adobe or stones, roughly covered with plaster. He looked up at the edge of the roof, seeing the thick mat of grasses and other growths that thatched it.

Ross wiped the sweat from his face and took off his boots. He tied them together with his scarf and hung them about his neck. Slowly, foot by foot, he worked himself up, digging his fingers into crevices, feeling the blood run from his nails, until at last the thatching brushed his sweating face. He pulled himself over the edge and lay flat, breathing hard, feeling the sweat run from every pore. He sat up and pulled on his boots. The light was stronger in the east. The rooftop was thickly layered with the dried grass and weeds. He wondered how strong the roof was. All he had to do was break through and the end would come in a hurry.

He walked softly across the roof until he reached the low wall at the front, part of the curving facade edge, that looked toward the dark motte. There was no movement out there except that of the swaying trees.

He lay flat, taking off his hat, thrusting his head between two clumps of the thick growth. Now there was nothing to do but wait with spidery patience for the Kid to appear, and God help Ross if the Kid knew or suspected that Ross had doubled back on him.

Slowly the full moon arose, lighting first the mountains far beyond the Pecos, then creeping across the Valley of the Pecos to touch the eastern hills of the mountains where flowed the Rio Dulces. Then it flowed across the lower flanks of the mountains and finally covered the mountains themselves, and suddenly Ross could see as clearly as though it was daylight.

He rested his head now and then. He felt unutterably tired. His old wounds ached dully and no matter how he lay they still ached. His bad knee throbbed. *I'm getting too old for this game*, he thought.

Once she came out of the mission and stood there in the moonlight, not fifteen feet below Ross. She looked toward the village, listening and waiting, and he knew then that the Kid was out there somewhere hunting for Ross. He grinned wryly. Hunt, you smart bastard, he thought.

Once the church bell rang softly. Maybe the Kid was up there.

The moon was slanting down toward the west when one of the horses whinnied softly.

Ross slowly raised his head. A man stood at the edge of the timber, looking to right and to left, and then he crossed the open space toward the mission. Ross tightened his sweaty grip on the Colt butt and his finger took the slack out of the trigger. The Kid was too far away for a clear accurate shot, and Ross wanted him alive.

The Kid stopped and looked back, fifty feet from the front of the mission. He stood there a long time listening.

Ross wet his dry lips. He edged closer to the edge of the roof.

The Kid turned. There was a puzzled look on his handsome face. He walked ten feet.

Ross sat up. The Kid did not look up. He stopped and turned.

Ross rolled over the edge, hung for a second with one hand and then let himself drop. "Grab some sky, Kid!" he cried. He struck heavily and his bad knee gave way. He went down on it as the Kid whirled, clawing for a draw.

For an infinitesimal fraction of time, they faced each other, thoughts racing through their minds, and then both of them fired. The Kid grunted in savage pain. He staggered back. Ross leaped to his feet and jumped to one side, fanning the hammer as fast as he could while two slugs whispered past his left ear. Ross' Colt ran dry, and the echoes fled across the plateau and died against the moonlit hills.

The Kid stared at Ross with white set face. The smoking Colt dropped from his nerveless fingers. "It had to be *you,*" he said hoarsely. "Somehow it ain't right."

Ross lowered his empty pistol. No man alive could stand there with six soft nosed .44/40s in his guts.

The Tascosa Kid went down on his knees, and bowed his head as though praying, then he fell face forward and lay still. A slow trickle of blood, black in the bright moonlight, stained the white caliche beneath him.

She came to the mission door. "Are you all right, Ross?" she said.

He nodded dumbly. Slowly he walked to the Kid and rolled him over. Somehow the Kid had died with that fleeting smile on his face, half amused, half sarcastic.

Ross stood up. "Get your things together, Maureen," he said in a toneless voice. He followed her into the echoing mission to help her. "I had to kill him," he said. It was almost as though he was talking to himself instead of to her.

"I know," she said softly.

She came to him, and this time it was her who comforted him. "I'll help you with the ranch," he said.

She shook her head. "I can't ever live there again. I'll sell the Shamrock. We can use the money to buy out your brother."

"You won't find the Canadian like the Rio Dulces," he said.

She rested her head against his chest. "Thank God for that," she said.

Ross loaded the body of the Kid on the mule and carried it to the old graveyard. The moon went down as he began to dig a fresh grave, but he worked by lantern light until the job was done. He rolled the Kid in blankets and tied them about his ankles, knees, waist and neck. He slid the stiffening body into the grave and placed the Kid's engraved and empty Colt atop the body. For a moment he stood there, head bowed in prayer, and then he filled the grave.

They sat silently until the dawn and then rode toward the Door of the Moon. At the edge of the village Ross turned in the saddle. "It's better this way," he said. "I've made a legend of him now. It is what he would have wanted."

Just as they reached the pass, the dawn wind crept across the plateau. Faintly, ever so faintly, came the ringing of the bell.

TAKE A LOOK AT BARRANCA AND BLOOD JUSTICE:

Two Full Length Western Novels

Gordon D. Shirreffs, Spur Award and Owen Wister Award winning author, tells the tales of the old west as they were meant to be told—with no holds barred action and adventure.

In *Barranca*, a dying blind man vows to reveal the site of a lost silver mine to two Civil War vets, but only if they will help him see through the quest. He knows he won't live long enough to enjoy the spoils, but he wants to die at least having the knowledge that it was found. The unlikely trio must deal with arid desert heat, hostile forces, crooked Federales, and treacherous cliffs to discover the lost valley where a silver treasure beyond their wildest imaginings awaits.

In *Blood Justice*, Jim Murdock had left Ute Crossing seven years before, with a posse hot on his heels and thirsty for blood. Now, he'd arrived back just in time to see another lynching. The three men who were supposed to have murdered the town's leading citizen were removed from the jail at midnight, taken to a hill, and hanged by their necks until dead. Someone was too anxious to get them out of the way, and Jim Murdock was going to find out why. He was going to track down the truth—and the real killer or killers—even if it meant putting his own neck in a noose...

"The joy of reading Shirreffs' work is in his mastery of pacing and his tough, gritty prose." – **James Reasoner, author of Outlaw Ranger.**

AVAILABLE NOW

ABOUT THE AUTHOR

Gordon D. Shirreffs published more than 80 western novels, 20 of them juvenile books, and John Wayne bought his book title, Rio Bravo, during the 1950s for a motion picture, which Shirreffs said constituted *"the most money I ever earned for two words."* Four of his novels were adapted to motion pictures, and he wrote a Playhouse 90 and the Boots and Saddles TV series pilot in 1957.

A former pulp magazine writer, he survived the transition to western novels without undue trauma, earning the admiration of his peers along the way. The novelist saw life a bit cynically from the edge of his funny bone and described himself as looking like a slightly parboiled owl. Despite his multifarious quips, he was dead serious about the writing profession.

Gordon D. Shirreffs was the 1995 recipient of the Owen Wister Award, given by the Western Writers of America for "a living individual who has made an outstanding contribution to the American West."

He passed in 1996.